BELA LUGOSI and the HOUSE OF DOOM

BELA LUGOSI
and the
HOUSE OF DOOM

By Dwight Kemper

Midnight Marquee Press, Inc.
Baltimore, Maryland, USA

Also available from the same Author:
Who Framed Boris Karloff?

Copyright © 2008 by
Cover Art by Frank Dietz
Interior Artwork by Dwight Kemper
Layout and Design by Susan Svehla
Copy Editing by Jim Nemeth

ISBN 13: 978-1-887664-93-6
ISBN 10: 1-887664-93-9
Library of Congress Catalog Card Number 2009921180
Manufactured in the United States of America

First Printing by Midnight Marquee Press, Inc., February, 2009

Dedicated to the memory
of Bud Abbott and Lou Costello—
two funny men who still make me laugh.

Acknowledgments

No book of this kind can be written without the help and support of many experts and enthusiasts in the Monster Kid and film scholar communities, as well as certain mystery readers. The following have contributed their time and expertise or criticism: Many thanks to Cathy Kemper for her editing and proofing skills and Gene Cothran for his probing questions and additional proofing; also thanks to Jack Theakston and Hal Lane on the Classic Horror Film Board for fact checking a detail about Bela, Jr.'s uniform; many thanks to Bob Furmanek and Ron Palumbo, the authors of *Abbott and Costello in Hollywood* (Ron was kind enough to share scene report information, as well as verifying certain facts about film locations, while Bob gave me full access to his production files, stills, and unedited outtakes to *Abbott and Costello meet Frankenstein*); and thanks to Gregory William Mank, author of the *Universal Filmscript Series* and other great works about classic horror. Special kudos go to Stephen Jacobs. He provided much needed information about Boris Karloff's family that I won't divulge here for spoiler reasons. Look for Mr. Jacobs' upcoming authorized biography from Tomahawk Press, *Boris Karloff: More Than a Monster*. And a big thank you to the Hungarian Yahoo group for help with certain key phrases in Bela Lugosi's native tongue.

Cast of Characters

Bela Lugosi—a Hungarian character actor typecast as Dracula, and amateur sleuth.

Lillian Lugosi—Bela Lugosi's wife.

Bela Lugosi, Jr.—Bela Lugosi's son.

Bud Abbott—a straight man, half of the comedy team of Abbott and Costello.

Lou Costello—a comic, the other half of the comedy team of Abbott and Costello.

Basil Rathbone—a British leading man typecast as Sherlock Holmes, and amateur sleuth.

Boris Karloff—a British actor typecast as Frankenstein's Monster, and amateur sleuth.

Lon Chaney—a character actor typecast as the Wolf Man.

Glenn Strange—a former cowboy heavy and Frankenstein's Monster in *Abbott and Costello meet Frankenstein.*

Lenore Aubert—an Austro-Hungarian actress.

Jane Randolph—an actress.

Bobby Barber—a court jester hired to keep Abbott and Costello from getting bored.

Charles T. Barton—a director, who frequently worked with Abbott and Costello.

William Goetz—a studio chief.

Leo Spitz—Goetz's partner.

Eddie Mannix—an M-G-M vice president.

Don Marlowe—Bela Lugosi's agent.

Dr. Fell—an inventor.

Kalara and Janika Skorzeny—brother and sister representatives from Hungarian Relief.

Dr. Kopf—a private physician.

Richard—a man of mystery.

Prologue

Weird Woman

Bela Lugosi's first conscious sensation was of being adrift in a sea of profound darkness. Gradually, the darkness gave way to light, a light that stung his eyes and forced them open. In an instant he was jolted by a skull cracking headache.

As he had done many times on the stage and screen in the role of Count Dracula, Bela threw his arm across his face to guard against the coming dawn. As he did, his nostrils were assailed by a terrible smell he couldn't identify.

Where am I, in a garbage dump?

He waited for his eyes to grow accustomed to the light. He squinted at his arm and down at his clothes and tried to focus, not sure if what he was seeing was real. It looked like he was wearing a tuxedo. More specifically….

This is my Dracula tuxedo.

He sniffed his sleeve. The awful smell came from his jacket.

Was I performing Dracula and the audience, they pelted me with garbage?

He noted that his costume was stained stiff with round yellowish-white blotches. The stains were splattered all over his dress shirt, tuxedo jacket and trousers.

Too addled to be cautious, Bela tasted the stains on his sleeve.

Custard?

He propped himself up on his elbows and realized he was in a cramped sleeping bunk with sunlight pouring in through portholes at his feet and behind his head.

Portholes? I am on a ship? I have been Chinesed away!

What he meant was "shanghaied," and he vaguely considered having been over-powered at the city dump by shanghaiing clowns with drug-laced custard pies.

That is just stupid!

He struggled to collect his thoughts.

I am in my Dracula costume—and in a sleeping bunk onboard a steamship bound for God knows where.

Bela noted a rectangular window to his left.

So I find out where God knows where is.

He rolled over to get a look outside, but his way was blocked by someone laying next to him, a curvaceous someone with long silky hair and who smelled of perfume. Lugosi's mind was all in a muddle as he felt the contours of the strange woman's hips and inviting roundness of her bottom. As she mumbled in her sleep, it occurred to Bela that he had never heard of *couples* being pressed into service on foreign steamships.

Perhaps we are lovers. It might even be my darling Clara!

Bela remembered Clara Bow, the It girl and their torrid affair, and the many love bites she left on his back. He smiled and patted the girl's bottom and felt content to just lay quietly with her.

...his way was blocked by someone laying next to him...

Only there was something keeping Bela from basking in contentment. It was an overpowering thought in his native Hungarian that came roaring through his fog-shrouded mind like a runaway train: *A feleslégem meg fog ölni!* Roughly translated: *My wife is going to kill me!*

Dear God, yes! I am married!

Which raised the question of this woman's identity—the weird woman he could not remember who was facing away from him and hogging all the blankets. Bela reached over and pulled back the blankets, expecting to see her naked flesh. Much to his relief, she was wearing a coat.

Stirred by the sensation of being uncovered, the mystery woman rolled over in her sleep and nuzzled the crook of Bela's neck. As she sighed contentedly, Bela realized that this weird woman wasn't a stranger at all, but was his dear wife, Lillian, who wrapped her leg around him, and dug a stiletto heel into his calf.

Through the sudden pain, it occurred to him that this meant he wasn't aboard some steamship bound for China or in some cozy lover's retreat, but was actually safe inside his own studio dressing trailer. He must have been making a picture. Only, for some reason, the title of the picture escaped him.

In fact, a lot of things seemed to escape him, almost as if an air raid warden had ordered a total blackout of his memory.

Bela slipped out from under Lillian's arm, disentangled himself from her leg, and rolled over and sat on the edge of the bunk. He rested his aching head in his hands, fretting over the prospect of another hangover—except this felt like no hangover he had ever experienced before. It was neither the morning-after-morphine blues, nor the pounding-headache-with-the-stale-aftertaste-of-whiskey pinks. He just felt—vague.

He ran his fingers through his hair and as he did, he became aware of something odd. Looking at his hands, he saw that his fingers were stained with black dye. Staring past his dye-stained fingers, Bela saw a foot peeking out from under a drawn privacy curtain. It wore a scuffed-up patent leather dress shoe. He could also make out the blue cuff of a dress uniform trouser leg with a white stripe running up the side.

Bela cautiously rose from the bunk on wobbly legs and slowly drew back the curtain. He found a young boy curled up on the floor in a sound sleep, and wearing a decidedly rumpled military school uniform covered in the same custard blotches. It took a moment for Lugosi to recognize the boy as his son, Bela, Jr.

We were all shanghaied by pie throwing clowns!—No, that is still stupid!

He stared at the slumbering boy, and then over at his sleeping wife, and desperately tried to remember how they all wound up like this. While it was possible that he and Lillian may have had one of their infrequent moments of passion, when the morphine and his advancing age had not robbed him of his libido, that still didn't explain why his son was asleep on the floor, or why he and Lillian were fully dressed.

This was all too much for Lugosi. He reached over and shook Lillian.

"Lillian," he croaked with vocal cords that wheezed like a disused pipe organ in a dusty crypt. "What has happened?"

She stirred, and then rolled over and fell back into a deep sleep, now completely cocooning herself inside the blankets.

Bela sighed wearily and sat back on the bunk. He rubbed his eyes, trying to force any remembrance about what had happened last night, but found it was like trying to recapture a dream before being fully awake. He decided this was pointless and pulled himself up by the privacy curtain, found his balance, and carefully stepped around Bela, Jr., stumbling around Lillian's and his steamer trunks, and toward the forward part of the trailer where his makeup table and chair were set up. He kept himself upright by using the trunks for support.

Wait, why are our trunks here?

He wondered if perhaps he and Lillian had been evicted. No, they had been staying with Hungarian friends while he and Lillian were in Hollywood. Had his friends thrown them out? Judging from how he felt, maybe he went on some kind of drinking binge and his friends asked them to leave. But no, that still didn't explain why he was dressed in his Dracula costume or why it was stained with custard—or why he remembered about the Hungarian friends but little else.

What do I remember?

He decided to take a brief inventory. He was Bela Lugosi, born Béla Ferenc Dezső Blaskó. He was an actor from Lugos, Austria-Hungary. He was in a dressing trailer with his fourth wife and ten-year-old son. He recalled that he resided in a small apartment in New York City, but had flown back to Hollywood to make a picture. But he could not remember last night or yesterday morning. He found his amnesia to be oddly selective that way. It was as if someone had erased from his mind everything that had happened to him in the last 24 hours. It wasn't just a black out—those recollections were censored somehow, locked up, forbidden to him. But there had to be a way to free them!

He lunged for the makeup table and turned on the light bulbs framing the mirror and looked into his haunted face. His hair was wildly unkempt from having run his fingers through it and his piercing blue eyes were framed by a mask of smeared black hair dye like a ghoulish raccoon. Bela almost laughed out loud, but his throat was too dry to let the chuckle escape, and his laugh was reduced to a rasping cough.

He shut his eyes and forced himself to think. He was no stranger to the after-effect of narcotics or alcohol. But this was something different, something stronger. Bela began to experience a growing feeling of paranoia, as if on some murky level of consciousness he was aware that something had been done *to* him, and this was not something he had done to himself.

There had to be something, some clue, anything to give him a hint about what had transpired in those missing hours. Bela looked at his reflection again and caught a glint from the inner pocket of his tuxedo jacket. He sat down in the makeup chair and pulled out a handful of glass cigar tubes. The stogies within must have been very expensive, and definitely not something Bela could afford. He opened one of the tubes, took out the cigar and sniffed along the length of it.

Cuban, his sensitive nostrils detected. *Definitely a Cuban cigar.*

He quickly felt around in his other pockets and found something in his pants pocket; a book of matches! Holding the cover up to the light, he read the words, *Phil's All Nite Diner.*

So he had been to an all night diner—dressed as Count Dracula.

BAH! That makes no sense!

But it told him that whoever it was that tried to hide things from him, they were in a hurry and they made the mistake of leaving clues behind.

Wait, why do I think that?

But that's exactly what he felt. There was someone behind this. Perhaps they thought Lugosi would just ignore those clues because they made no sense.

HA! They obviously do not know Bela Lugosi as well as they think they do!

He was now determined to uncover the mystery!

Still, mystery or no mystery, he had expensive cigars and a convenient book of matches. He decided to take advantage of the situation and bit off the end of the cigar, tore out a match, struck it alight, and rolled the cigar around in his mouth until the burning match coaxed an aromatic stream of blue smoke from the cigar tip. Exhaling smoke through his nostrils, he felt his head begin to clear. He searched the other inner pocket of his jacket and discovered—a notebook! In fact, judging by the imprint on the cover, it was a policeman's notebook.

Now we are getting somewhere.

Flipping through it, he was disappointed to find that some of the pages had been torn out. No doubt, they were important pages, too, which only added to Bela's growing frustration. He began to wonder if those pages had been torn out to deliberately keep him ignorant of what had happened to him.

What horrible thing might I have done that it would involve police?

He read some of the remaining pages. There were notes about bodies in a lake and a missing trailer. Frightened, he threw away the notebook and stood up. As Bela backed away from the dressing table, he became aware of something funny about the insides of his shoes. He sat back down, pulled off his right shoe, slipped his hand in and pulled out several pages of folded notebook paper. And judging by their size and the torn perforations at the top, these were the missing pages from the policeman's notebook!

Aha!

Invigorated by this discovery, he eagerly pulled off his other shoe, and as he did, he noticed his shoes were scuffed like his son's and they were covered with dried mud.

There is mud on my shoes, and bodies in a lake!

He reached inside the other shoe and found more notebook paper—and something else, something cardboard crumpled in the toe. He put the pages on the makeup table and shook the shoe out, slapped the rubber soles, shook again, and out fluttered a soggy and battered looking calling card. Bela carefully picked up the card, hoping the name printed on it would give him another clue. On the back was some barely legible handwriting. It may have been a telephone number and what looked like a faded "205." Turning the card over, Bela saw printed in green ink not a proper name, but a most peculiar symbol; the letter "C" with the drawing of a human brain inside it, a crown above it, and the motto *Semper Occultus* printed below it.

Bela wondered for a moment if someone was playing a joke on him and the paranoia he felt was from remembering the pranksters. He was making a picture, yes. So maybe he had been to a wrap party. He had been to other wrap parties, and often the actors came in their costumes. He set the card aside with a snarl of annoyance and tried to focus on the words scribbled on the pages of torn out notepaper. Perhaps if he could recognize the handwriting, he could identify the prankster. The ink was faded and bled through pages made damp from his foot perspiration, but he definitely recognized the handwriting on the first collection of pages.

It was *his* handwriting.

Squinting, he read:

Dear Basil Big Deal Celebrity Detective Rathbone:

Basil Rathbone? Lugosi tried to remember the last time he saw Rathbone. He couldn't be sure. He continued to read:

I am tired of you pretending to solve the case before Bela Lugosi, so here I will write down my conclusions and how I arrive at them before we close the case, and I will have this letter dated and witnessed to prove that I solve it first and I am the better detective!

Case? Better detective? He vaguely remembered once solving a mystery a long time ago with Basil Rathbone. It had something to do with fellow screen boogieman Boris Karloff. And Lugosi recalled that Rathbone had acted so infuriatingly superior playing in real life the role of Sherlock Holmes. But that was—when? Yes, it was while they were all working together on *Son of Frankenstein* back in 1938, and this was now—he wasn't sure. He flipped through to the last page of notepaper where indeed Bela had jotted down the day and time the notes were written.

26 February 1948, 2:00 A.M.

Had it really been ten years since he had taken on the real-life role of an amateur sleuth? And it must be February, because inside the trailer it was chilly, as it would be on an early February morning, even in Hollywood. He shivered as he glanced at the notepaper again and at a signature witnessing the document. It was signed, *Bud Abbott!*

Frowning, he flipped back to the first page and continued reading.

It was a kind of inexplicable, clawing, clutching, creeping—terror!

…I suspected from the beginning that you were not what you pretended to be! And Karloff—

Karloff! The very name grated on Lugosi's nerves. What does *he* have to do with this? Could it be that Boris Karloff was in trouble again?

…And Karloff, he too aroused Bela's suspicions when he spoke of Richard, and he handed to me the calling card to be used, "Should the need arise," he said.

He glanced at the calling card lying on the makeup table, then at the pages.

…I also did not trust Lou Costello's—

and the House of Doom

Bela's eyebrows arched with surprise.

Lou Costello?

He examined closely the second collection of papers that were written in someone else's hand. The notes were dated in the distinctly American form of month, followed by day and year: *February 26, 1948.*

And they were signed, *Lou Costello!*

Could it be that this mystery had something to do with baggy pants funnymen the likes of Bud Abbott and Lou Costello?

Lugosi got up and went to the nearest porthole, pulled back the curtain and raised the shade. Looking out, he realized the dressing trailer was parked on the lot at Universal-International Studios outside Stage 17. Extras were milling by in full costume—cowboys and harem girls, and a mermaid lying in a wheelbarrow flipping her colorful tail as a makeup man in a lab smock pushed her up the street. Lugosi vaguely recognized the mermaid as actress Ann Blyth.

Bela surveyed the inside of his dressing trailer and looked down at his costume.

Yes, that is why I am in Dracula's clothes. I am making a picture with Abbott and Costello! A funny horror picture!

He tried to remember the title of the production. It had something to do with Frankenstein. Then a sudden thought penetrated the gloom clouding his mind like a ray of sunshine after a storm.

Those two funnymen, they are all the time making practical jokes. This was just one more such joke!

Glancing down at his sleeping son, Bela felt a sudden uproar of fury.

How dare they give my son alcohol!

That was the only explanation. Abbott and Costello got the three of them drunk and left them this way in Bela's own trailer. He strode to the mirror and glared at his custard-stained costume.

They are always throwing pies around!

He was about to toss the two crumpled bunches of notepaper in the trash, when one phrase caught his eye:

…House of Doom…

Those three strange words inspired a strong reaction in Bela Lugosi. It was a kind of inexplicable, clawing, clutching, creeping—terror! It was the kind of terror that mystery writers usually exploited in pulp fiction. It was a terror that grabbed Lugosi's now rapidly beating heart and compelled him to sit back down in the makeup chair. It was a terror that forced him to read from the beginning his own words that he had no recollection of having written. But those words dredged up such peculiar and comically exaggerated visions he dared not believe them to be real.

Part One
Calling Dr. Death
Chapter 1

"Hey, Abbott," remarked short, pudgy Lou Costello as he gestured up a sweeping gothic staircase, "did you hear that somebody's gonna kill Bela Lugosi?"

"Now who would want to kill Bela Lugosi?" the tall, lanky Bud Abbott asked matter-of-factly to set up his partner's punch line.

"*Me*, if the guy don't wake up and get through this goddamn scene already!"

"Be patient, Lou," the darkly beautiful Lenora Aubert said. "I'm sure Bela is doing his best."

"His best ain't good enough," Costello complained. "We've been rehearsing *Vampire Descending a Staircase* all morning, and the guy hasn't got all the way through it once!"

The lovely blonde Jane Randolph frowned sympathetically. "Maybe he's sick."

"He ain't the only one," Costello grumbled.

Charles T. Barton shushed for quiet. "One last run-through before the cameras start turning, everybody," the roly-poly director said. "Okay, here we go. Cue, Bela."

All eyes turned to Bela Lugosi, the picture of European elegance. Dracula's lines to Abbott and Costello picked up at the cut point of the previous days' filming. "You should be careful. A person could get killed that way." Right on cue, Lugosi descended the staircase, keeping his hands hidden in the pockets of Dracula's paisley smoking jacket. Everyone thought he did this to conceal a Band-Aid on the index finger of his right hand. Actually, the Band-Aid was just an excuse Lugosi concocted to hide how badly his hands were shaking. He opened his mouth—and his mind drew a complete blank. The Hungarian actor gave his co-stars an apologetic smile, eliciting a grimace of frustration from Lou Costello.

"GODDAMN IT, BATS!" the comic exploded. "SHAKE THE COBWEBS OUTTA YOUR NOGGIN AND LET'S JUST DO THIS THING!"

"Take it easy, Louie," chastised Barton, who was used to Costello's tirades. The director frowned. "Bela, what's wrong? It's like you're in a trance."

"That's funny," Costello carped. "I thought Dracula was supposed to put *other people* in a trance." He felt his forehead. "I know I feel awful woozy right about now."

Ignoring the wise crack, Barton asked Lugosi, "Are you feeling all right? Frankly, the way you look right now, I really can't tell if you're sick or not."

To create the illusion that Lugosi at 65 was the immortal Dracula, makeup artist Bud Westmore hid the actor's aging features beneath a thickly applied greenish-gray pancake. Eyeliner and black eyebrow pencil diverted attention away from the bags under his eyes, lip rouge gave his mouth a youthful fullness, and jet black dye concealed his graying hair. On black-and-white film the illusion of vitality was very convincing, even in extreme close-ups, but in person Lugosi's makeup made him looked like a warmed over corpse.

"I am well," Lugosi lied in his trademark Hungarian accent.

He felt the eyes of his wife Lillian upon him. From his high vantage point he could see her sitting there in one of the ornate high-backed chairs decorating the hall of the castle set. She wore a gray coat over a blue polka dot dress. Sitting with her on the arm of the chair was their ten-year-old son, Sergeant First Class Bela G. Lugosi, Jr., on leave from military school. He was smartly attired in his dress blues and was smiling proudly at his father, but Lillian was not. Bela knew that look all too well. She was worried that his craving for morphine was affecting his work. Somehow she could see that the pain attacking Bela's legs would not go away, that it was consuming him, and that the craving was growing. He forced a reassuring smile, but her worried expression remained. Bela addressed his director and for his wife's benefit he pledged confidently, "Once the camera is rolling, I will do the scene with no problems."

"You better, Bats," Costello said. "Because right now I'm gettin' that French thing, what do you call it? When a guy feels he's relivin' the same thing over and over."

"*Déjà vu?*" Abbott suggested.

"Not since I got married," Costello joked.

Lugosi gave both the director and Lillian a confident nod, and then climbed the stairs. He hesitated, turned and looked to Bud Abbott's pretty niece. "My line, please," he requested.

Script clerk Betty Abbott cleared her throat. "*You should be careful,*" she read aloud, as Costello mouthed along, "*a person could get killed that way.*"

Costello turned to his partner with dismay and whimpered, "I'm gettin' bored, Abbott."

"What do you say to a pie fight?" the straight man suggested.

Lou perked up immediately. "I'd say, 'Hello, pie fight, how's the family?'"

They both ran to the prop table where a well stocked ammo dump of seltzer bottles and real cream pies were kept for just such an emergency. The comedians chose their weapons and made ready to let fly. Barton hurried to intervene and got caught in the crossfire, which put Abbott and Costello and the rest of the company into hysterics.

Lugosi alone remained taciturn, keeping a safe distance on the staircase.

Wiping lemon meringue out of his eyes, Barton complained, "Come on, you guys! No more horsing around."

"You oughta be ashamed of yourself, Charlie," Costello snickered, "gettin' pie-eyed this early in the morning."

"Very funny," Barton sneered as director's staff member Fritz Collins handed him a towel.

"Don't blame me for gettin' bored outta my skull," said Lou, jerking his thumb in Lugosi's direction. "Blame the *late* Count Dracula. He's drivin' me nuts! How many times do we gotta do this scene?"

"Now, now, Lou," Abbott chided, "Bela is a seasoned professional and he probably has a very good reason for being late this morning."

"Sure he does, Abbott. Dracula don't have an alarm clock in his coffin."

The call sheet had Bela reporting to makeup and wardrobe at 8:15, but he hadn't turned up until 9 o'clock, the hour Bud Abbott and Lou Costello were scheduled to check in. The comedy team arrived on time and ready to go. Unfortunately, since Bela was the focus of the scene, and it took Westmore over an hour to transform Lugosi into a vampire, this meant the rest of the cast and crew could do little more than twiddle their thumbs. Bud and Lou tried to kill the time posing for Joe Glaston, Lou's press agent. Joe took a few candid publicity shots of the boys and comic Bobby Barber messing around with a set of musical instruments. But the horseplay was all for show. In reality, Bud and Lou were pissed.

To make matters worse, not only did Bela delay production, he brought unexpected visitors to the set. In addition to his wife Lillian, who chauffeured her husband wherever he went, and his son, who was a frequent guest, the tardy actor was accompanied by two friends from his homeland, Kalara and Janika Skorzeny, neither of whom spoke a word of English.

"To be entirely fair," Abbott said, "Bela wasn't the only one late for work this morning." He pointed at their leading ladies who were all decked out for a Masquerade Ball. "Now suppose Bela had shown up on time? We'd still be in the same boat we are right now because of Lenore and Jane."

"You're right, Abbott," said Lou, taking the scene report from Betty. "Lenore had to report at 6:45 and Jane at 7:30, and they show up a half hour late." He slapped the report conclusively. "There's no excuse for it," Lou said, eyeing the prop table of pies, "so there's only one fit punishment." He picked up a Boston cream pie and eyed Lenore, who made a very sultry target dressed as she was in a Grecian toga.

"Don't you dare," warned Lenore, backing away. "You put that pie down!"

"You're right." Lou handed the pie to his partner. "A pie fight is too good for you girls." He stalked Jane, smirking like a wicked little boy about to give his babysitter hell. He wiggled his fingers.

"No, Lou, not that!" she begged, trying to keep her distance, but found herself backed up against a gargoyle-capped newel post.

Jane's Spanish Dancer getup bared her midriff, and Lou took full advantage of it, tickling her unmercifully, taunting her in his high-pitched little boy voice. "So, are ya gonna be late for work again, Jane, are ya, huh?"

"No!" she squealed, laughing hysterically and squirming. "That's not fair! Quit it! Come on, Lou! Stop! Uncle! UNCLE!"

Lenore came to Jane's rescue, chastising Lou with a wagging finger. "You are a bad boy!" she scolded.

With hands on hips, Lou climbed two steps up the staircase. "Hey, that's my line, toots," he said, giving the statuesque actress a comical eye-to-eye grimace.

Abbott shook his head reproachfully. "I can't take you anywhere," he said.

Barton put his fingers to his mouth and got everyone's attention with a long, shrill whistle. "Hey, everybody," he called, "back on your marks!" He looked up at Lugosi. "This one's for real, Bela."

Lugosi descended to the middle step and frowned at Betty Abbott. "The line, please?" he asked.

"*You should be careful—*," Betty began, interrupted by Costello waving to the dialogue director.

"HEEEEEY, NORMAN!" he called to Norman Abbott.

Bud's nephew hurried over. "Yes, Lou?"

"Help Bats with his lines before I take a wooden stake to the guy."

Norman smiled up at Bela. "Why don't we run lines in private, Mr. Lugosi?" he diplomatically offered.

With an arrogant wave, Lugosi said, "That will not be necessary," and ascended to his mark. "I am ready now! Roll the camera!"

Costello glanced up at the glowering Hungarian, and then whispered to his partner. "Hey, Abbott, where's Bobby? I got me an idea." With a mischievous twinkle in his eye, Lou cupped his hands against Abbott's ear and whispered instructions.

Abbott smiled, gave Lou the OK, and hurried to find Barber.

After wiping his face, Barton clapped his hands and shouted, "Okay, okay, fun's over, everybody. Get back on your marks. Cameras will be turning for real this time. Let's have quiet on the set." He became aware of someone muttering. "We're supposed to have quiet on the set, people. So who's yapping?" Barton spotted Lou's secretary, the lovely Aida "Dee Dee" Polo, talking to someone on the stage telephone. "Dee Dee," he shouted, "hang up! We're getting ready to roll."

She was too engrossed listening to the party on the phone to take any notice of Barton.

"*Now*, Dee Dee," Barton snapped.

"Sorry," she said, hanging up, and hurried over to Costello. "That was Dr. Fell on the phone. He says everything is all set for the demonstration."

Lou smiled and rubbed his hands together eagerly. "That's swell, Dee Dee."

The pretty girl frowned. "Your new accountant will be there, too."

"What's wrong? Why the long face?"

"Lou, it's about your accountant. I can't prove anything, but I think he's cheating you."

"Okay," said Barton, shooing Dee Dee away. "Come on, baby, out of the shot, please."

Costello gave his secretary a reassuring wave. "We'll talk about it later, Dee Dee. Don't worry so much."

Barton looked around. "Where'd Abbott go? Oh, there you are. Places everybody."

"Okay, Mrs. Lugosi," a voice behind the scenes said, "cross your legs and look pretty." It was Glaston taking more publicity pictures.

Lugosi cast Glaston a withering look of disdain for showing far too much interest in his wife's legs.

"Joe," Barton complained, noting Bela's glare of menace, "can you wait until we get this shot, please?" He indicated the fuming Hungarian with a nod. "Lugosi's distracted enough as it is."

"Sorry, Charlie," Joe said, "This'll only take a minute."

As Glaston hefted his camera, Eddie Sherman, Abbott and Costello's agent and studio go-between, nodded at Bela, Jr. "Let's have the kid stand beside her, Joe," he suggested. "It'll be real patriotic."

The boy tucked his white uniform cap under his arm and stood at attention, "Like this, sir?" he asked, while Lillian posed and smiled.

"Just like that, kid," Sherman said.

...a cloaked figure skulked behind him...

Glaston winked and raised his camera. "You're a beauty, all right, Mrs. Lugosi," he complimented.

"Thank you," said Lillian demurely, glancing up at her fuming husband.

It wasn't that long ago that they had reconciled after Lillian had filed separation papers in August of 1944, claiming that Bela was too controlling and jealous. He burned with that jealousy now, all too aware that Lillian was much younger than he. Years earlier Bela had commissioned an artist to paint Lillian's portrait, and she hadn't changed a bit. She had the same dark shoulder length hair and bright eyes. Bela, on the other hand, felt every second of his advancing years, and they weighed on him heavily.

"Okay," Glaston said. "Hold it!" He snapped the picture. "Perfect!"

"All right," Barton called. "This is it. Places!"

Jane and Lenore positioned themselves on chalk marks made yesterday when the previous scene wrapped. Lou stood a step below Lenore while Bud Abbott rested his arm on the railing, which wasn't in continuity, but signaled how tired he was getting of repeating the same scene.

Over by the grand gothic fireplace, dressed in a white doctor's smock and holding a clipboard, Charles Bradstreet was waiting for his cue. As Professor Stevens, he had the thankless job of playing the romantic male lead in an Abbott and Costello comedy.

Standing beside him were Lugosi's two Hungarian guests. Bradstreet was paying particular attention to the pretty Kalara Skorzeny. The girl was dressed in a long gray peasant dress that was buttoned up to her neck, and a pair of white gloves. Despite the concealing attire, it was obvious she had a curvaceous figure, which hadn't escaped

Bradstreet's notice. The handsome leading man gave her a flirtatious smile. Kalara's brother gave *him* a sneer of disapproval; at least Bradstreet thought it was a sneer.

Janika Skorzeny's face had been disfigured, giving him a permanent sneer regardless of his feelings. But judging by his threatening body language, Bradstreet decided it was safer to take a couple of respectful steps away from the girl.

Barton called up to the cameraman on the boom. "Is the camera ready?"

Behind the camera, cinematographer Charles Van Enger said, "Camera ready."

Assistant director Joe Kenny displayed the slate for the camera that identified *The Brain of Frankenstein* as production 1572; scene 100; shot 632; cameraman: Van Enger. He clapped the clapperboard, and dropped the slate out of the shot.

"Here we go," Barton said, cuing Bela; "All right."

Lugosi made his descent down the staircase. Unbeknownst to the actor, as he delivered his lines, "...a person can get killed that way," a cloaked figure skulked behind him and joined Lugosi where the actor was meant to pause on the staircase. Everyone burst out laughing. The camera stopped turning as Bela suddenly became aware of the intruder and roared at the diminutive Mr. Hyde. "GODDAMN IT! We should not be kidding when we are working!"

Comic Bobby Barber raised his mask, revealing a short, bald unassuming 52-year-old man. "Around here, kiddin' *is* working," he said.

"Aw, come on, Bela," said Abbott good-naturedly. "We're just getting you back for this morning."

Still laughing, Lou called up to the cameraman. "Did you get all that? Oh man, I hope you got the look on Bats' face."

"I got it," Van Enger assured him.

Costello snickered and waved to Betty. "That one's for me there," he said, which was his way of requesting a print of the outtake. Universal often processed private copies of outtakes as a favor to Lou, and at the studio's expense.

Lugosi was mortified. Brushing Barber aside he confronted Barton. "Is this how Bela Lugosi is to be treated? Like he is nothing but a Vaudeville serious man?"

"I think you mean 'straight man,'" Barton corrected. "Come on, Bela. The boys were just letting off a little steam. It's not like you don't deserve it."

"It is no wonder Karloff refused to do this picture! All the time these funnymen are throwing pies and spraying seltzer everywhere!" Lugosi stormed over to the prop table. "Seltzer and cream pies, they have no place on the set when you are filming a horror picture!"

Lou was still crying from laughter. "It is when it's a *funny* horror pi'ture."

"You think it is so funny, do you," Lugosi said, "showing Bela Lugosi such disrespect?"

"*Me* showin' *you* disrespect?" Costello's face turned bright red as he jabbed a pudgy accusing finger at the Skorzenys and exploded, "WHAT KIND OF RESPECT ARE YOU SHOWIN' *ME* BRINGIN' A COUPLE OF COMMIES ON MY SET?!"

Lugosi drew up indignantly. "Kalara and Janika Skorzeny are not *Commies*, as you call them! They are expatriates from my homeland who have only just arrived in this country! Why would you say such a thing?"

"Cuz if they was *real* patriots they'd speak English like Americans!"

"How dare you! Kalara and Janika sacrificed everything to come to this country. They represent Hungarian Relief, a worthy charity to aid refugees like themselves *fleeing* Communist tyranny. In the eyes of my people, they are heroes!"

Costello's eyebrows rose in surprise. "No foolin'?" he asked.

Bela gestured proudly. "They want Bela Lugosi to appear tomorrow at a fund raiser at the Hollywood Knickerbocker Hotel. This offer was made to me only this morning and just as I was leaving for the studio. There was much we had to discuss, so I bring the Skorzenys here to go over the details. *That* is why I was late getting here today."

Lou's expression softened. "Well, why didn't you say so," he asked, smiling broadly. "I'm all for charity, especially if it's against Communists. Right, Abbott?"

"Why sure," Abbott agreed. "That puts a completely different picture on everything."

Lou pointed at himself and his partner. "Maybe they'd like it if Bud and me showed up at this fund raiser with you."

"I could ask them," said Lugosi warily, concerned he might be upstaged if they came.

Costello waved his partner and his press agent over. "Hey, Joe, Abbott, come on." Lou approached the Skorzenys and gave them a broad smile as he shook their hands. "Welcome to the set!"

"They speak no English," Bela reminded him.

"So what," Lou said. "Everybody knows what it means to get your pi'ture taken."

The Skorzenys stood there looking stiff and puzzled as Bud and Lou got between them and Glaston got down on one knee. "Bud, Lou, put your arms around them," the press agent directed. "Make them feel welcome."

"How's this?" Lou asked, hugging Kalara tightly, which only made the girl look even more apprehensive.

"That's great," said Joe, ogling her as he raised his camera. "Smile everybody."

The flashbulb popped.

Kalara gasped. Her brother's dark eyes flashed with anger as he barked Hungarian expletives and gestured at the offending camera.

"What?" the press agent asked Bela. "What'd I do?"

Lugosi stepped in to pacify Janika. Translating, he explained to Glaston, "You threatened to steal his sister's soul with your camera."

"You've got to be kidding," Joe said.

"I am quite serious. In my country, it is a common superstition."

Lou snickered. "I guess that's one superstition *you* got over real quick."

Lenore frowned reproachfully. "You shouldn't joke about a thing like that. I'm Austro-Hungarian and such things are taken very seriously by my people."

"Aw, Bats knows I'm only kiddin'," Costello said. "Ain't that right, Bats?"

Had he not wished to appear ungracious in front of his guests, Bela would have given vent to his growing disapproval. He forced a thin-lipped smile.

Joe nodded at the Skorzenys. "Tell them I'm awfully sorry."

Bela translated. Janika nodded. He reached into his jacket and produced a Hungarian-to-English dictionary. Flipping through a list of phrases, he said finally in an accent to rival Bela's, "You are very welcome," and extended his hand in a gesture of forgiveness.

They shook hands.

"Okay," said Lou, "so we're all friends again, right?"

"Yes," said Bela. "Everything, it is smooth."

"You mean 'smoothed over,'" Costello corrected. "And just to show you there ain't any hard feelings," he took Bela aside and whispered, "I'm willing to let you in on the ground floor of something big. So how 'bout it?"

"Do I want in on the ground floor of something big?" Lugosi asked, confused. "You are investing in a high-rise hotel?"

Lou gave Bela a playful poke. "Man, sometimes you're a royal pain in the ass, but you kill me!" Costello gestured for Bela to lean in. He whispered, "It ain't a hotel, but it'll be *in* every hotel and casino in America. It's a new invention and I know the inventor. It's an investment deal that'll make you a lot of money."

Lugosi's brows knitted with skepticism. "What does this new invention do?"

Costello said with a smile, "I could tell you, but I'm gonna do better than that—today I'm gonna *show* you! I'm gonna show *everybody,* especially Goetz and Spitz. Those two guys are running this studio now, and would you believe it, they wanted to give Bud an' me the air to make a bunch of *prestige pi'tures.*" He snorted contemptuously.

Lugosi frowned. "Why is he making this funny monster picture then?"

Lou snickered. "Goetz and his prestige stuff nearly bankrupted this studio, is why." Adding with a smirk, "An' daddy-in-law Louis B. Mayer ain't about to bail Goetz's ass out of his financial troubles this time, neither! And Mayer's daughter's got expensive tastes, and if Goetz goes broke, he ain't gonna be able to buy no more oil paintings. Dr. Fell's invention could make him a lot of dough, so once Goetz gets a load of what I got, Goetz will get Spitz to want in, and I can spit in Spitz's eye 'til he's beggin' me to let him get in like Goetz. What do you say, Bats?"

Frustrated by Costello's wordplay, Lugosi complained, "What do I say? I do not even know what you are talking about!"

No doubt worried that Bela's temper was getting the better of him, Lillian insinuated herself into the conversation. "What's this about an invention?" she asked.

Lugosi glared impatiently. "I do not know. He refuses to tell me what it does."

Costello smiled and said, "Just be at the studio commissary at noon and you'll find out. Dr. Fell, he's got the whole thing set up. You'll meet the doc and he'll show off his invention. He needs investors to cover the start up costs for mass production. Me, I've already sunk in a bundle for what the doc calls 'research and development.' Bud's sunk in plenty, too."

"Lou, please," Barton pleaded, gesturing at the staircase, "while we're all still young."

"Keep your shirt on, Charlie," Lou said. He gave Lugosi a crafty smile. "Oh, and Karloff and Rathbone are real interested."

Both Lugosis were stunned. "Karloff and Rathbone?" Bela blurted out. "I thought Rathbone was in New York, and Karloff…he is so, how do you say it? Clutched with a dollar."

"You mean 'tight with a buck,'" Lou corrected. "All I know is Karloff in particular can't wait to invest. But, hey, never mind, if you'd rather let him make all the dough…." He left the implication hanging as he sauntered back to his position.

"Karloff in particular can't wait to invest."

Beneath his greenish pancake, Bela grew red with indignation. "WE WILL SEE WHO MAKES DOUGH FOR WHO!" he raged.

Smiling broadly, Costello said, "That's the ticket, Bela. You'll show 'em! Oh, and wear the whole Dracula costume. I'm havin' all the monsters dress up. It'll impress the investors."

Lillian took her husband aside. "Please, Bela," she whispered. "Can't you see that Mr. Costello is just using your rivalry with Mr. Karloff to get you to invest money you don't have?"

"What is the harm in seeing what is so special about this invention? If the demonstration is in the commissary, perhaps, I think it is a bread making machine."

Lillian stared quizzically. "Why would you think that?"

"Did Costello not just say that Karloff would be making dough?"

"He meant 'money.' 'Dough' is what Americans call money."

Shaking his head, Bela complained, "Americans and their ridiculous slang! Why do they not just say what it is that they mean?"

Overhearing the remark, Barton pointed at the staircase and fumed, "I'll say what *I* mean and mean what I say, *get up there and stand on your mark!*"

Bela scowled irritably as he mounted the stairs. He got halfway up, winced, and then climbed back down. He could ignore the craving for his medicine no longer. "Mr. Barton, I must take a break, but for only a few minutes."

"A break?" Barton exclaimed.

"Yes," Lugosi insisted, looming over the short-statured director, "Bela will be in his trailer. I will be only five minutes."

Lugosi left the soundstage amid a general murmur of growing discontent.

"Take five, everybody," Barton sighed.

Jane looked concerned. "I still think he's sick. I thought I saw him limping."

Bradstreet fidgeted with his clipboard. "I don't know about Lugosi, but I'm sure getting sick of waiting to say my lines."

Lillian turned to her son. "Darling," she said, "Wait here. I'll be right back."

"Is Dad all right, Mom?" he asked.

"Of course he is," she lied, and hurried after her husband.

Chapter 2

Wednesday, 25 February 1948
10:39 A.M.
Laemmle Blvd., Universal-International Studios

Lillian hurried out the side stage door and ran into a tall, dark-haired young man. She tried to get around him, but Don Marlowe matched her step for step.

"Lillian," he said, flashing a conniving smile, "where's the fire?"

"Not now, Marlowe," she said.

"Now hold on, babe," Marlowe said, doggedly blocking her way. "Does this have anything to do with Bela? He hurried on by and didn't say two words to me."

Lillian frowned as she tried to duck past. "It's really none of your business."

Marlowe grabbed her shoulders. "Hey, babe, if Bela's got a problem, it's my job to make it right. That's what an agent does. I got him his own trailer, didn't I? Face it, honey. I'm worth every penny of my ten percent. Why, if it wasn't for me, Bela wouldn't even be *in* this picture."

"I'll tell him you said so," Lillian said coolly, and pushed her way past.

"You don't have to, babe," Marlowe called after her. "He already knows."

A row of Airfloat trailers sat sheltered from the blazing California sun beneath overhanging soundstage awnings along Laemmle Blvd. The line began at the far corner of the Stage 17 building and continued all the way down to the adjacent Stage 6 build-

...she found the whole trailer had been ransacked.

ing, where the London hotel room, cellar stairs and hidden dungeon sets for the picture were located. The trailers were long, gleaming aluminum hulks with round porthole windows and corrugated trim. Bud Abbott and Lou Costello each had a trailer all to themselves, which spoke of their occasional spats, as well as their star power. Monster actors Glenn Strange and Lon Chaney had to share a special trailer set aside for Bud Westmore, the new head of Universal-International's makeup department. The last one in the line was the trailer displaying Bela Lugosi's name on a star next to the door. From inside the trailer came the sounds of someone tearing the place apart. Lillian hurried inside and closed the door after her. Flicking on the light switch she found the whole trailer had been ransacked. Her steamer trunk had been opened and her clothes strewn all over the floor. Kitchen cabinets and even the oven door were left ajar. She could hear, but not see, her husband frantically searching for his morphine.

Lugosi yanked back the blue privacy curtain that separated the sleeping quarters from the rest of the trailer, giving Lillian a start. He glared at her accusingly. Lillian could see that the cabinets beside the bunk had been stripped bare, their contents spilled haphazardly on the floor. "I cannot find my medicine," Lugosi fumed. "Where have you hidden it? I know it is here somewhere!" He quit the sleeping quarters and returned to his desperate search of the drawers of Lillian's steamer trunk. "Where is my medicine!" he demanded.

"You don't need it, Bela," she said, watching despairingly as the rest of her panties and bras went flying this way and that. "You've been taking too much of it lately."

"Do not tell me what I need or do not need! The pain in my legs, it is unbearable! And now Abbott and Costello want to upstage me at the Hungarian Relief fund raiser!" He shook out one of Lillian's hatboxes and tossed it aside with a frustrated grunt. His searching gaze rested upon his own steamer trunk. He began to claw at the latches, and then shook his head. "No, you would not hide it there."

Wincing, Bela pulled himself up and stumbled toward the bunk where he plopped down and began rubbing his thigh.

Lillian closed the oven door and reached for the coffeepot resting on the burner. "Let me make you some coffee."

"Coffee will do nothing," he whined, grabbing a throw pillow and fidgeting with it. "I need my medicine!" he demanded.

"The doctors say the pain is all in your head."

"It is *not* in my head!" Lugosi angrily shot to his feet and threw the pillow at her. "The pain is in Bela's *legs!*" he insisted.

"Bela, please," she begged, "people will hear you."

"LET THEM HEAR ME!" he roared. "This picture, it is a disaster! I should have done like Karloff and told the studio no!"

Lillian grabbed her husband and shook him. "Bela, please, this isn't like the old days when you could make demands and the studio would listen to you! We need the money! This picture could mean a new life for you!"

Lugosi shrugged himself free of Lillian's grip. "BAH! That is what they said about *Son of Frankenstein* and my role as Ygor! Nothing came of that!" He sat at his dressing mirror, rubbing his right side, "Nothing, except Bela getting shot! Oh, Bela solves a mystery, *yes!* But what happens after that? Rathbone and Karloff, they go on to better things, but what of Bela? Bela goes to Monogram pictures, the Poverty Row, and then nothing!"

"That's why we moved to the East Coast," said Lillian as she knelt down to gather up her clothes, "and why we live out of steamer trunks. And why Bela, Jr. lives with my parents." Frustrated, she balled everything up and stuffed her things in the trunk, shut it and locked it. "We all make sacrifices so you can find better work." She leaned against the trunk and blew a loose lock of hair out of her face.

"Better work? BAH!" Bela complained. "Endless road tours playing the Karloff part in *Arsenic and Old Lace!*"

He gazed despairingly at his reflection. Earlier in his career, Bela paraded before a mirror to convince himself that he *was* Dracula; now it was as if his scowling reflection had taken on a life of its own. Dracula was accusing *him* of turning the vampire into little more than a target for the antics of Bud Abbott and Lou Costello. Bela sighed. "I used to say that Dracula never ends. But I was wrong. Dracula will end, not with a stake through the heart, but instead he will drown in seltzer water."

As infuriating as it was to be the wife of Bela Lugosi, it was moments like this when Lillian felt the pangs of love that first drew her to him—or was it now sympathy? Lillian pocketed her trunk key and stood behind her husband and began rubbing his shoulders. "Don't get discouraged," she said.

He sighed. "Chaney is right," Bela lamented, "this movie, it makes the monsters into buffoons, things that inspire laughter, not terror." His head fell forward as Lillian kneaded his tired muscles. "Now I, too, am a buffoon."

"Dracula is not a buffoon and you *are* Dracula."

She could feel his muscles tense as Bela's burning stare returned to his reflection. "That is not what the studio thinks of Bela! Oh, yes, Karloff, the studio pleads with to play Frankenstein! But Bela, the studio says they can do better than Bela for Dracula!" He turned around and gazed at Lillian with wounded pride in his eyes. "My agent, he had to go to the executives and *beg them!*"

"I don't think Marlowe had to plead for you at all," Lillian insisted. "He just said that to justify his percentage."

"I would not even need Marlowe if you had let me answer this letter!" Lugosi opened the makeup table drawer and pulled out a letter dated a year earlier. The return address was from the Hungarian Foreign Affairs Office.

Lillian said with a sigh, "Not the letter again."

"It is not just any letter. It is an official invitation to return as the new Minister of Culture." His blue eyes burned with renewed pride. "Think of it, Lillian! We would have a fine house, the best of everything! Still, I am sure they would have me if only I agree to renounce my American citizenship! This would mean a new life for all of us!"

"Bela, you know why you turned them down." Lillian took the letter, stuffed it back in its envelope and returned it to the drawer.

Bela winced and glared at her accusingly. "Turn them down? You would not even let me write to them so that I *could* turn them down! Three times they made to me the offer, and three times you refused to let me answer them!"

"It could have been a trick." She gazed earnestly into her husband's eyes. "Once you were back in Hungary they might have made an example of you and had you thrown into a Gulag."

Bela reached down and rubbed his legs. "The pain, it is getting worse." He looked up at Lillian with a pinched expression of torment. "Please, my darling," he begged, "I need my medicine."

Lillian sighed, defeated. "Slip out of your smoking jacket and roll up your sleeve. I will give it to you." She added sternly, "Turn your back."

Bela did as he was told, removing his smoking jacket and turning his back as Lillian went to fetch the hidden injection kit. He rolled up the sleeve of his dress shirt, revealing a forearm dotted with needle tracks of previous injections. He took a length of rubber tubing from the makeup table drawer and used it to tie off a vein. He slapped his arm to raise a telltale bulge and as he did, he watched Lillian in the makeup mirror. She picked up the throw pillow and, while attempting to hide what she was doing with her body, revealed that the pillow contained a hidden pocket! Lillian reached inside and pulled out the small black velvet case containing a glass syringe, a small bottle of alcohol, and a small glass bottle of morphine sulfate. Lillian glanced back to make sure the hiding place was safe. Bela tried to look innocent by busying himself with his forearm. He smiled to himself, amused by his own cleverness. What he didn't know was that his wife was equally as clever.

Playing the role of reluctant nurse, Lillian made certain that Bela saw her uncapping the needle and disinfecting it with a cotton ball soaked in alcohol. She drew back the plunger and inserted the needle into the rubber membrane on the top of the morphine bottle, feeling Bela's eyes on her the whole time. She injected the bottle with air and pulled back on the plunger, filling the syringe not with morphine sulfate as Bela expected, but with distilled water. She soaked a ball of cotton with alcohol and readied Bela's arm for the injection. She hesitated, holding the syringe between her first and second fingers, her thumb ready to depress the plunger. "Are you sure about this, my love?" The needle glinted in the light coming from the dressing trailer windows.

Lugosi nodded. "Please. The pain."

Lillian sighed and let an arc of liquid spurt forth, insuring no air was left in the syringe. Then she administered the shot. Lugosi winced as she did. Lillian undid the rubber tubing. The placebo effect took hold almost immediately. Bela smiled with relief. "Thank you, my darling. Thank you."

She gave Bela a kiss. A knock and a familiar silhouette in the frosted glass porthole in the door gave her a start. "It's Marlowe," she hissed, and called out, "Just a minute!"

Lillian pulled down all the shades and drew the curtains across the portholes and gestured for Bela to roll down his sleeve. She grabbed the drug paraphernalia and hurriedly stowed the tubing, syringe, and bottle of "morphine" under the mattress of the sleeping bunk and drew back the privacy curtain.

Checking his reflection and his costume, Lugosi stood up and tied the belt on his smoking jacket. He gestured grandly. "Enter."

"Bela," Marlowe said, closing the door after him, "I hear you were late for work today. Anything I can smooth over?"

Lillian stepped between them. "What do you want, Marlowe? Bela has to be back on the set."

"I had a great idea for promoting Bela and I just wanted to run it up the old flagpole."

Lillian rolled her eyes, recalling the many ways Don Marlowe's schemes added to Lugosi's downward career spiral. "You mean like the midnight spook show?" she challenged.

The agent brushed Lillian aside. "Bela, how would you like to perform at the Silver Slipper in Las Vegas?"

Bela exclaimed with alarm, "Las Vegas? Never! That place is filled with gangsters!"

"Aw, you got it all wrong. Las Vegas is about showgirls and glamour. Believe me, Bela, if you go to Vegas, you'll get a real bang out of it."

"HA!" Lugosi scoffed. "That is what Bugsy Siegel got, a very large *bang-bang* in the eyes from when the gangsters shot him." He rubbed the scar on his side. "So there will be no Las Vegas for Bela Lugosi."

"Okay, okay. Forget Vegas." Marlowe switched tactics and nudged Bela with his elbow. "Say, did I hear right? Lou Costello is offering you an investment deal? Maybe I can close it for you. I've heard good things through the grapevine about this Dr. Fell."

Lillian glared at Marlowe. "You were eavesdropping?"

"I just happened to be hanging around behind the scenes, babe."

Lillian eyed the agent narrowly. "Do you know what his invention *does?*"

"I've heard a few rumors." He leaned in and whispered, "Some pretty weird stuff, if those rumors are even half right. You ever hear about something called cryonics?"

"Cry-whatics?" asked Bela, mystified.

"Cryonics, you know, freezing stuff. I hear Fell is doing some weird experiments having to do with deep freezing. They say he's some kind of German super-scientist working on stuff that would make Von Braun as green with envy as your face looks now." He gestured for Lillian and Bela to get in close. "I hear the government gave Fell a whole new identity. They had to so he could work on top secret stuff having to do with putting people on ice for space travel."

"Space travel?" Lillian jeered. "If he's working on things like space travel, why would he ask for investment funds from Lou Costello? It doesn't make sense."

Marlowe shrugged. "You got me. I'm just repeating what I've heard." He smiled. "Maybe the Feds decided they didn't want their flyboys turned into popsicles."

"I have to go back to the set, Marlowe." Lugosi stepped outside.

Lillian pushed Marlowe out ahead of her and closed and locked the trailer door. She took Bela's arm and together they headed back to the soundstage.

Marlowe padded after them. "By the way, Bela," Marlowe brashly inquired, "how are you feeling these days?"

Lugosi eyed his wife. "I have been better. Why do you ask?"

"No reason. It's just I've been talking to your doctor on the East Coast, and he wanted me to make sure you got the best possible care." Marlowe turned and waved over a man standing in profile and holding a little black medical bag. Whoever the physician was, he made a startling first impression. Clutched at a dramatic angle between the doctor's teeth was a long black cigarette holder. He removed the cigarette holder and held it in a distinctly European manner as he tapped the ashes from the tip. He was of medium height and had perfect posture. Lillian noted the sharpness of his profile, his coarse curly hair, and mustache. Even standing still, the physician radiated great force of will. But when he turned on his heel to greet them, Lillian was startled to see that the right side of the doctor's face was covered by a black half-mask.

Marlowe beckoned. "Here's your patient, Doc. Meet Bela Lugosi."

The doctor returned the cigarette holder to his mouth and approached. Although in his early sixties and slightly prone to plumpness, the doctor moved with the vitality of a much younger man. He forced a smile and Lillian felt his one good eye keenly scrutinize them from beneath his caterpillar eyebrow.

"Bela," Marlowe said, "this is Dr. Kopf. He's going to be your personal physician."

"His *what!*" Lillian exclaimed, looking the weird medico up and down. "Is this a joke?"

Dr. Kopf clicked his heels and bowed with a military attitude. "*Herr* Lugosi," he said with the hint of an accent, extending his hand. "I am so honored to make your acquaintance. I have followed your career with great interest."

Bela smiled and took the doctor's hand. "You are a fan?" he asked, noting at a glance that the doctor had nicotine stained fingertips, suggesting a chain smoker who didn't always use a cigarette holder. Lugosi also noted that the doctor's fingers were stubby, yet strangely elongated at the tips, and ending in oddly humped nails.

"Oh, yes indeed," the doctor said. "I have seen all your films. I even own prints of several of them."

"Really," Lugosi beamed, the doctor's flattery derailing his detective instincts. "Which role do you like most, if I may ask?" Considering how he was presently made up, Bela expected the doctor to say *Dracula*.

"Without a doubt," Dr. Kopf declared, "Roxor in *Chandu, the Magician* was your most mesmerizing performance." The doctor smiled apologetically. "No pun was intended."

Bela accepted the compliment graciously, if somewhat perplexed. "I am glad you enjoyed it, doctor." In reality, Bela felt the villain Roxor was beneath him, and he only took the role for the money, but a compliment was a compliment. Changing the subject, he asked, "Marlowe has told you of my pain?"

"Yes. Acute sciatica, the result of a bullet wound you received during The Great War in Hungary."

"Exactly," Lugosi said. "I was presented with the Hungarian Purple Heart, but I have suffered terribly ever since. The doctors and my wife, they try to wean me off my medicine."

"Oh, I disagree." Dr. Kopf patted his medical bag. "There is no shame in taking pain medicine, when you really need it." He reached into his bag and produced two vials of morphine.

Bela smiled gratefully. "That is just what I was telling Lillian." He reached for the bottles.

"I'll take those," Lillian insisted, snatching the bottles away. She eyed the doctor suspiciously. "You're a German?"

"Austrian, *Frau* Lugosi," Dr. Kopf corrected, clicking his heels. Lillian did not like the way he was looking her up and down, almost as if sizing her up as a conquest.

"You sound German to me," she sneered.

Bela put his arm around his wife. "You must excuse Lillian. She means well, and I love her dearly." He patted his chest. "Always I keep her picture in Dracula's tuxedo breast pocket next to my heart."

He reached into his bag and produced two vials of morphine.

Marlowe sniped, "Does it help deflect the wooden stake?"

Lillian grabbed Marlowe by the arm and took him aside. "Listen, Marlowe, I don't need you sending a for-hire pill pusher around to fill Bela's head with nonsense."

"I'm just looking out for my client, babe. After all, we wouldn't want Bela to needlessly suffer, now would we?"

Lillian glared menacingly. "If you *ever* do anything like this again, I'll see *you* suffer—plenty." She stuck the vials of morphine in her coat pocket. "Now, about this Dr. Kopf—is he the one spreading rumors about Mr. Costello's inventor?"

"You know your problem, Lillian? You're paranoid."

"Do you know *your* problem, Marlowe?"

"No, babe, what's my problem?"

"*Me.*"

Taking her husband's arm, Lillian made her excuses to Dr. Kopf. "We're sorry you came out here for nothing, doctor. I'll see you get paid for your time."

"Thank you, *Frau* Lugosi, but I will bill *Herr* Marlowe instead." He eyed the agent closely. "Do you have it?" he asked.

"In the trunk of my car, Doc," Marlowe assured him.

Lillian smirked. "Make sure he pays in cash. Now if you'll excuse us, Bela is needed back on the set." Eyeing Marlowe, she added, "*Alone.*"

As she and Bela returned to the soundstage, Lillian heard Marlowe remark to Dr. Kopf, "If Dr. Fell could bottle the cold shoulder that dame just gave me, he wouldn't need cryonics."

Chapter 3

Wednesday, 25 February 1948
12:10 P.M.
Universal Studios Commissary

The section of the commissary reserved for executives and A-List stars was a classy affair. Pleated curtains lined the walls; round dining tables were situated throughout with white tablecloths, cloth napkins and silverware. Bela Lugosi remembered once sharing a table with Gloria Holden, who was shooting *Dracula's Daughter* at the time. So it came as no surprise when Lugosi, with Lillian on his arm and flanked by Bela, Jr., joined the gathering crowd in full Dracula regalia, wearing his least favorite cape. It was made of shining satin with a lining that blended from gold to salmon pink and had a batwing-inspired fringe. Lugosi thought it was ludicrous looking, but apparently the special effects department needed a shiny material to perform an animated bat-to-human transformation for the picture.

Bela was not the only monster in attendance. Towering over the crowd was Glenn "Pee Wee" Strange as Frankenstein's Monster, his prune-wrinkled face and overhanging foam rubber forehead and drooping foam rubber eyelids painted a grayish green. Riding on his broad shoulder was his ten-year-old daughter, Janine, who looked like a pig-tailed kewpie doll beside her father's massive frame.

Lon Chaney, who had dropped the "Junior" from his billing, but not from his studio contracts, was in Wolf Man makeup minus the false teeth and hairy gloves. Paper towels were tucked into the collar of his dark blue shirt. A foam rubber appliance transformed his forehead, nose and upper lip into a wolfish snout. An elaborate full head reddish-brown werewolf wig and hairy brows had replaced Jack Pierce's tedious applications of yak hair.

"Remember," Chaney said to makeup artist Emile LaVigne, "the minute this dog and pony show is over, I want out of this getup."

"I know, I know," the diminutive, bespectacled LaVigne said, painfully aware of the actor's impatience with monster makeup.

Bela noted the bulge of a brandy flask in Chaney's back pocket and whispered to his wife, "I will wager he is drunk again." He gave Lon one of his patented disapproving scowls.

"Glass houses, my darling," Lillian warned.

Lugosi frowned. "What about glass houses? You hate gardening."

Lillian patted her husband's arm. "Just be kinder to Mr. Chaney. That's all I'm saying."

Bud Abbott approached Lugosi and took the Hungarian's hand, clasping it between both of his. "Glad you could make it, Bela," he said, smiling warmly. "I'm sorry about before. I really respect you as an actor."

"And I have respect for you as a comedian, Mr. Abbott," Bela said.

"Lou wanted me to tell you that he's sorry, too. It's just that, well, when it comes to Reds, Lou sees red, and when you brought those two foreigners on the set, he just got the wrong idea, you understand."

Bela forced a smile. "*Foreigners*, of course, I understand," he said. "But you must understand that your language, it is very difficult for Hungarians to learn. When first I came to this country, I had to learn the lines by the sounds."

"Phonetically," Lillian elaborated.

"Oh, don't get me wrong," Abbott explained hastily. "Lou isn't the only one on the lot who feels this way about Communists. Bob Arthur, our producer, is the same as Lou, a staunch Republican and real American Patriot. Now that you explained how your friends *fight* Communists, the Skorzenys are welcome on the set anytime."

"I see," Lugosi said, maintaining a pleasant demeanor. "That is most kind."

Abbott glanced around and whispered, "As a matter of fact, Lou's thinking of getting everyone who works on our pictures to sign a loyalty oath, he cares that much about fighting Commies in Hollywood." He patted Bela, Jr. on the back. "And some day, your boy will take the Reds on as a fine young officer."

Bela, Jr. saluted. "Yes, sir," he said, smiling.

"So just forget about this morning," Abbott assured Bela, "that's all water under the bridge."

Bela frowned. "Water under which bridge?"

"Aw, that's swell!" Abbott laughed. "You know that routine."

"Routine?" asked Bela, genuinely wondering what bridge Abbott was referring to.

Bela, Jr. tapped his father's shoulder. Lugosi leaned over to listen as his son whispered, "It's just an expression, Dad."

Bela nodded with understanding and smiled pleasantly at Bud. "Yes, a fine routine," he said.

Abbott looked relieved. "I'm glad there are no hard feelings."

"My feelings, they are very soft," Bela said grandly, then gestured at a stage situated at the head of the dining room. On the stage stood Lou Costello and a scientist who could have easily been mistaken for silent film director Erich von Stroheim. Closely cropped dark hair on his pate tapered to neatly shaved baldness around the ears and back of the head, emphasizing the egg-shape of his skull. His features were hard. Penetrating blue eyes peered from behind thick, black rimmed glasses. A thin dueling scar ran down the right half of his forehead from hairline to brow ridge, putting Lugosi in mind of the Frankenstein Monster's scar. His posture and a neck brace betrayed some spinal injury supported by a rigid corset hidden underneath his doctor's smock. He wore black rubber gloves as if prepared to operate. Standing on the sidelines were Eddie Sherman and Joe Glaston. Joe had his camera ready.

"That one," said Lugosi, pointing at the scientist, "he must be the inventor."

"Yes, that's Dr. Fell." Abbott tapped his temple. "He has a great mind."

"I understand you and Mr. Costello have invested quite a bit of money in…whatever it is the invention does."

"Lou has high hopes that we'll get back twice what we invested, maybe more. See that guy over there, the one standing with Dee Dee Polo? That's Lou's new accountant. Mike introduced Lou to Dr. Fell."

Lugosi noted the young man holding a briefcase. "I overheard earlier that Miss Polo does not trust him very much."

"They share a very small office at Lou's house that Dee Dee used to have to herself," Abbott explained. "It's a territorial thing, I guess." He gestured at two men standing near the foot of the stage. One was bespectacled and dark haired; the other husky with twin shocks of silver at the temples. Abbott said, "I just hope this demonstration impresses the bosses."

"Mr. Goetz," Bela said, pointing at the man with the glasses, "does not strike me as a man who is easily impressed."

"Well, you know how these intellectuals are. But Spitz is the man to impress. If we can wow him, then Goetz is sure to play along." He leaned in and whispered, "Spitz is very shrewd. He started out as an attorney and movie company advisor before accepting Goetz's offer to help run Universal-International."

Bela turned to his son. "Did you hear that, son? Mr. Spitz is an attorney." He explained to Abbott, "My son, he wants to be a lawyer when he grows up."

"You don't say." Abbott poked Bela, Jr. kiddingly. "So you want to be a bloodsucker like your old man?"

"Yes, sir," Bela, Jr. said with a smile.

Bela put a hand on his son's shoulder and nodded toward the stage. "Perhaps you ought to speak to Mr. Spitz. He may be able to give you valuable advice."

Lillian turned to her son. "That's a good idea. Why don't you have a look at the machine and get to know Mr. Spitz while your father and Mr. Abbott and I talk?"

"Okay, mom," Bela, Jr. said.

Jane Randolph and Lenore Aubert gave the passing boy a smile as they approached Bela and Lillian. Jane was still in her Spanish Dancer costume, and Lenore was every inch the femme fatale in a stunning black crepe evening gown and mink wrap. Lenore gestured at Bela, Jr. "You should be very proud of your son, Bela."

"I am, indeed," Bela said, gesturing broadly. "Does not my son look handsome in his uniform?"

"Very handsome," said Lenore.

Standing at the foot of the stage, and in uniform, Bela, Jr. looked like a soldier on leave at a carnival sideshow. Smiling at Lugosi, Abbott remarked, "That boy's the spitting image of you."

Bela gave Abbott an affronted frown. "You want to spit on my son?"

"No, no! It's just a saying," Abbott explained quickly, "like, 'never the twain shall meet.'"

"What train?"

Without missing a beat, Abbott replied in his staccato delivery, "The twain that wuns on twack twee."

"What?"

Lenore indicated the stage with a nod. "Lou has arranged quite a publicity stunt."

Jane gushed with enthusiasm. "Isn't this exciting? I wonder what that thing does."

Lillian asked Abbott matter-of-factly, "What *does* it do?"

"Just keep your eye on that cabinet, folks," he said, sounding like the fast-talking city slicker he played for laughs. "Believe me, the invention is very practical and will make investors a lot of money."

Bela watched Lou Costello with keen interest. The comic stood like a proud father beside an aluminum cabinet that made humming and grinding noises. "Keep your eyes right here, folks," he said, pointing at an empty glass sitting inside a vending compartment.

There to lend their moral support were Lou's wife, Anne, and their 12-year-old daughter, Paddy. Anne was a former burlesque dancer, and by Bela's standards, still very attractive. Paddy was decked out in her finest party dress and hopped up and down excitedly as the machine made a final gasp and three perfect cubes of fresh ice tumbled into the glass. With all the showmanship of a carnival barker, Costello raised the glass triumphantly, shaking it, making the ice cubes tinkle, and posing as Glaston captured the moment.

"There it is, folks! *Ice!* This baby makes *ice* like magic! No more trays! No more fuss! And no muss neither! Just hook up the hose to any faucet and the Wonder Icemaker makes ice by the bucketful!"

"Wow!" marveled Bela, Jr.

Lillian smirked. "So this is the great cryonic experiment Marlowe heard rumors about."

"Very disappointing," Lugosi said, shaking his head.

"Now don't be hasty," said Abbott. "Like I said, this is a very practical invention."

Lenore nudged Jane. "Let's get a better look—over there," she said.

Jane nodded. "Okay."

The girls slipped through the crowd and positioned themselves behind Joe just as the press agent screwed in a new flashbulb. "Can we get another shot, Lou? Every time I try to get a picture of the doc, he looks away or covers his face. "

"Sure," said Lou, throwing his arm around Dr. Fell and steering him toward Glaston's camera.

"I told you," scientist snarled with a trace of a German accent, "I don't wish to be photographed!"

"Why?" asked Costello. "You afraid Joe's gonna steal your soul or somethin'?"

"What? No." He squinted in the flash as Joe snapped a picture. Dr. Fell glared angrily as Joe quickly replaced the bulb and made ready to grab another shot.

Lou held up his hand and pointed into the crowd. "Wait a minute, Joe. Let's get Goetz in the pi'ture, too!"

"Thanks, but no thanks," the studio boss said. He turned to his partner. "What do you think, Leo?"

Spitz studied the machine with a critical eye. "How much ice can this contraption make an hour?" he asked Costello.

Lou played the excited little boy. "It makes lots, and lots! And lots more! So much ice Sonja Henie could skate on it!"

"Yeah, yeah, yeah," Spitz sneered. "Never mind the ballyhoo. I just want the straight dope."

Goetz shook his head wearily. "Just as I thought, a waste of time."

"Don't be so hasty, Bill," Spitz said, rubbing his chin thoughtfully. Gesturing at the cabinet, he asked Costello, "Well, how much ice does this thing make an hour?"

"So much ice that—"

Obviously unhappy with the comedian's hyperbole, Dr. Fell cleared his throat loudly. Lou took the hint and let the scientist take over.

"At the maximum setting, approximately one hundred gallons of ice an hour," Dr. Fell said. "It is only limited by the capacity of the bin and how quickly it is emptied." He raised the lid of the cabinet, displaying a bin full of perfect ice cubes. "There is a sensor in the collection bin. The sensor interrupts the process if it detects the bin is full." He picked up a cube with his rubber gloved hand and displayed it proudly. "Note how my quick-freeze process forms perfect cubes of ice, exact to within a fraction of a millimeter on all six sides. And the crystallization is flawless, giving the cubes a transparency heretofore unimaginable!" His magnified eyes grew wild with excitement. "And the transport system dispenses ice a glass at a time, or champagne buckets can be filled from the bin directly, which would be ideal for hotels and restaurants alike! Yes, this machine is capable of even greater speeds if the bin is emptied quickly so the sensor is not triggered!" The scientist's pride bordered on the megalomaniacal as he declared, "Did I say a hundred gallons an hour? Perhaps even a thousand gallons in an industrial setting, nay, perhaps even a million…"

Costello stepped in and said, "So like I said before, it makes lots and lots of ice."

Glenn Strange smiled with admiration. "What they won't come up with these days," he said in a gravelly voice with the hint of a Southwestern accent.

Chaney elbowed the Monster in the ribs. "Now if that thing can make ice cubes out of vodka, I might get one for Lenny's Ranch," he said, referring to the homestead named after his career-launching role in *Of Mice and Men*.

Dr. Fell glared at Chaney. "It doesn't matter what liquid you use, as long as the source is connected to the intake hose." He paused briefly as he reflected on the matter. "All you would need to do is to adjust the temperature to the freezing point of alcohol. And then, think of it!" His eyes were aflame as the possibilities excited his imagination. "Ice cubes of vodka for the perfect martini! Whiskey cubes for the finest whiskey sours!" He clutched at the air dramatically, declaring aloud, "We could rule the world!" adding in a calmer, more rational tone, "…of bartending and hospitality."

Costello smiled nervously. "He gets that way sometimes, he's such a kidder." Out of the corner of his mouth, he muttered, "This is how come I said to let me do all the talkin'."

Just then Bobby Barber arrived on the scene. "What's doin'?" he asked.

Lon Chaney became the enraged Wolf Man as he grabbed the little man by the lapels and shook him. "How dare you show your ugly face around me!"

Bobby's eyes widened with fear. "I said I was sorry!"

"Sorry? NOT HALF AS SORRY AS YOU'RE GONNA BE!" he growled.

The Frankenstein Monster interceded. "Hey, what's all the fuss?" asked Glenn.

"This little bastard ruined my transformation scene, Pee Wee," Lon explained.

Janine Strange gasped. "Oooh, Daddy, what he said!"

Glenn patted his daughter's leg reassuringly. "He don't mean nothin', honey. It's just angry talk." He gave Chaney a chastising frown. "Watch your language, Lon. There's ladies present."

The Wolf Man looked to the Monster for sympathy. "I'm sorry, Pee Wee, but this little—" He caught himself and said, "this little *so and so* ran onto the set in the middle of a take and shot off a firecracker! A *firecracker!* You can't mess up even one frame of those lap-dissolve shots and when he made me jump, he ruined everything!" He drew Barber in until they were nose-to-snout. "Thanks to this clown 10 hours of work was *junked!* Last week I did re-takes *all day* because of him!"

"Hey, what's all the fuss?" asked Glenn.

A bright flash startled the Wolf Man. Chaney snarled at Glaston, "Say, what's the big idea?"

The press agent smiled. "It was too good a shot to pass up."

The Wolf Man tightened his grip on Barber's lapels. "Be sure to make a print for this runt. It'll give the plastic surgeon something to work with after I take him apart!"

"Now just a minute, Chaney," Lugosi said as he stepped in between them like a referee at a prizefight.

"Gee, thanks, Bela," Bobby said with a sigh of relief. "For a minute there I thought—"

Lugosi said to Chaney, "You are not the only with a score to settle with Barber." He turned to the now sweating Bobby Barber and smirked. "So, Barber," he said, "I see you are again up to your old magic, spoiling people's takes."

"It's not magic, goddamn it!" Chaney growled. "It's *tricks!* Up to your old *tricks!* Jesus, Lugosi, haven't you caught onto the slang yet?"

Janine Strange gasped again and put her tiny hands over her ears. Glenn shook his head at Lon. "You gotta watch your language around my kid."

The Wolf Man rolled his eyes.

Lugosi detected strong alcohol on Chaney's breath. With a shrug, Bela said, "Tricks, magic, it is all the same to me. But nevertheless, Barber has made trouble for both of us." He leveled a menacing stare at the comic. "Perhaps *together* we should teach him a lesson."

Barber flinched. "Now wait a minute, fellas. Messing up your takes wasn't my idea. Lou put me up to it. Honest!" He looked imploringly to Costello. "Tell 'em, Lou."

Costello noted the two studio heads' looks of disapproval. "Come on, will ya?" he scolded Barber. "If you're gonna get beat up, take it outside." He patted Dr. Fell on the back. "This is the doc's show. Now scram, or it's the doghouse for you tonight."

"Aw, come on, Lou," Barber whined. "Not the doghouse!" A glint of recognition replaced Barber's pouting. "Say, I know you!" he said to Dr. Fell.

"I do not believe we have met," Dr. Fell answered icily.

"Maybe not, but I seen your act."

"Aw, no you don't!" Chaney grabbed Barber's lapel. "You're not gonna weasel your way out of this by changing the subject!" the Wolf Man insisted.

The elusive Bobby Barber slipped his arms out of his sleeves, leaving a nonplussed Wolf Man holding an empty jacket.

As Lon angrily threw the jacket down and glared at Barber, the little man scrambled up onto the riser and gestured at the doctor's tunic. "It was back in Vaudeville. You wuz in a white lab coat," Barber pointed at the icemaker, "and you had a big cabinet, bigger than this one even. You used it to turn a pretty dame into a gorilla and back again!"

Costello grew nervous as he pulled Barber aside and whispered, "Pipe down, will ya?"

Lugosi turned to Chaney and quipped, "I see the doctor, he has been up to tricks as well."

Goetz studied the fuming scientist. "Are you sure about that?" he asked Barber.

"I remember like it was yesterday," Barber insisted. He turned to Dr. Fell. "You played it like you wuz Eric von Stroheim in a mad scientist picture. That was your gimmick."

The scientist's hackles rose with indignation. "To you Americans, all of us Prussians look like von Stroheim!" He raised his hand to strike the comic. "How dare you compare me to a common stage magician!"

Costello broke into a sweat as he tried to hold him back. "Bobby didn't mean nothin' by it. See? He's always crackin' wise. That's what I pay him for."

"You *paid* him to treat me this way?" Dr. Fell said with a withering glower.

"Sure he did!" Chaney snarled as he mounted the stage and grabbed Costello's arm, "Just like he paid Barber to ruin my transformation scene."

"Yes," added Lugosi, joining Chaney on the stage, "just as he was paid to ruin Bela's staircase scene!"

Caught between the Wolf Man, Dracula and a fuming inventor, Costello slipped into character and emitted a series of scare-take gasps.

"N-n-no," Lou stammered. "I never paid him!"

"He's right," Barber said, thinking this was a routine. "I'm insultin' you guys for nothin'."

"WHAT!" Fell roared.

The crowd laughed uproariously, much to Dr. Fell's consternation. Goetz and Spitz remained stone-faced.

Tugging nervously on his shirt collar, Costello fell back on what he knew best. "HEEEEY, AAAABBOTT!" he cried.

Hearing his cue, Bud Abbott hurried to join his partner. "What's wrong now?" he admonished.

"It wasn't me, Abbott," Costello pleaded in his little boy voice. "It was Bobby!"

Bud turned on Barber and demanded, "What do you have to say for yourself?"

"Aw, all I said was that the doc reminded me of a Vaudeville magician I knew once."

"Is that so?"

"Yeah. That magician turned a lady into a gorilla and back again." Barber eyed Costello. "Looks to me like he hasn't changed Lou back yet."

"THIS IS AN OUTRAGE!" the scientist roared, slamming his fist down on the icemaker cabinet.

"I thought it was an icemaker," Lou wisecracked.

Frustrated, Dr. Fell gestured angrily at the machine. "It *is* an icemaker!"

"You said it was an outrage."

"The machine isn't an outrage! YOU ARE THE OUTRAGE!"

"I'm no outrage. I'm Italian."

Bud pulled on Lou's necktie to get his attention. "Now look here! When he says that this is an outrage, he doesn't mean that the machine is an outrage. He means the *situation* is an outrage."

"The situation ain't no outrage," Lou insisted. "The situation is supposed to be us givin' a demonstration. We're demonstratin' an icemaker."

"But you're making it an outrage."

Lou held up the glass of ice. "I ain't makin' an outrage. I'm makin' ice cubes!"

Bud rolled his eyes in comic frustration to the delight of the gathering throng. "Oh, you're impossible!" he grumbled.

"I ain't impossible. I'm Lou Costello." He grabbed his partner by the lapels. "Bud, don't ya know me?"

Bud shook himself loose. "I sometimes wish I didn't."

"I'll second that," said Goetz, who turned to his partner and gestured at the exit. "Come on, I've seen enough."

Spitz hesitated. "But what about the ice machine? This could really be worth something."

"As far as I'm concerned, the only thing worth investing in is art, not some crackpot's invention being touted by a couple of fugitives from Vaudeville. Which reminds me, I just got the Van Gogh framed. Come on, it's in my office."

"Is this a gag?" Mannix laughed uproariously at the disembodied appendage.

As they turned to leave, Goetz found his way blocked by a short, squat executive with a flat pug face. The man slapped Goetz on the back gruffly and guffawed, "Hey, Bill, what's your hurry?"

"What are *you* doing here?" Goetz asked warily.

"Stick around and find out," the tough guy said.

Lugosi instantly recognized Hollywood's most notorious scandal fixer and Louis B. Mayer's indispensible right hand man. "Mannix," he exclaimed under his breath, and then slipped away to join his wife.

"What is Mannix doing here?" Bela whispered to Lillian.

She shrugged. "Maybe the Mob sees a good investment and wants a monopoly on the invention."

"What do board games have to do with it?" Bela demanded as Mannix leapt onto the stage and got Lou and Dr. Fell in a crushing bear hug.

"This was terrific!" he effused. "The most entertaining goddamn demonstration I ever saw! I tell ya, this icemaker is the best thing since sliced bread! I'm willing to take the plunge and I know a bunch of guys who are just waiting to dive right in with me!"

"Gee, Eddie, you really mean it?" asked Lou eagerly.

"Sure I do, Louie." The executive slapped Dr. Fell on the back. "The name's Mannix, doc! Eddie 'The Bulldog' Mannix, Vice President of M-G-M! But you can call me Eddie! They call me 'The Bulldog' because when I see a good thing, I bite down and won't let go! Put 'er there!"

Mannix grabbed Dr. Fell's hand and shook it vigorously. To everyone's shock, Mannix's enthusiastic handshake pulled Dr. Fell's hand off at the wrist.

"Is this a gag?" Mannix laughed uproariously at the disembodied appendage. "That's a good one! I asked ya to put 'er there, and damn if you didn't! HAW! HAW!"

"Actually," the inventor said proudly as he rolled up his sleeve, revealing a metal forearm, "it is another invention of mine."

Dr. Fell took the mechanical hand back and attached it to a socket at the end of his wrist, then rolled the sleeve of the glove back over the forearm. Reaching with his good hand, he unbuttoned his tunic at the shoulder, exposing a padded leather body and neck brace. The sight reminded Lugosi of Peter Lorre's startling appearance in *Mad Love*.

"Sensors in my body brace accept commands from my remaining muscles," the doctor explained, "and those impulses are sent to the hand and elbow joints. Three motors in the hand, one to work the thumb and two to actuate the fingers, imitate *perfectly* normal articulation, but with a hundred times greater strength!"

Demonstrating, Dr. Fell grabbed the glass filled with ice cubes and pulverized it in a powerful, yet natural grip. "You see?" he said, clapping the powdered glass off his hands, "I was caught off guard by your handshake, but had I wished, I could have crushed the bones in your hand as easily as this glass."

"You don't say," said Mannix, scratching the back of his head.

"I lost my arm in The Great War," Dr. Fell explained, displaying his hand proudly. "But from that tragedy came this vastly improved instrument!" He smiled as a wild gleam returned to his eyes. "A whole array of specialized attachments can be fitted to the wrist and work at my command!"

Mannix gave the doctor a playful nudge and remarked suggestively, "I got a pretty good idea what those *specialized attachments* are good for, too. You get it, doc? Huh?" He winked and chuckled.

Dr. Fell eyed Mannix narrowly, and then slowly, he smiled. "Yes," the doctor said, reflecting on the matter, "I see what you're saying." He leaned over and muttered, "I should introduce you to my sister. She thinks as you do and makes such off hand remarks."

Mannix guffawed and slapped the scientist on the back. "Hey, that's a good one, doc! Off hand. I get it! HAW! HAW!"

Bela grimaced as he watched, confiding to his wife, "This Dr. Fell, he is crazy. But there is something else. I do not like him. I do not know why, but I do not like him."

"*I do not like thee, Dr. Fell,*" a familiar voice recited in hushed Shakespearian tenor.

Alarmed, Lugosi turned quickly to find Basil Rathbone standing behind him.

"Sorry, old fellow," Basil said. "I didn't mean to startle you."

"Rathbone," Bela sneered. "Costello warned me that you would be here."

Lillian studied Basil's aquiline features. "What was that you were saying?"

"Oh, just an old nursery rhyme my nanny taught me." The actor earnestly recited, "*I do not like thee, Dr. Fell, the reason why, I cannot tell. But this I know and know full well; I do not like thee, Dr. Fell.*"

Lugosi gestured impatiently. "You have not changed, Rathbone. Your jokes, they are still not funny. Where is Karloff?"

The gaunt, bronzed figure of Boris Karloff emerged from the crowd and joined Rathbone. "Hello, Bela."

"Hello, Karloff," Bela said begrudgingly. The Hungarian observed that Boris was sporting a mustache and looked infuriatingly dapper.

"You don't sound terribly pleased to see us," Karloff observed good-naturedly.

William Goetz and his partner chose that opportune moment to invade the scene. "Boris! Mr. Rathbone! It's a pleasure to have you on the lot."

Spitz nodded in agreement as he shook Karloff's hand. "We can't wait for you to get started."

Bela eyed Boris keenly. "Have you changed your mind about being in the picture?"

"No," Boris explained. "Mr. Goetz is merely paying me to promote your film."

Lugosi glowered at the studio chief. "Bela Lugosi can promote his own film!" he insisted.

Goetz gave Bela a condescending smile. "The public identifies Frankenstein with Mr. Karloff. Now, if the movie had 'Dracula' in the title, naturally we'd send *you* to New York." Addressing Boris, he said, "We'll even pay for your hotel if you will allow us to take pictures of you purchasing a ticket for *The Brain of Frankenstein*." He turned to Spitz. "Call a meeting of the advertising department. I want to test that ridiculous title, *Brain of Frankenstein*. What kind of a title is that for a comedy, anyway?" He turned back to Karloff and Rathbone. "Listen, when you've had enough of Lou Costello's antics, come by my office and we'll discuss the details over brandy and cigars. Mr. Rathbone, I'd very much like to talk to you about being in one of my prestige projects."

"Thank you," said Basil. "I'd like that very much."

Bela waited for the bosses to be out of earshot, and then leveled a hard stare at Rathbone. "Why are you here anyway, Rathbone? Obviously it was not to talk to Goetz."

"Oh, uh, I'm here on business."

"What kind of business? I thought you were in a play on Broadway." Lugosi gestured at Basil's arm. "I also heard you had broken your wrist."

The question seemed to catch Basil off guard. "Oh, uh, yes, a silly accident. Happened whilst I was walking the dog…in the park. Lost my footing." He displayed his right hand and flexed his wrist. "Quite healed now. Just a bit stiff. Caused a bit of a fuss on opening night. Had to do it in a cast. But, as they say, the show must go on and all that."

"So why are you here now with Karloff?"

"As I said, I'm in Hollywood on business." A nervous smile played on Rathbone's lips. "Boris and I ran into each other…at the Brown Derby. Yes, you see, he, uh, mentioned his meeting at the studio, so I, uh, invited myself…to tag along."

Bela eyed Rathbone narrowly. He suspected the actor was lying but couldn't figure out why. "I see," Lugosi said.

Lenore and Jane approached.

"Boris. Basil. There you are," greeted Lenore.

"A pleasure, Miss Aubert," Boris said, and then extended a hand to Jane. "Ah, Miss Randolph, I'm charmed to meet a fellow protégé of Val Lewton. *Cat People* and *Curse of the Cat People*, wasn't it?"

"Why, yes," said Jane slyly, "so nice of you to remember."

Lenore smiled. "I'm afraid the only cat I worked with was *The Catman of Paris* in a silly little shocker for Republic Pictures." She and Jane exchanged knowing looks, and then Lenore said, "But you know what Benjamin Franklin said about cats..." and together the girls chorused, "'…all cats are gray at night.'"

Lenore frowned at Jane while Jane gasped and covered her mouth. The blonde smiled sheepishly and whispered, "Sorry, I thought *I* was supposed to say it."

Basil arched his eyebrow and glanced at Boris. He cleared his throat and said to the ladies, "I, uh, prefer Theodore Roosevelt's famous quote, 'I speak softly, but carry a big stick.'"

"Ah, yes, I *see*," said Lenore, putting a strange emphasis on "see," and then asked, rather mysteriously, "Where?"

"The hotel," said Boris. "My suite."

"When?"

"Tonight," said Basil.

Lugosi glared accusingly at Karloff and Rathbone. "What kind of conversation is this? It all sounds very under the hand."

"Underhanded," Boris corrected.

"Whatever it is, you are all up to something, I think."

"Not at all," Rathbone flatly denied. "It's just business."

"You said your business was elsewhere."

"It is," said Boris. "At my hotel."

"Sounds like risqué business, if you ask me," commented Lillian.

"It's nothing of the sort," Boris insisted.

Bela pointed at Lenore. "Then why did you call her 'my sweet?'"

Karloff chuckled. "I didn't call Lenore 'my sweet.' I was referring to my suite at the hotel."

"So your wife is at the hotel?"

"My wife is home, but my suite is at the hotel."

"So there is at your hotel yet *another* woman?" Lugosi's eyebrows arched with masculine admiration. "I did not know you had it in you, Karloff."

Lillian tapped Bela's shoulder to get his attention. "Bela, he means his suite at the hotel."

"That is who I meant!" Lugosi addressed Karloff again. "So who is this sweet at your hotel?"

"I didn't mean—," Boris began.

Basil rolled his eyes. "Ye gods, Boris, let me have a go at it or we'll be at this all day!" He shook his head at Bela. "You've obviously been spending too much time in the company of Abbott and Costello." He braced himself and explained, "When Boris is talking about his suite at the hotel, he means his *room* at the hotel, a hotel *suite*, s-u-i-t-e."

"Exactly," said Lillian. "Do you understand now, my sweet?"

Lugosi glared at his wife. "We do not have a suite! We have my trailer."

"I didn't mean we *have* a suite, I was calling *you* my sweet, because that's what you are to me—my sweet. So when Mr. Karloff talks about *his* suite, he means his room, but when I talk about my sweet, I mean you. Understand?"

Bela glowered. "I think you are part of a conspiracy to drive me mad."

"Oh, honestly, Bela," Basil carped. "Sometimes you can be so—"

The exchanged ended abruptly when they all became aware that everyone in the commissary was staring at them.

Up on the stage, Costello nudged Abbott. "Did you get a load of that routine? We gotta use it in a pi'ture some time."

Mannix laughed uproariously as he leapt from the stage and rushed over to give Lugosi, Karloff and Rathbone a bone-jarring group hug. "If it ain't my old pals, the three B's! Boris, Basil and Bela! Been a long time, boys! Glad to see ya!" Slapping Boris on the back, he asked, "How's the new wife, Karloff? Sorry to hear about you and Dorothy splittin' up. She was a real sweet lady."

Lugosi snarled, "Do not start *that* again!"

Wincing from the blow, Boris rubbed his shoulder and asked, "How did you know about my divorce?"

Mannix frowned. "Gee, sorry, Karloff, I forgot about your bad back." He shrugged. "It's just I keep tabs on all my old pals."

"I see," said Boris, recalling his last encounter with Eddie Mannix. "I wasn't aware I was your pal."

"Sure you are!" Mannix said. "Look! Me and Toni are still together!" He displayed a gold tiger eye ring. "Boy, remember the trouble this little ring got me in?"

"Yes," Rathbone said with polite reserve, "it was quite a predicament, for all of us."

Eddie's eyes twinkled. "Say, why don't you guys bring your wives over and you, me and Toni will have dinner at my joint!"

"Uh, Ouida's in New York," said Basil.

"Evelyn really doesn't like dinner parties," said Boris.

"Lillian would rather die," said Bela, gesturing at his now embarrassed wife.

Mannix slapped Lugosi on the back. "HAW! HAW! Always speak your mind, don't you, Lugosi! That's what I love about you!"

"Yes," said Rathbone. "Boris and I are well aware of our friend's outspoken-ness."

"I am not outspoken!" Bela insisted. "I merely say what needs to be said!"

The crowd parted as Glenn Strange lurched clumsily on his built-up boots, all the while his daughter hugged his neck for support. "Hello, Boris!" he called. "What brings you to these parts?"

Obviously glad for the interruption, Boris waved and said, "Hello, Glenn. Come right over."

Glenn nodded at Janine. "This here's my little girl," he said, patting his daughter's leg. "Janine, this is Boris Karloff. He showed Daddy how to play the Monster when we worked together in *House of Frankenstein*. He's a real swell guy!"

"Hello, Mr. Boris," Janine said.

Boris smiled pleasantly. "Hello, my dear. I have a little girl, too. Her name is Sara Jane." He indicated Glenn. "And your Daddy makes a very fine Monster, don't you think?"

"Yes," Janine nodded, patting her father's flat head.

"Say," said Mannix, "that gives me an idea." He waved Joe Glaston over. "Hey, Joe, you want a swell picture? Take a shot of the two Monsters and me."

"I don't really think that's necessary," Boris said humbly.

"Sure it is," Mannix insisted, getting between them and posing for Joe's camera. "Say, cheese!"

Glaston got down on one knee and snapped the picture.

Satisfied, Mannix grinned like a big kid and then took Joe aside. "Make some copies for me, will ya?"

When Mannix was out of earshot, Glenn leaned down and whispered, "Sorry about that, Boris."

"Think nothing of it, Glenn. How are you holding up?"

"I'm doing just fine," the Monster said with a broad smile. "Westmore's foam rubber makeup makes playing the Monster a snap. Why, I even get dialogue this time!"

"Not that Tarzan dialogue, I hope."

"Well, mostly it's…" Strange fell into character, putting his daughter down and holding out his arms as he lurched toward Bela, intoning, "Yes, Master."

Lugosi grimaced. "Stop holding your arms out like that! I told you I only did that in *Frankenstein meets the Wolf Man* because I was supposed to be blind."

"I *am* blind." Glenn explained to Boris, "That's the only drawback with this getup, I can't hardly see nothin' with these eyelids on." He said to Bela, "If I don't hold my arms out, I'm liable to trip and fall flat on my face."

Bela relented. "I suppose that makes it all right."

Mannix came back, rubbing his hands together vigorously. "What do you say to a steak dinner tonight? It's on me."

Lillian noted two familiar figures hovering at the entrance to the commissary. "Here are the Skorzenys, Bela. Why don't you call them over and introduce them to Mr. Mannix?"

Bela was about to tell her exactly why he didn't want to introduce them to the likes of Eddie Mannix, when he turned to Glenn and suggested instead, "Show the Skorzenys how you play the Monster."

"Why, sure," Glenn said, and he lumbered in their direction.

The reaction "Pee Wee" got was not what Bela expected. Kalara Skorzeny's eyes became wild, and her face blanched in stark terror. She backed up against her brother, pointing at Glenn's Frankenstein Monster, while crying in alarm, "*A kárhozat háza! A kárhozat háza! Halál! Halál!*"

Costello hurried over. "What happened? Did somebody try to take her pi'ture again?"

Mannix shrugged. "Search me. I can't make out a word she's sayin'."

"It is Hungarian," explained Bela. "She speaks no English."

Boris held Glenn back. "You'll have to convince the poor girl you're only an actor in makeup. Show her that your daughter isn't afraid."

"Good idea," Glenn said.

Janine clapped her hands over her ears to block out Kalara's hysterical screaming as her father picked her up and said with a broad smile, "It's okay, lady, it's just a costume. See? This is my little girl. She's not scared at all."

Unfortunately, even a paternal Frankenstein Monster can seem awfully menacing and Kalara responded with more hysterics.

Basil steered him away. "Glenn, perhaps it might be better if you got out of sight."

"I guess I better." Squinting, Strange looked around calling, "Hey, Emile, lead me outta here, will ya?"

Glenn hugged his daughter as he lurched out of the commissary by way of the back door, led by the makeup man and followed by Lon Chaney's Wolf Man, who obviously didn't want to make matters worse with his own frightful appearance.

This proved all too much for the Hungarian girl. She pointed and screamed, "*A kárhozat háza! Halál!*" and fainted in her brother's arms.

Boris rushed to help Janika as he carefully lowered his sister to the floor.

"Mannix," directed Basil as he knelt beside her, "keep everyone back." Rathbone undid the buttons on the unconscious girl's sleeve and bared her forearm.

The Bulldog turned on the pressing crowd and barked, "Give the dame some air! Come on, you guys, everyone, get the hell back! Move it, or I'll brain ya!"

"Maybe somebody should call a doctor," Bud Abbott suggested. "Is there a doctor in the house?" he asked the crowd.

"Hey, what about Fell?" said Mannix. "He's a doctor." He waved him over, shouting, "HEY, DOC, GET YOUR ASS OVER HERE!"

Remaining by his invention, Dr. Fell explained, "I am not a medical doctor. I'm a scientist."

Basil felt for Kalara's pulse, and then paused in the act, his eyes narrowing.

Bela knew that look all too well. Something had peaked Rathbone's amateur detective instincts.

Janika glowered and slapped Rathbone's hand away, tugging down Kalara's sleeve.

"Please," Basil urged, "I'm trying to help her."

Basil reached to loosen Kalara's collar. Again Janika pushed him away, protesting vehemently in Hungarian.

"We have to loosen her clothing," Rathbone tried to explain as Janika continued to protest. "Bela," he implored, "tell him that we need to loosen the young lady's clothing. Circulation to the brain, don't you know."

While Lugosi tried to reason with Janika in Hungarian, a familiar figure wearing a black half-mask pushed his way through the startled crowd. "Let me through, I'm a doctor!"

"I thought I sent him home," Lillian remarked coolly.

"Lillian!" Bela scolded. "The doctor only wishes to help."

Janika didn't take kindly to Dr. Kopf and his remarkable appearance. Lugosi had to explain that Kopf was a real doctor, and his private physician, so it was all right to let him examine Kalara.

Janika reluctantly agreed.

Dr. Kopf examined her pupils. "She's in deep shock," he concluded.

"I'll elevate her feet," said Rathbone as he removed his jacket and bunched it up. "We need a blanket or something to keep her warm." Spying Lenore's wrap, he asked, "Might I trouble you for your coat, please?"

"Of course," said Lenore, handing over the mink. Basil took the wrap and tucked it under Kalara's chin.

The doctor smiled. "I see you've done this before, *Herr* Rathbone."

"You pick things up in No Man's Land," Basil said offhandedly.

"You were in The Great War?"

Basil flashed a rakish smile. "I was a patrol officer with British Intelligence." Basil noted the mask. "I take it you were in The Great War yourself."

Two studio nurses arrived. With Rathbone's and Dr. Kopf's assistance, the nurses lifted the unconscious girl onto a wheeled stretcher.

Costello shook his head. "Pee Wee's makeup sure gave the poor kid one heck of a scare."

"Yeah," Abbott said, frowning with concern as the nurses strapped Kalara down. "Maybe we should rethink the whole idea of doing a comedy monster picture."

Lugosi addressed the doctor. "Have Kalara taken to my trailer."

Dr. Kopf said, "I'm sure the studio has an infirmary."

"No, I insist she be taken to my trailer. She should be made comfortable."

The doctor bowed. "Very generous, *Herr* Lugosi."

Bela turned to Janika and explained where they were taking his sister. Janika walked with the stretcher, holding his sister's hand as they rolled Kalara out.

Bela turned to Lillian. "I must report back to the set, or I would stay with her. Do not let Kalara out of your sight." Bela motioned his son over and whispered, "I want you to see that no one but the doctor and Janika see Kalara. If anyone else comes, you find out their name and you write it down. Do you understand? You are a soldier, and I am putting you on guard."

Bela, Jr. saluted. "You can count on me, Dad."

Lillian eyed Bela keenly. "Something worries you, too."

"I do not think that Frankenstein frightened her at all."

Lillian nodded as she and Bela, Jr. hurried to catch up with the stretcher.

Abbott tapped Bela on the shoulder. "Hey, what gives?"

Rathbone arched an eyebrow, casting a sly look in Boris's direction. "I think Mr. Lugosi is being a trifle melodramatic."

Bela glared narrowly. "If you spoke Hungarian, you too would take such precautions."

Costello asked, "So what did she say that's got your boxers in a knot?"

"'*A kárhozat háza,*'" Lugosi repeated as he gave Costello a fierce look. "It means 'House of Doom.'"

Lou swallowed hard. "And what was that other thing she said?"

Glaring at Costello as only Dracula could, Bela intoned ominously, "Death."

"Yes, I suspected something like that," Basil said, nodding conclusively.

Lugosi glared. "How could you suspect such a thing? You do not speak Hungarian."

Rathbone gestured at his wrist. "I saw the evidence tattooed on Miss Skorzeny's forearm—serial numbers."

Lenore pressed her hands together with concern. "You don't mean…?"

"Yes," said Basil. "Miss Skorzeny, and her brother, too, I expect, were inmates in a concentration camp."

Chapter 4

The company was dismissed around 6 o'clock. Bela emerged from Stage 17 as Dracula in all his vampire glory followed by Lenore, Jane and Bradstreet. They had been shooting scenes in the castle's bedrooms, hallways and laboratory and were ready to call it quits for the day. Barton had the cameras moved to Stage 28 for tomorrow's filming of the Masquerade Ball scenes.

While his co-stars headed for the makeup trailer, Lugosi stopped to talk to his son. "Did anyone other than the doctor or Janika try to see Kalara?"

"No one, Dad," Bela, Jr. assured him.

Bela glowered suspiciously at Karloff and Rathbone, who were keeping watch with Bud Abbott outside Bela's trailer. "What are they doing here?"

"They're worried too, Dad."

Bud Abbott anxiously pace back and forth, glancing at a calling card he was holding.

"What became of the esteemed Dr. Fell?" asked Boris.

Abbott shrugged. "Dr. Fell said he wasn't feeling well, so he asked if he could catch a ride home in Dee Dee's car. I think maybe Mike went with them."

"Just where does the good doctor reside?" asked Rathbone.

Abbott smiled nervously. "Oh, he lives in a spooky old joint off Wilshire Boulevard. I think it used to be a funeral home back in the day. That wreck surrounded by all these new postwar houses really makes it stick out like a sore thumb." He fidgeted with the calling card. "Uh, I could draw you a map, if you want."

"That would be helpful, yes." Rathbone motioned him over, took the card and slipped it into Abbott's breast pocket. "And do keep *that* to yourself, old boy. Later, I'll brief you on how and when to use it."

Bud Westmore opened the door to the makeup trailer and stepped aside to make room for a now human looking Glenn Strange. The former stunt man and movie heavy had traded Frankenstein's black jacket and pants for jeans and a checkered shirt. Janine paused in the doorway. Glenn picked her up. She felt his cheek and said, "Now you look like Daddy again."

He kissed her and said, "Daddy thought he was gonna drown when Bud here pulled that headpiece off, there was so much sweat."

Janine giggled.

Westmore motioned to Bela. "Hey, come on, you're next, Dracula."

"I will be there in a moment," Lugosi said. "Let Bradstreet go next."

Westmore shrugged. "Suit yourself." He motioned Bradstreet inside and closed the door after them.

Lugosi asked Rathbone, "Any news yet of Kalara?"

Before Rathbone could answer, Lou Costello pulled up in a studio buggy. "HEEEY, AAABBOTT!" he shouted excitedly. "Eddie's a done deal!" Costello jumped out, rubbing his hands together gleefully. "Sherman's wrapping things up right now!"

Abbott smiled weakly. "That's fine, Lou, just fine."

"Fine? It's great!" Lou gave his partner a pinched frown. "Smile, will ya! Why do you have to be such a Gloomy Gus all the time?" He noted everybody's faces. "What is this, a funeral?"

"Lou, there's a poor girl fighting for her life in there."

"Aw, she'll be okay. Cheer up, already! We're gonna be rollin' in dough."

Abbott shushed him and looked around anxiously. "Lou, please, the audit is coming up." He leaned in and whispered as he fingered his breast pocket. "Listen, what if I told you there might be a way to get the IRS off our backs?"

"Who are you kiddin'? It ain't the IRS you're worried about. It's your bookie. Well, don't worry. We'll be able to pay off your gamblin' debts *and* the IRS and still have plenty left over to get that swimmin' pool started." Costello turned to Lugosi. "As for you, Bats, if you want in, you better hurry and make up your mind. Mannix has big plans for the Wonder Icemaker."

"Yes," Lugosi sneered. "Mannix has friends that need many things kept on ice."

"You mean because Eddie's like this with the Mob?" Lou crossed his fingers.

Abbott held up his hands and winced. "Lou, ixnay. If Eddie hears you talkin' like that—"

"Aw, don't worry, Abbott. Who doesn't know about Eddie and the Mob?" Lou asked with a shrug. "But, hey, their money is as good as anybody else's, ain't it?"

"If you live to spend it," Lugosi countered.

"Look, enough business talk," Lou said, changing the subject. "Is the girl okay?"

Rathbone shook his head. "We haven't heard yet."

"Gosh," said Glenn. "I sure am awful sorry I got the gal so upset."

Rathbone looked around. "Where is Mr. Skorzeny?"

Bela gestured back at the soundstage. "He is telephoning Hungarian Relief. He wants to cancel the fund raiser, but I said I would do it anyway and dedicate my appearance to Kalara."

Janika emerged from the soundstage, glowering as he approached.

"Bela," said Glenn, "tell the guy how sorry I am."

Bela translated what Strange said just as Lillian came out of the trailer, holding the door open for Dr. Kopf.

"If *Fräulein* Skorzeny should become agitated during the night," the doctor said, handing her a bottle of pills, "have her take two of these. They're fast acting and she'll sleep for hours. I'll call back in the morning."

"Thank you, Dr. Kopf." Lillian added apologetically, "About the way I behaved toward you earlier...."

"Nonsense, *Frau* Lugosi. *Herr* Marlow mentioned nothing to me about your husband's morphine addiction. You were right to put me in my place. As for the girl, I will assign a nurse to watch her."

"That won't be necessary," Lillian assured him. "I'll stay with her tonight." She put a hand on her son's shoulder. "I'm calling a cab for you and your father."

"But, Mom," Bela, Jr. protested, "I'm on guard duty."

"You're relieved."

"But—"

"She is right, young man," said Dr. Kopf. "You are a very brave soldier, but as a soldier, you must obey orders. And for someone your age, there is no higher ranking officer than *Mutter*."

Janika confronted the doctor, making demands in Hungarian. Lugosi stepped in to translate. "He wants to know about his sister's condition."

The doctor noted Janine Strange with a glance. "We should not speak in front of the children." He saluted Bela, Jr. "Soldier, would you escort the young lady over there?"

Glenn put his daughter down. "Go with Bela, Jr., honey. We got grown up talk to do."

"Okay, Daddy," Janine said, smiling and taking Bela, Jr.'s hand.

Once the children were out of the picture, Dr. Kopf addressed Skorzeny's question. "Tell *Herr* Skorzeny that the *fräulein* has suffered a severe mental trauma. She is in catatonic shock and must rest."

Bela explained the situation. Janika nodded and asked a question. Bela translated, "He wants to know if she will be well enough to take back to the hotel tomorrow."

"I can tell better in the morning."

As Lugosi relayed the message, Abbott gestured at Janika. "Bela, tell your friend that I'll gladly call a cab and I'll personally take him back to his hotel. I'll even buy him dinner, if he likes. I'm sure he doesn't want to be alone at a time like this."

"That is very kind of you, Mr. Abbott." Bela conveyed Bud's offer to Skorzeny. Skorzeny scowled at Abbott, but his tone of voice registered gratitude. "He accepts your offer, Mr. Abbott," Lugosi explained. "Janika also apologizes that he cannot smile. His facial muscles, they were damaged."

"*Herr* Lugosi," the doctor said, "you might be able to clear up a small mystery. In her delirium the *fräulein* kept mumbling something in Hungarian."

"Was it, *a kárhozat háza?*" asked Bela.

Janika was visibly shaken by the phrase. The doctor noted the reaction and asked, "That sounds like it, yes. What does it mean?"

"It means, 'House of Doom,'" said Bela.

Rathbone pressed, "Ask Mr. Skorzeny what that phrase means to him."

As Bela questioned him, Skorzeny grew agitated and related his painful memories, speaking so quickly that Bela had to ask him to slow down a few times. When at last he fell into a grim silence, Bela explained, "He said that the House of Doom was a secret Nazi laboratory in a castle near Budapest and that it looked very much like the castle set in our picture."

Costello looked Skorzeny up and down. "No wonder they wuz so shook up before about gettin' their pi'ture took." He asked Bela, "So what happened in this House of Doom?"

"What he described to me about Kalara's horrible experiences, I would rather not say in front of the ladies. But it is why she and Janika now fight for a better Hungary."

Dr. Kopf frowned. "She kept asking for a doctor, a doctor named Halál."

Janika cried out, "*Doktor Halál!*" His eyes filled with burning hatred and he began ranting Hungarian vitriol at such a furious pace Lugosi struggled to keep up.

"Janika says that Doctor Death was the chief scientist—and it was believed that he was dead. He thinks that Kalara saw him alive today—in the commissary. Now he fears Doctor Death will try to kill Kalara—to silence her."

Rathbone asked, "Why can't Skorzeny point this war criminal out to the authorities himself?"

Bela relayed the question. Skorzeny ranted again, covering the lower half of his face with his hand.

Bela explained, "Janika says that no one except Kalara ever saw Doctor Death without his surgical mask."

Skorzeny continued, cutting a vertical slash in the air as he spoke, pointing at Glenn Strange.

"Kalara told Janika once that Doctor Death had a scar, a scar on his forehead like this." Lugosi described a line extending from hairline to brow. "Like Frankenstein."

"Gosh," said Glenn, "no wonder the poor kid screamed when she saw my ugly puss."

"Dr. Fell, too, has such a scar," said Lugosi, who directed a challenging leer in Lou Costello's direction.

Costello folded his arms and shrugged. "So do a lot of guys," he insisted. "That don't make 'em all escaped Nazi scientists. For all we know, the poor kid goes nuts when she sees any kind of scar." He pointed at Kopf's half-mask. "What about this guy? He's got a puss that'd scare anybody."

"Now, Lou," Abbott chastised, "don't be like that."

"Be like what?" Costello shot back irritably.

The doctor shook his head. "How they both must have suffered, that poor girl especially. The horrors she suffered are imprinted upon her body." Putting a hand to his half-mask, he added grimly, "Just as they are on mine. See for yourselves." He rolled up his sleeve and displayed serial numbers tattooed on his forearm. "I, too, am a survivor. I have seen such horrors before."

Rathbone noted the tattoo. "Can you describe the girl's injuries, doctor?"

Dr. Kopf rolled his sleeve down and buttoned it, and as he did he described matter-of-factly, "Her hands and feet show signs of having been exposed to extreme frostbite." He tugged at the cuff. "I have heard of the Nazis conducting such low temperature experiments. They wanted to see how long it would take for a human being subjected to extreme cold to die, and if they should die, if they can somehow be revived."

"Those monsters!" Lenore snarled.

"Those side-winding bast—," Glenn began, and then remembered there were ladies present. "*Rustlers*," he substituted, "side-winding *rustlers*."

Lillian shuddered with revulsion. "And on both her breasts, tattoos—strange insignias tattooed right where it would hurt the most."

"No!" Jane exclaimed, crossing her arms over her breasts as if staving off a similar fate.

"Can you describe these tattoos?" Basil asked pointedly.

"What's it to you?" Lillian demanded, annoyed at what struck her as Rathbone's prurient interest.

Boris frowned apologetically. "You must forgive Basil. He takes this Sherlockian stuff too much to heart."

Basil eyed Lillian. "Was one of them something like a bat with a battle axe?"

Lillian started. "How did you know?"

"A what and a what?" Bela exclaimed.

Lillian gestured and nodded. "It was a bat and a battle axe. The tattoo on the other breast was even stranger."

"An open palm, perhaps?" Basil suggested.

"No—a telephone."

"A telephone!" exclaimed Boris.

Basil nodded and smiled. "Yes, Boris, a telephone. No doubt displayed within a hexagon."

Lillian started. "Yes, but…how did you know?"

Jane gulped and clutched her hand to her throat. "This is too weird for me. Lenore, will you walk me to my car? I suddenly don't want to be out alone."

"I feel the same way."

Strange gallantly offered his arms. "It would be my pleasure to escort you lovely ladies back to your cars."

"Thank you, Glenn," said Lenore, entwining her arm with Glenn's as the former cowboy heavy called for Janine to join them.

Jane took the little girl's hand and Glenn's other arm and said, "Good night, everyone."

Boris said, "Good night, ladies."

Dr. Kopf handed Lillian and Bela each a business card. "If *Fräulein* Skorzeny's condition should change, call me. This will put you directly through to my answering service."

Lugosi glanced at the card and noted the name: *Dr. Tod N. Kopf.*

Lillian said, "Thank you, Dr. Kopf. Can we call you a cab?"

"No need, *Frau* Lugosi, I am parked in the executive lot." The doctor clicked his heels together and bowed. "*Auf Wiedersehen.*"

Rathbone pulled out a black leather-bound notebook and began writing something in it as Lugosi overheard Karloff remark, "Perhaps we should call Richard for instructions." Bela noted the way Karloff kept a wary eye on the retreating Dr. Kopf.

Rathbone glanced up as the doctor turned a corner and disappeared between the paint and electrical shops. "I really don't think that's necessary. Although," he said, indicating the notebook, "R. S. might be able to look up these serial numbers."

"Good show, Basil! I'm sure he can."

Bela looked over Basil's shoulder to see what he had just written, and then studied the pair closely. "Who is this Richard you speak of? Why would he know about concentration camp serial numbers?"

Rathbone smiled nervously as he snapped the notebook shut. "Oh, uh, Richard is just a fellow I have business dealings with. He's retired from the British consul service with connections that might prove useful. Nothing you need be concerned about."

As he pocketed the notebook, a business card fell out. Lugosi picked it up before Basil could retrieve it. There was a strange emblem printed in green ink, a letter "C" with a brain inside it, a crown above and the words, *Semper Occultus* printed below. As he examined the card, Bela's eyes narrowed with suspicion. "This man would be useful for what?" He pointed at Basil's pocket. "And why did you just write down the doctor's serial number, if all that concerns you is the girl's?"

Rathbone shrugged, smiling nervously. "No reason. I just found it interesting."

Gesturing at the card, Lugosi asked, "And what nonsense is this? You must take me for a fool. It is obvious that you two are on a case and it has to do somehow with this card and with your knowledge of Kalara's tattoos. You are investigating a mystery, admit to it!"

"Nah," Costello interjected, looking at the card. "Rathbone'd have on a Sherlock Holmes hat if he was. I'll bet this card means he's in Little Orphan Annie's Secret Society."

Skorzeny casually glanced at the card.

Basil smiled disarmingly as he addressed Bela, but kept a wary eye on Skorzeny. "My days as a detective, real or fictional, are behind me, old boy. Actually, uh, that is the calling card," he hesitated, and then brightened, "of my business associate. Yes, that's just what it is!"

"What kind of calling card is this?" Bela scoffed. "There is no name on it."

Rathbone spoke at a rapid-fire pace. "It represents a circle of private investors that wish to maintain their anonymity. But the point is, Richard is the chairman, and he has heard about Mr. Costello's scheme. I was sent here as, uh, their representative, yes, exactly, to see if Dr. Fell's invention was something they'd be interested in." Smiling confidently, he added, "I think I can definitely recommend that they take the plunge."

With a voice dripping with suspicion, Lugosi asked, "Why did you not say so before?"

Rathbone straightened up, taking on a superior air. "I told you, they wish to maintain their anonymity. I wasn't to reveal my true intentions until I was sure the scheme was viable."

Lou beamed. "You really think this Richard guy and his friends would want in?"

"Most definitely," said Basil.

"That's great!" Costello's enthusiasm gave way to regret. His face fell. "Oh, wait. I just made a deal with Eddie. I can't do nothin' until I okay it with him."

Basil frowned with mock disappointment. "Oh, what a shame," he said, snatching the strange calling card away from Bela, much to Lugosi's consternation. "Ah well, no sense crying over spilt milk." He pocketed the card and turned to Boris. "Just so my trip to California isn't a complete waste of time, we ought to take Mr. Goetz up on his offer for a chat. He did mention something about a role for me in his next prestige picture."

Bradstreet emerged from Westmore's makeup trailer. "You're next, Lugosi," the makeup man called.

"In a minute," Lugosi sniped. He glared disapprovingly at his fellow boogiemen. "You would think of investments and film deals when in my trailer a poor girl suffers? I am ashamed of both of you!" He glowered at Costello. "And you, too!"

"Gee, you're right," Lou said, frowning with shame. "I'm a heel."

Looking genuinely remorseful, Boris said, "Bela, really, if you must know—"

"BELA!" Westmore shouted. "Get in here or you can go home wearing that getup!"

Lugosi snarled and waved the makeup man away. "What did you want to say, Karloff?"

"Never mind, Boris," Basil interrupted hastily. "No need for explanations."

Karloff shot Basil a disapproving frown, but relented. He mumbled uncomfortably, "I suppose you're right," before delivering a very heartfelt, "My apologies to you both." He reached into his pocket and produced a notebook similar to Basil's. He unclipped a pen and slipped one of the strange calling cards from a pocket in the notebook's cover. "We're staying at the Knickerbocker Hotel. I'm in Suite 205." He jotted his room number and the hotel's telephone number on the back of the card and handed it to Bela. "If anything should happen, do let me know." Glancing sideways at Skorzeny, he added mysteriously, "Present this card...if the need should arise."

Taking the card, Lugosi glared narrowly. "What is *that* supposed to mean?"

Rathbone grabbed Boris's arm and said hastily, "He means if you should decide to join the investment group." He coaxed Boris along with a cheery, "Come, Boris. I understand Mr. Goetz has acquired a rare Van Gogh," followed by a snarling whisper, "What were you playing at?" and then smiled nervously, bidding all an unconvincingly pleasant, "Good evening," before steering his reluctant companion down a bystreet leading to Goetz's corner office.

Bela and Lillian stared after them, confused. Lou just scratched his head, while Abbott nudged him and whispered, "Lou, that's what I wanna talk to you about—in private."

Suddenly a stagehand emerged from Stage 17 and waved Lou over. "Mr. Costello, you have a phone call," he said.

"Hold that thought, Abbott." Lou hurried to answer the phone.

Lillian gestured after Boris and Basil. "What was *that* all about?" she asked.

"I do not know," said Bela. He stuffed the calling card in his pocket and declared with Hungarian determination, "There is something strange going on, and I feel that they know more than they say. But Bela the detective, *he* will investigate and he *will* find out!"

"Detective?" asked Abbott.

"Yes, detective! Bela is the finest there is!" He nudged Skorzeny and explained what was going on as Bela, Jr. frowned.

"Uh, Dad," the boy said, tugging on his father's cape.

"What, my son?" he asked. "You wish to help investigate?"

"No," Lillian said. "He's wondering what I'm wondering." She gestured at Lugosi's clothes. "You want to go sneaking around looking like that?"

Lugosi looked down at his costume and felt his face. "I am still in makeup!" He hurried toward Westmore's trailer just as the makeup supervisor was locking it up. "Where are you going?" Bela demanded.

"You made your coffin, now you can lie in it." Westmore headed back to his studio, leaving Lugosi to haunt the lot as Dracula, whether he liked it or not.

He returned to Lillian and said with a dismayed shrug, "I will just have to investigate looking like this."

Lillian shook her head disapprovingly. "I really don't think you should be spying on your friends."

"It is not spying, it is investigating. There is a difference."

"It isn't investigating when there isn't a crime to investigate. You're just being nosy."

Lou Costello returned just as Bela said, "My Hungarian intuition tells me otherwise. First there was that strange conversation between Karloff and Rathbone and Jane and Lenore, and talk of a late night meeting, then there is Kalara. No, there is more here going on than meets my eyes. Bela solved a mystery once before as a detective, and Bela can solve this mystery as well."

"What'd I miss?" Lou asked eagerly.

Abbott gestured at the soundstage. "What was the phone call about, Lou?"

"It wasn't nothin' important, Abbott. Joe said he was gonna stay on the lot and finish developing the pi'tures at the studio photo lab." He nudged Bela and jerked a thumb at Janika. "Uh, don't tell your friend, but Joe said that in spite everything, he got a swell action pi'ture of the Hungarian dame and this guy nearly punchin' Joe's lights out."

Lugosi glowered. "I told you how Janika feels about having their picture taken."

Lou shrugged. "He don't understand what I'm sayin', so don't tell 'im." Changing the subject, he asked, "Anyway, did I hear right that you were once a real detective?"

Lugosi proudly pointed at himself. "I solved a murder," he bragged, and then waved at his surroundings. "It happened on Stage 7 on this very lot. Sometime, I tell you all about it."

Lillian smiled. "Mr. Rathbone and Mr. Karloff helped. Just remember that when you tell the story." She playfully poked him in the ribs. "So did I, remember?"

Lugosi waved dismissively. "*They* were very little help." He put his arm around Lou's shoulder. "I tell you what really happened. Karloff and Rathbone, they would never have solved the case without Bela." Glancing at his wife, he added reluctantly, "Or Lillian."

A twinkle of mischief glinted in Lou's eye. "Say, if you're gonna play Sherlock an' investigate Karloff and Rathbone, can I be your Watson? I'll even drive ya wherever ya want."

This gave Bela pause. "You will drive Bela, all right," Lugosi said, appraising the pudgy little comic, "drive Bela mad." With a reluctant nod, the Hungarian said, "But, yes, you can be Bela's Watson. Come, we must follow Karloff and Rathbone."

"In that getup?"

"Yes, in this getup. Now we go."

Puffing out his chest, Costello grabbed Bela, Jr.'s military cap and set it on his head at a jaunty angle. He gave Bela a snappy salute. "Lou Costello, Junior G-Man is at your service." He jumped in the driver's seat of the studio buggy and gestured at the empty seat next to him. "Hop in, Sherlock! You, too, Abbott," Lou said, jerking his thumb at the back seat.

"Uh, sorry, Lou," Bud replied nervously. "I don't think we ought to bother Mr. Karloff and Mr. Rathbone."

"Neither do I," said Lillian.

Abbott gestured at Janika. "Besides, I'm looking after Mr. Skorzeny."

Lou leveled a withering glare. "Ah, don't be such a wet blanket."

Janika asked Bela what was going on. Bela explained. Janika gestured at the studio buggy.

"What's he sayin'?" Lou asked.

"He would like to be a detective, too," Bela said.

"Hey, great! The more, the merrier. Tell 'im to hop in."

Janika got in, followed by a reluctant Bud Abbott. "I don't know about this, Lou. Seeing that Janika's sister is sick and all."

"Hey," said Lou, "if he wants to do somethin' to keep his mind off his troubles, that's his business."

Bela, Jr. stepped forward and saluted. "Excuse me, Mr. Costello, sir," he said with military bearing.

"You wanna be a detective, too?" asked Lou.

"No, sir." The boy pointed at the cap on Lou's head. "If you please, sir, I'd be out of uniform if I didn't have my cap."

"Are you sure this is your hat?" Lou teased. "It fits me real good."

"It is, sir. Look inside."

Lou took off the cap and looked inside the sweatband. *B. Lugosi* was handwritten in white ink. "This is your hat all right." Glancing at the embroidered initials, E.N.M.S., across the front, Lou said in mock seriousness, "Say, I didn't know your military school also made chocolate candy."

"Sir?" Bela, Jr. asked as he took the cap back.

Lou reached into his jacket pocket and pulled out a brown pouch of M&Ms. "See? En and Em's."

"Oh, no, sir," Bela, Jr. said seriously, placing the cap on his head. "It stands for 'Elsinore Naval and Military School.'"

"You don't say. You learn somethin' new every day."

Bud Abbott leaned forward. "Come on, Lou, quit teasing the kid."

Lugosi pointed ahead. "No more jokes, funnyman. We have a mystery to investigate."

"Okay, Bats. Like Sherlock Holmes says, the game is 12 inches."

"What do you mean by that?"

"It means the game's a foot."

Lugosi rolled his eyes. "I think Bela may regret this."

"Bela," Lillian said, pointing at her shoulders. "At least take the cape off."

Lou shook his head. "Leave the cape on. You look more natural that way."

Before Lillian could protest, Costello took off for the Administration Buildings and Scenic Gardens where William Goetz had the corner office. Lou pulled over across the way and pointed at an open casement window.

"Well, look at that," he said. "We couldn't ask for a better place to eavesdrop." Costello got out of the studio buggy and made an inviting gesture to Lugosi. "After you, Dracula."

"No, Watson," said Lugosi, getting out and bowing slightly, "after *you*."

The two amateur sleuths tiptoed over to the adobe style buildings and crouched under the open window to Goetz's office.

"You mean to say," they heard Rathbone remark, "that this self-portrait is a recent discovery?"

Bela peered over the sill. Inside William Goetz's spacious office Lugosi saw Karloff and Rathbone standing by a generously stocked wet bar. They were admiring a gilt framed portrait of artist Vincent Van Gogh displayed on a brass easel.

"That's exactly what it is," Goetz said proudly while watering a hanging plant by the open window.

Boris gestured at the painting with his brandy glass. "I assume you had it authenticated."

Spitz sat in an overstuffed chair and took a puff of his cigar and smiled. "Mr. Goetz wouldn't pay 50 grand for a work of art without first getting an expert appraisal."

"I should say not," Goetz said. "Jacob Baart-de la Faille himself made the appraisal."

"And the title?" asked Basil.

"*Study by Candlelight*. It's the pride of my art collection."

"I say, Boris," Rathbone said enthusiastically, "do you think Vinny would be interested in seeing this?"

"Oh, definitely," Karloff said, with equal zeal. "I think he'd be awfully put out if we *didn't* tell him about it."

"Vinny?" Goetz asked, pausing in his watering.

"Vincent Price," said Basil.

Spitz sat up straight. "Vincent Price, the actor?" he asked incredulously.

"The three of us worked together on *The Tower of London*," Boris explained.

"He played the Duke of Clarence," Basil elaborated, "and did it brilliantly."

"It was our second collaboration with director Rowland V. Lee." Clearing his throat, Boris muttered to Basil, "With far less drama behind the scenes than *Son of Frankenstein*, I might add."

"That goes without saying," Basil agreed. "Now," he said to Goetz, "if there's a chap you want in a prestige production, Vinny is definitely your man."

Goetz smirked. "Forgive me for saying this, but I hardly think the actor who appeared in *Green Hell* could fully appreciate something like *Study by Candlelight*."

"On the contrary," said Basil, "he's quite the art connoisseur."

"You don't say."

"I do say."

"In fact," added Boris, "I wouldn't be surprised if dear old Vincent couldn't give your Van Gogh expert Mr. Baart-de la Faille a run for his money."

"Is that so?" asked Spitz, eyeing his partner.

"Indeed," said Basil. "We definitely ought to invite him over for a look, a meeting of one Vincent with another, you might say."

Goetz frowned. "I'll think about it." Having finished watering his plant, Goetz stuck the watering can out the window, dumping the excess on the eavesdropping detectives, and then closed and latched the window.

Costello spat an arc of water and sighed. "So what did we learn from that?"

"We learned," Bela grumbled, "that we are not so good at spying."

They headed back to the studio cart. Abbott did his best not to laugh. "I'm not the kind of person to say I told you so, but I told you so."

"Yeah, yeah, yeah," Costello grumbled as he grabbed Abbott's pocket hanky. A calling card fell from Bud's pocket. "Hey, what's that?" Costello picked up the card. Printed on it in green ink was the now familiar brain inside a large letter 'C.' "This is one of Rathbone's cards," he said.

"Uh, I can explain that," Abbott began.

Bela took out the calling card Karloff had given him and compared the two. "They are exactly the same." He eyed Abbott narrowly. "Which of them gave to you this card, and why?"

Lou's face turned bright red with anger. "I know what this is all about!" He pointed accusingly at his partner. "You wuz gonna join Rathbone's secret investment group without me!"

"Lou, please, you gotta listen to me," Abbott said helplessly.

"Forget it! You wanna make deals behind my back, fine! But I'm buyin' you out of the Wonder Icemaker. I don't need no traitors in Lou Costello Enterprises!" He jerked his thumb menacingly. "Get outta my studio buggy!" He glared at Janika. "If you're sidin' with Abbott, you can get out, too!"

"Lou, please," Bud pleaded.

"Save it," Costello said, getting behind the wheel.

Janika started flipping through his Hungarian-to-English phrase book.

Costello angrily gestured back at Skorzeny. "Lugosi, tell the guy to get out!"

Bela explained that the two comics fought often, but made up later, and that Janika shouldn't take it personally. Skorzeny appeared not to understand, refusing to get out of the studio buggy. Abbott patted Skorzeny's shoulder to get his attention and gestured for him to follow him, pantomiming as he spoke, "We…go…eat. But first…," he hoisted an imaginary glass and emptied it in one imaginary gulp, "…we *drink*."

"Ah, *drink!*" Janika said, understanding at least one word of English, and he eagerly followed Abbott out of the studio buggy.

Costello said, "Come on, Bela. We'll go to my joint an' plan our strategy over dinner." Glaring at Abbott, he added, "Bats an' me are gonna solve the mystery all by ourselves! As for you," he said with a sneer, "when this pi'ture is finished, so are we!"

"Lou, you can't mean it."

"See if I don't!"

Lou stamped down on the accelerator, leaving Bud alone with Janika Skorzeny.

Chapter 5

With the Wonder Icemaker secure in the rear of Lou's Woody station wagon, Bela Lugosi found himself being chauffeured to Sherman Oaks.

"How are ya doin' back there, Bela?" Costello asked, tickled at seeing Count Dracula in his rearview mirror.

Bela and Paddy shared the back seat. He sighed, dismayed at still being in costume and makeup. "As well as can be expected," he grumbled, all too aware that the girl wouldn't stop staring at him.

"I can see ya in the mirror," Costello commented. "I thought vampires wasn't supposed to have reflections."

"Very funny. Just keep your eyes on the road."

Paddy studied Bela keenly. "Boy, wait 'til I tell the gang I had Dracula in my car." She pointed at the rear compartment. "But shouldn't you be lying back there in a coffin?"

Lugosi glared menacingly.

Anne turned around to scold her daughter. "Paddy, you behave yourself." She smiled at Bela. "Don't worry, Mr. Lugosi, you can borrow my cold cream to get that makeup off."

"Thank you," Bela said. He gestured at his attire. "But that will not help me with my costume."

"You can wear some of my duds," Costello offered.

The six-foot-tall Hungarian glared at the much shorter and far stouter Lou Costello. "I do not think we are the same size."

Paddy asked, "Didn't you have normal clothes in your dressing trailer?"

Bela glowered at the girl. "I did not want to frighten Kalara. Looking as I do now, and in her present condition, she might have died of fright." He crossed his arms. "And why am I telling you?"

Lou said, "Okay, so what's wrong with keepin' the penguin suit on? You'll be all fancy for dinner." He pointed ahead. "We're comin' up on our spread now."

Lou Costello lived on a ranch in Sherman Oaks, less than ten minutes from the studio. Carved on each of the front gates were the initials L.C., Lou Costello's brand. As they drove up, Lou said with a great deal of pride, "This was just a one-story joint when I first bought it. Now look at it." He pulled up in front of the two-story, twenty-four-room mansion situated on more than an acre of land. They were greeted at the door by Lou Costello's butler and maid. As Anne gave her coat to Ophelia, Lou smiled at the butler. "Watch your throat, Mitch," Lou joked, "we got a vampire for dinner tonight!"

The butler smiled, thinking Lou was only joshing. He went pale with fright when Lugosi appeared and handed him his bat wing cape. Recovering himself, Mitch swallowed hard and handed the cape off to Ophelia, and asked, "Uh, would you like me to put the car away, sir?"

"Yeah, thanks. And be careful when you unload the Wonder Icemaker."

"Yes, sir," Mitch nodded, edging past Lugosi, keeping a wary eye on him. "I'll get the gardener to help me, sir."

Lou nudged Bela and pointed at the retreating butler. "Hey, Bats, I'm your Watson an' Mitch is *my* Watson."

Lugosi frowned. "I do not understand what you mean."

"Mitch's last name is Watson, for real."

As Bela entered the huge formal living room he was nearly knocked down by a fleeing ten-year-old girl. She dashed past Lou and Anne, leaving a trail of foul smelling purple smoke in her wake. She was immediately followed by a harried-looking young governess brandishing an overcoat. "Young lady, come here this instant!"

Anne shook her head in despair. "Not again," she lamented.

Lou appeared more amused than angry. Still, he shouted sternly, "Carole Lou Costello, come here this minute!"

The dark-haired girl slunk in from the dining room with her hands behind her back. Whatever she was holding, it emitted a curling stream of rising smoke. "Hello, Daddy. Momma," she said, affecting innocence.

With hands on hips, Anne scowled. "What did you do now?"

The governess said, "She was playing with her chemistry set!" She held up her coat. "She deliberately poured chemicals all over my new coat!"

Carole shrugged as she held up the test tube of smoking, smelly chemicals. "I was makin' perfume. I wanted to give Cookie a surprise."

"She gave me a surprise all right!" Cookie exclaimed. "This odor will never come out!" She held the coat away from her, wrinkling her nose in disgust. "And it smells awful!" She waved back at the stairs. "The whole upstairs is choked with fumes from that stuff!"

Anne gave her wayward daughter a stern look. "Carole Lou, how can you do these naughty things? I carried you under my heart for nine months, and massaged your little body so you can walk today."

Lou smirked. "She can run pretty good, too."

Paddy looked up at Bela. "And I'll bet you thought the spooks in *your* castle was scary. My sister would frighten Frankenstein."

Lou took the governess's coat. "Don't worry about it, Cookie. I'll buy you a new one." He glared in Carole's direction. "And it's comin' out of your allowance." He held out his other hand expectantly. "Come on, hand it over."

Carole sighed. She put a black rubber stopper in the test tube and gave it to her father. Smiling prettily, she said, "I'm sorry, Daddy."

Lou was obviously a pushover. "I can't stay mad at you," he said, throwing his arms out to give his daughter a hug.

"But I sure can," said Anne. "Young lady, you're not to play with that chemistry set for a month."

"Gee whiz, a whole month?" Carole asked, bitterly hurt.

"Another word out of you and you won't have it for two months."

Carole covered her mouth.

"Now off with you," her mother ordered.

As Cookie took Carole upstairs, Lou gave his wife the stinky smelling coat. Anne gave Lou a disapproving shake of her head.

"You spoil that girl," she accused.

"Ah, kids gotta be kids," Lou said as he stuck the test tube in his jacket pocket without thinking.

Anne sighed and followed Cookie up the stairs. Bela could hear her frustrated howling as she got the full impact of Carole's "perfume" experiment. "Oh, quick, Cookie," said Anne, "open a window! Open all the windows!"

Lou snickered as he turned to Bela. "Come on, Bats, we can have a drink before dinner. There's also somethin' I wanna show ya." Walking up to a well-stocked bar, Lou asked, "What's your poison, Dracula, a Bloody Mary?"

Lugosi ignored the joke. "A brandy, please." As Costello served Lugosi his drink, Bela gestured at the grandiose spread. "Your home, it is quite marvelous."

"We like it," Costello said. He leaned in and whispered, "A lot of this furniture comes from my pi'tures. Just between you an' me, I sometimes pick up things here an' there."

"Another one of your 'gags'?" asked Lugosi.

Costello shrugged. "Eh, it's all in good fun."

"It sounds to me more like stealing."

Lou flashed a sly grin. "I'll bet you kept a coffin or two from your pi'tures."

Lugosi gave Costello a narrow look. He decided to change the subject. "I am surprised you do not have a swimming pool," he said.

"We do have a swimming pool," Lou said. He grew silent for a moment. Bela detected a hint of sadness in the comedian's eyes. It came and went with an obvious force of will. "What makes you think we don't have a pool?"

"I heard you say to Mr. Abbott about having money enough to start construction of a swimming pool."

"Oh, that." Lou came out from behind the bar and gestured for Bela to follow. "I'll tell ya about that after dinner. Come out back, I wanna show you somethin'. You'll get a kick out of it."

Lugosi hesitated a moment, wondering if Lou had meant to literally give Bela a kick. He remained wary as he followed the little man. Walking into the backyard where a swimming pool and a small guest house had been erected, Lou said, "See? We got a pool. But that's not what I wanna show ya. Let's go to the garage." There was a room off the garage area. Lou led the way. The room was dark except for two hand-painted peacocks glowing phosphorescently under ultraviolet lights. Lou flipped a switch and revealed a private movie theater with seats for twelve. As Lou flipped another switch, Bela realized that the peacocks were decorating velvet theater curtains. The curtains drew back to reveal a large movie screen. Between the chairs and the movie screen was a luxurious pool table. Lou selected a pool cue and gestured at the table. "Do you play?"

"Sorry," said Bela, "I am afraid I have never learned."

Lou selected a pool cue, chalked it up and offered it to Bela. "Here, I'll show you how. It's easy."

Bela put his drink down on the edge of the pool table. Something glinting inside the corner pocket caught his eye. He reached in and pulled out a small bottle of Jack Daniels. With a half smile, Lugosi observed, "I see the table, it also serves as a bar."

Costello frowned as he took the bottle and shook his head. "She's hidin' bottles again," he muttered. Costello set the bottle aside and took Bela's hands and positioned them on the cue. "See," said Lou, "you just put your fingers like this," he spread Bela's fingers on the felt tabletop, "an' let the cue slide through like that."

Lugosi nodded as he straightened up. "That seems easy enough." He indicated the bottle of Jack. "Your maid, I suppose."

Lou smiled as he racked up the balls and positioned the cue ball. "This white one is the one you gotta hit into the colored ones. If the white one drops in the pockets, you lose a turn. I'll break."

Bela watched Lou as he took his position at the head of the pool table and expertly scattered the colorful balls. "Is this what you wanted to show me?" asked Bela.

"Nope," Lou said slyly. He flipped another switch and a hidden projector came to life. On the screen appeared the old Universal Studios logo, an airplane travelling around the world, followed by the familiar strains of *Swan Lake*. An art deco bat appeared with the following titles superimposed:

Carl Laemmle
Presents
"Dracula"
By Bram Stoker

"You have a print of *Dracula!*" Lugosi exclaimed.

"I sure do," Lou said. "Six ball in the corner pocket." He made the shot with the finesse of a billiard hall hustler. "I just wanted to show ya that I'm a big fan." He repositioned himself around the pool table and pointed with his cue. "Four ball, side pocket." As Bela watched the opening scenes of the carriage ride through Borgo Pass, Lou made explanations as he sank ball after ball and announced his shots in parenthetical interruptions. "See, this whole pi'ture was my idea. (Two ball, corner pocket.) Originally, I wanted to do something on Broadway, you know (eight ball, side pocket) where Bud an' me meet the monsters. Bob Arthur (seven ball off the nine ball into the side pocket) decided to take my stage show idea an' make a movie. Between you an' me, the script was crap. Paddy could have written somethin' better than the junk they handed me." Lou looked up and said earnestly, "I was the guy who insisted you be in the pi'ture or I wouldn't make it. The studio wanted some guy named Ian Keith to play Dracula. I told Goetz that nobody but Bela Lugosi could play Dracula. (One ball, side pocket.) I got Goetz to see it my way. I usually do."

"*You* insisted they use me?" Bela asked, astonished.

"I also got you your own trailer. I said you're a big star an' you oughta be treated like a big star." Lou indicated the pool table. "Five ball off the cushion and into the far side pocket." Lou put the cue behind his back. "Watch this." Again he executed a perfect shot. He smiled. "Wanna see me do it blindfolded?"

Lugosi was too busy absorbing what Costello just told him. "So, Marlowe lied when he said he begged the studio to hire me!"

"Who's Marlowe?"

"My agent." Bela glowered. "For the time being, anyway." He gestured dismissively. "He is what my son would call a wheeler-dealer. My wife, she does not trust him. Much like your secretary mistrusts your accountant."

"Yeah, Dee Dee is pretty dead set against Mike." He nodded to a door off at the far side of the theater. "They share an office here at the homestead."

"I understand it is this accountant who introduced you to Dr. Fell."

"Yep. Mike's got a good head for business." Lou proceeded to sink the last few balls.

"How did you come to hire this accountant?"

"Well, one day he came up to me an' he said he wanted to handle my affairs. I said, okay." He pointed at the remaining ball. "Game ball, corner pocket." He closed his eyes, looked away from the table and sank the ball as if it had been remote controlled. He straightened up and smiled mischievously. "You oughta see how I can sink a basketball."

Lugosi frowned. "You hired this man without seeing his references?"

Lou tapped his temple. "I got me an instinct for business. He was clean cut an' really impressed me. Besides, he plays a mean game of pool."

"I see," said Bela. He gestured at the table. "Speaking of pool, when will it be my turn?"

Lou put up his pool cue. "Oh, didn't I tell ya? The game's over. I won." He took the cue from Bela and handed the Hungarian his drink. "Come on, dinner's ready."

Lugosi looked up at the screen. He saw himself posed on the broken stone steps of Castle Dracula, holding a candelabrum and intoning over howling wolves, "Listen to them, the children of the night. What music they make."

Costello led Bela to the dining room where the family was already seated. The kids giggled as Bela sat in the chair next to Anne.

"What is so funny?" Bela asked.

"You're all green," Carole said.

"Louie," Anne scolded, "what were you thinking? Let poor Mr. Lugosi take that makeup off."

"Nah, it's more fun having Dracula at our table." He smiled at Bela. "I hope you're hungry," he said, and then called, "HEY, OPHELIA, BRING OUT THE GRUB!"

The maid presented the family with a turkey dinner on a large silver platter, and as she did, she was obviously trying to ignore Lugosi's appearance. "He looks hungry," remarked Lou as he stood up and sharpened the carving knife. "Do vampires like white or dark meat?" he asked. "Maybe you'd rather nibble on Ophelia."

"I prefer a drumstick," said Bela, handing Lou his plate.

"Suit yourself." Costello shrugged and smirked at his maid. "Sorry, Ophelia, it looks like Dracula's on a diet."

As Bela received his drumstick, he asked, "How long have you been doing business with this Dr. Fell?"

"We don't talk business at dinner time," Lou insisted. "But you wuz gonna tell me about the mystery you solved with Karloff and Rathbone."

The kids perked up immediately.

"A mystery!" said Paddy. "You solved a mystery?"

"Like a real detective?" Carole asked.

"How many bodies were there?"

"How'd they die?"

Lugosi counted in his head. "Four or five, I think." Adding with a shrug, "Bela is not too sure. There were so many."

Lou froze in mid-carving. "No foolin'?" A look of boyish excitement crossed his pudgy face. "What, the killer wuz bein' paid by the body?"

Lugosi smiled proudly. "The plot, it was very complicated. But Bela the detective, he was too smart for them."

Anne interrupted with, "Mr. Lugosi, would you like to say grace?"

Bela thought he detected strong alcohol on her breath; he also noted that her words were slightly slurred. He thought back to the bottle of Jack Daniels and wondered if Mrs. Costello was the one hiding liquor bottles. Without betraying his suspicious, he said pleasantly, "I would be honored, Mrs. Costello."

"Aw, Mom," whined Paddy, anxious to hear Bela's story.

"You hush," Anne said. She turned to Bela. "Call me Anne. Everybody does." She took a sip of what appeared to be water. Judging from her reaction, Bela suspected it was either gin or vodka.

After bowing their heads and after Bela said a Catholic prayer of thanks, the family dug in. As the meal continued, Bela noted that with every swallow of "water" Mrs. Costello was becoming more unsteady. Occasionally he caught Lou giving her angry looks, and then hiding his feelings with a joke or funny face. Bela decided to diffuse the situation. "I do not suppose you would like to hear a story about the murder Bela solved, not over the dinner table."

"Are you kiddin'?!" Carole exclaimed.

"Tell us all about it!" Paddy begged.

"Yeah," said Lou.

"I tell you everything," Lugosi assured them. "It began when Karloff asked Bela to catch the killer who had framed him." He related the story; and as he did, Bela couldn't help exaggerating his role in the case. In his version of events, it was Bela who had questioned all the suspects and who followed the trail leading to a notorious Hollywood house of ill repute, and how he had made all of Basil Rathbone's deductions. Unfortunately, this meant placing himself where he couldn't have been, since he had been shot and sent to the hospital midway through the investigation. Fortunately, his audience wasn't terribly concerned about details.

Carole looked earnestly at her father. "Daddy, tell Errol Flynn that Mr. Lugosi is my new hero!"

Lou gave Bela a wink. "That's a pretty big deal, Bats. Carole's got a big crush on Flynn."

Lugosi gave Carole a warm smile. "Now I tell you about how I spit in Bugsy Siegel's eyes. I put on him a gypsy curse. It took a while, but I understand the Mob, they shot out his eyes when they killed him. They think it was their guns that killed Siegel. But take Bela's word for it, it was the curse."

"Gosh," marveled Paddy.

Lou nudged his daughter. "Daddy did a lot of gamblin' at the Flamingo. Boy, how I used to tick Siegel off!"

Lugosi's face grew stern. "He got what came to him."

"I think you mean 'what he had coming to him,'" Lou corrected.

"Same thing!" Bela insisted. He gestured broadly. "But, now it is time for Bela the Detective to relate to you the most exciting part of the case...."

Bela was just about to tell how he, and not Basil Rathbone, had clashed makeshift swords with the murderer at Hollywood Presbyterian Hospital when Anne smiled and said, "So you wanna know about Dr. Fell? I can tell you about Dr. Fell. He's a genius, isn't he, Louie?"

"Go easy on that stuff, Anne," Lou cautioned. "Paddy, pass me the carrots."

"Louie is always sinking money in inventions," Anne continued. "People are all the time coming up with these wild ideas."

"I see," Bela said, trying to be polite. "I will admit, the icemaker, it appears to be a very good idea." He turned to Costello, who was sending dagger stares at his wife. "I heard that Dr. Fell, he was involved with government work, something to do with outer space."

"Yeah," said Lou, perking up, "that's what sold me on Dr. Fell. Anne's right about me investing in some pretty wild schemes before — "

"The oil wells," said Paddy.

"The diamond mines," said Carole.

"Race horses," said Anne.

"Hey," said Lou. "Those race horses are winners!" He smiled at Bela. "But they're right, most of the inventions lay an egg, but not the Wonder Icemaker. It's gonna make a mint."

"Sure it is," Anne said, taking another drink of "water."

By the end of dinner, Anne was obviously plastered. She tried to get up from the table and teetered precariously. Lou called for the maid. "Ophelia, I think it's past Mrs. Costello's bedtime. You wanna help her upstairs?"

"Sure thing, Mr. Costello."

The maid took Anne by the arm and gently directed her toward the stairs. Anne waved at Bela. "G'night, Dracula," she said with a drunken smile.

Lou addressed his family. "Okay, kids, get ready for bed. Dracula an' me gotta talk."

The children each kissed their father good night and said good night to Bela. When they were alone, Lou led his guest to the bar and poured two brandies. Lou selected a cigar from a box and offered Bela one. Bela noted that the cigar was kept in a glass tube, very expensive. He withdrew the stogie and savored the aroma. "A fine tobacco, Mr. Costello," Bela complimented.

They lit up. Lugosi took pleasure in the taste.

Lou took a handful of glass enclosed cigars and tucked them in his inner pocket. "Hey, none of that 'Mr. Costello' crap," the comedian chided. "You're Bela, and I'm Lou."

Lugosi became aware of his reflection in the large mirror behind the racks of liquor bottles. "I really should take off this makeup," Bela said.

"Sure thing, but first," Costello stepped from behind the bar and slapped the Hungarian on the back, "let's take a walk."

He led Bela out to the backyard. The night air was crisp, but the brandy and fine cigar kept Bela pleasantly warm. They strolled leisurely around the swimming pool until Lou gestured at an empty deck chair. "Sit down, Bela, I wanna tell you somethin'."

As Bela took his seat, Lou sat down in the deck chair next to him and said earnestly, "I guess you noticed that Anne likes to drink a little too much."

"I had not noticed," Lugosi lied.

"You're a bad liar, Bats." Lou fell silent for a moment. "Anne didn't always drink so much. She didn't used to hide liquor bottles all over the joint neither. She's only done that since—" His voice choked. "You see, Bela, that pool you heard me talk to Abbott about was a pool for the Lou Costello, Jr. Youth Foundation. It's important that little kids learn how to swim."

"Lou Costello, Jr.?" asked Bela. "Your son, he was not at dinner. Is he ill?"

Costello gave Bela a searching look. "You mean, you don't know?" The comedian sat back. "Gee, I thought everybody heard that radio broadcast." The humor left Lou's eyes. "My boy Butch accidentally drowned." He gestured at the shallow end of the pool. "When I came home, my son was lying dead—over there." His eyes welled up with tears.

Lugosi was caught off guard. "I am sorry. I hope I did not—"

"That's okay, Bela. I just thought everybody knew."

Imagining how he might have felt if such a tragic thing had happened to *his* son, Lugosi placed a comforting hand on Lou's shoulder and asked solemnly, "When did it happen?"

"I'll never forget that day. It was November 4th, 1943. I'd spent almost a year in bed with rheumatic fever. That day was my first day back to work on the Abbott and Costello radio show. Oh, man, I was stoked. I was ready to take on the world. When I left for the radio station that morning I told Anne, 'Anne,' I says, 'keep Butch up tonight, because I wanna see if he can recognize my voice on the air.' Mitch drove me to the NBC studios. Man, I was happy. We were goin' on the air at seven. Our guest star that night was Lana Turner. I was on top of the world, playin' around, pullin' gags. Like I said, I was stoked. In a couple of days it was gonna be my son's first birthday, and Anne was out shopping, buying a stroller for Butch. Butch was playing in his playpen that was set up near the pool. The only one around was my secretary at the time, Marty. She didn't know that she was the only adult in the house. Anne came home with the stroller and she and Marty put it together. Suddenly, they remembered about Butch and went to check on him. He wasn't in his playpen. Somehow he got out and crawled to the pool and fell in. Then…around six o'clock…Anne's sister called the studio. She asked Eddie Sherman to bring me home."

"How horrible."

"That's when I saw my son, my little Butch, just lyin' there. It was like the whole world landed on top of me."

Lugosi nodded solemnly. Then something occurred to him. "Wait. If this terrible thing happened, why was there a radio broadcast?"

"I did it for Butch. I knew wherever he was, he'd be listening. I wanted him to hear his daddy's voice." Lou pulled up his right sleeve and revealed a copper bracelet with *Butch* inscribed on it. "I had this welded to my wrist so I'd never forget that day." He took a drink of brandy. "How does that song go? 'Even though your heart is achin', laugh clown, laugh,' right? That's how it's been ever since. Sometimes I blow up at people when I don't mean to." He looked at Lugosi. "Since you're a detective, there's something about that day that still eats away at me, a real mystery."

"What is that?"

"My son's knees, they wasn't scraped. If he crawled outta the playpen himself, why wasn't his knees scraped? That's been naggin' at me for years. I can't believe anyone in the family or on my staff would hurt Butch, but the fact that my son's knees wasn't scraped still haunts me."

Lugosi gestured helplessly. "I do not know what to say. I have met your family and your servants, and I cannot believe any of them would harm a child, even accidentally."

"I feel the same way. Still—" Lou shrugged, giving Bela a sad smile. "I didn't mean to bring you down, Bats. I just thought if we wuz gonna work together, you oughta know I ain't just a baggy pants clown. It's funny, but ever since then, when I hear a phone ring, I think it's bad news."

Mitch appeared at the entrance to the patio. "Sir, Mr. Barber is on the phone. He says it's urgent."

Lou smiled. "Now ain't that a coincidence?"

He got up and waved for Bela to follow him into the living room. Bela lingered in the patio doorway as the butler handed Lou the telephone.

"Hey, Bobby, what's up?" He snickered. "Are you getting scared bein' all by yourself, you big sissy?" It amazed Bela how quickly Lou's demeanor could change from tragic to comic. Suddenly Lou's face registered confusion and annoyance. "What's that supposed to mean?" he asked. He paused to listen, and then said, "Look, will ya calm down an' talk sense." Costello jumped with alarm. He shouted, jiggling the hook, "BOBBY! HEY, BOBBY! ARE YA THERE?" but got no answer. He hung up and turned to Bela with a look of urgency. "We gotta get back to the studio right away!"

"What happened?" Bela asked. "Where is Barber?"

"In the doghouse," said Lou cryptically as he rushed Bela onto the patio. Lugosi stood his ground.

"In the doghouse? Is this more American slag?"

"He's in the doghouse," Lou insisted. "I mean for real."

"What do you mean by that?"

Lou explained, "For a gag, I got a big doghouse with Bobby's name on it set up on Stage 28. He's there right now. All I know is that I heard Bobby gasp and the phone went dead! If that don't sound like a mystery, nothin' does."

Mitch appeared with Lugosi's Dracula cape. "Your cape, sir," he said, offering to drape the cape on Bela's shoulders.

Lugosi fastened the cape around his neck. "Thank you," he said, and then remembered about his face. "What about my makeup?" he asked Costello.

Lou shoved Bela toward the garage. "Worry about gettin' the makeup off later. Come on, Sherlock, the game is a hand and a foot!"

Chapter 6

Wednesday, 25 February 1948
8:15 P.M.
Universal-International Studios

Traffic on U.S. Highway 101 at Ventura Blvd. was bumper to bumper. Costello took a detour up Vineland Ave. to pick up Lankershim from State Highway 134, also known as Moorpark Street. But again, traffic on Moorpark had slowed to a crawl. He continued up Vineland, hoping to catch Lankershim where it intersected with Victory Blvd.

"Traffic's kinda heavy tonight," Lou said.

The reason soon became obvious. On the far shore of the Los Angeles River, huge clouds of black smoke belched into the nighttime sky and over the greens of the Lakeside Golf Course of Hollywood, and motorists were slowing down to watch the spectacle. Costello gave Bela a nudge and pointed. "Hey, will ya look at that? That's one hell of a fire."

"It almost looks as though the fire is where we are going," Bela remarked.

"Yeah," said Costello nonchalantly, and then did a double take. "It *is* where we're goin'!" Suddenly overtaken by fear, Costello shouted, "JOE!" and gave Bela his own reasons to be fearful as the comic began weaving in and out of traffic, driving over medians, sideswiping the occasional car, and not averse to taking a detour on curbs while ignoring things like the occasional panic-stricken pedestrian.

"WHAT ARE YOU DOING?" Lugosi bellowed over the sound of complaining car horns and people screaming. He dug his fingernails into the dashboard and prayed to the Blessed Mother as Costello stuck his head out of the window and shouted, "Get outta my way!" and sent the station wagon careening across the bridge spanning the "mighty" Los Angeles River. Bela kept his eyes shut, but couldn't help picturing a fiery death involving a brief but frightening plummet to their doom at the bottom of the nearly dried lakebed that Hollywood residents call a river. No one was more relieved than Lugosi when the car miraculously reached Universal Studios in one piece.

"Slow down!" Lugosi commanded. "You will get us both killed!"

"Can't ya see? Joe was working late developing his pi'tures, and it's the film lab that's on fire!"

The laboratory was one of the adobe façade buildings lining the road passing the front lot and gate. Smoke poured from every window and the BUY VICTORY BONDS billboard displayed on the roof was covered in black soot. It looked like the Universal City hook and ladder crew had already gotten the blaze under control. Firemen on the ground ran hoses into the building, while firefighters on extended ladders kept the fire from spreading by sending jets of water over the roofline of the lab and other nearby buildings. Firemen and police were helping to get evacuees from the administration building and lab to ambulances waiting in the parking lot across the street. Police had set up a road block and were diverting traffic, but Lou Costello took matters into his own hands and drove through the barrier and turned into the front gates, honking for the guard. The guard ran out and waved the station wagon away.

"Sorry, Mr. Costello," he shouted over the sirens, "you gotta turn around. Can't you see? The lot's being evacuated."

A traffic cop charged up, threatening Costello with his nightstick. "Say, what's the big idea?" he demanded. "Didn't you see me signaling for you to turn around?"

Costello ignored the fuming flatfoot and revved his engine. "Open those goddamn gates," he shouted at the guard, "or I'll drive right through 'em! My press agent's in there and I'm gonna save 'im!"

"Get out of that car," the cop ordered, grabbing the driver's side door handle. "You're under arrest!"

Costello jammed his foot down on the accelerator. The station wagon lurched forward. The guard waved him back and glared at Costello as he hurried around to open the front gates. "If you get killed," he warned, "don't come cryin' to me."

"Hey!" the cop shouted, his sleeve caught in the door handle. He ran beside the car as Costello sped through the gateway. Lugosi said another silent prayer as the station wagon made a hard right onto Rosabelle that disentangled the patrolman and laid him out on his keister. The station wagon came to a screeching stop scant inches from the back end of a parked fire engine. As Bela crossed himself and gave a prayer of thanks, the Fire Captain charged toward them, angrily waving his fist.

"You can't park here," he commanded. "We gotta keep this area clear!" He did a double-take at the sight of Count Dracula in all his green-faced glory getting out of the car, along with a panic-stricken Lou Costello. "What the hell...?" he gasped, and then grabbed Lou as he tried to make a run for the building. "Are you nuts?" He tried to hold Costello back, but found he was tangling with a wild man.

"Joe is in there! We gotta help 'im!"

"Let *us* worry about saving people!" the Fire Captain protested. "Now get outta here!"

Two ambulance attendants came down the back stairs bearing a stretcher with a blanket-covered body. Costello took one look, shouted, "JOE!" and gave the Fire Captain a swift kick in the shin and hurried to catch the attendants.

The Fire Captain was literally hopping mad as he winced and snarled and held his aching shin. "Why that little...!"

Just then Bela Lugosi spotted Boris Karloff and Basil Rathbone coming from the direction of the administration building, with Bill Goetz following after them. "Where are you going?" Goetz shouted. "We're supposed to evacuate!" It was obvious to Lugosi that his rivals in detective work wanted to question the attendants. Bela knocked the hopping Fire Captain to the ground as the ambulance attendants tried unsuccessfully to get past Lou Costello.

"Get out of the way," the attendant with curly brown hair demanded. "He's very badly burned. We have to get him to the hospital."

Lugosi gruffly blocked Rathbone and got to the attendants first. "Who is this man?" he demanded as he pulled back the blanket, uncovering the victim's face. It was the ash smeared face of Joe Glaston. Bela eyed the attendants narrowly. "You said he was burned. Look, there is not a mark on him." He pulled the blanket back even further and found Glaston was trussed up in a straight jacket. "What is this?" he demanded.

Glaston groaned and then shouted, "No! Wait! Help! Help!" just as the limping traffic cop spotted Lou Costello.

"HEY!" the cop shouted, brandishing his nightstick.

The brown-haired attendant turned to his blond partner. "We better get going, Carl."

"Right, Hans."

Ignoring Glaston's protests, the attendants slid the stretcher into the ambulance. Bela grabbed Hans by the shoulder. "What is going on here? Where are you taking him?"

"Bela!" Rathbone warned.

Karloff shouted, "Behind you!"

The blond attendant gave Bela a stunning blow to the back of his head, while Hans kayoed Rathbone with a right cross. Boris wheeled the blond-haired man around and delivered a blow to Carl's midsection, and then grabbed his hand in pain. The blond-haired attendant used his right arm like a club, knocking Karloff to the ground. He stood over the fallen actor, ready to bludgeon him further when Hans cried, "Come on, Carl!" He slammed the ambulance doors and ran to the forward cab. "Leave them!" He pointed at a second ambulance pulling up beside Costello's car and the approaching traffic cop. "We have to go *now!*"

Turning his whole body to look where his partner was pointing, Carl shouted, "Right!" and left Karloff groaning on the ground. He sprinted for the driver's side door of the ambulance just as Lou Costello sprang into action.

"Hold it, you bastards!" Lou shouted, grabbing the back pocket of Carl's trousers. At the same time, the traffic cop grabbed Lou Costello.

Carl kicked.

The pocket tore.

Lou took a tumble and so did the cop — again.

The ambulance sped away with sirens blaring just as the two attendants from the second ambulance got out and hurried over to render assistance.

"Hey, did you see that?" said a white coated attendant.

"I sure did," said his partner, helping the cop to his feet. "Those ambulance guys must be nuts."

The Fire Captain grimaced as he limped to meet them. "I don't know about those attendants, but these other two guys," he said, casting a withering glare at Lou and Bela as Rathbone and Karloff helped them to their feet, "they're crazy!"

"I got you now!" the traffic cop said, grabbing Costello by the collar.

"Are you both all right?" Basil asked, keeping a tight hold on Lugosi's arm.

Wrenching himself free, Bela protested, "Of course I am all right! Is it Bela's fault that those men do not fight fairly?" Rubbing the back of his head, he winced and grumbled, "What did the blond one use, the brass knuckles?"

"I don't know," said Boris, shaking his stinging hand. "But he had a stomach as hard as steel."

Bela chanced to glance up at the building across the street that housed the cutting rooms and film vaults. Perched up on the roof, obscured by smoke and a line of trees, was what appeared to be an oddly shaped figure working an old style movie camera. "Who is taking pictures?" he asked.

Rathbone looked where Lugosi was pointing, but by that time, the figure had picked up the camera and shuffled out of sight. "I don't see anyone," he said. "Perhaps it was a Movietone news photographer."

"Nobody from Movietone ever looked like *that*."

"Mr. Costello," asked Boris, "are you all right?"

"Oh, he'll be just fine," the cop said, getting out his handcuffs.

Lou held his chest and tried to catch his breath. "We gotta...get after...those kidnappers. They're... gettin'... away." His knees buckled.

"Aw, now don't pull any funny stuff," the traffic cop warned.

"Can't you see he's ill?" said Boris, pulling Costello up. "You should be in hospital."

The attendants hurried to help. "Thank you, Mr. Karloff. We'll take it from here."

"Nah," said Lou, shaking his head. "It's nothin'. I had rheumatic fever a couple of years ago. I can't take a pratfall like I used to." He smiled weakly, pointing at his car. "Set me over there. I'll be all right." The attendants eased Lou onto the rear bumper of his station wagon. "Just give me a minute," Costello assured them.

"Do try to rest, old man," Basil said.

"Oh, he'll get plenty of rest," said the cop, "in a jail cell!" He counted the charges off on his fingers. "Resisting arrest, assaulting an officer, reckless driving—oh, he's gonna have a nice *long* rest."

With everyone's attention on the comic, nobody noticed Bela as he spied a wallet on the ground. Figuring it was a kidnapper's wallet lost during his scuffle with Lou Costello, Lugosi grabbed it. A quick examination of its contents revealed a number of ID cards, all with different names and occupations. One card in particular excited Bela's attention—an old American Bund membership card! He smiled wickedly, having found evidence that Rathbone and Karloff had overlooked.

"Nazis," he muttered conclusively. "I wonder..."

"I say, Bela," asked Basil, giving Lugosi a start, "do you need a ride home?"

"A ride?" said Bela, quickly pocketing his discovery. "I have no need of a ride from you, Rathbone. We came here because a friend of Costello's called for help. We must go there now."

"Go where?" asked Basil. He gestured at Lugosi's attire. "Dressed like that?"

Lugosi eyed him narrowly. "As if I would tell *you*. And never mind how I am dressed!"

Boris frowned. "I really think you and Mr. Costello should see a doctor. If someone on the lot needs help, you should tell security and let them handle it."

"Mr. Karloff is right," said the second attendant. "I saw the whole thing. After a blow to the head like that, you could be really hurt, Mr. Lugosi." He led Bela to the ambulance and sat him down on the rear bumper.

"Nonsense," Lugosi insisted as the attendant examined him. "We Lugosis are very hard-headed."

"So we've noticed," Rathbone quipped. "What is your opinion, sir?" he asked the attendant.

"We should at least get him to a hospital for some X-rays."

"Out of the question," Bela said. "We are on a case."

"A case?" The attendant eyed Lugosi with concern. He took out a penlight and noted how Bela's pupils reacted to light. "Can you tell me what day it is?"

Bela squinted. "Of course Bela knows what day it is! What, you think maybe I am stupid?"

Lou smirked. "Nah, he just thinks you're bats from that hit on the head."

Arson investigators arrived on the scene as a fireman emerged from the smoking building carrying a melted gasoline can and an object too small for Lugosi to get a good look at. Reporting to the Fire Captain and the investigators, the fireman said, "It looks like the fire was deliberately set." He handed the smaller object over to the lead investigator. "It's a photo developer's timer. It was wired into a wall socket and used as a kind of detonator."

Rathbone held out his hand. "May I have a look at that?"

The investigator held it out. "You can see it, but I'll handle it."

Rathbone glanced at the device. "Quite ingenious," he said. "See there, Boris? It uses a mercury switch. Wired to the electrical outlet, it causes a spark that ignites the petrol and *whoosh!*"

"Instant three alarm fire," Boris said, finishing Basil's thought.

"I'll take that," the Fire Captain said. "It looks to me like Costello's photographer is the one we want. I'll bet this timer belongs to him. It's pretty open and shut."

"Not quite so open and shut," said Rathbone, arching an eyebrow. "That timer is standard darkroom equipment. Besides, I doubt this sort of thing is within Mr. Glaston's expertise." He smiled condescendingly. "No. This is definitely the work of a professional arsonist."

"All the time, talk, talk, talk," Lugosi complained. As Goetz approached, the Hungarian gave the studio head an appraising leer. "You," he demanded, "has anyone threatened you?"

Goetz acted as if Bela were invisible. "Can we go now?" he asked Boris and Basil. "Leo is waiting for us across the street."

"Yes," said Rathbone. "We've satisfied our curiosity here."

The Fire Captain said, "You can go back to your office, if you like, Mr. Goetz. We've got the fire out now. And don't worry. We were able to save the film drying and cutting rooms, so I don't think too many of the dailies were destroyed."

"Oh, good," said Goetz, almost sounding disappointed. "Good job, Captain."

Boris gave Goetz a smile. "It's a good thing, too, Bill. It just occurred to me that in all the excitement you forgot to rescue your Van Gogh."

"Yes, that was stupid of me."

Goetz turned to leave but had his way blocked by Bela Lugosi. "Do not evade my question," he said. "Did someone threaten you?"

"You mean, besides you?" Goetz retorted.

"Maybe this art expert, this Baart-de la, whatever his name is, maybe he threatens you for some reason?"

"How do you know about Baart del la Faille?"

"Nothing escapes Bela, the Great Detective!"

Rathbone turned to the ambulance attendants. "I believe Mr. Lugosi needs a sedative. Wouldn't you agree?"

"Mr. Lugosi," said the first attendant, smiling patronizingly, "you really ought to let us take you to the hospital." Talking out the corner of his mouth to his partner, he muttered, "Get the sedative, Frank."

"Right, Pete." Frank climbed into the ambulance

Pete got a firm hold of Bela's arm.

"Do not listen to Rathbone!" Bela said with indignation. "He and Karloff, they are trying to keep Bela from whatever case they are investigating!"

"Sure, sure, they are, Mr. Lugosi," Pete said, trying to appease his apparently delusional patient. "Hurry up, Frank," he called.

Frank emerged with a syringe. "Don't worry, Mr. Lugosi, this is just something to help calm you down."

For the first time in his life, Lugosi flinched at the sight of a needle.

Boris looked very uncomfortable. "Bela, really," he said, "we're terribly sorry." He shook his head regretfully and followed Basil back to Goetz's office.

Bela raged, "COME BACK HERE! KARLOFF!"

"Now, now, Mr. Lugosi," said Pete. "We don't want to have to restrain you, now do we?"

Lugosi begged, "Costello, do something!"

"Aw, no you don't," the cop warned Costello as he gestured at the ambulance with his nightstick. "You're going in that ambulance and I'm riding with you." He pulled Lou up gruffly. "Now let's get going!"

"Hey, Bats," Lou said, hesitating. "Did you know my partner Bud has epilepsy?"

Bela glared angrily. "What does that have to do with anything?"

Lou smiled at the ambulance attendants and the traffic cop. "Do you guys know what I do to snap Bud out of one of his spells?"

"No, what?" Frank asked.

Without warning, Lou gave Frank and the arresting officer punches to the solar plexus. Lugosi caught on and did likewise to Pete. As they all doubled over in pain, Costello grabbed Lugosi and they bolted for the station wagon and made their getaway up Laemmle Blvd. without looking back.

Suddenly Bela shouted, "STOP THE CAR!"

Lou slammed on the brakes and looked for signs of trouble. "What? What is it?"

"Go back, something is wrong!" Bela demanded, pointing at the soundstages and at the trailers lining the street.

"What's wrong? I don't see nothin'."

"My point exactly! There is something not there that should be. Go ahead and back up."

"Make up your mind," Lou complained, falling into the *U-Drive* routine without meaning to, "do you want me to back up or go ahead?"

The withering look Lugosi gave him was enough to convince Costello to reverse gears. He stopped under the awning of Stage 17 where Lugosi got out and stood on the spot where his dressing trailer *used* to be. "WHERE IS MY TRAILER?" he raged. "IT WAS RIGHT HERE!"

Costello joined him and waved his hands in the empty space. "It's gone, all right."

Lugosi grimaced at the comic. "This is no time for jokes, funnyman! Where is the trailer?"

"Take it easy, will ya. They probably just moved the trailer because of the fire."

"Then why are *those* trailers still here?" Lugosi gestured angrily at Abbott and Costello's trailers, and at the Westmore makeup trailer.

"I dunno, but why don't we go ask Abbott? The light in his trailer's still on. Maybe he saw somethin'."

"We shall see." Lugosi strode up to Abbott's trailer and pounded loudly on the door. When he got no answer, he tried the door and found it unlocked. He barged inside and, much to his consternation, found Abbott sprawled out on the floor, blacked out and stinking of whiskey. Lugosi grabbed him by the lapels and sat him up. "Wake up!" he snarled, shaking him roughly. "Wake up!"

Costello stuck his head in. "Is Abbott in here?" Seeing his partner on the floor, he gasped and hurried to help. "Abbott! Are you okay?" He patted his partner's face. "Abbott?" He looked anxiously to Bela. "Is Abbott all right?"

"Yes," groused Lugosi. "He has obviously been drinking." He nodded at the empty bottle of J&B brand whiskey on the floor beside the insensate straight man. "And drinking too much." Lugosi noted there were two glasses on the table in the breakfast nook. "And he did not drink alone."

Lou shook his partner. "This don't look like a bender to me. I think he had a fit or somethin'." He checked Abbott's pupils—they were fixed and dilated. "Hey, I think he's been slipped a Mickey."

Bela glared irritably. "What does the Disney rodent have to do with this?"

"Not that kind of Mickey, I mean a Mickey Finn—knock out drops." He got up and pulled back the privacy curtain and pointed at the bunk. "Come on. Help me get him in bed."

Lugosi glared sternly. "Right now I do not have sympathy for Mr. Abbott. I want to know where my wife and son are! And Janika and Kalara, too." He shook Abbott again. "Wake up and tell me where they are!"

Abbott groaned and looked up at them bleary-eyed. "Sorry, Skorzeny," he slurred, "I guess I dozed off." He suddenly became aware of his surroundings and found himself staring into the ghoulish face of Count Dracula. "HOLY SMOKE! IT'S THE DEVIL!" he shouted.

Lugosi shook him again. "I am worse than the devil! I am Bela Lugosi who wants to know where are the Skorzenys? Where are my wife and son?"

Abbott grabbed his head. "Ohhh," he moaned, "my head is killing me."

"*I* will kill you," Bela threatened, "if you do not tell me what became of my wife and son!"

Abbott looked around the trailer. "What time is it?"

"After 8 o'clock," Costello answered.

"You mean I've been out for nearly two hours?" Abbott said disbelievingly. "I only had one shot."

Lugosi pulled Abbott roughly to his feet. "WHERE IS JANIKA?" he roared. "WHAT DID YOU DO WITH HIM? YOU WERE WITH HIM LAST!"

"I don't know!" Bud exclaimed nervously. "The last thing I remember, we were having a couple of shots before I called us a cab. Next thing I know you're yelling at me!" He frowned and shook his head. "Maybe I had a blackout or something."

Costello pulled Lugosi back. "I'm tellin' you, Bats, he didn't just have a blackout. I think somebody drugged him, and I think that somebody was your pal Skorzeny."

"Ridiculous," said Bela. "Why would Janika do such a thing?"

"I'll bet he's a Commie, just like I thought he was!"

"Impossible! He is a hero!"

"Sez who? Skorzeny? I'll bet he had somethin' to do with your trailer goin' missin' and maybe even that fire and those kidnappers."

"You believe he would take a trailer when his own sister is sick in there? Do not be ridiculous!"

"Hey, I'll bet Bobby has a line on where your wife and kid are and I'll bet he even knows about Skorzeny bein' a Red! That's probably what he wanted to tell me about when he got cut off!"

"Then we must go now to the Phantom Stage!" Lugosi glared at Abbott as he staggered to his makeup chair and sat down. "We should take *him* with us."

Lou shook his head. "Abbott's in no condition to go detectin' around with us." He put his hand on his partner's shoulder. "Listen, pal, you stay here an' rest. Or maybe you should go over to Goetz's office. Karloff and Rathbone are over there right now. I'm sure those guys'll take you home, seein' that you're all in cahoots."

"Lou, about that," Abbott began pitifully, "I wasn't going behind your back, honest. There's a real good chance Rathbone and Karloff can get the IRS off our backs. All I have to do is a little favor for them."

Lugosi glowered. "What kind of *little favor* do they want from you?"

Abbott shook his head wearily. "I can't say, I've been sworn to secrecy." He gazed earnestly at Costello. "But I'm doing it for *us*, Lou, for you and me—honest."

"Okay, pal, I believe you." Costello gave his partner a reassuring smile. "Are you strong enough to walk over, or do you want I should drive you to Goetz's office?"

Abbott put his hand on his partner's. "I'll be okay in a minute, Lou. If Bobby needs you, you better hurry over and see him."

Lou turned to Bela. "We better go see Bobby right now."

"Very well," said Bela, giving Abbott a narrow stare. "But know this, Mr. Abbott: If my wife and son are harmed and I find that you are in some way responsible, I will kill you with my bare hands. I may be old, but this bat still has fangs that are sharp."

Chapter 7

Lugosi and Costello used their star power to get two night watchmen to open Stage 28.

"I sure don't like being on the Phantom Stage at night," the first night watchman said. He was short and stocky and hunted for the right key amongst a ring of keys hanging on his belt. "This place gives me the willies." He looked up at his taller lantern-jawed partner. "That's why I let Herman patrol this place without me."

Herman eyed Costello suspiciously. "Say, Al, isn't he the guy who pulls all those practical jokes?"

"That's him, all right," Al said, trying a key in the lock.

"How'd you two get on the lot with a fire going on, anyway?" Herman glared at Lugosi. "And why are you in that Dracula getup?"

"Never mind how I am dressed." Lugosi urged, "We are concerned about a man's life. Open that door immediately!"

Al's hand was visibly shaking as he inserted another key into the lock. "You gotta see it my way, Mr. Lugosi. Mr. Costello's got sticky fingers so you can't be too careful letting the guy onto a closed set."

Affecting innocence, Costello said, "You got me all wrong." Bela now knew where Lou's little daughter had learned that look.

The metal door's hinges creaked eerily as Herman turned on his flashlight and shined it around inside.

Al whispered, "I remember one picture where Mr. Costello was playin' a ghost. The director told me that nobody was supposed to move the props, something to do with special effects. Well, sir, Mr. Costello swiped some of them props right out from under my nose and almost got me fired."

"Aw, it wasn't me," Lou denied, putting on his best angelic face. "I'll bet it was one of the stagehands."

The taller night watchman eyed Lou suspiciously before following his partner inside.

Lou took Bela aside and whispered, "Sittin' on my mantle is a little antique clock with a secret door. I sneaked it out when the watchman wasn't lookin'." He put a hand to his mouth and suppressed a snicker.

Lugosi glared disapprovingly and pointed inside the soundstage. "Get in there, funnyman."

While the shorter watchman hunted around for the control board that ran the stage lights, the taller asked, "So what's this Barber guy doin' in here anyway? It's against Studio policy for a guy to be in here after hours."

"I snuck him in for a gag," Costello explained. "But we're worried he might be hurt."

Al pulled a lever; harsh white light illuminated the backstage area with its upstairs gallery of dressing rooms. To the left was the permanently standing opera stage. Stepping out on the boards, they saw that the Paris Opera House's audience section had been transformed into the exterior set for *The Brain of Frankenstein's* Masquerade Ball, a huge outdoor dance pavilion complete with pond, hanging paper lanterns and locker rooms. The cameras and lights were all in place for tomorrow's shooting schedule, but for some strange reason, the cameras were all focused at the Opera House stage.

"The cameras," Lugosi said, straining to listen, "I can hear them turning. Someone is filming us." He strained to see. "But there is no one behind the cameras."

"Oh, yes, there is," Al said with a shudder. "I'll betcha it's *his* ghost pulling one of his pranks." He pointed up at the opera boxes hidden behind the pavilion's nighttime cyclorama. "He's usually up there. That's where his ghost lives. Remember, Herman, I told you about the ghosts, about Lon Chaney and *The Phantom of the Opera?*"

"I remember, Al." Herman shook his head, "You and your ghosts."

Al shined his light up at the opera boxes. "They say that Lon Chaney, Sr.'s ghost still haunts Box 5, that box seat right there by the stage. But that ain't all." The watchman pointed at the catwalks. "Folks say the ghost of a stagehand haunts them catwalks. The poor guy fell to his death." He gulped. "He died right over there. They say Chaney's ghost pushed him so he'd have another ghost for company. I guess it must be lonely haunting this place all by yourself."

Lugosi sneered, "What nonsense." After a moment's hesitation, he crossed himself and kissed his thumb. Noting the amusement on Lou's face, Lugosi declared, "Bela Lugosi, he takes no chances."

Al nudged his partner. "Herman don't believe in ghosts. Do you, Herman?"

"It's all nonsense."

As if on cue, the soundstage lights went out and a low moan filled the darkness.

Costello sidled closer to Lugosi. "I *do* believe in spooks!" he said, repeating Bert Lahr's famous line from *The Wizard of Oz.* "I do, I do, I *do!*"

Al nervously drew his gun while Herman shined his flashlight around. "That's the ghost! I told you, Herman! I told you!"

The weird moaning came from the backstage area.

"It's coming from that big doghouse," Herman said, directing his light at the source of the moaning. Over the man-sized doggy doorway, a sign read:

OFFICE OF
Roberto Barber
PRESIDENT OF
ABBOTT & COSTELLO PRODUCTIONS

Costello breathed a sigh of relief. "There ain't nothin' to be scared of." He bent down to look inside. "That's just Bobby clownin' around." He reached in to shake the sleeping figure and reacted with one of his scare takes, running to Bela for protection. "Th-th-that ain't Bobby," Costello stammered. "Th-th-that guy's got hair!"

Lugosi squared his shoulders and demanded, "Come out of there, whoever you are!"

A man grumbled and slowly crawled out of the doghouse.

Lon groaned as he got slowly to his feet. "I don't remember nothin'."

Herman shined his flashlight in the man's face.

"Get that goddamn light outta my eyes," the stranger complained. "It's givin' me a headache!"

"CHANEY!" Bela exclaimed. "What are you doing here?"

Lon groaned as he got slowly to his feet. "I don't remember nothin'." He winced, holding his aching head. "I guess I musta come here after LaVigne got the makeup off my puss." He reached into his back pocket for his brandy flask. He tried to take a swig and found the flask empty. "Where am I?"

Herman said, "You're on the Phantom Stage, Mr. Chaney. I'd like to know how you got in here."

"So would I," said Costello, eyeing Chaney suspiciously.

Lon looked around with a half smile. "I guess Pop wanted me to come by for a visit." He ran his fingers through his hair. A streak of red smeared on Chaney's forehead.

"Let me see your hands," Lugosi insisted.

Lon drunkenly swatted Bela away. "Oh, get off me."

Bela grabbed one of Chaney's wrists. "It is just as I thought! Your palm is red!"

Lou joked, "I didn't know you could tell fortunes."

Lugosi eyes narrowed. "I mean there is blood on it, you fool!"

"BLOOD!" Al exclaimed.

Costello switched from joking to serious, grabbing Chaney by the shirt and shaking him angrily. "Ya dirty drunk, what'd you do to Bobby?"

Lon shoved Costello away. "Aw, keep your mitts off of me!" He shook his head wearily. "I didn't do nothin' to nobody. Hell, I don't even remember comin' here."

The two guards had to restrain Costello. The comic's face went three shades of crimson as he ranted, "YOU WERE MAD AT BOBBY! I'LL BET YA FOLLOWED

'IM TO THE PHANTOM STAGE AN' BEAT 'IM TO DEATH!" Lou was livid with rage. "TALK, YOU SON OF A BITCH! TALK OR I'LL BREAK EVERY BONE IN YOUR BODY!"

Chaney grabbed his head. "Goddamn it, Lou, keep your voice down. My head is killin' me." He leaned against the doghouse and slipped. Barely catching himself, he squinted at the floor. "What the hell's that stuff?"

Lugosi kneeled down and touched the wet spot in front of the doghouse. "It is blood," he concluded. He stood up and noted smears on the knees of Lon's trousers. "See here. Chaney got blood on himself when he crawled into and out of the doghouse. It is the same for the blood on his hands. I think that Barber, he stuck out his head and someone hit him," Bela rubbed his still aching head, "someone whose hand is very hard."

"Now that that's settled," Chaney said, "all of you, go away and let me sleep it off." He crawled back inside the doghouse and made a pillow with his forearms. Moments later he was snoring like a hibernating grizzly bear.

Suddenly the backstage lights flickered back on.

"Keep an eye on them, Al," Herman said, turning off his flashlight. "I'm going to call the head office about this."

Al cleared his throat and said overbearingly, "Okay, you guys, no sudden moves until my partner gets back."

Costello tried to reason with him. "Look, if Chaney didn't hurt Bobby, then maybe he's still in here someplace." He cupped his hands and shouted, "Bobby! Bobby, can ya hear me? BOBBY!"

There was no answer.

"Wait a minute," said Lugosi, sniffing the air. "Do you smell that? It smells like gasoline."

"Of course I smell gasoline," Costello said. "We were just at a fire. We're gonna stink with smoke and gasoline for days."

"And the lights, they went out and came on again." Lugosi pointed at the fire hose. "Quickly, unwind the hose!"

"What do we need a fire hose for?" Costello said. "There ain't no fire!"

"Why wait until the last minute?"

Al held up his hand. "Now hold it! You guys stay right where you are."

Bela pointed at the alarm. "Sound the alarm! Do it now!"

"Are you crazy?" Al sputtered. "Turning in a false alarm's against the law."

Bela shoved Costello forward. "You do it, funnyman! Quickly!"

"Awright! Awright!" Lou reluctantly did as he was told.

The fire alarm clanged loudly as Lou unwound the hose. The guard grabbed the fire hose away from Costello and glared angrily as he shook the nozzle at him. "I've had enough of your monkey business!" He handed Lou a pair of handcuffs. "Now get Chaney up and put the bracelets on 'im."

Lou reached inside the doggy doorway and grabbed Chaney's right wrist. "I'm doin' it, you don't have to be so bossy about it!"

Too groggy to resist, Chaney squinted and asked, "Got any coffee? I could really go for some coffee."

Lou was about to cuff Chaney's other wrist when Bela said, "Be quiet!" The Hungarian looked around warily. "I hear a noise!"

Al grimaced. "Quit tryin' to spook me!" He marched to the exit. "I'm gonna get Herman and we're takin' you to see Mr. Goetz." He grabbed the door handle and yanked, but the door wouldn't budge. "Hey, what gives here?" He rattled the handle and called over his shoulder. "The door's locked!"

Bela hushed him. "Quiet, I said! I hear ticking!"

"Now cut that out!" The nervous night watchman strode up to Bela, threatening him with the fire hose nozzle. "You guys locked us in here when my back was turned, didn't you?"

There was a loud *BANG!*

Flames erupted from behind the light board.

Bela shoved Lou forward. "Turn on the water!"

Lou ran to the water valve and gave it a quick turn. The sudden pressure shot the nozzle out of Al's hands, slapping him in the face and blowing him down. Like a crazed serpent, the hose writhed around wildly, sending streams of water in all directions, drenching the light board, the fuse box and Lou, Bela and Al.

In the now dark soundstage, Lou blindly grabbed something. "I GOT IT!" Lou shouted. "I GOT THE HOSE!"

"That is my leg, you idiot," Lugosi growled.

"I thought that hose felt kinda scrawny."

The fire erupted anew, bathing the soundstage in an eerie orange glow. Flames ran up the curtain legs framing the proscenium to the private opera boxes and their decorative mustard colored curtains.

They all made a jump for the dancing, spewing fire hose. Bela's now soaking wet velvet cape threatened to encase him like a straight jacket as they crawled over each other.

Al pointed at the water valve. "WE GOTTA TURN THE WATER OFF SO WE CAN GET CONTROL OF THE HOSE!" he shouted.

A wall of fire rose up between them and the water valve.

"I'll do it!" Lou volunteered.

"Wait," said Lugosi, unclasping his cape. "This will keep you from getting burned."

He put the dripping wet cape over Lou's shoulders. Lou pulled the high collar up over his head and wrapped himself in the cape. He ran through the flames unharmed and reached the burning hot valve, and then used the cape to get hold of it and twisted the valve shut.

The hose dropped limply to the floor.

Lugosi helped the guard to his feet. Al grabbed the nozzle while Bela held onto the hose itself. The watchman took aim and commanded, "Turn on the water now!"

"Aye, aye," Lou said with a jaunty salute. "Left standard rudder!" He spun the valve open.

Bela and the guard braced themselves against the pressure as the hose inflated and a jet of water shot out at the burning walls.

"HOLD THE HOSE STEADY WHILE I SOAK THEM OPERA BOXES," the watchman ordered.

As Bela and the guard worked the hose, Lou grabbed a fire extinguisher off the backstage wall. He looked a sight wearing a wet Dracula cape as he tried to put out the rain of smoldering fallout with billowing white jets of CO_2. Water slammed into the permanently standing sets, tearing down flaming curtains and soaking opera seats. If Lon Chaney's ghost had indeed been occupying Box 5, he would now be soaked to the ectoplasm.

Just then a fireman's axe sent the soundstage door crashing to the floor as a brigade of firemen forced their way in. The Fire Captain commanded, "GET ON THAT HOSE! GET THOSE MEN OUTTA HERE! AND DON'T LET NOBODY KICK YOUR SHINS!"

Firemen ushered out Lou, Bela and the guard. "Wait!" said Lou, running for the doghouse. "Chaney's in there! He'll be killed!"

"Hey, Dracula, Jr.'s not fooling!" a fireman standing by the doghouse called out.

He reached in and pulled the sleeping actor to his feet. Chaney squinted. "Say, you got any coffee?"

"Sure we got coffee," said the fireman, "outside."

Lon nodded sleepily and smiled. "I take mine black, no sugar."

As the first fireman led Lon outside, a second fireman grabbed Lou. "Come on, you too!"

"Wait! Bobby's in here somewhere! We gotta find him!"

The Fire Captain pointed at the exit. "Leave that to us. Now get outta here!"

Costello allowed himself to be ushered outside where Bela, Chaney and Al sat wrapped in gray blankets on the running board of the fire truck. Lou gave Lugosi a smile as he handed him his cape back. He took a blanket offered by one of the firemen and then sat down. Looking down at his wet clothes, he shrugged and said, "Look on the bright side; at least we don't got to take a bath Saturday night." He pointed at Bela's face. "You got most of the green makeup off, too."

Ignoring Costello's remark, Bela asked, "Do you know where Dr. Fell lives?"

"You don't think the doc had anything to do with this?"

Lugosi eyed Costello narrowly. "Answer my question. Do you know where this Dr. Fell lives?"

"Sure. What, you think I give money to people whose address I don't know?"

Resisting the urge to tell Costello that was exactly what he thought the comic might do, Bela turned to the watchman. "You stay here with Chaney. Mr. Costello and I have business elsewhere."

They were about to leave when the taller night watchman blocked their way. "You're not going anywhere," Herman insisted.

"Herman! Where'd you go?" asked Al, getting to his feet. He screwed up his face and let loose with an explosive sneeze. He sniffled and rolled his eyes. "Great! Now I got a cold!" He pointed accusingly at Lugosi and Costello. "These jokers nearly got me killed locking us in!"

"Us?!" Lou exclaimed. "We didn't lock nobody in nowhere."

Al glared menacingly. "Well, somebody locked us in, and I know it wasn't Herman. So if it wasn't Herman and it wasn't me, that means it had to be you!"

Drawing his weapon, Herman said, "Never mind, Al. I just got off the phone with Mr. Goetz. He wants to see these jokers pronto." He gestured at Lou and Bela. "You two are comin' with me." He grabbed Chaney by the arm and tried to pull him up. "You, too."

Chaney wrenched his arm free. "I ain't goin' nowhere 'til somebody gets me some coffee!"

"Now look," Herman began.

Bela shook his head. "He will not listen to you," he insisted. "I will speak to him." Lugosi smiled warmly at Chaney and cooed, "You want coffee. There is plenty of coffee at Mr. Goetz's office. All the coffee you want."

Lon Chaney smiled like a contented two-year-old. "No foolin'?"

"No fooling," Lugosi assured him. He gestured at Herman. "This man knows where the coffee is."

Chaney nodded and got to his feet. He shoved the watchman forward. "Let's go then," he said.

Herman was as tall as Chaney and stood his ground. "None of your rough stuff!" he warned. He made sure both of Lon's wrists were locked in the handcuffs. "There!" he said with a nod, and then pointed with his gun. "Now get going. We're all going for a little ride in my patrol car." He shoved Chaney forward. The drunken actor fell flat on his face with a thud. The watchman gestured at Costello. "Come on," he sighed, "help me get him up."

As they got Chaney to his feet, the actor mumbled, "You gotta watch that first step."

Lugosi glanced to his right. He thought he saw something strange hidden amongst the lumber piles of the Studio saw mill across the way—a Movietone style newsreel truck and a weird, boxy caricature of a man standing atop the truck operating a movie camera mounted up on the roof. Before Lugosi could alert the night watchman to the mysterious truck's presence, it sped away down the paved road that led to the Studio back lot. Maybe his eyes were playing tricks on him, but Lugosi could have sworn that the truck had no driver.

Chapter 8

William Goetz's executive secretary was still frazzled after the evacuation. She sat behind her desk with her coat and hat on—just in case she had to make another quick exit. As the pretty girl sat there nervously filing her nails, she looked up and barely acknowledged the men standing before her—until she did a double take. Three men were held at bay by a tall night watchman: A soaking wet Lou Costello and a waterlogged Bela Lugosi each had an arm supporting a barely conscious, blood-stained Lon Chaney.

"What on earth—," she began.

The lantern-jawed night watchman said, "Mr. Goetz is waiting to see us."

She eyed Lou skeptically. "Is this another one of your jokes, Mr. Costello?"

Just then Don Marlowe entered with Eddie Mannix. "Hey, baby," Marlowe chirped, "Mr. Mannix would like a word with your bosses."

"Marlowe!" Lugosi exclaimed. "What are you doing here?"

"I might ask you the same question."

Mannix stared quizzically at the trio of soaking wet actors. "Did you two guys go skinny dippin' without takin' your clothes off?"

The secretary buzzed Mr. Goetz on the intercom. "Yes?" Goetz said.

"The night watchman is here to see you, sir." She glared at the dripping wet stars. "And he's not alone. Mr. Costello, Mr. Lugosi, and Mr. Chaney are here."

Goetz sighed. "Send them in," he said resignedly.

"Go on in," the secretary said.

Inside William Goetz's spacious office, a familiar looking traffic cop smiled in triumph and said, "That's him, that's the guy I want!" jabbing an accusing finger in Lou Costello's direction. Bud Abbott was seated opposite Leo Spitz and nursing his aching head with an ice bag, while Karloff and Rathbone lingered around the Van Gogh.

Lou and Bela held up a swaying, drunken Lon Chaney. The handcuffed actor squinted and asked, "Anybody got any strong coffee?"

Goetz smirked at Costello. "You can't keep out of trouble tonight, can you, Mr. Costello?" He addressed the night watchman. "What's this all about?" and then glowered at Costello. "And kindly stop dripping on my oriental rug."

Mannix sat on the edge of Goetz's desk. "I can't wait to hear this one!" He crossed his arms expectantly.

"Well, sir," Herman explained, "Mr. Chaney was found in a drunken stupor inside a large doghouse on the Phantom Stage, and he has blood on him."

Mannix was enjoying this immensely. "You mean a Universal Studios horror star was found at the scene of the crime by a security guard? And it looks suspicious?"

Herman nodded. "Yes, sir, it looks very suspicious."

Mannix slapped his knee and smirked at Karloff. "Boy, does this take me back!"

"Yes, it does seem a rather familiar scenario," Boris commented. "Wouldn't you agree, Basil?"

"Oh, definitely," Rathbone agreed.

The cop had a smile a mile wide. "Oh, you're going up the river for a long time for this!" he said to Costello.

Goetz sighed and addressed the watchman. "So what happened after you found Chaney on the set?"

"I went to telephone you about it, Mr. Goetz. When I got back, the Phantom Stage was on fire."

Goetz took the news calmly. "I see."

Lugosi glared accusingly. "First the kidnappers take away Joe Glaston, and now those same kidnappers take Barber. They also kidnapped my wife and son and the Skorzenys!"

Chaney frowned. "Say, where's that goddamn coffee at?"

Rathbone's expression grew sympathetic. "Yes, Mr. Abbott told us what happened."

Boris approached Bela and squeezed his shoulder reassuringly. "But don't worry, Bela. We're here to help you."

"Yes," Rathbone said, extending his hand in a gesture of camaraderie. "Just as before, all for one and one for all."

Bela shrank away angrily. "I do not trust either of you!" He glared at Mannix and pointed accusingly. "*You* had something to do with this! Admit it!"

Chaney squinted. "What'd I do?"

"NOT YOU!" Lugosi barked. "I meant *him!*"

"Me?" Mannix said. "Come on, Lugosi, I have nothin' against you or your family."

"You are a *fixer*, yes? Maybe you are fixing things, and to fix things people must disappear!"

"I can vouch for Mannix," Marlowe said, putting an arm around the tough guy's shoulder. "He was with me." Mannix glared at him. Marlowe shrank back. Clearing his throat, he repeated, "He was with me."

"Yeah," said Lou. "And when Mannix wasn't with him, he was with my agent Eddie Sherman."

"Still, Marlowe is not to be trusted!" Bela glared at his agent. "My wife, she has always been suspicious of you. Now I see why. Why are *you* here, Marlowe?"

"Doing what an agent does best—arranging a meeting of the minds to make big deals, while I earn my usual ten percent."

"There was nothing mysterious about it," Mannix insisted. "Marlowe was acting on Goetz's behalf to arrange a real estate deal, that's all."

Spitz waved anxiously. "Uh, they don't have to know about that."

Lugosi confronted the studio heads. "Could this be why someone is trying to burn down your studio? And why my wife and son have been kidnapped?"

Costello insisted, "I think it's just like I said. Skorzeny is a Red and he has your wife and kid!"

"No," Lugosi denied. "Lillian and Bela, Jr. were looking after Kalara!"

"Maybe she was fakin'!"

"She was not faking! Dr. Kopf said she was ill! I still say that your Dr. Fell has something to do with this! We know there are kidnappers, and that Kalara saw Dr. Death in the commissary! It is obvious the kidnappers and Dr. Death are connected somehow, and they took the trailer to silence her forever!"

Rathbone arched an eyebrow. "I must say, you really…."

"I do not have time for your praise, Rathbone."

"I was going to say, that you really jumped to conclusions."

"Yeah," said Lou. "I still think your pal Skorzeny is the guy we want."

Lugosi produced the kidnapper's billfold. "Then how do you explain *this!*"

"What is it?" asked Lou.

"This wallet fell from the pocket of one of the kidnappers. It has evidence that these kidnappers, they have many aliases and they might even be Nazis!"

"Nazis!" exclaimed the cop. "I think you're all crazy."

"Mind if I have a look at that?" Basil asked.

Bela grimaced. "Yes, I mind!" He threw the wallet to Eddie Mannix while trying to keep Lon Chaney on his feet. "Look at this and tell Bela to his face that you did not hire this man to fix things for you while you make the alibi!"

Mannix shuffled through the ID cards. "I didn't hire this guy to do nothin'," he took out one of the cards and showed it to Goetz, "but Lugosi's right about the guy maybe bein' a Nazi sympathizer. This card is an American Bund membership card. That's the American branch of the Nazi party." He eyed Lugosi closely. "So this is on the level?"

With a leer of contempt, Bela said, "Of course it is, as you say, level!"

"Honest, if this guy is with the Mob, I ain't never heard of 'im." Mannix showed Goetz the rest of the ID cards. "How about it, do any of these names sound familiar?"

"Of course not," Goetz replied, barely glancing at the evidence.

"Are you sure you paid your 'dues' to the Stagehands' Union?"

The studio chief remained cool. "It can't be the Stagehands' Union."

"How 'bout the Teamsters?"

Spitz rubbed his chin thoughtfully. "We paid our 'dues' to the Teamsters, too."

Mannix shrugged. "Then you got me. Unless you guys owe gamblin' debts I don't know about."

The night watchman cleared his throat. "So what do we do with these guys?" he said, indicating Bela, Lon and Lou. "Let this cop take charge of them?"

Mannix smiled. "Aw, Lon can sleep it off in my guest bedroom. Toni'll get a real kick out of it. She's got a thing for the Wolf Man."

Goetz studied the trio appraisingly. "No, I have a better idea." He pointed at Costello. "As far as I'm concerned, *you're* Mr. Chaney's handler." He addressed the watchman. "Mr. Chaney is now Mr. Costello's responsibility. Let him go."

"*Me?*" exclaimed Lou. "What am I gonna do with him?"

Goetz smirked. "You're going to see that Chaney stays sober, or else."

"What about Barber?" the watchman asked while removing Chaney's bracelets. "Do you want me to file a missing person's report?"

"That guy's not missing!" Spitz glared at the actors. "It's a put-on by these jokers. I'll stake my life on it."

Lou whispered, "You shouldn't oughta say things like 'stake' in front of Dracula. It'll give the guy heartburn."

Lugosi snarled, "You are not helping." He gave Goetz and Spitz a glare of menace. "Someone is trying to destroy your studio. Maybe to extort money or maybe it is revenge. Whatever the reason, you should remain on your guard." Bela turned to Lou. "Come, we go change into dry clothes." He released his hold on Chaney and headed for the door.

"Go where?" Lou asked, struggling to hold up Chaney all by himself.

"We drive to Dr. Fell's house." Lugosi insisted.

"Now hold on!" the traffic cop ordered as he took out his handcuffs. "I didn't agree to none of this. As far as I'm concerned the only place the little guy is going is with me."

Mannix grabbed Chaney's other arm. "Look," he said to Costello, "just to show I'm on the level," he turned to the traffic cop and declared, "I'm Eddie Mannix, and Mr. Costello and Mr. Lugosi are pals of mine."

The cop frowned. "Aw, now you can't—"

"You can take it up with your Captain," Mannix insisted. "M-G-M contributes big money for the Policemen's Benefit, ya know."

Sighing, the cop reluctantly put away his handcuffs. "Yeah, I know."

Giving Chaney's arm back to Bela, Mannix reached for his wallet. "Say, you look like you've been through a lot tonight. I know a place in the Hollywood Hills that'll get you a good massage." He slipped the cop the address of a certain brothel and a folded bill. "Are we all square now?"

The cop smiled and pocketed the bribe. "We're square." He scowled at Lou. "Just stay out of my way," he warned, and then stormed out.

"Boy," Costello said to Eddie, "They don't call you a fixer for nothin'."

"You better believe it," said Mannix. "Now, if you like, I'll get my friends on the force to keep their ear to the door about this kidnapping business."

"What?" Bela asked.

Basil explained, "He means he'll use his influence to locate your family."

"Yeah," said Mannix. "If these guys are pros, somebody's gotta know about 'em. If the cops can't help, I'll get my pals in the Mob to look into it. I'm on your side." Mannix offered his hand in a gesture of cooperation. "Let me help."

Lugosi hesitated. "Why do you want to do this?"

Lou smiled. "I keep tellin' you, Eddie ain't a bad guy, once you get to know him."

"Yeah," Mannix said, extending his hand further. "Come on, Lugosi. Let's be pals."

Rathbone stepped between them. "Bela, don't do it. You know what Mannix is capable of. You'd be making a deal with the devil."

Bela glowered with imperious disdain. "Look who it is that calls the pot black, Mr. Secret Investment Group Spokesman." Bela took Mannix's hand and shook it. "I trust you, Mannix. For now."

"Okay, now we're cookin' with gas," Mannix said with a smile.

"So now, we are three," Bela declared, "Mannix, Costello and I."

"Hey, I'm in," slurred Chaney. "I was in a Charlie Chan once."

"Wasn't you the bad guy?" asked Costello.

"Oh yeah." Chaney shrugged. "But I wanna help anyway." He squinted at Lugosi. "Got any coffee?"

Lugosi sighed. "Very well, we are now four." He gestured broadly in Abbott's direction. "Unless Mr. Abbott, he would like to join us."

Costello waved his partner over. "Come on, Abbott! We can be detectives together, just like we wuz in *Who Done It?* Only for real."

"I wish I could," Abbott said, glancing nervously at Rathbone. "But I don't have it in me."

"That's okay, pal," said Costello with an encouraging smile. "You've been through a lot, so you just go home and sleep it off."

Abbott smiled wanly. "I just don't want to let you down."

"How can the best straight man in the business let me down? Bela an' me can solve this mystery."

Mannix gestured at their wet clothes. "Not the way you guys are dressed."

Bela looked down at his wet and rumpled Dracula costume. "What can Bela change into? My clothes, they were in the trailer."

Lou gave Bela a playful nudge. "Don't worry, Bats, I know where all three of us can get a change of clothes."

"Fine," said Mannix. "You go change, and we'll meet up in the Executive Lot. Meanwhile, I'll make some phone calls." Mannix grabbed the phone on Goetz's desk.

"And we'll go make ourselves all presentable. Come on, Bats." Costello led Bela to the door, leaving Lon Chaney without any visible support. Lon dropped to the floor with a thud. Costello and Lugosi ran back to pick him up.

"This way, sleeping beauty," Lou said.

Chapter 9

Costello and Lugosi struggled to keep the tipsy Lon Chaney upright as they hurried to a waiting studio buggy. They were each dressed in costumes straight from the racks of *The Brain of Frankenstein*. Lou had on his "Wilbur Gray" tan gabardine suit and a plaid deerstalker left over from one of Basil Rathbone's *Sherlock Holmes* pictures, Bela was attired in yet another of Dracula's tux and tails, and Lon looked like a new man in his "Laurence Talbot" gray flannel suit. Bela was still winded from their struggle to dress the uncooperative actor, and was finding it difficult to steer Chaney in the right direction. But he was even more concerned with his present appearance, gesturing despairingly at his costume. "Again, I am dressed as Dracula!" he complained to Costello. "You expect for me to be taken seriously this way?"

"What would you rather look like," Costello asked, "a classy bat or a drowned rat?" He suddenly frowned and stopped short. "Wait a minute."

"What is wrong?"

Lou patted his pockets. "Hold Chaney up a minute, I think I forgot 'em."

"Forgot what?" Lugosi asked, struggling under the burden of Lon's slumping form as Chaney blinked and squinted and wiped his huge hand down Bela's face. "Where's that coffee?" he mumbled.

Lou sighed with relief and pulled out a handful of glass tubes. "Whew! For a minute, I thought I left 'em in my other suit."

Lugosi glared angrily. "Cigars? Give me those!" He shoved Chaney at Costello and confiscated the stogies. "Now help me with Chaney! He is very heavy."

They steered Lon to the studio buggy and loaded him into the back seat.

"Come," said Lugosi, getting in the passenger seat, "we go to your car now."

Lou gestured at Bela's pocket. "Come on, hand 'em over," he said.

"No," Lugosi said. "I want you to concentrate on the case, not on your cigars!"

Costello got behind the wheel. "Gimme just a couple," he said. "Come on, Bats, they're mine!" He gave Bela a cherubic smile. "We can share-zies; half for you and half for me."

"When we finish with the case," Lugosi insisted. "Now drive."

Costello drummed his fingers on the steering wheel, giving Bela an appraising once over.

"What are you staring at?" Bela asked with annoyance. "I said no cigars until the case is solved."

Lou shook his head. "It ain't that."

"What then?"

"I was just thinkin' you look half-dressed without the cape."

"Very funny," Bela grumbled. "Now drive!"

"Awright! Awright!" Lou griped, stamping on the accelerator. "I'm the guy who oughta be pissed. Those are *my* cigars!" They sped up the road to the Phantom Stage. "Shouldn't we get Karloff and Rathbone to help?" he asked.

Lugosi glowered. "Those two? Never!"

Costello parked the studio buggy next to his car. The fire department was locking up the Phantom Stage as Lou ran his finger in a layer of black soot that had settled on the hood. "Wouldn't ya know it," he lamented. "I just got the car washed."

"Never mind about that." Lugosi pointed at Chaney's slumped form and at the station wagon's rear compartment. "Let us lie him down in the back. He can sleep it off there and not get in the way."

"Good idea." Costello opened the rear door and together they coaxed Chaney to his feet and steered him toward the back of the station wagon. Lugosi ducked Chaney's head down and they shoved him inside. The tipsy actor stretched out in the back and began snoring contentedly.

"What a great Watson he will make," Lugosi sighed as Costello slammed the door. He eyed Costello's deerstalker. "It is bad enough I am dressed as Dracula. Do you have to wear that silly hat?"

Costello turned the hat around so the visors faced sideways. "Hey, now we're both Sherlocks." He stuck his hand in his jacket like Napoleon and posed proudly. "Scared of the competition?"

Lugosi shook his head as he got in the passenger seat and Costello got behind the wheel.

Lou insisted, "I still think we oughta get Karloff and Rathbone's help on this. They seem to know a lot."

"They know much, but say nothing. Karloff and Rathbone are not to be trusted!"

Costello drove down Laemmle Blvd, and then took an unexpected sharp right.

"Where are you going?" Lugosi demanded. "Drive to Dr. Fell's house."

"We gotta meet up with Mannix first, don't we? He's supposed to help." Lou was about to turn down the street to the Executive Parking Lot when Lugosi slapped his hand on the dash board. "NO! We do not wait for Mannix! If he finds out something, we ask him later. There is not a moment to lose."

Costello shrugged. "Okay, you're the head Sherlock." He made a U-turn and drove to the front gate.

The guard leaned out of the guardhouse window. "Good night, Mr. Costello."

"Good night," said Lou. "And I'm sorry for yellin' at you before."

"That's okay, Mr. Costello." The guard smiled. "Mr. Abbott left in a taxi just now. He was looking mighty worried. Are you two guys having another spat?"

"Oh, it ain't nothin' like that. It's just Bud's been through a lot tonight." Lou waved. "See you tomorrow."

The instant he pulled out into traffic, Bela said, "Go back."

"Go back?" Lou carped. "What for?"

"I want to question the guard," Lugosi grumbled. "Now go back!"

Amid complaining car horns and screeching tires, Lou made a U-turn and drove back to the guardhouse.

"Did you forget something?" the guard asked.

Lou pointed at Lugosi. "Bela's got some questions."

Lugosi squeezed Lou against the seat as he leaned across. "Did you see a dressing trailer leave the studio earlier this evening?"

The guard shook his head. "Nope," he said. "Sorry. No dressing trailers, coming or going." He pointed up the street. "Did you check on the back lot?"

"Hey, the back lot," said Lou. "Maybe we oughta search the back lot."

"That is true," said Bela, remembering the strange newsreel style truck. "Before, I see a strange van driving to the back lot." He shook his head. "But no," Bela insisted. "We must question Dr. Fell before he can escape."

"You really think the doc has anything to do with this?"

"I do."

Lou looked worried. "Dee Dee drove him home. You don't think…?"

"Why did you not say so before? We must go there now! But first," Lugosi got out of the car and marched up to the guardhouse. "I must use your telephone."

The guard handed Bela the handset. "What's the extension?" he asked, his digit waiting in the finger hole of the dial.

"Give me Goetz's office."

Moments later, William Goetz's weary voice said, "Yes?"

"This is Bela Lugosi."

There was a frustrated groan. "What do you want now?"

"The kidnappers could have taken the trailer to the back lot. You must organize a search."

"Should I hire extras with torches and pitchforks while I'm at it?"

Lugosi grimaced at the handset. "This is not a laughing matter! Many lives are at stake and in particular the lives of my wife and son."

"Mannix called in a favor to a friend in homicide. I'll have the Lieutenant check the back lot first, if that will that make you happy."

"What will make me happy is finding my wife and son alive." Bela gave the handset back to the guard. "Hang that up hard. I am very angry."

The guard slammed the handset back on the hook.

Lugosi nodded his approval. "You do that very well."

"I've been married twenty years," the guard said. "I get lots of practice."

Bela got back in the car. "We go now," he said, rubbing the back of his head, "but first we stop at a drugstore for some aspirin. I have a headache."

"Right!" Lou switched gears and gave the gate guard a childish wave of wiggling fingers. "Toodle-loo!" he chirped and drove off.

As Lou headed down Lankershim Blvd., Bela asked, "Where does Dr. Fell live?"

"Around Crescent Heights," Lou said, adding with a mischievous smile, "an' since we're goin' that way, I know the perfect drugstore for your headache."

Lugosi winced. "No! You do not mean—"

Chapter 10

Lou Costello parked out front of the famous Hollywood drugstore with the large neon sign over the entrance blinking, "Schwab's." Neon signs in the windows offered "Breakfast, Luncheon, Dinner" and "Prescriptions" with "Free Delivery." It was here that a tuxedoed Bela Lugosi was trying to look inconspicuous as he and a Sherlockian Lou Costello stepped inside.

Lou pointed at a couple of phone booths standing side by side in the corner. "I'm gonna make a quick call."

Lugosi pulled Lou back. "We have no time for that. As soon as I am done here we must go to Dr. Fell's house." He grabbed Costello's hat and turned the visors the right way around. "And do not embarrass me any more than you have!" he complained.

"Fine, but I wanna make sure Abbott got home okay." Lou gestured at a nearby soda fountain stool. "Have a seat an' get your headache powder. I'll be right back."

Bela begrudgingly sat down at the counter as a soda jerk wearing a white uniform and jaunty cap leaned forward and asked, "What'll it be, Mister?"

"A headache powder," Lugosi said. He watched as Costello waited by the occupied phone booths. One of the occupants, a distinguished looking gentleman, attracted Lugosi's attention. There was something oddly familiar about both him and the black leather notebook in his hand.

The soda jerk selected a glass. "How would you like your headache powder, in a glass of soda or plain water?"

"Soda," said Bela, still watching the man in the phone booth keenly. "Make it a ginger ale."

"Sure thing," the soda jerk said. He deftly flipped the glass into the air and caught it in his other hand. After filling the glass with ginger ale, the young man added a measured portion of BC Headache Powder and stirred. Offering Bela the glass of fizzing remedy, the soda jerk's eyebrows rose with sudden recognition. "Say, aren't you—," he began excitedly.

Ordinarily, Bela enjoyed fan moments like this, but tonight he had no patience for it. "Yes, I am he," he said irritably. "Leave me alone." He ignored the young man by keeping his eyes on the gentleman in the phone booth.

"Boy," the soda jerk said with a broad smile, "I can't wait to tell Mr. Schwab that I met Boris Karloff!"

Bela nearly choked on his headache remedy. "I am Bela Lugosi! How dare you confuse me with Karloff!" He gestured curtly at his Dracula costume. "Especially dressed as I am!" He gulped the rest of his remedy, slammed his glass down, and marched over to Costello. "Come, funnyman," he demanded. "We must go!"

"Aw, keep your shirt on. This'll only take a minute." Lou turned around and bumped into the gentleman just as he was exiting the phone booth, causing the man to drop his notebook. "Sorry, Mister," Lou apologized. "Lemme get that."

"I do beg your pardon," the gentleman said in a British accent.

They bent down simultaneously to collect the notebook and bumped heads. The gentleman straightened up and stared accusingly at Costello. "I say, are you trying to be funny?"

"Oh, I don't hafta try to be funny. It just comes natural."

"Indeed." Again the gentleman bent down to collect his notebook and again Lou Costello instinctively did likewise. Their noggins collided with a decided thud. The man was obviously taking umbrage with this routine. "Will you kindly stop doing that!"

Lugosi grew impatient. "Please," he said, "allow me." He pushed Lou back and collected the notebook, noting the calling cards that had spilled out on the floor. They had a familiar insignia printed in green ink, a capital "C" with a brain inside it, a crown above it and with the motto "*Semper Occultus*" printed below. "Where did you get these calling cards?" Lugosi asked.

Lou took the card and asked, "Hey, your name wouldn't be Richard, would it?"

The question seemed to unnerve the gentleman. "I have never heard that name before," he denied, taking back his notebook and calling cards. "And kindly leave my property alone, if you please," he said, returning the notebook to his inner jacket pocket.

"I know your face," Lugosi said. There was definitely something vaguely familiar. The man was in his sixties and wore a tweed suit and brown waistcoat. His silver hair was combed back. He wore a trim mustache and had a deep bronzed complexion, suggesting he was possibly of a mixed East Indian heritage.

Costello was the first to put two and two together. "Say," said Lou, wagging his finger with recognition, "did anybody ever tell you that you look an awful lot like Boris Karloff?"

The gentleman grew quite vexed at the suggestion. "How dare you!"

Costello tried to explain, "Look, I wasn't tryin' to insult you or nothin'. I know Boris Karloff personally an' he's a swell guy."

Staring Costello down, the gentleman declared, "To even use that name in my presence is not only insulting, it's degrading!"

Lugosi sympathized. "I know exactly how you feel," he said. "Just a moment ago that young man over there mistook me for Karloff."

"I told you," Lou chastised jokingly, "you shoulda wore the cape."

The soda jerk tapped Bela on the shoulder. "Say, that'll be a nickel, Mr. Lugosi."

Bela searched his pockets, coming upon the photograph of Lillian he kept in his tuxedo, and the water logged calling card Boris had given him, but not his wallet. "I left my wallet in my trailer with my regular clothes." He nudged Lou. "You pay him. I pay you back later." He showed the stranger the calling card. "Karloff gave me a card very much like yours. Excuse it being so wet."

"I see," the gentleman said, examining the card and eyeing Bela with kinder eyes. He handed the card back. "Please," he offered, reaching into his pocket, "allow me." He gave the soda jerk a quarter. "There you are, young man," he said. "Keep the change."

The eyes bugged out of the soda jerk's head. "Wow, thanks!"

"...be sure to show them—should the need arise."

Gesturing after the retreating soda jerk, Lugosi nodded pleasantly. "That is very kind, considering."

Costello smirked. "I guess it's like Karloff said; show the card if the need should arise." He addressed the gentleman. "So, what, is it like the Masons?"

"Not at all," the gentleman said. "It's just that I had no idea you were *the* Bela Lugosi."

Lou frowned. "Like there's another Bela Lugosi?"

Sighing, Bela gestured at his companion. "And, as you may have guessed, this is *the* Lou Costello."

"Of course," the gentleman said. "Here you are," he reached into his notebook and pulled out two cards, "a nice fresh one for each of you," adding with an equally mysterious air, "be sure to show them—should the need arise."

Lou pointed at the telltale bulge as he pocketed the card. "So, what's with the gun?"

The gentleman gave Lou a disarming smile. "Oh, that," he said. Growing serious, he leaned in and whispered, "Can you two keep a secret?"

Lou and Bela nodded earnestly.

"So can I." Without another word of explanation, the gentleman departed.

"That," Lou said, eyeing the fellow as he left the drug store, "is one really weird guy."

"Forget about him." Bela pushed Costello toward the phone booth. "Make your phone call. Every second counts."

Lou sat in the phone booth, but left the door open. Bela leaned against the booth as Costello dropped a coin into the slot and dialed. "Hello, Betty? It's Lou. I'm just callin' to make sure Bud got home okay." Costello listened and frowned. "He didn't? ...No, I'm sure he's okay. You know Bud. He probably went to Murray's house, or stopped at a bar for a nightcap, or somethin'." He cast a worried look at Lugosi. "Listen, Betty, *if* Bud shows up," he hastily corrected himself, "I mean, *when* Bud shows up, leave a message with my butler. I'll get it later. Okay, bye." He hung up. "You think the kidnappers got Bud?" he asked Lugosi.

"Is there any place besides home that Mr. Abbott would go?"

Lou thought a moment and snapped his fingers. "I know the place!" He dropped in another coin and dialed. "Abbott's got his own bar, Abbott's Backstage. He hangs out there with his cronies all the time."

Lugosi frowned. "Mr. Abbott owns his own bar?" He shook his head. "That would be like a child owning his own candy store."

Lou grinned. "You're tellin' me." He listened as the phone kept ringing. "There ain't no answer." He hung up, giving Bela a determined look. "We gotta go there an' see if Bud's okay."

"We do not have time for that," Bela insisted. "Surely one of these cronies of Mr. Abbott you mentioned, they can investigate instead."

"Hey, that's a good idea." Lou dialed. "I'll call Murray Teff. He's Abbott's right-hand man." He waited for Teff to pick up. "Hello, Murray, this is Lou Costello. Is Bud there? He isn't, huh? Okay, now listen, I want you to go over to Abbott's Backstage an' see if Bud's over there."

Lou listened, and as he did his face flushed red. "WADDA YA MEAN YOU'RE IN THE MIDDLE OF A CARD GAME?" he shouted. "Listen, Teff, you get your ass over to Abbott's Backstage, and whether Abbott is down there or not, you call my house and leave a message with my butler! If ya don't, I'll come down to your joint an' shove them cards right down your goddamn throat! You got me? GOOD!"

He hung up loudly and glared at the payphone. "The nerve of the guy," Costello grumbled.

"Now that we have taken care of that, we must go to Dr. Fell's house."

Lou followed Bela outside. "You think Abbott's okay?" he asked.

Getting in the car, Lugosi said, "I do not know. But I have a feeling that Dr. Fell, he has all the answers."

Part Two
The Frozen Ghost
Chapter 11

Wednesday, 25 February 1948
9:52 P.M.
Wilshire Blvd.

As they drove to Dr. Fell's house, Bela tried to think of a subtle way to bring up an indelicate question, but Lugosi wasn't one for subtlety. The best he could manage was to clear his throat, which he did repeatedly until he finally got Lou's attention.

"You got a sore throat or something?" Costello asked.

"I have questions," said Bela. "It concerns your son."

The comic grew serious. "What do you have to bring that up for?"

"You are helping me to find my son; I want to put your mind at rest about yours."

The sadness in Lou's eyes was illuminated by headlights reflected in his rearview mirror. "There's no way you'll ever do that, Bats. Drop it."

"You asked me, as a detective, to find for you an answer, why there were no scrapes upon your son's knees. I have questions to help me get a clearer picture of the problem."

"You think you got questions I haven't already asked myself about a million times? Asking questions don't do any good, Bela. Like I said, drop it already."

"But perhaps you are too close to the problem. I may think of something you may not have thought of, or you are afraid to think of. Please, just a few questions."

Costello sighed and pulled the car over. Draping his arm over the seat, he looked askance at Bela, and said irritably, "So, go ahead, ask."

"On that horrible day, how was your son dressed?"

Lou winced and emitted a quiet sob; a tear ran down his cheek. The comedian looked away as he said, "Butch was wearin' a white shirt...and blue shorts."

"Was he wearing shoes?"

"No. He wore socks. White socks." Lou glared at Bela. "Why?"

"The socks, were they dirty?"

There was a deathly, lingering silence before Lou said, "I saw Mitch pick up one of Butch's socks that he found by the pool. It musta come off when Butch crawled out of his playpen."

"I see." Lugosi nodded. "How fast could he crawl?" he asked.

"He could crawl real fast."

"And yet," Lugosi said, mulling things over, "he had no scrapes upon his knees."

"No," Lou snarled, "which is why the cops were treating my wife like she was a goddamn murder suspect." He rubbed his hand over his pudgy face, trying to stifle his temper. "Look, I appreciate you wanting to help, but can we just stick to the case we're on right now?"

"I am sorry I caused you pain," Lugosi said humbly. "But if it helps to console you, I do not believe your son was murdered."

"That's where you're wrong, Bela," Costello said bitterly. "Butch *was* murdered. And I know the bum who did it."

The color drained from Lugosi's face until he was as pale as Count Dracula. "Who could have done such a terrible thing?" he gasped.

Costello's eyes grew hard. "You wanna know who killed Butch? I DID! There, I said it!"

"Impossible! I do not understand."

"Ever since I was a kid I wanted a swimming pool, but back then my family couldn't afford one. So when I made it big, I go and have built the biggest damn pool I could fit in my backyard! Ironic, ain't it? I wanted a pool, and it drowns my only son! So scrapes on the knees, or no scrapes on the knees, it don't matter! *I killed him* because if I didn't build that swimming pool, Butch would still be alive today! So, can we please change the goddamn subject?" Lou grabbed the steering wheel and pulled back into traffic, cutting off a passing car. The other driver swerved and leaned on his horn. Two bright headlights illuminated the sleeping form of Lon Chaney.

Bela looked in Costello's rearview mirror. "We are being followed," he said.

Lou glanced back. "It's probably the guy I just cut off."

Lugosi hunted through the glove compartment. "Do you have a gun?"

Costello rolled his eyes. "Sorry, Bats, I left my gat in my other suit."

"Do you have a blackjack or a lead pipe?"

"Why, because I'm Italian you think I got me an arsenal in my car? Relax, will ya? The guy ain't following us. It's just your imagination."

Costello turned off Wilshire Blvd. onto a cul-de-sac. He pointed at a boarded up old house hidden by tall palm trees and overgrown bushes. "That's the doc's house over there."

Lugosi looked behind them. The mystery car also turned onto the cul-de-sac. "Do not look now, but my imagination is still behind us."

Costello tightened his grip on the wheel. "Let's try and lose the guy."

"If they are the kidnappers, they know where my wife and son are."

"So what do we do? You got a plan?"

"Yes. If we cannot threaten them with weapons, we must let them capture us, so they take us to where Lillian and Bela, Jr. are being held."

"That's the plan? Let 'em kidnap us?" Lou shook his head. "That's the crummiest plan I ever heard."

"Have you a better one?"

"Yeah," said Costello, pulling over. "We wait for the guy to walk over here, and then when he's in just the right spot, we knock him on his ass by opening the car door as hard as we can, and then before he can get up, jump him and beat the hell out of him to make him talk."

Lugosi nodded. "Yes, that *is* a better plan."

The mystery car passed under a street lamp before parking in the shadows. Lugosi noted it was a maroon Chevy coupe fresh from the dealership. The driver's side door opened and a shadowy figure emerged.

"Get ready," Lou said, keeping his eye on the rearview mirror and gripping his door handle.

Lugosi did likewise. "He is coming this way."

"Remember," said Costello, tightening his grip on the handle, "if he comes on your side, open your door as hard as you can."

Lon Chaney groaned from the rear luggage compartment. "Anybody got any coffee?"

"NO!" Lugosi barked.

Rolling over on his side, Lon said, "Wake me when there's coffee." He curled up and went back to sleep.

Lugosi kept his eye on the rearview mirror. "He is coming to my side of the car."

A lone figure knocked on the passenger window.

"NOW!" Lugosi shut his eyes and pushed the door open with all his might, sending the figure tumbling backward. Bela leapt from the car. With eyes shut, Bela punched blindly at the stranger sprawled under him, ranting, "SO YOU WOULD DARE TO FOLLOW LUGOSI? I SHOW YOU WHAT A LUGOSI IS MADE OF!"

"Will ya quit that?!" said a familiar voice.

"Hold 'im, Bela!" Lou said. He began throwing punches. "Didn't know I was a boxer when I was a kid, did ya, ya bastard?!"

"YEOW! Geez, Lugosi! Costello! Knock it off before I murder you guys!"

Bela and Lou froze. Lugosi looked down at his prostrate foe. "YOU!" he said.

Eddie Mannix shoved Bela off of him and sat up. "Were you expecting maybe Boris Karloff?" he asked sarcastically.

"Now that you mention it—," Bela began. "Why were you putting on us the tail?"

"What's the mystery? You guys tried to ditch me, so I followed you." Mannix got up and brushed himself off. "I thought I could help out, you know, by giving you guys some muscle. Looks like you can do fine by yourselves." He adjusted his tie and ran his fingers through his thinning hair. "Boy, I sure feel sorry for anybody that tangles with you two." He jabbed a stubby thumb at the old house. "So what's the plan? Look for an open window and sneak in?"

"Actually," Lou said. "We was just gonna go up to the front door an' knock. The guy knows me."

"Makes sense to me," Mannix said. He slapped Bela and Lou on the back. "Let's go and do some business."

The scene was suggestive of many a Poverty Row chiller Lugosi was forced to make for Monogram Pictures. A cool February wind blew dried leaves on the overgrown property. On the lawn out front was a faded sign that read, "Willoughby & Son Funeral Home." The porch creaked as Lou, Bela and Eddie climbed the worm-eaten steps.

"Are you sure someone lives in this joint?" asked Mannix.

Lou reached for the knocker. "If you think this is spooky, wait 'til you meet the butler."

Mannix snickered. "There's a butler?"

Before Lou could use the knocker, a man appeared from around the house. "Hold it right where you are," he demanded, aiming a double barreled shotgun. He was dressed in a bathrobe, slippers and pajamas.

Lou and Bela put their hands up.

Mannix remained unfazed. "So who are you, the old family retainer?" he asked with a cocky snicker.

The man looked flummoxed. "Me? No, I live next door."

"Aimin' at folks with a shotgun ain't exactly the good neighbor policy, pal."

The man lowered his weapon. "There's been strange things happening, Mister, and with him looking like Dracula," he said, indicating Lugosi, "well, I figured you might have something to do with the monster."

"Monster!" exclaimed Costello. "What monster?"

"The big iron monster, that's what monster. It's an ugly looking bastard. Big head, big eyes, pointy metal teeth." The man visibly shuddered at the recollection. "Gives me the creeps just thinking about it."

Bela drew up indignantly. "You are trying to make Bela appear foolish! What you describe is the Iron Man from my serial *The Phantom Creeps*." He sneered, "Perhaps you should stay away from the children's matinee if it gives you such nightmares."

The man in pajamas eyed Bela narrowly as he raised his weapon. "You want to take a look at the hole in my fence, Mister? It broke into my yard and trampled my wife's prize flower beds and got tangled in my ham radio antenna."

"Hey, Gridley," Mannix said, "You mind aiming that thing someplace else?"

"Oh, sorry. The monster's got me all on edge." The man pushed the release lever, unhinged the shotgun and rested the open barrel in the crook of his arm. "The name's Bill, by the way, Bill Connor, like O'Connor, but without the O."

"Pleased to meet ya, Bill," said Mannix. "I'm Eddie Mannix, this is Lou Costello, and the penguin is Bela Lugosi."

"Is this on the level?" Bill asked in star-struck awe. "Could I get your autographs?"

Lugosi glowered impatiently. "Perhaps another time. Besides monsters, did you see anything else suspicious, perhaps maybe an ambulance?"

"No, no ambulance," said Connor, "just the hearse."

Grinning, Mannix asked, "There's a hearse?"

"This old place used to be a funeral home." Connor gestured down the driveway. "It's parked around back in the carriage house."

Costello whispered to Lugosi, "Maybe the monster drives it."

Connor shrugged. "Then there was this pretty girl in a sports car…"

"A pretty girl, you said?" Bela reached into his tuxedo and produced Lillian's picture. He approached the man and showed it to him. "Was it this woman?" he asked.

The man squinted at the photo, held it up to the street light, shook his head and handed it back. "No, the girl I saw was a blonde. She drove up with that creepy looking doctor and some other fella."

"Oh," Costello explained, "that was just my secretary."

Connor nodded toward the house. "Are you fellas planning on going in there?"

"That's the general idea," said Mannix.

"Lots of luck," he said, and then headed back to his house.

Mannix chuckled and counted off on his fingers. "Let's see, we got a spooky house with a butler, a spooked neighbor, a monster on the loose, and a hearse. All we need now is Arch Obler tellin' us that it's later than we think."

"Enough of this," Lugosi said impatiently, mounting the porch. "What are you waiting for?" he said to Costello. "Knock the knocker."

...his eyes were drawn to an ashtray on a small table by the staircase.

"I'm knockin', I'm knockin'," Lou said as he banged the knocker.

Moments later a tapping and footsteps could be heard approaching from inside. The front door creaked open. A tall man wearing round dark glasses and holding a white cane appeared. Cocking his head to listen, the blind butler asked in a deep, raspy voice, "Yes, who is that?" It struck Bela that there was something strangely familiar about the butler's long white hair and droopy mustache.

"Hello, Grimes," said Lou. "It's Lou Costello and Bela Lugosi. Oh, and Eddie Mannix. We're here to see the doc."

"Come in," the butler said. He held the door open and gestured at a hall tree bench in the vestibule. "If you have hats and coats, you may hang them there."

"We're fine," said Eddie. He noted the butler's attire. "Say, what's with the old fashioned greatcoat, Jeeves? Do you chill easy?"

The butler was stone-faced as he explained, "It gets very cold...in *certain* parts of the house, sir."

Bela hesitated at the threshold. He found the butler disquieting, and he couldn't decide why. The musty dankness within the house and the creaking floorboards as he took his first tentative steps inside only added to his apprehension.

"Come on, Bela," Lou said, urging him forward. "It's the Watson that does all the scare takes, not the Sherlock."

Lugosi glowered. "I am not frightened! I just do not tread easily where angels fear to go."

Dominating the entry hall was a rickety, cobwebbed-laced staircase. Bela tried to see what was waiting at the top, but saw only murky shadows. The tapping of the butler's cane along the wainscoting added to the Hungarian's unease. Bela became aware of a hint of tobacco amongst the stench of dry rot. He sniffed the air and his eyes were drawn to an ashtray on a small table by the staircase. Resting in the ashtray was a cigarette burning at the end of a long cigarette holder similar to the one Lugosi remembered seeing Dr. Kopf using.

"Nice place ya got here," Mannix complimented, running his finger along the dusty banister, "it looks real lived in."

"Yeah," Costello said, playing scared. "I heard tell this joint made the cover of *Better Morgues and Cemeteries*."

Grimes stopped by a set of pocket doors off to the left of the entry hall and groped for the door pulls. He explained, "The doctor keeps the house this way to scare off curiosity seekers."

Mannix said with a smirk, "Isn't that what the monster roamin' around outside the joint is for?"

"Monster, sir?" asked the butler.

"Yeah," said Costello, "we ran into a neighbor friend of yours armed with a shotgun."

"He said he saw a big metal monster in the bushes," Mannix chuckled.

"Imagination has a way of running away with one, sir," the butler rasped, pulling the doors open. Lugosi expected them to squeak noisily along their tracks. The doors moved silently, which Bela found even more off-putting. The butler bid them to enter. "Please wait in the parlor with the other guests."

The room beyond was once the viewing parlor of the funeral home, and now just an ordinary room for receiving guests. It was bathed in a wavering orange glow cast by a crackling fire. The dancing shadows played across the sheet covered furniture, giving the impression that the parlor was occupied by lounging ghosts.

"What other guests?" Bela asked warily. "Is Dr. Kopf here?" He gasped, not from seeing the mysterious physician with the half mask, or from having come upon some loathsome apparition, but because he spied two annoyingly familiar faces. "Karloff and Rathbone!" he exclaimed.

"Well," smiled Basil as he stood up, "fancy meeting you here."

"And look Basil," Boris said. "Eddie Mannix is with them."

"Amazing how we keep bumping into each other," Basil quipped.

"Indeed," agreed Boris.

The butler paused at the entrance. "I will tell my Master that you are here." He closed the pocket doors; the tapping of his cane faded down the hall.

Mannix pointed at a gilded bas relief mask hanging on the wall by the fireplace.

"I'll lay ya odds that a pair of shifty eyes appears from behind that mask!" he chuckled.

"It is all a bit theatrical, isn't it?" Rathbone agreed as he surveyed the room.

"What brings you here?" asked Boris casually.

"We got business with the doc," Lou said. "You guys wouldn't by any chance be tryin' to make a deal behind my back, was ya?"

"I should say not!" Karloff said, insulted.

Lugosi glared. "With my wife and son in danger, why are you not using those great detective minds to find them?"

"How do you know we're not?" Rathbone retorted.

The scene was interrupted by the arrival of Dr. Fell. "Good evening, gentlemen," Dr. Fell said. "Ah, *Herr* Costello, your arrival is unexpected."

"Good evening, doctor," said Basil pleasantly. "As I explained on the telephone, our partner is very interested in that mechanical hand of yours."

"I knew it!" Lou shouted accusingly. "Listen here, Rathbone, the doc an' me are partners, and now so is Eddie Mannix. You wanna talk to the doc, you gotta do it through Lou Costello Enterprises!"

"Please, *Herr* Costello," said Dr. Fell. "The invention I was about to demonstrate for *Herr* Rathbone and *Herr* Karloff has nothing to do with the icemaker."

"It don't matter," Lou insisted. "Lou Costello Enterprises gets first dibs on anything you invent, includin' that hand!"

"I think you will agree there is enough profit to go around once my invention is presented to the public."

Mannix smiled. "Well, I know I'm always game for a good investment, and a new hand like that will make a mint if we get the Veterans Administration interested."

"Actually," said Dr. Fell, "I have another invention, one that puts this hand and my icemaker to shame." Bela noted that the doctor's mechanical hand now appeared as a flesh-colored replica of a normal human hand, right down to the fingernails.

With an inviting gesture, the doctor said, "Now, if you will follow me to my laboratory—"

Dr. Fell led everyone down the hallway to a door beneath the staircase. He opened the door and waved his guests inside. "The basement is this way, gentlemen."

"What?" asked Mannix. "No secret passageway?"

"I beg your pardon?" asked the humorless inventor.

"Skip it." Bidding the others to follow, Mannix said, "Come on, boys. I can't wait to see what the doc's got cookin' down there."

The door leading to the basement laboratory creaked on rusty hinges. Bela all but expected a Monogram Pictures camera crew to be waiting for him at the bottom of the stairs. Dr. Fell threw a switch, illuminating the anteroom that had once served as the embalming room for the funeral home and where a number of parkas hung from a coat rack. Dr. Fell handed one to each of his guests. "You will need these. It's quite cold inside." Bela and the others exchanged looks as they donned the parkas. Having dressed himself, Dr. Fell reached for the latch to a large freezer door.

Lou Costello gulped. "Please tell me you keep sides of beef in there."

"Something like that," Dr. Fell answered cryptically.

Bracing himself for the sight of dead bodies on slabs, Lugosi followed the doctor and the others inside a metal walled room lined with many morgue freezer doors on one side, and ending with a bank of control panels and a glass observation window opposite the entrance. The air was chilled enough for Bela to see his breath. The Hungarian shivered. "Why is it so cold?"

Mannix was grinning from ear to ear. "Aw, come on, boys. Where's your sense of humor? This is great!" He nudged Dr. Fell with his elbow. "So what's the setup, doc? Ya keep stiffs on ice in here, or what?"

Dr. Fell gave Mannix a thin smile. "In a manner of speaking, yes."

The doctor turned a knob on the control board. The lights in the room beyond came up, revealing a bank of eight crystal cabinets.

Mannix's jaw dropped. "Jeez, will ya look at that!"

Bela felt an unnerving sense of familiarity. The cabinets stood like upright coffins against the walls and held human-shaped silhouettes behind frost encrusted glass.

Gesturing dismissively at the display, Lugosi sneered, "What kind of nonsense is this?"

In the center of the room, lit from above by a single baby spotlight, was a metal embalming table. The table was bolted to the floor and surrounded by Tesla coils.

"Did Kenneth Strickfaden put you up to this?" Boris asked as he perused the control board. "This looks *exactly* like the sort of equipment I've played with before."

"Quite," added Basil, approaching the window. He felt the glass, and instantly withdrew his hand. "The glass is painfully cold!" He turned to Dr. Fell, gesturing at the frozen figures. "I trust you have a permit to keep human cadavers here."

"Those are not human cadavers," assured Dr. Fell. "They're alive." He indicated the metal slab. "They are test subjects placed in a hibernation state by my metabolic de-animator." He pointed at a glass canopy suspended over the table. "That is the containment module for the liquid nitrogen and a special gas."

Rathbone rubbed his hands vigorously as he crooked an eyebrow. "Are you trying to tell us that those people volunteered for this experiment?"

"They feel no pain. They feel nothing, in fact. My method suspends life itself, gentlemen. Metabolically speaking, not so much as a second in time passes for them."

Karloff looked skeptical. "Assuming that all of this isn't an elaborate prank, I take it you can revive them safely."

"Ah, therein hangs the dilemma. In theory, I should be able to revive my subjects many months or even years later, completely unharmed, not having aged a single day."

Lou frowned. "What, you mean, you can't?"

"I can *now*," Fell assured him. "I made a recent breakthrough." He pointed at the ceiling. "You met one such subject already, my butler. But in reviving him, there was a mild side effect."

Basil stiffened. "His blindness, you mean."

Mannix roared with laughter. "Oh, this is *great!* What a spook show!" He slapped Rathbone on the back. "Don't ya see? This is all a gag!" He smiled at the doctor. "Did Goetz put you up to this? HO! HO! What a joker!"

Karloff gave the doctor a hard stare. "Exactly who are your test subjects?"

Dr. Fell shrugged. "Does it really matter? They're the derelicts of the world who agreed to my terms in exchange for food and drink and the promise of eventual payment. I have their signed waivers on file. But before we begin, I must disclose the absolute truth about myself." Dr. Fell looked grim. "What *Herr* Barber said at the demonstration was quite true. I am, in fact, a former stage magician."

Costello was crestfallen. "So all this is a gag?"

"No," Dr. Fell insisted. "I wanted to keep my past as an illusionist a secret for fear you would think my de-animator was merely a parlor trick. I assure you, back in Germany I *was* a chemical and mechanical engineer. My field was low temperature physics." He rolled up his right sleeve and held up his mechanical hand. "You wondered how I lost my hand."

"You said you lost it in the War," said Basil.

"In a sense I did, yes. Experimenting with such dangerously low temperatures does not come without risks." He led them to a stainless steel worktable on which a tall metal cylinder stood. "Allow me to demonstrate." He reached for a bright red rubber ball and bounced it with his good hand, catching it with his mechanical one.

Pointing at the fragments, Lou exclaimed, "Yikes! I'll bet that musta smarted."

"You work that thing really good, doc," Lou said, impressed.

"Thank you, but that's not what I meant to demonstrate. Observe." The doctor opened the cap sealing the cylinder. White mist spilled heavily along the sides and onto the tabletop. "Liquid nitrogen, gentlemen," he said with a flourish. He took handling tongs from the table and used them to pick up the red rubber ball. "Now watch." He immersed the ball in the liquid nitrogen. After a moment he removed the ball, now frozen dead white and smoking with an icy aura of mist. "This is what happened to my hand." Dr. Fell raised the tongs high above the table and released the ball. The frozen rubber ball landed on the tabletop where it shattered like a fragile Christmas ornament.

Pointing at the fragments, Lou exclaimed, "Yikes! I'll bet that musta smarted."

"Okay," said Mannix, obviously still amused by the freak show, "so what do you do for an encore?"

"Now," said Dr. Fell, "I shall demonstrate an interesting side effect of my new revival process."

"Besides blindness," Rathbone countered.

"Yes," Dr. Fell smiled. "After months of countless failures—"

"By 'failures'," said Rathbone, gesturing at the morgue freezer doors, "you mean deaths."

Ignoring Basil, Dr. Fell gestured at two unoccupied glass coffins. "I was successful with two others."

"Who might these 'subjects' be?" Rathbone asked pointedly.

Dr. Fell ignored the question as he selected a pair of goggles from a row hanging on one wall. "Not only have I successfully revived my subjects, but in doing so, I discovered a rather startling side effect. The test subjects awakened with their cellular structure completely regenerated!"

"What does that mean in English, doc?" asked Mannix.

"With the aid of this machine, I shall grow a new hand."

"You're gonna do what?"

"You heard correctly, *Herr* Mannix. I shall grow a new hand."

After placing the welder's style goggles over his glasses, he gestured for his guests to do the same. "These goggles have been specially treated and will protect your retinas from the intense light generated by the re-animator." As Bela and the others followed suit, Dr. Fell pressed a button causing a metal door that connected the observation room with the operating room to slide open. "Wait here. This wall and the lead-impregnated glass will protect you from the radiation."

"Is this guy on the level?" asked Lou.

Even behind the dark goggles, Bela's skeptical grimace was very apparent. "I think we are being prepared for a magic trick."

"You may well be right," said Basil.

They could see Dr. Fell approach the metal slab. He slipped off his parka, set it aside, and drew down a microphone like a ringmaster at a prizefight. "You will see that this is no trick. It is quite real. First, I shall freeze myself, and then program the re-animator to revive me. During this process, my cellular structure should regenerate." He stripped to the waist down to his body and neck brace.

"That's impossible," Karloff insisted.

"Not at all," said Dr. Fell as he unbuckled and removed his mechanical arm and hand, revealing an extremity amputated above the elbow. "The regenerative phase is what makes revival after freezing possible. When you freeze human tissue, the invading ice crystals destroy cellular integrity. But, by employing a special serum derived from certain sea creatures and reptiles, I have succeeded in complete cellular regeneration." He discarded the mechanical arm and eased himself slowly up on the metal preparation table.

Bela whispered to Karloff, "You are not going to believe this nonsense, are you?"

Boris shrugged slightly. "I confess that his explanation seems reasonable."

Basil smirked. "In a rather unreasonable way, I suppose."

They watched as Dr. Fell laid back and pushed a button mounted next to his good hand. Restraining bands emerged from the slab and encircled him as the glass canopy lowered. Soon Dr. Fell was completely covered like so much pheasant under glass. An illuminated sign over the observation window announced, "FREEZING PROCESS INITIATED."

"You gotta admit," said Mannix, "the guy's got showmanship."

"Watch, gentlemen," Dr. Fell said from a microphone mounted inside the canopy. Slowly a white gaseous smoke crawled over the doctor's body. "The gas is the preserving agent that will revitalize—my—c—c—cells—once the—" There was an audible gasp. Moments later the mist inside the canopy dissipated, revealing a frozen Dr. Fell.

"Wow," marveled Lou. "Ain't that somethin'?"

Suddenly the Tesla transformers roared to life, sending currents of electricity through the air and lightning bolts dancing across the glass canopy. Lights dimmed and brightened. The illuminated sign changed to read, "REVIVAL PROCESS INITIATED." Suddenly there was an intense flash that made Bela involuntarily shut his eyes despite the protective goggles. When he opened them, the glass canopy was rising from the table, bringing a whiff of smoky gas with it. Metal bands disappeared back into the metal slab and Dr. Fell sat up, flexing his newly created right hand. Standing up, he felt his neck and lower back, and smiled triumphantly. Leaping nimbly from the slab, he quickly unbuckled the straps that held him confined inside the medical corset and stripped off the back and neck brace. Before the startled eyes of his guests, Dr. Fell rubbed his neck and gave it a few test turns to the right and left, and reached down and touched his toes. He was completely healed of all his wartime injuries.

"Impossible!" Rathbone exclaimed.

"Remarkable!" Karloff gasped.

"Bullshit!" Lugosi declared.

Costello was aghast. "But we all saw it! It really works!"

"I don't believe it," an astonished Eddie Mannix said.

Dr. Fell donned his medical tunic and parka and hurried back into the antechamber. He removed his goggles and offered his arm for examination. "Judge for yourselves, gentlemen. As they say, seeing is believing, but touching is knowing."

Each man gingerly touched the arm. "It's real!" marveled Lou.

Lugosi would hear none of it. He pushed the others aside and grabbed the arm roughly. "We shall see how real it is!" He grabbed Dr. Fell's thumb and bent it back. The doctor screamed in pain. Lugosi quickly released the thumb. "It is true! That is a real hand!"

Rubbing his aching thumb, Dr. Fell glowered. "Yes, quite real. So are you now all convinced?"

Mannix ran to the observation window. "This thing is worth a fortune!" He grabbed Dr. Fell. "Name your price, doc! Whatever it is, I got people that can get it!"

Dr. Fell smiled. "I was hoping you would say that." He flexed his new hand. "Originally, I had U.S. government funding."

"You lost your funding?" asked Karloff. "What happened?"

"Much like the fictional *Herr Doktor* Frankenstein, my experiments were thwarted by those who did not share my vision."

"In other words," said Rathbone, arching his eyebrow, "you were only allowed to experiment on animal subjects."

"Chimpanzees are hardly a worthwhile substitute." Dr. Fell went to a wall telephone. "Now I am forced to seek out private investors." He lifted the receiver from the brass drop hook and pushed one of a series of servant call buttons. "Grimes, come," he said into the mouthpiece. The instant he hung up the receiver the basement door opened and Grimes stepped in, tapping his cane on the metal floor.

"You called, *Herr Doktor?*" Grimes rasped.

Costello leaned in and whispered, "How'd he get down here so fast? Did they shoot 'im out of a cannon?"

"Show these gentlemen out." Dr. Fell turned to address his guests. "You will forgive me. I must rest. The process is quite draining. Hang up your goggles before you go."

Basil slipped off his goggles and strode up to Grimes, grabbing the butler's hand. Grimes flinched stiffly. "So sorry," said Basil. "I should have warned you of my intentions. I merely wished to give you my goggles."

"I do not like being touched, sir," the butler explained.

"Of course you don't." Rathbone handed his goggles to Boris. "Do hang those up, old fellow?"

"Certainly," said Boris.

Basil smiled at the butler. "Don't trouble yourself about the door. We can see ourselves out."

"As you wish, sir," said Grimes.

"Let's go, gentlemen," said Basil with a smile of satisfaction.

Lugosi followed, all the while having the distinct feeling he was missing something. Once outside, Bela glowered at Basil and demanded, "What did you see? You are smiling like the cat that ate the bird!"

"Canary," corrected Basil.

"Same thing!"

"Nothing at all, Bela," Basil said with an annoyingly superior air. "However, I will leave you with this question: If Dr. Fell usually works alone and he wasn't expecting either you or Mr. Costello this evening, why did he have all those extra parkas and pairs of goggles?"

Lou nudged Lugosi. "Hey, he's right. An' Fell never took me to the basement before."

Rathbone consulted his watch. "It's getting quite late, and Boris and I have to contact our fellow investor. Come, Boris." Thrusting his hands in his pockets, he recited cheerfully, "*I do not like thee, Doctor Fell. The reason why, I cannot tell...*"

Boris continued the rhyme. "*...But this I know, and know full well. I do not like thee, Doctor Fell.*"

Lugosi turned to Costello. "They know something! Rathbone has figured it out!"

"Figured what out?" asked Lou. "We saw it for ourselves. The doc grew a new hand. You felt it for yourself!"

"What we saw was a trick!" Lugosi glared at the house. "Dr. Fell, he wants to make a fool of Bela, but Bela is too clever!"

Lou gestured for Bela to follow. "Come on, Bats, let it go," he said, heading back for his car. "Meanwhile, I guess I got me a houseguest." He glanced in the rear compartment and did a comic double take. "Oh no! Now Chaney's gone!"

Bela caught sight of something in the bushes surrounding the house. "I know where Chaney is," he said.

"You do?" asked Mannix.

Chaney emerged from the bushes, zipping up his fly. "Boy, that's better," he said. Shuffling up to Mannix, Lou and Bela he asked, "You guys know where I can get some eats? I feel like ham and eggs."

"Sadly," said Bela, "the kidnappers, they have failed to rid us of Chaney."

Chapter 12

The "All Nite" diner where Lou and Bela took Chaney was a refurbished 1920's dining car that had definitely seen better days. Doris Day's *It's Magic* was playing on the jukebox. Eddie Mannix was inside a phone booth at the far end of the counter. Lon Chaney occupied a window seat booth where he was busy wolfing down a large plate of ham and eggs. Lou Costello and Bela Lugosi sat opposite and watched Lon with queasy fascination.

"What'd that plate of ham and eggs ever do to you?" Lou asked Lon.

Lon was in heaven. "Man, I'm famished!" He grinned happily. "These are the best eggs I ever had! Only one thing'd make 'em even better." He grabbed a bottle of catsup, unscrewed the cap, and slapped the upturned end of the bottle, unleashing a large blot of coagulated tomato paste. "Perfect!" he said.

Lugosi could only sit in mute horror as he reached for a paper napkin to wipe away a splash of catsup on his cheek.

With egg on his chin, Lon asked, "So let me get this straight. Some doctor wants you to invest in an ice machine that can grow a guy a new hand?"

"We saw it happen," Lou insisted. "And it ain't an ice machine. The doc calls it a de-animator."

"Goddamn, Lou, if you ain't the most gullible bastard I've ever met," Lon said, and gulped down what remained of his coffee.

"What's that supposed to mean?"

"It means you get taken to the cleaners by every two-bit con artist with a crazy invention that nobody but *you* would believe could work!" Lon smirked at Lugosi. "His wife told me all about Lou's get-rich-quick schemes." He scooped up another helping of eggs and catsup. "Like Lou really needs the money."

"It just so happens I *do* need the money, wise guy." Lou explained to Bela. "The IRS is on my case for back taxes. I need to make a big bundle to pay it off."

"Jesus Christ, Lou," Lon said, "if you just gave 'em the money you waste on this crazy crap, you wouldn't be in debt." Holding out his cup, he called, "Waitress! Can I have a refill?"

"Sure thing, Mr. Chaney," said the pretty buxom blonde as she came out from behind the counter with a fresh pot. She poured steaming coffee into the cup and asked, "Either of you gentlemen want anything?"

Lugosi shook his head. "I think Mr. Costello and I, we have lost our appetites."

"Keep the eggs coming, honey," Chaney said, tucking a five-dollar bill in the waitress's uniform skirt pocket.

"Sure will, Mr. Chaney!" The waitress's blue eyes were beaming with star-struck adoration.

Chaney winked. "Call me Lon, sweetie."

"Right away—Lon!" She burst into giggles and trotted back to the counter. "PHIL!" she shouted in a voice more becoming of a drill sergeant, "ANOTHER PLATE OF HAM AND EGGS!"

"Keep your shirt on," Phil griped from the kitchen.

"As much as it pains Bela to say," Lugosi said to Lon, "I must agree with you. I, too, think that what we saw tonight was a magic trick."

"How can you be so sure?" asked Costello.

"Because I have worked with magicians before, I know these things."

Lon frowned. "What magicians have *you* worked with?"

Lugosi shifted uncomfortably in his seat. "Last year, to make extra money, Bela had to work…." The rest of the sentence trailed off into a humiliated mumble.

"In a what?" Lou asked.

Through gritted teeth, Lugosi repeated, "In a *spook show!*"

This tickled Lon no end. "Wait a minute, Bela Lugosi in a midnight spook show? That's rich!"

Glowering, Bela insisted, "It was a quality production! Bill Neff himself was the magician! It was, as he called it, a first class show! But the point is, I have seen how his magic tricks work. I think that what we saw tonight was very similar to the Suttee!"

"What's furniture gotta do with magic?" Costello asked.

Lugosi sneered. "Not settee, funnyman, *Suttee;* the Burned Alive Illusion!" He turned to Chaney. "A pretty girl, she is placed on a table. The table, it is covered by a box. The magician drops a match into the box. Smoke rises from within as the girl, she screams in pain. The sides drop down, revealing the girl is now reduced to smoldering, blackened bones."

He asked Costello, "Does that sound familiar?"

"But the doc wasn't turned into a pile of bones," Lou insisted. "He grew a new hand."

"I believe it was done the same way." Bela gestured. "The table, it makes a substitution."

"Substituting what? A new hand for no hand?"

"No, you poor excuse for a Watson—substituting one man missing a hand for a man not missing a hand!" Lugosi pounded his fist on the table in triumph. "*That* must be what Rathbone observed! He touched the butler's hand! But I noticed something else!"

Lou pointed. "Speaking of hands, you're gonna break yours if you hit the table like that."

Bela waved Lou away. "Never mind my hand! It is the butler's face I noticed! The butler's face, it was like mine!"

Chaney smirked. "Now that would scare anybody."

"Now wait a minute," said Costello, "Grimes don't look nothin' like you, so what are you talkin' about?"

Lugosi glared impatiently and gestured at his face. "He wore the same disguise that I did in *Dark Eyes of London*, a disguise that I wore in a duel role as a criminal pretending to be a blind man!" He jabbed an index finger in Chaney's face. "I will stake my life that the hand Rathbone touched was mechanical, because the mad scientist and butler switched roles!" He sneered at Costello. "And that, funnyman, is how the butler got down to the basement so fast!"

Costello frowned. "I don't get you."

"The table has a false bottom, and a secret passage that comes out just outside the basement door. While the Dr. Fell with the real hand, he keeps us distracted, the Dr. Fell with the fake hand disguises himself as the butler."

"This is some mystery," Lou complained. "The butler did it."

Lugosi slammed his fist down on the table. "Now I remember!" he exclaimed.

"You remembered how to break your hand?"

"No! I remember where I see those cabinets before!" Bela smiled triumphantly. "They were set pieces on *The Black Cat!*"

Chaney frowned. "You mean the horror picture you did with Karloff?"

"Yes! Karloff kept his dead wives in those cabinets! Those very cabinets, they are from the Universal Studios prop warehouse! And those Tesla coils, they are from the studio, too!"

Costello shrugged. "Well, maybe he got the props from the studio when International bought out Universal and maybe Fell made 'em into the real thing."

Chaney shook his head smugly. "Sure, Lou, that's gotta be it."

Bela pounded the table with his fist. "That explains it!"

Costello gawked. "What? Why you keep hittin' the table like that?"

"No! It explains why Marlowe knew so much about Dr. Fell! He did not get that information about Dr. Fell being a super-scientist from the grapes as he said he did!"

"'Grape-vine,'" Chaney corrected.

"That, too! Lillian was right about Marlowe! Marlowe got the information about Dr. Fell from Dr. Kopf, because Dr. Fell *is* Dr. Kopf! I saw Dr. Kopf's cigarette holder in an ashtray in the hall! At least he is the Dr. Fell who has a hand! Marlowe, he is also doing business with Goetz and," he cast a glare at the phone booth, "with Mannix!" Lugosi raised his finger in triumph. "Dr. Fell's equipment is from the studio, and the studio, it is going up in flames; somehow one has to do with the other! Where there are professional arsonists, there is the Mob, and where there is the Mob, there is Eddie Mannix!"

Costello nudged him and murmured out the corner of his mouth, "Speak of the devil."

Mannix approached with a broad smile on his face. "They found your trailer!" he announced. "It was ditched on the studio back lot."

Bela stood up, his face simultaneously radiating hope and fear. "Lillian and my son, were they found alive?"

Mannix shook his head. "Not a trace of anybody, just the abandoned trailer."

"We must go there now!" Lugosi insisted, pushing Lou to get out of the booth.

"Awright! Awright!" Costello protested. "Take it easy. I'm gettin' out!"

"Goetz and the Lieutenant are waitin' for us." Mannix nodded at the door. "Come on, Lugosi, I'll take ya in my car."

"Aw, no you don't," insisted Costello. "I'm Bela's Watson. Where he goes, I go, too." He pointed at the phone booth. "I gotta make a call first." He jerked a thumb at Chaney. "You guys can babysit the Wolf Man."

"Have it your way," said Mannix with a shrug.

Lugosi asked Mannix, "What of Janika? Is there any news of him?"

Mannix frowned. "Who?"

"Janika Skorzeny. You met him at the commissary. His sister Kalara, she faint-ed."

"Oh, yeah, you mean the guy with the pushed in face."

"Exactly! My wife was taking care of Kalara when the trailer was stolen."

Mannix scratched the back of his head. "The Lieutenant didn't say nothin' about him. When was the last time anybody saw Skorzeny?"

"He was last seen with Mr. Abbott under very mysterious circumstances." Bela nodded toward the phone booth. "Now both he and Abbott are missing. Costello, he is very worried. I fear that one disappearance has much to do with the other."

"Hey, what's all the mystery?" Lon asked as the waitress took away his empty plate and substituted a full one. "Maybe Skorzeny went back to his hotel."

"That's an idea," said Mannix. He asked Bela, "Where's he staying?"

"The Hollywood Knickerbocker Hotel, the same hotel where Karloff and Rathbone are staying," Lugosi scowled, "and such a coincidence, it is very suspicious."

Lou came back looking worried. "Murray Teff didn't find nothin', and Abbott's still not home. I'm real worried now and so's Betty."

Chewing loudly, Chaney asked, "So how do you know Abbott's not on the lot somewhere?"

"Because the guard at the main gate saw Abbott leave in a cab."

"Did the guard say Bud was in the cab by himself?"

"He didn't say so, no."

"Okay," said Chaney, his mouth full of eggs, "so maybe this Skorzeny guy was in the cab with Bud. They're probably tying one on in the hotel bar right now."

Lugosi frowned. "Considering what happened the last time Mr. Abbott and Janika shared a drink together, that is not very likely."

"What's that supposed to mean?" Chaney asked.

"We found Abbott out like a light," Costello explained. "It looked like Skorzeny might have drugged him." He eyed Chaney narrowly. "Say, you didn't happen to have a drink with Skorzeny too, did you?"

"To tell the truth," Chaney said with a smirk, "I sneaked a couple of shots right under Westmore's nose."

"Okay, now it's my turn to ask," said Costello. "What's *that* supposed to mean?"

Chaney shrugged. "I keep a little extra whiskey hidden inside spirit gum jars." He smirked and scooped up another forkful of eggs. "Westmore don't suspect a thing and I got my stash right out in front of him."

Lou turned to Lugosi. "Say, you thinkin' what I'm thinkin'?"

"That someone drugged Chaney's whiskey? Yes, I think that, too."

"Okay," said Mannix, "so suppose Abbott was unconscious when the guard saw him leave in the cab, and suppose Skorzeny shanghaied him back to the hotel."

"Gee, you think?" asked Costello.

Lon shrugged. "It sounds screwy to me, but maybe you oughta go check out the hotel just to be sure."

"We cannot," Lugosi insisted. "We must go to the back lot."

"Fine," said Mannix, "so like I said before, I'll drive Dracula to the back lot, Lou can go check out the hotel."

"What about Chaney?" Lugosi asked.

Chaney smiled. "I'll sit here and finish my eggs."

He was about to scoop up another helping of eggs when Mannix grabbed his fork hand. "I got me a better idea," Mannix said. "Since Lou's gotta babysit you anyways, you can both check out the hotel together." He shouted for the blonde waitress. "Hey, baby! Put the ham and eggs in a doggy bag, will ya?"

"Sure thing," the girl beamed. She stuck her head through the pickup window and shouted, "PHIL, A DOGGY BAG FOR THE WOLF MAN!"

"All right, all right," Phil complained. "Quit your hollerin'!"

Mannix paid the check and left a tip, and then headed toward the exit. He stopped abruptly when he noticed Lugosi wasn't following him. "What's wrong now?"

Lugosi frowned. "This is just what the kidnappers want to do, divide us and then conquer."

Costello nodded. "Yeah, we outta stay together."

Mannix smiled. "Don't sweat it, either of you guys. I got me a way so we can all keep in touch no matter what happens."

Lugosi glared skeptically. "How, you have with you a crystal ball?"

"Even better."

Mannix led them outside to his car. "Ain't she a honey?" he said proudly. "It's the latest model Chevy coupe straight from the factory show room. I buy a new one every year, and always in maroon." He caressed the fender. "Maroon's my favorite color."

"Considering all the blood you have spilled," Lugosi remarked sarcastically, "I should think so."

"You're funny, Lugosi." Mannix traced the lines of the car with his hand. "She's got a sweet exterior, all right." He paused when he reached the rear end. "But like they say, it's what's on the inside that counts." He opened the trunk and revealed a metal box containing an amalgam of glowing vacuum tubes and wires. "Take a look at this!" he invited.

"Gee," Costello marveled, his eyes wide with excitement. "What's it for?"

Like a used car salesman, Mannix made an oily pitch. "My friend, you are lookin' at the marvel of the modern age! This here is an emergency radio telephone!"

"Radio telephone!" exclaimed Lugosi. "You mean to tell me that you can place a call from your car?"

"That's what I mean to tell ya!" Mannix pointed as he described each component, "That's the receiver, that's the transmitter, and that's the logic circuit. That wire there, that's the antenna, and that cable goes to the telephone mounted on my dashboard." He led them to the driver's side of the car. They saw what looked like a dial and a telephone handset fixed to a board on the dash. "Any call I can make on a regular phone, I can make from my car."

Lou was in gadget heaven. "That's the most goddamn amazing thing I ever seen! A whole telephone station in the trunk of your car! Oh, I gotta get me one of these!" He gazed at Eddie like a kid sitting in Santa's lap. "You gotta tell me where I can get me one!"

"Sorry, Lou," said Eddie. "Bell Telephone won't be makin' this available to the public until later this year, and then, only after the FCC quits their hemming and hawing about radio bandwidth, but I got connections and now I'm one of the official product test guys."

Gesturing at the diner with his bag of ham and eggs, Lon frowned questioningly. "So if you got this great rig here, why were you on the payphone?"

Mannix sighed. "As great as this thing is, it's got a few bugs. The transmitter runs directly off the car battery. It draws a lot of juice. Use the phone too much, and you're flaggin' down cars for a jump." He gazed earnestly at Costello. "So don't call unless it's important."

"Sure thing, Eddie," Lou said eagerly. "So what's the number?"

Mannix jotted the phone number down on a piece of paper and offered it to Costello, and then had second thoughts and withheld the paper. "Remember," Mannix cautioned, "a call to let us know you got to the hotel, and one to give us the low down. Got it?"

"I got it, Eddie," Lou assured Mannix. "I got it."

Eddie gave him the paper. "Another thing, keep it short. This ain't the Kate Smith Hour. The less time you're on the blower, the better for me."

"I got it, Eddie. Keep it short." Costello opened the paper and smiled. "You're kiddin', right?"

Mannix frowned. "Kiddin' about what?"

"The number, ALexander-2222. This is a gag, right?"

"I don't see what's so funny about it."

"Abbott an' me got a routine—forget it." Costello straightened his deerstalker and beckoned Lon to follow him. "Come on, Watson, the game's a foot and a half!"

Mannix slammed the trunk shut. "Well, Lugosi, it's time I took you for a ride."

Bela warily eyed the tough guy. "I do not like the sound of that," he said.

Mannix smirked as he got in the driver's seat. "The only time you got to worry about *that* kind of ride is if you're ridin' in the trunk."

Lugosi got in and gestured behind him. "Your trunk is full of equipment. It must, as they say, cramp up your style."

"Oh, there's ways to fit a guy in there." Mannix started up the engine. As he glanced behind to back out, he remarked, "Of course, you need a junkyard compactor to do it."

Bela eyed him keenly, not sure if the studio head was kidding or not. He was going to ask, and then thought better of it.

Chapter 13

Wednesday, 25 February 1948
11:10 P.M.
Universal-International Studios

Mannix pulled up to the front gates and honked.

The guard grabbed his clipboard and held it up to his face. "Sorry," he said in an oddly exaggerated gruff voice. "The studio is closed."

"I'm Eddie Mannix and this here is Bela Lugosi. We're expected."

The guard turned his back and checked his clipboard. "Oh yeah," he said, and stepped out of the guardhouse to open the gates. He kept his hand on the visor of his cap, pulling the cap down over his eyes as he pointed with his other hand. "The Lieutenant is up on the back lot by Lubin Lake. Go all the way up Laemmle Blvd., follow the road all the way around. You can't miss it." He ducked back into the guardhouse, keeping his back to Mannix.

"Thanks," Mannix said. His eyes narrowed as he tried to catch a better look at the guard. "Say, haven't I seen you someplace before?"

The guard coughed and grabbed a handkerchief from his pocket and held it up to his face. "Humph," he chortled. "No," he said in a far more cultured voice, and then in a deeper register, "no. I'm just a guard. Move along please." He waved them on.

Mannix shrugged and said to Bela, "It takes all kinds."

The service road took them past relics from Universal's golden age, a period that reigned under the watchful eye of "Uncle" Carl and Junior Laemmle. Together, father and son took acreage that was once a chicken ranch and transformed the land into a field of Hollywood dreams. But "Uncle" Carl's extravagance and poor business dealings had bankrupted the studio, and Junior had succumbed to a mysterious illness. Universal had changed hands several times, but always the back lot remained, and was still in use, with large permanently standing outdoor sets seen in countless B-movies. Tableaus of frozen time dotted either side of the valley road like a crazy quilt of clashing history. But while some sets stood as reminders of the past, others were gone forever. Beyond the crest of a hill there once stood the lavish million-dollar Monte Carlo set for Erich von Stroheim's *Foolish Wives* that existed now only in postcards. Looking to his left, Lugosi had a commanding view of the valley. By day a pall of gray smog hung over Tinseltown like a mournful ghost, reducing its majestic ring of mountains to little more than a hazy outline. But at night the crosshatching pattern of Burbank's city lights and moving traffic gave the valley basin a twinkling starry brilliance that couldn't be dimmed by pollution, or by Bela's career disappointments.

As Mannix drove up to the man-made pond named after director Harry Lubin, Lugosi pointed ahead and exclaimed, "The scenery, it has been built already!"

"Yeah, so?" asked Mannix with a shrug.

Bela glowered, pointing at the fully realized *The Brain of Frankenstein* "pier on the island" set. "The scenes, they are not to be shot until next month, and yet the set is sitting here in February. You are Vice President of a movie studio. Does that not strike you as strange?"

Mannix shrugged again. "Maybe Barton likes to have things set up ahead of time."

"BAH!" Lugosi said. "You are of no help at all."

The abandoned dressing trailer and an ambulance were just ahead. The trailer's lights were on, which meant the generator was running. Parked a few feet away from the dressing trailer were Bill Goetz's limousine and a black Oldsmobile sedan. Waiting by the sedan was a burly looking figure in a derby and a trench coat. He used his flashlight to signal Mannix to park his car by the sedan. Eddie left the engine running, just in case Lou Costello should phone, and his headlights on to help light the scene. The police lieutenant approached and reached through the open window to grab Bela's hand. He gave it a vigorous shake. "It's a real pleasure meeting up with you again, Mr. Lugosi!" His spoken words appeared as frosty puffs in the chilled night air. "Ford's the name. Lt. Fred Ford, Homicide! It's been a while!"

"I know you?" asked Bela incredulously.

"Yeah," Lt. Ford said. "Don't you remember? We met at Hollywood Presbyterian Hospital a couple of years ago. You got shot."

"Yes, now vaguely, I remember you."

"Well, you were kinda loopy from the medication." He noted Bela's attire. "Dressed kinda spiffy for a crime scene investigation, ain't ya?"

"I have no time for jokes!" Bela got out of the car and demanded, "Do you know where my wife and son have been taken?"

"Look, let's not get ahead of ourselves." Ford shined his flashlight at the dressing trailer. "My partner and Mr. Rathbone are waiting for us inside."

Lugosi scowled. "Rathbone is here?"

Ford smiled. "Rathbone got here before me and my partner did. Goetz is nosing around the boathouse." Ford shined his light at a large van with a rotating antenna idling by the lake. "What do you guys make of that?" he asked.

Lugosi saw cables that led from the van out to one of two camera platforms set up in the middle of the lake. "Why is there a television camera out there?" he asked.

Mannix smiled. "I'll bet they're gonna do some kind of remote TV publicity stunt."

Bela scoffed, "I was not told about any such publicity stunt."

"Maybe they're gonna use Karloff. That's what Bill's paying him for, ain't it, to promote your movie?"

"I had not thought of that," Lugosi snarled.

"I had a look-see in the van," said Ford. "The engine's running but nobody's home." He led them to the van and shined his light in the back windows. "Have a look yourself," he said. "See? It's empty except for transmitting equipment running off the engine."

Lugosi peered inside and saw blinking colored lights, and banks of flickering monitor screens, but no sign of anyone.

Mannix pointed at the rotating antenna array on the roof. "This is some pretty sophisticated stuff."

Ford nodded. "It might even be remote operated. Imagine that."

"Did you run the plates?"

"Sure did. The van's legit, registered to Universal-International as a commercial vehicle. Goetz claims he don't know anything about it, though. So if somebody *is* tinkering around with remote television equipment, they're doing it on company time, but on the Q.T."

Mannix surveyed the set dominated by a Gothic stone wall with ornate iron gates rigged so the Frankenstein Monster could tear the gates off their hinges. "You find anything else that's queer?"

"You mean besides these weird footprints?" Ford pointed at several boxy depressions surrounding the van. "Rathbone found tire tracks, lots of 'em." Mannix and Lugosi followed Ford to the hitch end of the trailer. He shined his flashlight at the ground. "There were two cars. One was hooked up to the trailer. The other was parked there between the trailer and the ambulance." He led them to the back of the ambulance.

"The doors are wide open," Lugosi commented, and pointed at a stretcher that was hanging halfway out of the ambulance by two wheels. "The stretcher, it was abandoned."

Lt. Ford nodded. "Yeah, it looks to me like the kidnappers were in the middle of transferring the hostages to the second car when they were interrupted." His flashlight revealed the side of the ambulance was riddled with bullet holes.

"Interrupted by whom?" Lugosi asked, running his hand over the holes.

"That's the big question," said Lt. Ford. He shined his light on the ground. "At least one guy got hit. See the blood there?" He bent down and felt the blood drops. "The blood's still kinda wet, so it didn't happen too long ago." He nodded at the mystery van. "But that van got here after the fireworks, I'll bet my badge on that. There ain't a scratch on it." Straightening up, he said, "There's evidence somebody was waiting here for quite a while." He shined his light on several cigarette butts. "A foreign somebody by the looks of it."

Bela picked up one of the butts and closely examined it. "You are right. This is not an American brand of cigarette," he observed. "It is too large and there is no brand, despite it having been manufactured, and not one you roll yourself."

"Rathbone thinks these are Russian cigarettes."

"Russian!" Mannix exclaimed. "You think the Reds had anything to do with this?" He pointed at the van. "You think that's some kind of spy van?"

"Beats me," the Lieutenant said. "But whoever smoked them cigarettes was a killer."

"How do you figure?" asked Mannix.

"From evidence we found by the dock."

Mannix and Bela followed Lt. Ford down stone steps to a pier dressed with balsa wood crates and barrels. Reddish-brown streaks of blood led to the end of the pier and a detachable wooden ladder. Moored by the ladder was a small motorboat.

Ford shined his light at the boat. "They might have used that motorboat to dump the bodies. You can see the traces of blood in it from here."

Lugosi felt growing panic. "Did you drag the lake for my wife and son's bodies?" He ran to the edge of the pier calling, "Lillian! Bela, Jr.!" He braced himself to leap into the cold black water.

Mannix held him back. "There ain't no point in jumpin' to conclusions, or off the pier." He asked Ford, "Uh, Lugosi *is* jumpin' to conclusions, right?"

"There may be bodies, but I don't think they'd be Lugosi's wife and son." Ford led them back to the gates. "The watchman patrolling the back lot on the morning shift disappeared and nobody's heard from him since. There's dried splashes of blood on the steps, and that's not all." He shined his flashlight on something by the wall. "Take a look at this."

The detective pointed out a tripod and a pole hidden under ferns and other shrubbery. "That's a surveyor's level and a ranging pole," said Lt. Ford. "See the blood on the telescope there? It looks like somebody got whacked in the head with that thing earlier today." He gestured at the surrounding area. "My guess is the bodies we're lookin' for belong to the two surveyors and our AWOL studio guard."

Bela eyed Mannix with growing suspicion. "The meeting Marlowe was arranging between you and Goetz, what kind of 'business' was it that you were discussing together? There was talk of real estate!"

Basil Rathbone appeared from behind the dressing trailer and frantically waved them over. "Lt. Ford! Come here quickly, man! Your partner needs you!"

"Come on," said Ford.

Mannix hurried after him as Lugosi struggled to keep up.

"This is not over, Mannix!" Bela shouted.

Inside the trailer, Bela had a strange sense of *déjà vu*. They found Lt. Ford's plainclothes partner sprawled out on the floor of the dressing trailer.

"MICKEY!" Ford knelt down and shook the unconscious man vigorously. "Mickey! What happened? Mickey!" He looked up at Basil. "Is he—?"

Rathbone crooked an eyebrow and scoffed, "Dead? Hardly." He used his handkerchief to pick up an empty coffee cup. "The fool gulped down this cup of coffee, and before you can say, 'poor crime scene protocol,' he lost consciousness." He put the cup down and thrust his hands in his pockets. "His heartbeat is slow, but steady. I'd say judging from the dilation of his pupils, he's been drugged." He clucked his tongue reproachfully. "Not to be judgmental, but it serves him right."

Lugosi picked up the cup and poked at the bottom with his finger and noted something grainy. "What is this? I do not think it is sugar."

Basil took back the coffee cup and, after tasting a bit of the substance with the tip of his tongue, declared, "No doubt a tranquilizer of some sort."

"Wait a minute," said Mannix. "You mean somebody doped the coffee?"

"So it would seem."

Lugosi nodded. "This happened before with Mr. Abbott."

"Yes," remarked Basil, "he told us all about it." He gestured at the cup. "But upon further examination of Mr. Abbott's trailer, I observed no telltale residue in the bottom of his glass."

"So what are you saying?" asked Lt. Ford. "We got two sets of kidnappers using two different kinds of KO powder?"

"One would assume so," said Basil.

Groaning, Mickey sat up and squinted. "Say, what is this, a lineup?" He took one look at Lugosi in his tux and let out a bloodcurdling scream and cried, "OH, JESUS, IT'S THE DEVIL! I'M DEAD!"

Lugosi glowered. "How dare he! This time I am not even wearing the makeup!"

Ford slapped his partner's face. "Aw, calm down! That's Bela Lugosi."

Mickey squinted. "Lugosi?" He let out a sigh of relief. "Thank god! For a minute I thought I bought me a one way ticket to Tombstone City."

"You nearly did, you dope." Ford indicated the coffee cup. "You doped yourself! What'd you do a dumb thing like that for?"

Mickey shrugged. "It's been a long night and I thought, what the hell, free coffee."

Rathbone sighed and massaged the bridge of his nose. "Remarkable," he muttered.

Lugosi caught sight of something on the floor, and picked up a medicine bottle and a slip of paper.

Rathbone leaned in to kibitz. "What are those?" he asked.

Lt. Ford grabbed the slip of paper, earning a scowl of disapproval from Bela. "Say, this looks like a room service bill," the Lieutenant said.

Basil took the paper. "It's an itemized dinner list."

Lugosi snatched it back irritably. "And it is from the Hollywood Knickerbocker Hotel. This was a meal ordered by a Hungarian, for Hungarians."

"How do you know for sure?" Ford asked.

"There are six orders of goulash." Lugosi glared at Rathbone. "Obviously, this was not a bill for an Englishman. But *this*," he declared, brandishing the medicine bottle, "proves that Lillian was the one who drugged the coffee to escape from the kidnappers!"

Rathbone arched an eyebrow. "And how did you reach *that* conclusion?"

"I tell you how," Bela sneered. "It is, as you would say, elementary! The doctor, he gave Lillian these pills for Kalara to take should she become agitated. There were many pills before, but now it is empty." He gestured at the coffee pot simmering on the stove. "It should be obvious where all the pills went."

Suddenly the trailer was jarred by a huge explosion.

"What the hell was *that?*" Mickey asked.

They ran outside to find mushrooming orange plumes of fire erupting from a row of gasoline drums. The boathouse was in flames.

"The arsonist, he has struck again!" Lugosi declared.

Cries of *HELP! HELP!* came from the burning boathouse set.

"That sounds like Goetz," said Mannix.

Goetz appeared in the boathouse doorway, struggling to drag out a body. "Hurry!" he shouted. "There's another one in there!"

"Stay here," warned Basil as he and Ford dashed into the burning building.

Lugosi tried to follow, only to be driven back by the intense heat. "Did you see my wife and son in there?" he called, shielding himself with his arms.

Basil and Ford came out with a second victim slumped between them. "There was another body in there," said Ford, as he and Basil set the man down on the ground next to the first victim.

"He was wearing a studio guard's uniform," said Rathbone, glancing back at the boathouse that was now totally engulfed by fire.

Ford shook his head. "There's no way to get to him now."

Rathbone made a quick examination of the body. "This man's been shot!" He felt for a pulse. "He's dead!"

Ford did likewise with the first man. "This guy's head's bashed in." He rolled the body over and retrieved the victim's wallet. "Lay you odds that they're the missing surveyors." Ford checked for his ID and found a business card. "Yeah, they're the surveyors, all right!"

"I'll get a couple of blankets," said Mickey, running back to the sedan.

Ford glared at Goetz. "What happened?"

"I tripped on something, and suddenly the whole place went up."

Rathbone looked up accusingly. "You fool! You blundered into the arsonist's trip-wire. I told you to watch out for booby traps!" He felt the shirts of the two victims. "Their clothes are damp," he observed. "In fact, they're soaked to the skin." He glanced out at Lubin Lake. "I think these were the bodies that the killers discarded in the lake."

Lt. Ford wrinkled his brow. "So they were dumped in the lake, and then dragged into the boathouse?"

"So it would appear." Basil examined the bullet wounds. "The first man was shot with a small caliber weapon, perhaps a .22."

Ford glanced back at the ambulance as Mickey approached with a couple of blankets, followed by Eddie Mannix. "Judging from the bullet holes in the doors," said the Lieutenant, "I'd say those guys were packing 9mm automatics."

"That means we got two sets of guys." Mickey nodded back at the sedan. "I put in a call to the fire department, and to the coroner for the meat wagon, but dispatch says it's gonna be a while, something about a multiple homicide that's got every wagon in the joint tied up." He spread the blankets over the dead bodies.

Rathbone glared at the studio chief. "Are you absolutely certain you haven't received any extortion threats?"

"Not a one," said Goetz.

"What about the Van Gogh? Did you come by it legally?"

"I most certainly did," Goetz insisted. "I acquired it through a very reputable art dealer in New York."

Lt. Ford confronted the studio chief. "Well, *somebody* is out for blood! Think hard."

"Look, I make prestige pictures, not enemies."

"When you bought the studio, you might have made some enemies."

Goetz paused briefly, and then said, "Well, we *did* cut back on personnel."

Lugosi jabbed an accusing finger at Goetz. "What sort of business are you and Mannix involved with that would require the surveyor men to be killed?"

Mannix nudged the studio chief. "Come on, Bill, spill it. There's no reason to keep a lid on it now."

"It's none of their business, Eddie. And you keep your mouth shut."

"Okay, then." Ford twisted Goetz around, and then put the cuffs on him. "Maybe a night in the drunk tank will help you see things differently." He dragged Goetz back to the sedan and forced him into the back seat. "You can use your one free phone call to call your lawyer," the Lieutenant gruffly said.

"Wait a minute, Fred," Mannix said. "I'll tell ya."

"Eddie!" Goetz cautioned.

"They're gonna find out sooner or later, Bill." Mannix turned to Ford and fessed up. "Goetz and Spitz want to sell off this acreage to some developers I know. That's what the surveyors were doing here, getting an accurate appraisal of the back lot property. We're gonna turn all this into luxury apartments."

Rathbone observed, "Obviously someone is trying to sabotage the deal."

"Yeah," said Mickey, "they scare off all the other buyers and buy the land cheap."

"Good thinking, Mickey," Ford said. "About time, too."

Mickey shrugged. "Hey, I got my moments."

Goetz glared at Ford and twisted around to expose his handcuffs. "Can I get out of these now? I have to make a call to the insurance company about this."

"Yeah, we're done. If I got any questions, I'll call you." He dragged Goetz from the car and unlocked the bracelets. "Go on, get lost."

"I'll speak with you later, Eddie," Goetz said, rubbing his wrists. He got into his limousine and drove away.

Mickey turned to his partner. "So where do you suppose Mrs. Lugosi ran off to? You think she went home?"

"We are boarding in the home of Hungarian friends," Lugosi said. "I do not think she would place them in danger by going back there. Nor do I think she would go to her parents, or to my cousin for the same reason."

"If I wuz her," said Mickey, "I'd probably hide out at a roadside hotel."

The police dispatcher on the car radio said over heavy interference, "Lt. Ford, code 1, over!"

Lt. Ford reached into the sedan for the radio microphone. "Ford, over," he said.

More crackling static, followed by, "We can barely copy, over."

"There's a van with electronic equipment close by. I think it's causing the interference, over."

Bela glared down at his foot and, without warning, grabbed Basil's shoulder for balance as he raised his left leg.

"What on earth are you doing?" Rathbone asked.

"Something is stuck on the bottom of my shoe." Bela removed the object and examined it in the headlights of Mannix's car.

Mannix put on his reading glasses. "Hey, what is that thing?"

There was a glint of gold and an insignia, a battle axe superimposed over a bat with its wings spread, similar to the tattoo Lillian described on Kalara Skorzeny's breast.

Mannix quipped, "What's that, Dracula's tie pin?"

Basil leaned in between them. "Mind if I have a look?"

Lugosi hid the pin. "Of course I mind!" Sticking the pin in his pocket, Bela glared menacingly. "For once, Bela Lugosi will have the upper hand!" He marched toward his trailer. "It will be a cold day in Hell before Bela shares his clues with you!"

"Where are you going?" Basil asked over the sound of approaching sirens.

Bela tugged on the lapels of his tuxedo jacket. "To change out of this costume!"

"Change into what?"

Lugosi gestured impatiently. "Into the clothes I have in my trailer! What kind of stupid question is that?"

"There are no clothes in there."

"WHAT!" Lugosi stormed into his trailer. It was only now that he noticed that both his and Lillian's trunks were gone! He went to the closet and found only empty hangers. He wheeled around with a crazed look in his eye. "WHO WOULD DO THIS?" he raged to no one in particular.

A sudden twinge of pain attacked his legs. Wincing, he lunged desperately at the embroidered pillow lying on the floor. He all but tore the pillow in two. Lugosi's heart sank as he discovered that the hidden pocket was empty! Angrily casting the pillow aside, he moaned, "The kidnappers, they have taken everything!" Remembering that Lillian had hidden the syringe and vial under the mattress, he tore at the bunk, but found nothing. The pain in his legs struck like a knife. He collapsed on the bunk, massaging the knotting muscles. Lugosi glanced over at the makeup table and recalled that Lillian had taken possession of extra morphine bottles from Dr. Kopf. Perhaps she had hidden the extra bottles in one of the drawers. Forgetting his pain he sprang at the table and tore open the drawers. Suddenly a voice behind him said, "You won't find them there."

Lugosi wheeled around and saw Basil Rathbone standing in the doorway. The Hungarian snarled, "How dare you invade my privacy!" He ran his fingers through his tousled hair, trying to appear nonchalant. "What do you mean I won't find them there? Find what?"

"You know what I'm talking about." Basil flashed a knowing half smile as he stepped inside and closed the door. He reached into his pockets and produced the black velvet case and extra bottles of morphine. "I believe these belong to you," he said. "Really, Bela, aren't you a little old to be a dope fiend?"

Bela cast him a wrathful glare, his fists clenched. "I have a prescription for those!"

Rathbone clutched the bottles as he eyed Bela mistrustfully. "There are two possible explanations for what's been going on around here. One of them has to do with these bottles. Are you quite sure these are prescription medications? If your supply comes from an illegal source, the kidnappers could be working for the Mob."

"I have pains in my legs," Bela explained with a sneer. "I show you the doctor papers if that will satisfy you!" He opened a makeup table drawer and produced a manila folder.

"Files can be forged," Rathbone countered. "Again, on your word of honor, did you obtain these drugs legally?"

"YES!" Lugosi barked as he stuffed the file back in the makeup table drawer and slammed it loudly. The force dislodged a tiny microphone from the frame of the makeup mirror. It was the size of a collar button and dangled on a thin wire.

Basil's eyes fixed on it. He continued speaking while gesturing for Bela to keep up the conversation. "So," said Rathbone, "if your medication was legally obtained, that rules out one possibility." He slipped the vials in his pocket, and peered at the device.

All Bela was interested in was the velvet case in Basil's other hand. "Give me my medicine!" he demanded.

Rathbone casually tossed the case to Bela, sending the Hungarian into a panic as he fumbled to recover it.

Basil produced a small magnifying glass. "There was a letter," he said, blowing on the glass to fog it, and then wiping it clean with his hanky, "quite a tempting offer." He began a close inspection of the tiny microphone. "What did you tell them?"

Bela shoved Rathbone aside and searched one drawer, and then the other. The letter from Hungary was gone. Basil reached into his pocket and produced the letter. "Did you accept the offer?"

Bela trembled with rage as he made a grab for the letter. "You take too many liberties, Rathbone!"

Basil held it out of Bela's reach and then stuffed it back in his pocket. "Yes, yes, yes," Basil impatiently said as he returned to his examination of the microphone. "I'm a brute and a cad." He smiled in triumph and held the magnifier so Bela could look through it. "But, uh, you haven't answered my question." He gestured for Lugosi to have a closer look. "Did you answer the letter?"

But Lugosi was too angry to care. "That is none of your business!" he said.

Basil frowned impatiently and pulled Lugosi aside.

"And take your hands off me!" Bela demanded.

In his effort to break Basil's hold on his arm, Lugosi sent the medical case flying across the room. Bela tried to dive for it, but it was too late. The case sprang open as it bounced off the stove and landed face down on the floor with a crash. Staring in dismay, Lugosi's worst fears were realized. His precious hypodermic syringe had been reduced to glinting shards of broken glass.

"Never mind about that," Basil insisted as he renewed his grip on Bela's arm and shook him. In a low, snarling whisper he said, "Can't you see? Your trailer is bugged."

"How dare you!" Lugosi hissed. "I do not have bugs!"

Rathbone sharply shushed him and pointed at the wire dangling from the mirror. "A radio listening device, you stubborn fool. Your trailer is wired for sound." He leaned in and whispered in Lugosi's ear. "Someone is spying on you."

Bela glared skeptically. "Who would do such a thing?" he whispered.

"I don't know, but it may have to do with your letter." Rathbone nodded at the miniature microphone. "If my suspicions are correct," he whispered, "the letter and what you have in your pocket are connected in a very significant way."

Lugosi eyed Rathbone narrowly. "Do you know what I think?" Without warning, he spat on Basil's shoe, causing the sleuth to jump back, shocked. "That is for you, Rathbone," he declared, pointing at the wet spot, "a curse upon you for trying to deceive me!"

Basil looked up from his toe, quite astonished. "I beg your pardon?"

Lugosi approached the makeup mirror and yanked the listening device off its wires. He shook it at Rathbone accusingly. "*You* put this here when you were searching my trailer!" he said. "You try to fool Bela, but he sees through your schemes!"

Basil cast an affronted frown. "Now really, old boy," he began, only to be interrupted by a loud pounding on the trailer door.

"Open up, you guys!" Lt. Ford ordered.

Bela pushed the door open and pointed at Basil. "Arrest Rathbone! He is a thief and a bugger!"

Basil's eyebrow arched indignantly. "Careful with that last accusation. It's not what you think it means."

"Can't you guys get along for five minutes?" Lt. Ford sighed as fire trucks pulled up outside and firemen hurried to fight the blaze. Bela was about to make further charges against Rathbone when the Lieutenant grumbled, "Forget it, Lugosi. I need you to come with me right now."

Bela grabbed desperately at Lt. Ford's arm. "Is it about my wife and son?"

"No, but we found that friend of yours, that Skorzeny guy."

Bela was taken aback. "You have! He is dead? I am to identify the body?"

"Your friend Skorzeny is the suspect in a multiple homicide. I need you to translate his testimony. Come on."

As Lugosi and Rathbone hurried to Ford's sedan, Bela overheard a fireman say to his Chief, "Three times in one night. Someone must really have it in for this studio."

The Fire Captain shrugged. "Everybody's a critic."

Intermission

Interior, Lugosi's Trailer
Morning

Lugosi's recollections were interrupted by a loud banging at his dressing trailer door. He looked up from the mysterious notebook pages and wondered if the intruder was a stagehand sent to bring him to the set.

"LUGOSI!" the voice of Lou Costello raged, "GET OUT HERE SO I CAN KILL YA!"

"Now, Lou, please," came the muffled, quiet voice of Bud Abbott, "calm down. I'm sure Bela has a good reason for doing what he did, whatever it was."

Bela wondered exactly what he had done to make Costello so mad. He reluctantly unlocked the door. The knob pulled out of his hand as the feisty little comic stormed in red-faced and ready to deliver on his promise.

"SO," Lou snarled, "IT LOOKS LIKE YOU BEEN ON A DRUNK TOO!" He looked around the trailer and saw Bela, Jr. curled up on the floor and Lillian lying in the bunk. "What the hell's been goin' on in here? Did they throw you outta your hotel or what?" Costello displayed his right shoe and pant cuff that were inexplicably covered in tar. "And what the hell was *this* all about!?"

Abbott tried to hold his partner back. "Lou, please, why don't you give Bela a chance to explain himself? Obviously whatever happened to us must have happened to him, too. Look." He pointed at Bela's muddy shoes, and then at his own shoes and trouser cuffs that were also caked with dried mud. "So simmer down and let him talk."

"I don't give a damn about the tar or the mud or me wakin' up in your trailer on the goddamn floor!" Costello clutched a page similar to the pages Bela found in his shoe and shook it angrily. "I wanna know about this! What the hell is this!? You think what happened to Butch is something you can play for a gag?!"

"Do you mean the son that was drowned?" asked Bela, too confused and nervous to be tactful.

"YOU GODDAMN KNOW THAT'S WHO I MEAN!" raged Costello, crumpling the paper, the copper bracelet peeking from his sleeve as he shook his fat fist angrily.

Abbott politely removed his fedora and struggled to explain. "Lou and I woke up with one hell of a hangover. Lou was in my trailer and I was in his, and we can't remember anything that happened last night, like we were on the worst bender ever in our whole lives. Now he's on the warpath about whatever it is you wrote in that letter."

Lugosi nodded earnestly. "Yes, I, too, woke up that way," he said, and gestured at his still sleeping wife and child, whose only reaction to all the commotion was to roll over in their respective sleeps. "As you can see, my wife and son, I found them, too, under circumstances I cannot easily explain."

"WELL, EXPLAIN THIS!" Costello insisted, shoving the note at Bela.

The Hungarian took the note in his trembling hands, almost afraid to read it. Smoothing out the crumpled paper, he found once again the penmanship to be his own and he still had no recollection of having written it.

"READ IT!" Costello angrily insisted.

Lugosi began to read silently.

"OUT LOUD!" Costello yelled.

Bela cleared his throat. "'Dear, Lou: I have thought very carefully about your son Butch and how he was found...'"

"Yeah," snarled Costello, "I found that in my goddamn shoe, all right! I wanna know how you done it! What'd you do, slip Abbott and me a Mickey and then stick that note in my shoe, or what?"

He was about to punch Lugosi, but his partner held him back.

"No, Lou," Abbott pleaded. "Let him explain!"

"And that's your signature there, ain't it?" said Lou, pointing angrily at the letter.

"Yes, it is," Bela nervously confirmed. "If you look there," he said, gesturing at the notepaper lying on the makeup table, "you will see testimony in your own handwriting. And like Bela, I think you will have no memory of having written any of it."

"Oh yeah?" Costello gruffly shoved Lugosi out of the way and grabbed up the scribbled memos, knocking the strange calling card to the floor. As he shuffled through the papers, Bela concealed the calling card with his foot and used his toe to scoot the card under the makeup table. As he did, Bela watched the color drain from Lou's chubby cheeks as he read. The comic sat slowly down in the makeup chair, stunned. "Is all this on the level?" he asked.

"That is your handwriting, yes?" asked Bela, satisfied that the card was safely hidden.

Lou absently nodded as he read, and as he read, he began to remember...

Chapter 14

Wednesday, 25 February 1948
11:42 P.M.
1714 North Ivar Avenue

"Sherlock" Lou Costello, accompanied by his "Watson" Lon Chaney, entered the eleven-story Hollywood Knickerbocker Hotel. They couldn't help but gawk at the lobby's famous grand crystal chandelier like a couple of tourists and Chaney wolf whistled in admiration, much to the annoyance of D. W. Griffith. The all but forgotten silent film director of *Birth of a Nation* was seated on one of the hotel's many over-stuffed couches. Griffith glared at Lon over his copy of *The Atlanta Journal* and hissed a complaining; "Shhh!"

Ignoring the cantankerous Southerner, Chaney turned to Costello. "You go call Eddie and I'll search the bar."

Lou pulled Chaney back. "Ah, no ya don't," he said. "I finally got you sober, and you're stayin' that way."

Chaney sighed. "Fine, if that's how you feel about it, then *I'll* search the bar and *you* go call Eddie."

"That's different."

Chaney happily trotted off to the bar, leaving Lou Costello doing a double-take. "Well, I'll be damned," he said to himself, "that really works."

Shrugging, the comic hurried to a bank of phone booths. After closing the door, he dropped a coin into the payphone slot. The coin wended its way down into the coin box with the musical accompaniment of tinkling *dings!* And a final *ker-plunk!*

The payphone didn't have a dial, so Lou waited patiently until the dial tone was interrupted by the operator.

"Number plea-uzz," said the operator in an exaggerated nasally voice.

Costello fought the sudden sensation of comedy *déjà vu* and said, "Operator, gimme ALexander-2222."

"Number plea-uzz," she repeated.

Lou glared at the phone. "Okay, this is gettin' weird," he muttered to himself. He repeated louder, "Gimme ALexander-2222!"

"Would you speak a little louder, plea-uzz?"

This was spookily like Bud and Lou's "phone call" routine. Costello peered outside the booth, expecting to see someone playing a gag. He got back in the booth and closed the door, shouting, "*ALEXANDER-2222!*"

"Can you say that a little louder, plea-uzz?"

Unable to resist, he delivered the scripted punch line, "If I say it any louder, I won't have to call the guy; he'll hear me!"

"I am connecting your call, sir."

"About time," Costello grumbled.

There was a ring tone and the eventual *click*. "Mannix," the studio boss said gruffly over crackling static.

"Heeeeey, Eddie," Costello squealed with delight, "It's Lou Costello. Can you hear me?"

"Yeah, I hear ya. Did you get to the hotel okay?"

"Lon and me are at the Knickerbocker right now. I'll let you know the minute we find out somethin'." Lou giggled. "Hey, put Bats on, I wanna see what he sounds like on your phone."

Mannix sighed. "I can't, he's in the cop car ahead of me."

Lou started. "Well, what'd they arrest him for?"

"They didn't arrest him, you dope! Lugosi's pal, Skorzeny, is the prime suspect in a homicide and they need Lugosi to translate."

"Who'd he kill?"

"Are you sittin' down?"

Lou looked down at the wooden phone booth seat. "Yeah, what's up?"

"I'm sorry to say, it looks like Skorzeny shot the doc."

The color drained from Lou's face. "Dr. Fell's dead?" His downcast expression would have drawn peals of laughter, had anyone been watching. His lower lip trembled pitifully as he whimpered, "So I guess that means our deal is off?"

"Sorry, Louie," said Mannix, sounding genuinely sympathetic. "That's the way the cookie crumbles sometimes. I'll fill ya in just a soon as I know somethin' solid."

"Okay, Eddie. Good-bye." Lou glumly hung up.

He opened the door and promptly collided with someone leaving the booth next door. The other man dropped something. They bumped heads as Lou and the other man bent down to retrieve an all too familiar black leather-bound notebook and a completely unfamiliar small, disk-shaped gizmo. Holding his aching noggin, Costello straightened up and said, "Sorry, Mister. I—"

The rest of what he was about to say choked off as both he and the other man exclaimed simultaneously, "You again!"

It was the distinguished British gentleman from the drugstore. "Really, young man," the older man said, glaring contemptuously, "are you trying to persecute me?"

"I ain't persecutin' nobody," Lou denied. "Now don't move a muscle! Just stay there!"

Costello bent down and picked up the leather-bound notebook and glanced at the first page, which contained an itinerary that included things like, "*Call 'C'*, *Meeting with Billy*, and *Skull session tonight*." He also noted the calling cards stuck in the inside pocket. Taking out a card and looking at the strange insignia in green ink, Lou said, "I see you're still carryin' around Monopoly cards."

The gentleman grabbed back his notebook. "They are *not* Monopoly cards!" He snapped it shut and gestured at the disk as Lou picked it up. "And kindly return that to me."

Lou dug into his pocket and produced the calling card the gentleman had given him back at the drugstore. "Hey, remember, I'm in the club, too, see? 'Show the card when the need should arise.' Well, I need to know what this doodad is."

The gentleman sighed impatiently. "Kindly do not abuse the privilege."

Costello held up the device. "It looks kinda like the innards of a microphone."

The gentleman curtly grabbed the device. "It's something like that, yes." He looked past Costello to a young woman just entering the lobby. "Now please stay out of my way. But heed this warning," he added ominously, "beware Madame Z."

"What the hell is *that* supposed to mean?"

"Pray you never find out."

Costello eyed the gentleman as he met up with his attractive rendezvous. "Oh, I get it. It's the name of your little girlfriend. How do you like that, he's lookin' down his nose at me, when all the time he's meetin' up with a dame young enough to be his—" Lou shut up when he recognized the woman beckoning the gentleman over.

"Lenore!" he gasped, hurrying back into the phone booth to spy on the pair unobserved.

Indeed, it was Lenore Aubert. She was holding a big black clutch purse and dressed to the nines in a slinky black dress, mink stole and pearls. She smiled pleasantly as she and the mysterious gentleman met under the large chandelier.

Lou couldn't make out what they were saying, so he quit the phone booth and sat next to Griffith, all the while wondering if Lenore was a member of Rathbone's secret investment club. He grabbed the director's newspaper away and hid behind it.

The film director didn't take kindly to this at all. "How dare you!" he said.

Lou took out the sports section and handed back the rest, giving Griffith a stern, "SHHH!" Costello strained to listen.

"I should be angry with you, Richard," Lenore said.

When Lenore called the old gentleman "Richard," the hairs on the back of Lou Costello's neck prickled up.

Richard said, "Oh, why is that, my dear?"

"Jane and I were both a half an hour late for work this morning thanks to you," she replied, adding coquettishly, "Charlie Barton was as mad as a scalded cat. But you know what Benjamin Franklin said; 'all cats are gray at night.'"

"Really, my dear, that's hardly necessary."

Lenore stiffened as she opened her clutch purse and reached inside. "Considering what's been going on, I would prefer to be sure." She kept her hand inside the purse and repeated forcefully, "All cats are gray at night."

Richard smiled, obviously amused by Lenore's caution. "Very well, to quote Teddy Roosevelt; 'I speak softly, but carry a big stick.'" He chuckled. "If I didn't know better, I'd think 'C' was indulging in *double-entendre*."

Lou reached into his pocket and glanced at the calling card with the large initial C, and then listened as Lenore relaxed and closed her purse.

"It certainly aroused Bela's suspicions," she said. "Is Jane upstairs?"

Richard nodded. "Yes, as a matter of fact."

Gesturing toward the elevators, Lenore asked invitingly, "Shall we go?"

"Oh, please, my dear, ladies first."

Had Costello not known of Lenore's spotless reputation, the love she had for her Jewish husband, the fact that she told Sam Goldwyn where to go when he tried to get her on his casting couch, he might have thought she was about to do the mattress mambo with the old guy. He was what? Pushing 60? And what was all that malarkey about cats and sticks?

Suddenly a shocking thought took hold. He glanced at the calling card again and in particular at the logo with the brain inside the large letter "C" and the emblazoned motto *Semper Occultus*. Lou Costello's patriotic heart leapt into his mouth. "It's 'C' for Communists," Lou concluded. "They're Commie spies, just like Skorzeny!"

He reached the elevators in time to see Richard and Lenore step inside and an elevator boy in a red uniform, white gloves, and cap ask, "Floor?"

"Two, please," said Richard.

"Sure thing, Mr. Pratt," the elevator boy said.

The doors closed and the floor indicator arrow gradually moved to "2," where it stopped.

Lou hesitated, wondering if he ought to take the next car or hurry up the stairs. "If they're part of some Communist operation, I'm gonna need some muscle."

He ran to the bar.

Chapter 15

Wednesday, 25 February 1948
11:50 P.M.
Bar and Lounge, Hollywood Knickerbocker Hotel

Costello found Lon Chaney sitting at the end of the bar sharing a laugh, cocktails, and his breakfast leftovers with a stunning wasp-waisted brunette that had "femme fatale" written all over every shapely curve.

"Mmmm," she purred, savoring the cold scrambled eggs the way other women savor a kiss. "The catsup, it makes the eggs so…decadent." She spoke in a foreign accent that sounded to Lou's ultra-patriotic ear like Russian.

"You're pretty decadent yourself," Lon said, resting his cheek on his fist, gazing at her while exuding animal magnetism.

"Aww, you are so sweet," the temptress cooed. A white military cap barely large enough for her head was carelessly perched at a drunken angle and fell off as she leaned in to give Lon a kiss.

Lon caught it and gallantly placed the cap back on her head at a jaunty, but more secure angle. "There you are," he said, "pretty as a picture."

"And such a gentleman, too." She caressed Lon's cheek with tapered fingers encased in long, shiny, black skin-tight leather gloves. "You American men and your flattery."

"No, I mean it."

"Do you, darling?" She posed on the bar stool, thrusting out her ample chest. "Do you think that I am ready for Hollywood screen test?"

Costello thought, *More like she's ready to get arrested for indecent exposure.*

No stranger to the burlesque circuit, Lou had seen dancers decked out in some pretty bizarre outfits before, but this dame took the cake. It was like she was wearing her underwear outside of her clothes—and some pretty scary-looking underwear at that. The hourglass-defining black leather corset she wore was cinched so tightly that her heaving bosom was threatening to erupt with the drawing of every breath from a very low-cut black leather bustier. Her shiny red velvet lined black leather skirt was slit up the side, revealing a pair of shapely gams encased in black stockings and shiny black leather boots with stiletto heels.

"I'll bet this broad is a Red," Costello said to himself, "a red hot Red."

The Commie cutie licked her full, dark red lips and batted her long black lashes, displaying to her best advantage severely arched eyebrows, a black beauty mark on her left cheek, and straight cut bangs that all served to give her a vampiric veneer.

Chaney was smiling like a dope, laying on the charm. "You're very…photogenic," he said. "And that accent sure sounds a lot sexier on you than it sounds on Bela Lugosi."

Dracula's Daughter switched from seductress to gushing schoolgirl as she squealed, "I am so impressed you know Hungary's greatest living actor!"

Lon boastfully pointed at himself. "I'm makin' a movie with him right now."

"Tell me more about your friend, Bela Lugosi, and also about studio mogul with phone in car." She rested her chin on her laced together fingers. "You think this Mr. Eddie Mannix, he would find me…photo-genetic, too?"

Costello had seen enough. It was obvious to him that this dame was fishing around for information, or maybe she was just another would-be starlet trying to sleep her way into pictures. Either way, enough was enough. Lou insistently tapped Lon on the shoulder. "Come on," he said, "Lenore and Jane are in the hotel. They're up in a room together right now with some old British guy."

"Good for them," said the pretty vampire woman. "In decadent America they say that a woman, she may bed any man that she fancies. And if old man wants two women at once and they are all consenting, I say God bless America."

This gave Lou pause. "God bless America? You really mean that?"

"But of course," the beauty said.

"But you're a Russian."

"Correction, I am proud Hungarian who seeks political asylum." She raised her glass in a toast. "To George Washington, father of this wonderful country where a woman is free to pursue her fancy!" She downed the last of her drink and smiled seductively at Lon, leaning over and grabbing his knee. "And Zizi, she fancies you *very* much." She snarled aggressively like a tigress in heat.

Lon snickered as he made introductions. "Lou, this is Zizi. Zizi, this is Lou Costello."

"Hello, Mr. Lou," Zizi said, offering her hand. "A pleasure."

Lou took her hand and gulped. "Did Lon say your name was…Zizi?"

"Yes," she said.

Costello gulped again and patted her hand. "You wouldn't sometimes be called a Madame, would you?"

"Would you like to call me Madame?" she asked, gazing at Lou with bedroom eyes. She reached under her skirt and produced a riding crop that had apparently been hanging from her hip the whole time. She patted the business end of the crop in her hand, leering wickedly. "I hear you are bad boy."

Chaney snickered again and smirked at Costello. "Zizi is quite a handful, ain't she?"

"You don't know the half of it," Lou mumbled nervously. "Come on. Let's get outta here."

"Aw, do not leave yet," Zizi pleaded. She reached into her cleavage and pulled out a room key. Dangling it, she purred, "Zizi has room in hotel. If old man can have two girls, surely girl can have two boys." She added with a salacious whisper, "I even let you use riding crop on Zizi's bottom. I have been *very* bad girl."

"I don't doubt it, lady," said Costello. "But Chaney's married, and so am I."

"Are you *happily* married?" Zizi asked.

"So my wife tells me."

Zizi shrugged. "So what? I am not asking for long commitment, this is just for recreational sex." She smiled at Lon as she put her military cap on his head. "We play game," she said. "You are U.S. soldier who interrogates lovely Hungarian spy. You like to play games?"

"Sure do," said Lon. "You ever hear of a game called 'Post Office?'"

"Is not 'Post Office' a child's game?"

Simultaneously, Chaney and Costello said, "Not the way I play it." Lon glared at Lou.

"Sorry," said Costello, "it's a reflex." He got hold of Lon's arm. "Look, never mind that. Didn't ya hear what I just said? Lenore and Jane are upstairs with some guy called Richard that Lugosi thinks is mixed up with Karloff and his weird cards! And I'll tell ya somethin' else, too, I think they're all Reds."

With a dubious sneer, Chaney asked, "Where'd you get a dumb idea like that?"

Lou showed him the calling card. "See that 'C'? It stands for Communist. The guy's runnin' some kind of Commie spy ring, and Karloff, Jane and Lenore are in on it."

The Hungarian girl noted the card and frowned. "You think this means that they are Soviet agents?"

Chaney waved dismissively. "Oh, don't listen to this guy. He's all the time gettin' fired up about Commies takin' over Hollywood."

"You mean like I read about in American newspapers, about House Un-American Activities Committee investigating movie industry?"

"That's right, lady," Lou said impatiently. "In fact, this Richard guy said I should watch out for a dame called Madame Z, an' you sure fit the description." He grabbed Lon's tie. "Now let's get goin' or I'll tell Patsy on ya." He grabbed the hat off Chaney's head. "And take that off!" It suddenly struck him that he had seen that hat before. Costello noted the E.N.M.S. embroidered on the front. "M&Ms," he mused aloud.

"What about M&Ms?" Chaney asked.

Looking inside, Costello saw *B. Lugosi* written in white ink on the sweatband. "This is Bela, Jr.'s hat," Lou concluded. "He was wearin' it earlier today!" He glared at the brunette. "Where'd you get this hat, lady?"

"Zizi, she will never tell," the brunette declared drunkenly, giving Lon a sexy smirk of defiance. "I *am* this Madame Z you mention, a secret Soviet agent and have been trained to endure all forms of torture." She frowned with mock worry. "All but one, I fear. Whatever you do, please do not gang up and tickle Zizi, especially not under arms and soles of her feet at same time." She unzipped her right boot and slipped her foot out and then held up the boot and let it drop to the floor. "Zizi wants three-way, one way or another." She extended her leg invitingly at Costello, nylon clad toes wiggling provocatively. "If we cannot have sex, I get sexy torture instead."

"Look, lady," Lou protested, "this is no gag. There's a little boy that might be in trouble and this is his hat. Now where'd you get it?"

The drunken brunette pressed her lips together and mimed locking them up with an imaginary key, and then dropped the "key" down her cleavage. She put her hands behind her head, lacing her fingers tightly together, exposing armpits with tufts of curly black hair.

Definitely a European dame, Lou thought. He shrugged in defeat and gave Lon a nudge. "Well, I guess we better do it," he said.

"Do what?" asked Lon.

"You heard the dame, she obviously wants us to both tickle it outta her, so we gotta tickle it outta her."

"Aw, I was just flirtin' before. I can't really do nothin' with this dame. Patsy would kill me."

"Oh, like Anne ain't gonna kill me if she hears about this?" Taking off his deer-stalker, he folded it up and stuck it in his pocket and then put on the military cap and grabbed Zizi's ankle. "But we gotta," Lou insisted. "Don't worry; I'll keep quiet about it, if you do."

"Okay," Lon said, getting up from his stool and cracking his knuckles. "Get ready to talk, Zizi."

The Hungarian girl shook with anticipation as Lon got behind her and slowly reached under her arms, pausing to create suspense. He waited for Costello to get on the stool and put Zizi's foot in his lap. "Ready, Secret Agent Costello?" he asked.

Lou's heart wasn't it in. "Yeah, yeah, just start ticklin' her already."

"No! No!" Zizi begged. "Not that! Anything but that!"

Costello noticed the bartender was watching, and no doubt wondering what was going on. The comedian said, "Uh, she's auditioning for a part in a pi'ture."

Chaney lightly brushed his wiggling fingers against Zizi's exposed armpits. She shuddered and writhed on the barstool.

"No! Mercy, please!" she begged.

"No mercy?" Lon teased. "You got it, Zizi," and he dug his fingers in deeper.

Zizi bit down on her lower lip and stubbornly refused to laugh.

Lon was determined to make her crack. He dug in deeper and wriggled his fingers harder. This made Zizi jerk and struggle, but she still wouldn't laugh. After a few minutes, Lon paused and asked, "Are you gonna talk?"

Zizi exhaled a loud sigh of relief and gazed up at him with mock disdain. "Do you think that you *alone* can break the will of the villainous Madame Z? I will never tell!" She cleared her throat and wriggled her toes. "Not even if you *both* torture me at the *same time*."

Chaney glared at Costello. "Hey, Lou, do your part. She wants us both to do it."

Costello sighed and shrugged nervously. "Look, it's one thing to tickle a dame I know, like I tickled Jane this morning, but I don't even know this girl. This just feels weird."

"Come on, Lou."

"Yes, come on, Lou," Zizi insisted and wiggled her foot in his lap.

"Look, lady, just tell us where ya got the hat from and quit foolin' around."

"No, never," Zizi declared stubbornly. "I never tell!"

"There, you see," said Lon. "Either the both of us tickle her or she'll never tell us nothin'."

"Please, Mr. Lou," Zizi pleaded, "listen to big sexy man who employs double negative."

Costello sighed. "Awright, awright. I'll play along, but I won't like it."

"Good," said Zizi. "Now where were we?" She cleared her throat and got back into character. "I will never talk! Never! Never! Never!"

"Oh, yes you will!" said Lon. And as he returned to tormenting Zizi's underarms, Lou began to half-heartedly rake his nails against the sole of Zizi's foot. Her reaction was volatile.

"AHHHHHH!" she shrieked, exploding into the brassiest guffaws that Lou Costello had ever heard outside of a burlesque house. "NOT THAT! NOT THAT!" Encouraged by her reaction, Lou tickled her foot harder. Zizi was so beside herself that she began pleading for mercy in Hungarian and was kicking so hard that Lou had to wrap his arm around her leg to hold her down.

"Where'd you get the hat?" Costello pressed.

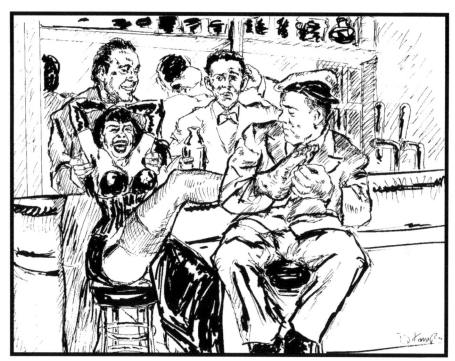

"NOT THAT! NOT THAT!"

"I NEVER TELL!" Zizi screamed between laughs.

With a look of determination, Costello treated Zizi's foot like a banjo, strumming his nails furiously over the sole of her foot, while Chaney worked his fingers down inside Zizi's corset. She screamed louder and looked like she was ready to crack.

"You gonna talk?" Costello asked.

Between gasps of laughter, she shrieked, "NO! NO!"

Chaney dug his fingers in further and probed for Zizi's other weak spots. He must have gotten her good, too, because the girl could take the torture no longer and pleaded, "HOKAY! HOKAY! I TELL! I TELL!"

Lou kept up the torture anyway. "Are you sure you're gonna talk?" he asked as he began playing "This Little Piggy" with her toes.

"YES! YES!"

"No more foolin' around?" He playfully pinched and wiggled her toes. "This piggy's got roast beef, an' this piggy's gettin' plenty more where this comes from!" He dug his fingers in between her toes and sent Zizi into fits of laughter so hard that her leather-clad behind practically bucked right off the barstool.

"NO! NONONONONONO! NO MORE! I TELL YOU! I TELL YOU ANYTHING I KNOW!"

"Okay, Lon," Costello said, letting go of the girl's foot, "I think the kid has had enough."

As Lon extricated his fingers from Zizi's corset, and as Zizi tried to catch her breath, Lou grabbed the hat off his head and asked forcefully, "Now, where'd you get this hat from?"

and the House of Doom

Panting, she said, "I steal…from man…you think…is spy," she swallowed hard. "The hat looked cute, so Zizi take."

"You mean Karloff and the other guy, they got the kid?" Costello asked, shocked. He glared at Chaney. "No wonder they need the dames up there. They're holdin' the kid hostage and need Jane and Lenore to look after 'im!"

"Oh, now come on," Lon scoffed. "You really think Boris Karloff, one of the nicest guys I know; you think he'd kidnap Lugosi's kid?"

"Karloff's a liberal, ain't he?" Costello retorted. "He helped start a Commie union, didn't he?"

"You mean the Screen Actors' Guild? That's no Commie union. I belong to it, and so do you."

"I belong to it, but I don't like it. If you ask me, all unions are Communist."

Zizi slipped her foot back into her boot and said, "Mr. Lou is right. That is why I escape Hungary to find new life in America. But now, I see that the Communists are taking over."

Chaney frowned at the girl. "Oh, come on. Don't tell me you believe what he's saying."

"You do not know what Zizi has seen." She invited them to lean in and she whispered, "Can you keep secret?"

Costello glared at her. "If you say, 'So can I' after Chaney an' me say 'yes', I'm gonna give you such a pinch."

"Maybe later," Zizi said with a saucy smile. "But I tell you truth about Zizi. I *am* a spy, but I am loyal agent working for United States." She gave them a tiny salute.

"No foolin'?" asked Costello.

"No fooling," said Zizi. "In fact, the man you encountered is dangerous Soviet agent, and head of large Communist cell working in Los Angeles."

"What did I tell you?" Costello said to Chaney.

"That's ridiculous," Chaney scoffed.

The girl crossed her bosom. "Is truth, so help me, cross heart and hope to be dead."

"So give us the low down," said Costello. "Who is this Richard guy, anyway?"

"His name is Richard Septimus Pratt, a double agent from England posing as retired diplomat. But I see through his disguise and have been as you Americans say, keeping on him the tabs. That is why I stole hat and have been wearing it here in bar, hoping to lure spies into Zizi's trap. Maybe I can count on you big, strong and loyal American men to help Zizi get the goods on the bads?"

Costello nodded. "You can count on us, lady."

"Good," Zizi said. "Now we make official. Zizi will swear you in as deputy agents."

Costello put the hat down on the bar, placed his hand over his heart and raised his right hand, while Chaney glared at them both like they were nuts. "Is this some kind of rib?" he asked.

Zizi smiled. "Later you play with Zizi's ribs, but for now, take oath."

Chaney reluctantly complied, while the bartender shook his head and muttered, "It takes all kinds."

Chapter 16

The elevator doors parted. "Second floor, all out," the elevator boy announced, all the while gawking at Zizi. As she stepped from the elevator car, the kid gave her a wolf whistle. Costello and Chaney followed Zizi as she strutted provocatively. Glancing back at the elevator, Lou noticed the elevator boy was watching Zizi's swaying hips with great interest.

"Look, are you sure you're a spy?" Costello asked her, gesturing with the military cap at her getup. "I mean, ain't spies supposed to be inconspicuous?"

Stopping to adjust the hem in her stocking, and bending over quite far, she asked, "What mean inconspicuous?"

Lon was admiring the view as he explained, "It means blending in, you know, not drawin' attention to yourself."

"Oh," said Zizi, straightening up and smiling. "Well, that works for men who are spies; ladies, not so much."

"That's a good thing," said Costello, "because you really stand out."

Zizi looked down admiringly at her breasts and then smiled at Lou. "I have been *standing out* since I was 12 years old."

"That ain't what I meant." Costello waved it off. "Skip it. Where did you say they was keepin' Bela, Jr.?"

She pointed and whispered, "The spy ring is this way." She put a finger to her lips. "Shhh. Be very quiet and walk this way."

As she tiptoed down the hall, Lou and Lon watched her with great interest.

"If I walked that way," said Costello, putting the military cap back on, "I might hurt myself."

Outside Suite 205, Zizi put her ear to the door, and motioned for Costello and Chaney to do likewise. All Costello could make out was an unintelligible murmur.

"I can't understand nothin'," he whispered.

"Me neither," said Lon.

"Zizi, she comes prepared." She reached under the slit in her skirt and produced a stethoscope.

As she put on the stethoscope, Costello pointed at Zizi's skirt and asked, "You got two extra pair of those things under there?"

Lon noticed a room service cart by the suite across the hall. It was piled with dirty dinner dishes, a half-eaten frankfurter sandwich, and several dirty glasses. "Hey," he whispered, "maybe we can listen with them glasses."

"Good idea," Costello whispered. He went over and got two of the glasses, handing one to Lon. As Chaney pressed the open end of the glass to the door, Lou did the same; only he put his glass the wrong way around, getting an ear full of milk dregs.

Zizi suppressed a giggle as she placed the bell of the stethoscope against the door.

Lou looked at the glass, rolled his eyes, sighed, and used his pocket hanky to wipe out his ear. Turning the glass the other way around, Costello pressed his ear to the bottom of the glass. It made a perfect amplifier.

"And you think that's the pattern?" asked a voice that was definitely Karloff's.

"I think so," said the voice of Lenore Aubert, "the film lab was processing Lon Chaney's changing into the Wolf Man scenes."

"Poor Lon," Jane said. "He's going to feel just awful when Charlie tells him they'll have to do the whole thing all over again."

Lon started and moaned, "OH NO!"

"What was that?" said the voice of Richard Septimus Pratt.

Zizi gasped. She pushed Chaney and Costello down the hall and around the corner, running into a well fed lady walking her Great Dane. The lady pulled back on the dog's leash and glared angrily. "You two idiots and your floozy should watch where you're going!"

The dog snarled.

Lon responded with his best Wolf Man growl. The dog squealed in fright and pulled his owner down the hall by his leash. Peering around the corner, the alluring spy and her two would-be operatives saw Boris Karloff check the hallway just as the woman was dragged along by the loping canine.

Karloff shrugged. "It must have been a dog," he said, and closed the door.

Zizi gave Lon a suggestive leer. "Zizi cannot wait to get you alone on full moon."

"I hated to do that," Lon said. "I like dogs."

Lou glared at Chaney and scolded, "What did you go and yell like that for, anyway?"

"I'm awful sorry," Chaney said, "but if you only knew what it's like shooting those damn Wolf Man transformations! They take all day and you can't move or nothin'! It's enough to drive a man to suicide."

"Just pipe down, will ya!"

Zizi motioned them onward. "Come, we go back."

The three of them tiptoed back to the suite. Costello and Chaney put their respective glasses to the door again while Zizi used her stethoscope.

"What about the serial numbers?" Costello heard Karloff ask.

"The young lady's serial numbers are legitimate," said the voice of Richard. "We traced them using records recovered from a clinic outside of Budapest; the laboratory was involved with certain diabolic Nazi experiments."

"Well, that's a relief, anyway," said Karloff. "Not about the experiments, but that Miss Skorzeny and her brother's stories are confirmed. That means we can cross them off the suspect list."

"Let's not jump to conclusions, Billy, please."

Lon tapped Costello on the shoulder. "Psst! Who's Billy?"

Costello shushed him.

Pratt's voice kept fading and growing stronger; Lou figured he was pacing. "According to Section 6, Kalara and Janika Skorzeny are *not* with Hungarian Relief."

"DGSP, do you think?" asked Lenore.

"Obviously. But I can't figure out what they want with Lugosi."

Lon frowned at Costello. "Psst! What's DGSP?" he whispered.

"Pipe down," Costello whispered back.

"Wouldn't that make it 'PD'?"

"SHH!"

"It is rival counter-counter espionage ring," Zizi hastily whispered.

Costello heard Karloff ask, "What about Dr. Kopf?"

"Tod N. Kopf?" remarked Richard sarcastically. "I'll say this; he has a wicked sense of humor. The serial numbers on the good doctor's arm belonged to a Fredek Vivas, a special effects and makeup artist for the Weimar Republic UFA film studio."

"So Dr. Kopf is really Fredek Vivas?" asked Jane. "I'm confused."

"The real Fredek Vivas died in the House of Doom's gas chambers."

"So this Dr. Kopf, whoever he is, has stolen Vivas's identity?"

"A common ruse used after the War," Richard said. "Nazi war criminals often disguised themselves as concentration camp victims to escape the liberating armies. But Tod N. Kopf is obviously a joke name, yet another alias. We believe that the culprit is actually Dr. Sigmund Rache, known to the inmates at the laboratory as *Doktor Halál*. But enough about Rache; Billy, have you or Rathbone had any luck locating the gold?"

"Basil did some checking," Karloff said. "After his little tussle in Central Park eight months earlier, he was able to trace the gold shipment to an Argentine steamer. Lenore, what did you find out?"

"My sources," said Lenore, "traced the ingots on their route to the West Coast. It took three months."

Jane added, "They were smuggled disguised as scene flat weights for a twelve city tour of *Arsenic and Old Lace*."

"Don Marlowe arranged the tour," Lenore said.

"Oh, yes," said Pratt. "Marlowe. I looked into his background. He's rather shady, lies frequently—"

Karloff chuckled. "The very definition of a talent agent."

Pratt stopped pacing, obviously irritated with having been interrupted, "—*but* his oafishness may be a cover."

"Any trace of Lillian or Bela, Jr.?" asked Karloff.

Lenore sighed. "We don't know *who* has them now."

Costello stared at Zizi. He stepped away from the door and motioned Zizi and Chaney to join him. "Hey," he said to Zizi, "I thought you said they got Bela, Jr. in there."

"Yeah," Chaney agreed, "in fact, they sounded to me like cops or something."

Zizi shrugged, pointing at the cap on Lou's head. "How then do you explain Pratt and the hat?"

"You got me there," said Lou, returning the glasses to the cart. He noticed the half-eaten frankfurter sandwich, the bite marks especially. "Hey," he said, "this looks like a kid was eatin' this."

Lon shrugged. "Yeah, so what?"

Zizi pointed at the cart. "This is where I found cap, on this very cart." She gestured at Karloff's suite. "Only before, it was over there."

Costello picked up the plate and pointed at the frankfurter. "I'll bet these are Bela, Jr.'s teeth marks. Maybe Pratt is keepin' the kid in this here other suite."

Chaney frowned incredulously. "But you heard what they said. They don't know who has Bela, Jr. any more than we do."

"Well, maybe because of your hollerin', they knew we wuz listenin'." Costello put down the plate and grabbed a glass. "I'll bet they got the kid in there to throw anybody lookin' for him off the trail." He put the glass to the door and got it the wrong way around again. He grabbed the hanky from his pocket. Costello looked to Zizi as he wiped out his ear. "What do you think?"

Zizi confiscated the glass. "I think you need to invest in stethoscope."

Lou angrily gestured at the door with his hanky. "I mean about the kid."

Lon motioned for Lou and Zizi to move away from the door. He whispered, "Okay, say Bela, Jr. is in that room. How are we gonna get in there to prove it?"

Costello stuck his hanky back in his pocket as he thought a minute, and then got an idea. Smiling, he said, "Well, supposin' a drunk husband is lookin' for his wife and he makes a mistake an' bangs on the wrong door?" He glanced at Zizi. "And his sexy drunk wife shows up with the cute little fat guy she's been double-timin' on him with."

The Hungarian girl pointed at Chaney. "Not to be offensive, but why am I not double-timing with big, strong American brute on little, tubby husband?"

Chaney frowned. "Yeah, how come?"

"Cuz it's funnier my way."

"Hokay," Zizi relented. "Have it your own way."

Lou gestured at the door. "So what are you waitin' for?"

"Okay," Chaney said, waving down the hall. "You guys stay out of sight and come in when it feels right."

Zizi grabbed Lon and planted a big kiss. "Good luck, Mr. Wolfy," she said.

Costello dragged her away and they waited around the corner where Lou gave Chaney the hi-sign to start the act.

Balling up his huge fist, Chaney banged loudly on the door. "MIRIAM! LET ME IN! I KNOW THAT LITTLE FAT RUNT IS IN THERE WITH YOU!" He banged even louder. "MIRIAM! YOU OPEN THIS DOOR RIGHT NOW!"

The door was yanked open by a foreigner with black hair and a handlebar mustache. "What meaning of this?" he asked in a thick Hungarian accent.

Chaney shoved belligerently past him. "DON'T TRY AND PROTECT THAT LITTLE WEASEL! WHERE'S MY WIFE?"

"You will leave room," the mustachioed Hungarian insisted, "or I call house detective!"

That was Lou's cue. "Don't worry, toots," he slurred, putting an arm around Zizi's waist, "Harry won't suspect nothin'."

"Oh, I hope not," Zizi slurred back, "my husband, he is very jealous."

"SO THERE YOU ARE!" Lon barked, grabbing Costello by the collar and dragging him inside. Mr. Mustache, as Costello mentally labeled the Hungarian man, was about to intervene, when Zizi held him back and began vamping him.

"So tell me, big boy," she said, playing with the curls of his mustache, "does mustache tickle when I kiss you?"

Mr. Mustache was dumbstruck as Zizi drew his lips to hers and she planted a long, hot kiss.

Chaney pushed Costello up against a couple of steamer trunks. "I SEE YOU GOT MY WIFE'S BAGS ALL PACKED!" he accused loudly.

"You got me all wrong," Costello said, acting the coward. "Uh, see, it ain't what you think." He glanced down at the tags on the trunks and saw they belonged to Bela and Lillian. "Bingo," he said.

"It ain't what I think, huh? Well, we'll see about that!" Chaney stumbled to a telephone by the couch, glowering at Mr. Mustache. "So you're gonna call the house detective on me, huh? And here you are makin' time with my wife too! Well, maybe *I'm* the one who's callin' the house detective on *you!*" He picked up the handset and gave the dial a bleary-eyed stare as Costello hurried over to Zizi and pointed back at the trunks.

"They're Bela and Lillian's trunks," he said. "Bela, Jr.'s definitely around here someplace."

"Good boy." Zizi reached into her cleavage for her room key. "I am sure you are right," she said, closing the door and using the key to lock it.

"Hey," Lou said, pointing at the key as Zizi returned it to her bountiful repository, "how come your key fits in that—" Realization suddenly hit home. "Uh oh."

Chaney began dialing when Mr. Mustache grabbed the handset away. "Don't think you can get tough with me," Lon warned.

Costello ran over and tugged on his arm. "Zizi's got the key. Zizi's got the keeeey," he said in a nervous sing-song musical delivery.

Chaney glared at him. "What's gotten into you?"

"The double agent's doin' a double cro-oss," Lou whisper-sang.

Mr. Mustache turned to Zizi. "What is this?" he demanded. "These are not MI6 agents." He pointed at the hat perched on Costello's head. "I thought plan was to lure Pratt's agents here with hat."

Costello nervously pulled Chaney by the lapel. "Quick, maybe we can make a run for it out the bedroom window!"

With a bewildered Lon Chaney in tow, Lou made a beeline for the bedroom just as the door opened a crack and young woman peered out. "What is going on out here?" she asked.

Lou did a double take and gasped. "Kalara Skorzeny! You're Kalara Skorzeny!"

Kalara opened the door wider, revealing that she was holding a Makarov Pistolet in her gloved hand.

Costello raised his hands. "And it looks like this is a stickup."

"Say, what's going on around here?" asked Lon, confused.

"Mr. Chaney! Mr. Costello!" said a familiar voice from inside the bedroom. Bela, Jr. had been lying on the bed reading a comic book. He leapt off the bed to run to them, only to have his way blocked by a muscular thug with his right arm in a sling. Costello labeled him "Wing Man." Using his free hand, Wing Man pushed the boy back onto the bed.

"You will not move, boy!" he growled as he drew out a gun.

Zizi barked an order in Hungarian. Lou gulped as he saw Wing Man cringe with fear. He holstered his Pistolet and made imploring gestures as he pleaded with Zizi in Hungarian.

"Kalara," Zizi ordered, "tell the others to come out. We must be hospitable to our American guests."

Kalara opened the bedroom door wider and gestured.

The first to emerge had a scar, a long scar, a scar that ran around his face from forehead, to cheek, to jaw line, around to his forehead again. This man Costello dubbed, "Scarface" for obvious reasons. The next was a young man with girlish good looks and smelled of toilet water. Costello nicknamed him "Pretty Boy."

Kalara pushed Wing Man out of the bedroom and then, while keeping Lon covered, she extended her free hand invitingly to Bela, Jr. "Come, darling boy," she cooed. "No one will harm you."

Bela, Jr. ran to Chaney, who shielded the boy while glaring at Wing Man. "Lucky for you she's got a gun on me," he said, nodding toward Kalara, "or I'd tear your god-damn head off!"

"Silence, fool," Mr. Mustache snarled, poking the barrel of his gun into Lou's back.

"What are you threatening me for?" asked Lou, pointing to Chaney. "He's the guy with the big mouth."

"Tovar," Zizi scolded. "If anybody is to say, 'Silence, fool,' it will be me." She drew out a gleaming brass framed pistol from a garter holster, an antique 1863 pocket Remington. "This has been fun game we play, boys. But now Madame Z has new game."

Lou raised his hands higher. "I'm guessin' it ain't 'Post Office.'"

A Brief Interruption

Interior, Lugosi's Trailer
Morning

"Post office!" Lugosi glared at Costello as he grabbed back the notes. "Are you sure you are remembering right?" He slapped the pages. "This sounds to me like one of your comedies."

Lou grabbed the notes back. "Hey, who was there, you or me?"

Abbott shook his head and pointed at the pages. "I have to side with Bela about this, Lou. I think you're exaggerating."

"I ain't exaggeratin' nothin'," Costello insisted. "What I said happened, happened just like I said it did."

"Including that business about tickling the lady spy?"

"Yeah."

"Aw, come on now." Abbott eyed his partner skeptically. "If you ask me, the two of you are hallucinating."

Lugosi pointed at his notes. "You yourself witnessed these conclusions that I do not remember having written."

"I did?" Abbott grabbed Bela's notes and stared confounded at his own signature. "This is a rib," he insisted. "It has to be a rib."

"It is not a rib," Bela insisted. "If by that you mean a joke." He grimaced at Costello. "At least *I* am not the one who is making the rib."

"Okay, Bats," said Costello, returning Lugosi's grimace with a challenging leer. "What do *you* remember happening while what was happening to me happened like I said?"

"Well, it was not anything the way you say." Lugosi referred to his notes and scowled at the comic. "*This* is what happened." He radiated authority and declared, "We were driving to Dr. Fell's house...."

Chapter 17

Bela sulked in the back of the police sedan, looking over at Rathbone, glaring at the actor's angular profile sharply contrasted in Mannix's headlights. Rathbone turned his head to gaze out the window at the passing scenery. Bela glanced down at Rathbone's pocket, and the bulge made by the three precious vials of morphine sulfate resting inside it. Seeing an opportunity, Bela reached over slowly in an attempt to pick the actor's pocket.

"Don't even think about it," Basil warned.

Bela glared angrily. "What, you have eyes in the back of your head!"

"No, I have a car window with your reflection in it." He gave Lugosi a smarmy smile. "Nice try, though." He returned his gaze to the window. "If you want your medicine, you'll have to be a great deal more cooperative."

Lugosi crossed his arms defiantly. "Never!"

Rathbone shrugged. "Suffer. See if I care."

He returned his gaze to the window, and as he did, he reached into his pocket and casually clinked the glass bottles together. The noise grated on Bela's jangled nerves until at last he could stand it no longer.

"Stop it! I show you! I show you!" He thrust his hand in his pocket and handed Basil the pin. "You are the devil," he complained bitterly.

"Believe me, it's nothing personal." Rathbone studied the bat and battle axe emblem. "The insignia means nothing to you?" he asked.

"Nothing!"

"Do the initials DGSP mean anything to you?"

"No!"

Basil reached in his pocket. "Now, about this letter…what did you tell the Hungarian government regarding their invitation?"

Lugosi returned the pin to his pocket. "I did not answer them at all." He scowled. "Lillian, she would not let me."

Rathbone nodded. "Yes, I suspected as much."

"I answered your question, I let you see the pin; now return to me what is mine," he gestured at the front seat, "or I make Ford make you give it back to me!"

Lt. Ford glared at them from the front passenger seat. "What's goin' on back there? Do I got to make Mickey pull this car over?"

Lugosi pointed angrily at Rathbone. "He started it! He has my medicine and he refuses to give it to me!"

"Medicine," Basil scoffed. "It's morphine sulfate, and Lugosi is growing far too dependent on it."

Bela snarled, "That is none of your business!" Addressing Ford, he said, "I have a doctor's prescription! It is for my leg pain."

Lugosi pointed angrily at Rathbone. "He started it!"

Lt. Ford sighed and rolled his eyes. "Come on, Rathbone, give the guy back his medicine. If he's got a prescription, it's legal."

"The legality of it isn't the point," said Basil. He gave Lugosi a challenging leer. "You haven't complained once about your sciatica since hearing of Skorzeny's arrest."

"What does that have to do with it?"

"It demonstrates that the pain you're occasionally suffering from is purely psychosomatic."

"I do not know from psycho…whatever you call it, but there are times Lillian, she tells me the pain is all in my head." He stared angrily. "I tell her, the pain it is real. I was shot in the line of duty once, and the pain has grown worse over the years."

"So has your career," observed Basil.

"What is that supposed to mean?"

"It means that while the source of your pain may be a legitimate medical complaint, I believe its severity is exaggerated by depression."

"What?"

Basil rolled his eyes. "The pain is all in your head." He reached into his pocket and produced the three vials. "I noted that only one of these bottles has been used recently." He held up the bottle in question. "This is the only one with needle marks in the rubber top. Is this the medicine you've been taking?"

Lugosi eyed the bottle hungrily, much as he did in *Dracula* when Dwight Fry cut his finger. "It is the medicine Lillian has been giving me, yes."

Basil nodded. "It's distilled water. It says so if you peel away the label that reads, 'morphine.'"

Lugosi grabbed the bottle and glared disbelievingly. "Lillian, she played me a trick!"

Basil gazed earnestly. "Listen, Bela. You fancy yourself a detective. Well, Sherlock Holmes had his own romance with the needle, and Watson often scolded him for it."

"I suppose now you are going to tell me Holmes, he died tragically from an overdose."

"Actually, he fell to his death struggling with Professor Moriarty at Reichenbach—" He waved. "But that's beside the point. Your health will suffer if you continue with this madness. For your family's sake, if not for your own, I urge you to give it up."

"I wish that I could," Bela admitted.

Lt. Ford pointed ahead. "We're here. Pull in there, Mick."

Mickey parked in the funeral home's driveway behind two beetle-shaped automobiles. The usually quiet circular court was abuzz with excitement. There were patrol cars with red flashing lights, and three coroner's wagons. Cops were questioning neighbors clad in bathrobes, including one who looked very familiar to Lugosi. Other policemen were milling around, poking in the bushes, peering into the funeral home's windows.

A cop hurried over to Ford's car and saluted. "Evening, Lieutenant," he said.

"What's the skinny, Pat?"

Shaking his head and speaking with a brogue, the cop said, "We ain't never seen the likes of it before. That spooky old house ain't what it appears to be at all. There's two decedents inside, but we think there might be more." He gestured at two taxis with their engines idling and their meters running. "We're just wrappin' up gettin' a statement from those two." The cabbies were leaning against their respective yellow cabs, grabbing a smoke and talking to police. One of the drivers was a short, tough-looking mug, the other a tall colored man.

Eddie Mannix pulled in behind Ford, left the engine idling, and got out. He approached the copper and slapped him on the back. "How's it going, Pat? Hell of a night, ain't it?"

Pat chuckled and shook Mannix's hand. "Eddie! What brings you here? No, now don't tell me. It's because of Bud Abbott, I'm guessin'."

"Abbott?" exclaimed Mannix. "Bud Abbott is here?"

"Yeah, he's in that house, and he's in a peck of trouble, as if you didn't know. That *is* why you're here, ain't it?"

Lt. Ford nodded toward the cabs. "Can I talk to those fellas now?"

The police questioning the cabdrivers closed their notebooks.

"Yeah," said Pat, "it looks to me like we're done with 'em."

As Ford and Mickey got out of the car, Mannix pointed at the house. "I'm gonna go see what kind of trouble Abbott's gotten himself in."

Ford opened the passenger door for Bela. "I guess that means you get to tag along with me and Rathbone."

Lugosi glared at Basil before getting out. "I am thrilled," he grumbled.

Approaching the cab drivers, Ford flashed his badge and said, "Evening, fellas. I'm Lt. Fred Ford, Homicide. What's been going on around here?"

The first cab driver shrugged. "You got me. When I moved here from New York, I thought I'd seen the last of stuff like this. Boy, was that a lot of hooey."

"You're tellin' me, brother," said the other cabbie. "This kind of thing, I don't need." He gawked at the tuxedoed Bela Lugosi. "Say, ain't you—"

"Never mind that," said Mickey. "Who was your fare?"

"Mine was a foreigner," the colored driver said. "Didn't speak no English, just kept talkin' to me with a damn dictionary."

Lugosi nodded. "It must have been Janika."

"What do you think, Rathbone?" Ford asked, finding himself talking to thin air while the actor was puttering around the two beetle-shaped cars. "Hey, Rathbone," the Lieutenant called, "get over here!"

Basil waved, and then casually crossed over, and much to Lugosi's annoyance, he was smirking to himself. "Sorry, Lieutenant," Rathbone said, "I was merely poking about." He nodded back at the cars. "I was just noting the Volkswagens, Hitler's car for the average working man."

"Well, stay with me," Ford scolded. "You're good at playin' detective, but I'm the one who's official." He turned to address the shorter cabbie. "What about you?" he asked.

"Lucky me," he said, "I got me a movie star; Bud Abbott. Only he was like this guy." He pointed at Basil.

"How do you mean?"

"He was playin' detective. Told me to pull up to the house and keep out of sight. We just sat here, him in the back seat, and the meter runnin' the whole time, actin' like we wuz at a stake out or somethin'."

"Did you see anything suspicious?" the Lieutenant asked.

"You mean besides some joker in a bathrobe carrying a shotgun?"

"A what?" Ford exclaimed.

Lugosi pointed back at the sidewalk. "He is the neighbor man over there. A monster trampled his flowerbeds."

"Sure it did," Ford said. He turned back to the cabbie. "Anyway, you were saying?"

"There was a bunch of guys in dark coats. All of 'em was carrying suitcases."

Basil's eyebrow crooked. "Really? What time was that?"

"I dunno, at least five bucks in cab fares ago. They pulled up in them beetle-shaped cars over there."

"How many guys?" Mickey asked.

"I didn't bother to count 'em, maybe five or six."

"More like eight, I think," commented Rathbone.

"How would you know?" challenged the cabbie. "You wasn't here."

"Elementary." He smiled at Ford. "Each Volkswagen seats four." He turned to Lugosi. "Remember when I pointed out the extra parkas and goggles? They weren't intended for us at all. Fell's demonstration was merely a dry run."

Lugosi sneered. "Yes, yes, yes. I deduced that myself hours ago."

Ford asked the cabbies, "Is there anything else you can tell us about those guys?"

The short cabbie said, "I could tell right away they were Krauts. After they goose-stepped their way into the old house, Abbott started snoopin' around in the bushes."

"I guess I pulled up soon after that," said the colored cabbie.

"More like twenty minutes later," the first corrected.

"Either way, my guy got out and knocked on the door. Somebody answers the door. The next I hear is *bang, bang!*"

and the House of Doom

Bela glowered at Ford. "Enough questions! We go in now!" He crossed the circle court and mounted the rickety porch but had his way blocked by a cop guarding the door.

"Are you the undertaker?" he asked, noting Lugosi's attire.

The actor drew up proudly. "I am Bela Lugosi, Master Detective!"

"Sorry. Nobody's allowed in but police and the undertaker."

Lt. Ford approached and smiled. "It's okay, he's with me. Let him in."

"Lieutenant, I don't think you realize how bad it is in there."

"Let me through!" Lugosi demanded and barged his way in.

The county coroner was in the foyer. He sat on a pile of coats thrown over the hall tree entry bench. He looked up from his clipboard and nodded. "Hello, Lieutenant," he said, gesturing with his pen. "Damnedest thing I ever saw, and I've seen a hell of a lot." He shook his head and continued writing.

"Wow," said Mickey, scratching the back of his head. "This is like somethin' out of *Inner Sanctum Mysteries*."

"Indeed," Rathbone remarked.

Police and crime scene investigators were buzzing around the dead bodies that were presumably Grimes the butler and Dr. Fell. Grimes was lying face down in a pool of blood by the stairs. Dr. Fell was slumped against the closed and blood-spattered pocket doors, clutching a .22 caliber revolver in a death grip. Grimes had been shot in the back, Dr. Fell through the heart. But the most startling detail: It was only by their clothing that Lugosi or anyone else could identify the decedents. The heads and faces of both men were hidden behind war surplus gas masks! The gray masks with their round black lenses and anteater filter snouts made the corpses appear comically grotesque, almost as if they had been murdered at a fancy dress ball.

"Where are the first officers on the scene?" Ford asked.

The coroner gestured beyond the foyer to the entry hall stairs where Janika Skorzeny and Bud Abbott sat handcuffed to each other. Mannix stood by the staircase, witnessing the proceedings. One patrolman held the alleged murder weapon in a handkerchief, while his partner shined a flashlight in the suspects' faces. No matter what question was put to him, Skorzeny's answer was always the same snarling reply; "*A kárhozat háza!*"

"Now, listen, you," the first officer said to Skorzeny, "quit talkin' gibberish! We caught you red-handed with this gun! Just admit you came here to kill the doc!"

"But, fellas," Bud said, "you gotta listen to me—"

"Shut up! When we're ready to talk to you, you'll sing plenty!"

"Hey," warned Mannix, "you go easy on my pal if you know what's good for you."

"Who the hell are you, anyway, his lawyer?"

"I'm Eddie Mannix. Are you new around here?"

The second cop grabbed Skorzeny roughly. "Spill it, Russkie! You can't weasel your way out of this with that Commie double-talk!"

Skorzeny again snarled, "*A kárhozat háza!*" and jerked his head at Dr. Fell's body.

Lt. Ford stepped in. "Jesus Christ, don't you jokers know you can't question a guy that don't speak English?"

The two patrolmen came to attention. "Evening, Lieutenant," the second officer said.

Ford was about to return the salute, but waved impatiently instead. "Never mind the protocol; just gimme the lowdown."

"We found these two guys running from the crime scene."

Ford was about to say something when two crime scene investigators entered from the back door, one of them carrying two crowbars. "Evening, Lieutenant," he said.

"Evening, Harry." Ford gestured at the crowbars. "What the hell are those for?"

The second investigator grabbed Dr. Fell's feet.

"Hey, hold on a minute," said Ford. He turned to the coroner. "Is it okay with you if those guys move the body?"

"It's fine by me," the coroner said, not looking up from his paperwork.

Ford wasn't satisfied. "Did you get pictures?" he asked a photographer.

The crime scene photographer was changing the flashbulb on his camera. Without looking up, he said, "Yeah. I got plenty, enough to wallpaper his tomb." He gestured at the door under the stairs. "I'm gonna go take shots of that Frankenstein lab. Let me know when you guys get those doors open."

The first investigator dragged Dr. Fell by his feet, leaving the body beside the butler's corpse, and a telltale smear of red on the floor. Returning to the pocket doors, the second investigator handed his partner a crowbar. "If this doesn't work, we may have to dynamite." Together they inserted the crowbars into the crack between the doors and tried, without much success, to pry them open.

"What's the problem, Charlie?" Lt. Ford teased. "You lab rats too puny to force open a couple of sliding doors?"

Charlie gave Ford a dirty look as he struggled with the crowbar. "Up yours, Fred," he growled as the veins in his forehead stood out. Charlie grunted as he and Harry put their backs into it. The crowbars slipped. Charlie banged his hand on the molding.

"Damn it! That's gonna leave a scar," he complained, shaking his hand and sucking on the wound.

Lt. Ford smirked. "Here, let a real man do it." He grabbed the door pulls and yanked, but the doors wouldn't budge. "Mickey, come'ere and give me a hand."

Ford took one door, Mickey the other. Together they pulled and strained.

Harry glowered. "Save your strength. Those doors are impregnable."

Lt. Ford grew frustrated and hit the doors with his fist. "Ow!" he grabbed his aching hand. "What the hell?"

"The wood paneling is just a façade," said Charlie, hacking away with his crowbar, exposing bare gray metal. "Underneath, it's like battleship armor."

Lt. Ford put his hand on the metal. "What's in there, Fu Manchu's rumpus room?"

"I was in there earlier this evening," commented Basil. "It's a rather unassuming viewing parlor."

Harry pointed. "If you go outside, you'll see the bay windows are closed off from the inside with steel shutters."

"We think the room might even be air tight," added Charlie.

"Air tight?" marveled Ford.

"Remarkable," said Basil as he stepped forward to investigate. "Do you suppose the Germans might be in there?"

Harry smirked. "If they are, they ain't saying much."

Charlie pulled a stethoscope from his coat pocket. "I listened with these, but couldn't hear a thing. I'm thinking their goose is cooked."

Lugosi gestured at the butler. "These men, they are wearing gas masks." He sniffed the air. "Do you smell any gas?"

Mannix grinned. "If you do, it's probably me. I had chili for lunch."

Bela glared at him. "I am being serious! Why are they in gas masks?"

Rathbone examined the door frame. "If this is a death trap of some sort, the gas masks suggest that Fell and the butler were planning to go back into this room to retrieve something." He smiled knowingly. "Suitcases, perhaps."

Lt. Ford glared at the two arresting officers. "Just exactly what went on around here?"

The first patrolman consulted his pocket notebook. "At approximately 11:26 P.M. we received a call from dispatch about a neighbor complaining of shots fired. When we arrived on the scene we found two yellow cabs parked out front. We questioned the cabdrivers. We were about to investigate the crime scene when we caught these two guys—," he nodded at Abbott and Skorzeny.

"Suspects," Ford corrected. "They're called suspects, for Christ's sake!"

"We found these two *suspects*; one identified as Bud Abbott, the other Abbott says is a foreigner named Skorzeny. Like I said, they were running from the scene."

"I wasn't running away," Abbott tried to explain, "I was chasing Skorzeny! *He* was running away!"

"Either way," said the second policeman, "Skorzeny was carrying this pistol in a shoulder holster. But we got the drop on him."

Rathbone pointed expectantly. "May I see the weapon?" he asked.

"Should I let him see it?" the patrolman asked Ford.

The Lieutenant nodded. "Yeah, Rathbone knows all about handling evidence."

"No need for me to actually handle it, Lieutenant." Basil gave the weapon in the patrolman's hand a momentary glance. "It appears to be a 9mm semi-automatic weapon. Judging from the five pointed star on the grip, and the design, it's a Makarov Pistolet from the Soviet Union."

"Hey," remarked Ford, "and those cigarettes back at lake were Russian, too."

"Precisely," said Rathbone with a nod as he resumed his probing around the pocket doors.

Lugosi overcame his superstitions about touching the dead and knelt beside the butler's body, rolled it over, and slipped the gasmask off the corpse's head.

"Hey, Lugosi," Ford warned, "you can't interfere with a crime scene like that!"

The Hungarian sleuth sneered, "I am *not* interfering, I am investigating." He reached down and ripped open the front of the dead butler's shirt, exposing the bullet-riddled corset of a medical body brace. "Aha!" He grabbed the snout of the gasmask and pulled it off the butler's head, and along with it a foam rubber mask that covered the dead man's head and shoulders. "There, you see!" Bela said, straightening up. "*This* man is the Dr. Fell missing an arm disguised as his butler! This mask, it hides the neck brace. Just as I suspected, the doctor and the butler, they change places using a Vaudeville quick change and a magic trick like the Suttee!"

Abbott asked, "What's furniture got to do with it?"

"IT HAS NOTHING TO DO WITH FURNITURE!" Lugosi raged, throwing the mask down.

Basil casually looked up from what he was doing. "I made the same deduction when I touched the butler's hand and felt the prosthesis."

Lugosi grimaced. "I knew before Rathbone! And that man," he declared, approaching the dead doctor, "he is Dr. Kopf, also pretending to be Dr. Fell!" Lugosi pulled off the gasmask expecting to find Dr. Kopf's face beneath it. Instead there was a Dr. Fell mask that came off with the gas mask, revealing a man with curly brown hair. Lugosi pulled out the foam rubber mask from inside the gas mask and stared disbelievingly at the dead man. "It is the second ambulance man!" he exclaimed.

"The who?" Ford asked.

"He kidnapped Lou Costello's press agent disguised as an ambulance man." He looked back at the butler's body. "They both were ambulance men and that one missing the arm, he wore a blonde wig and a mask, and he hit me over the head with his metal hand!"

Lt. Ford bent down to examine the first decedent's mechanical arm. "You're right, his arm's a fake."

"Aha!" Basil rejoiced. "I think I've found it."

Ford joined Rathbone by the doors, leaving Lugosi to glower angrily at being upstaged by Basil's discovery. "What'd you find, Sherlock?" Lt. Ford asked.

"Why, the proverbial secret button, Lieutenant." Basil pushed on the molding of the doorframe. "*Open, Sesame,*" he dramatically intoned as the pneumatic doors parted and the stair hall was overcome with the smell of death.

The bodies of eight Nazi officers were twisted into ghastly death contortions, their uniforms stained with vomit and other bodily excretions. Three of them lay stretched out on the floor before the pocket doors, their deeply tanned faces twisted into masks of desperation. They were piled atop each other, dying in the act of trying to claw their way out. The rest had attempted an unsuccessful escape through the shuttered windows.

Lt. Ford gestured at a table. "Are those what I think they are?" he asked.

There were eight suitcases, seven lying open on a coffin display bier now utilized as a table, and one suitcase opened face down on the rug. Basil stepped nonchalantly over the bodies and examined the contents of the suitcases. "If you think these are gold bricks, Lieutenant, then, yes, that's exactly what they appear to be." Basil hefted one of the gold bars. "Each weighs about, oh, I'd say, 400 ounces."

From the hall, Skorzeny cried out, "*A kárhozat háza!*"

Mickey asked, "What's that he keeps sayin'?"

Bela was about to translate when Rathbone upstaged him by explaining offhandedly, "It's Hungarian for 'House of Doom,' a secret Nazi laboratory near Budapest."

"No," Lugosi insisted as he backed away from the doorway. "He means *this* is the House of Doom." He crossed himself. "No one else step over the threshold! It is cursed!"

Basil rolled his eyes as he approached with the gold brick. "You claim to be the better detective," he said with an infuriating smirk, "I suggest you behave like one." He held up the gleaming brick and pointed at a mark stamped into the metal, the German eagle atop a Swastika. "Please note the mark. Very convenient, don't you think, the Nazis marking their gold for us like this?" He smiled at Mannix. "It makes this gold so much easier to identify than the stuff laundered through 'Lucky' Luciano's Swiss bank accounts, eh, Eddie?"

Mannix drummed his fingers on the newel cap. "Look, if you're implyin' that I had anything to do with this—"

"Perish the thought," said Basil, returning to the bier. He put the brick down on the table and examined the fallen suitcase more closely.

Bela glared at him from the doorway. "Come back here, Rathbone! I sense death in there!"

Basil sighed. "What was your first clue, all the dead bodies in the room? Now either help me look for clues, or stop interfering." He crooked an eyebrow as something caught his eye.

Lugosi's shoulders hunched with indignation. "You have been interfering from the start! And now all I want to do is save your life! You are very ungrateful!"

Lt. Ford pulled him aside. "Look, Bela, take it easy."

"Yeah," said Mickey, leaning against the doorframe, "you're gonna blow a gasket."

Before Bela's startled eyes, the pocket doors slammed shut!

Chapter 18

Thursday, 26 February 1948
12:02 A.M.
Dr. Fell's House, Crescent Heights

Mannix, Ford, Charlie and Harry all strained to get the pocket doors open, two men to a crowbar, while Mickey was on the phone to Headquarters. All the while Bela Lugosi was scolding them. "You ridiculed Bela for his beliefs," he said, "but still the house has taken Rathbone! Maybe next time you will listen to Bela!"

"Give it a rest, Lugosi," Mannix snarled, a vein popping in his forehead as he yanked on the crowbar with all his might.

"Goddamn it!" Frustrated, Ford pounded his fist on the doors. He sucked on his aching hand as he glared angrily at his partner. "Mickey, what the hell did you do?"

"I don't know!" Mickey said, hanging up and joining them. "But the Chief says it'll take twenty minutes to get the battering ram over here. Rathbone'll be dead by then."

"Forget Headquarters," Ford said as he began searching for the hidden switch. "Help me find the gimmick that'll get these goddamn doors open!"

Mickey felt all along the molding. "I must'a hit somethin' when I leaned against the door!"

"Gee, ya think?"

Mannix dropped the crowbar and grabbed his chest, huffing and puffing.

"Hey, Eddie, are you okay?" Harry asked, helping the tough guy ease down on the floor.

"Yeah, Eddie," said Ford. "You don't look so good."

Mannix mopped his forehead while Charlie took his pulse. "I'll be okay. The doc says I got a bad ticker is all." He shoved the crime scene investigator aside and struggled to get up. "But who listens to their doctor, right?" He picked up the crowbar and inserted the claw end into the seam.

Lugosi grabbed the crowbar away and pushed Mannix aside. "Killing yourself will do Rathbone no good, you fool! Go sit down over there with Mr. Abbott!" Lugosi put his ear to the door while Mannix gave him the fish eye and reluctantly did as the Hungarian suggested, easing himself down on the steps below the two prisoners. "RATHBONE," Bela shouted through the door, "CAN YOU HEAR ME?" He turned to Charlie. "Give me your heart listener!"

"You mean my stethoscope?" he asked, reaching for the instrument.

"Yes, whatever it is called!" Lugosi put on the stethoscope and listened at the door. "I hear nothing!"

Ford shouted, "BASIL, TELL US HOW TO OPEN THE DOORS!"

Bela listened carefully and shook his head. "Still there is nothing!"

Harry and Charlie and Mickey each took a section of molding and ran their hands up and down either side of the door frame.

"There must be a button or a lever here somewhere!" Harry said.

Charlie shook Mickey. "Hey, maybe if you do like you did before."

"You mean lean against it?" asked Mickey.

"Say, that's not a bad idea," Ford said. "Well, what are you waiting for, Mick?"

Mickey's eyes grew wide with fear and he slowly raised his hands over his head. "That's not what you did before, is it?"

Mickey shook his head and nodded toward the stairs. "I didn't have a Hungarian mug pointing a gun at me before."

"What are you talking about?" Lugosi said, and then looked where Mickey was pointing. Bela dropped the bell of the stethoscope and let it dangle from his ears as he raised his hands.

Everyone else raised their hands, too. They had all been so distracted by the crisis, including the arresting officers keeping an eye on Abbott and Skorzeny, that no one paid any attention when Skorzeny reached for the gun on the hip of the cop nearest him.

While Abbott shut his eyes tight and kept his hands up, Skorzeny was keeping everyone covered with the gun. "Please to put up your hands, all of you!" Skorzeny commanded in English tinged by a heavy accent. Mannix tried to make a move to disarm him, but his angina attack had made his reaction time way too slow. Skorzeny pressed the muzzle of the policeman's special to the back of Eddie's head. "No one makes the funny moves or the dog-faced man dies first."

Mannix sighed as he reached for the ceiling. "What a revoltin' development *this* is," he complained.

The coroner sitting on the bench in the foyer glanced up from his paperwork a moment, began writing again, and then did a double take.

"What'd I tell you, Lieutenant," one of the arresting officers said as he kept his hands up, "I told you the guy could speak English!"

Skorzeny gestured at the cop's belt and displayed the handcuffs chaining his wrist to Bud Abbott's. "Please to give over key!" the Hungarian said, and pulled back on the hammer of the gun for emphasis.

"At least the guy's polite about it," Mickey commented. The officer handed Mick the handcuff key and he stepped forward to unlock Skorzeny's handcuffs.

"Carefully," Skorzeny ordered as Mickey tried to steady his shaking hand and insert the key. "Or I shoot dog man."

"Now take it easy there, pal," Mannix said, raising his hands as high as they would go and staring straight ahead at the coroner, speaking volumes with his eyes. "I got a weak heart. I guess that's what a doctor's for, right? *To save your life.*"

The coroner looked around for something he could use as a weapon. He got up slowly, hefting his clipboard, and then thought better of it. He waved at Lugosi to get his attention. Bela scowled, thinking the coroner was trying to wave hello. The coroner pointed at Skorzeny and made yak-yak motions with his other hand, trying to tell Lugosi to keep Skorzeny talking.

Lugosi frowned, completely baffled and started mimicking the coroner's hand gestures.

Skorzeny was distracted by Bela's antics. "What you do there?" he asked, now free of the handcuffs, and gesturing for Mickey to step away.

Bela shrugged. "Shadow puppets, I think," he said. He gave up in frustration and yanked the stethoscope from his ears. "I have had enough of this silliness!" Bela glared at Skorzeny and shook the stethoscope, chastising his fellow countryman. "I am very disappointed with you!"

Lt. Ford smiled nervously. "Uh, Lugosi, we don't want to upset the nice man with the gun."

"Stay out of this!" Bela commanded, and then addressed Skorzeny again. "So you were only pretending to not know English! You make a fool of Bela who tries to translate for you!"

"I had to pretend," Skorzeny explained in his defense. "It was not my intent to insult you. I have only great respect for Bela Lugosi, Hungary's finest living actor."

Mickey muttered to Ford. "At least he's living for now." Ford shushed him.

Skorzeny smirked. "The things men will say when they think you cannot understand them, it would amaze you!"

"Aha!" Bela exclaimed. "So you understood Lou Costello when he told to me that the photographer Glaston took your picture!"

Skorzeny nodded in the affirmative. "I cannot allow my picture, or Kalara's to be taken. Not for reasons of superstition, which is the fruit of religion and religion is the opiate of the people. No, it is to conceal our identities as espionage agents for glorious DGSP."

Bela frowned. "Rathbone mentioned DGSP before." He reached into his pocket and held out the pin. "What have you to do with this pin?"

Skorzeny tugged on his lapel, revealing a similar pin hidden beneath it. "All agents wear such a pin. It is symbol of our glorious spy ring."

"So that is why *you* drugged Mr. Abbott!"

"Yes," Skorzeny confessed proudly. "It is true that I drug Abbott and I leave him to steal back negative from Glaston man."

"And it was you who set laboratory fire!"

"I did not start fire!" Skorzeny looked insulted. He glared at the bodies of Dr. Fell and Grimes. "*They* started fire and kidnapped Glaston man. They did it because camera-man took a picture of *Doktor Halál* and he wanted all evidence destroyed."

Lugosi snarled in frustration. "None of this matters now!" He pointed at the pocket doors. "A man's life hangs in the balance! Put down the gun so we may save Rathbone!"

All this time the coroner had been searching under the pile of coats for a weapon. He still wasn't having much luck as Skorzeny sneered, "What do I care what happens to Rathbone? He is MI6 secret agent, I am DGSP. We are enemies. If he dies, it is no nose off my skin."

Lt. Ford's mouth dropped open. He shook himself out of it and said, "Wait, you think Rathbone is a spy? No, you got it all wrong. He's an actor."

Skorzeny stood up. "Enough talk! You will now give me keys to vehicle!" He pointed his gun at Bela. "I take Lugosi with me."

"You better let him have it," Ford told his partner.

Mickey nodded and slowly reached for his car keys. "Hold on a minute," he said, assuring Skorzeny, "they're clipped on my belt, see?" He turned around and displayed his rear end by pulling up his jacket. "I'm just getting the keys. No sudden moves."

Skorzeny frowned. "I prefer you move quickly. I am not enjoying looking at you from this angle."

Mickey got the keys off the key ring and held them out to Skorzeny. Grabbing them, Skorzeny said to Bela, "You will now come with me."

"I will not!" Lugosi said stubbornly. "Why should I?"

Skorzeny shrugged. "Because if you refuse I will shoot you and it will hurt."

The coroner was hoping to find a gun or a blackjack in the pockets of one of the coats, but he kept coming up empty. The most menacing thing he found were car keys and a roll of Lifesavers. Skorzeny waved Mannix to get out of his way as he descended the stairs. He backed into the foyer while keeping his gun trained on Lugosi. "We go now," Skorzeny commanded.

Out of desperation, the coroner grabbed a coat and threw it over Skorzeny's head.

The move startled Skorzeny.

The gun went off.

Lugosi flinched.

The bullet missed Bela's shoulder.

It splintered the door frame behind him.

Skorzeny was wrestled to the floor.

The pocket doors parted with a pneumatic hiss.

The overwhelming stench of death and bodily excretions invaded the stair hall again.

Standing inside the parlor amid death and decay was a very calm Basil Rathbone, holding a gold brick in one hand, and pinching the nostrils of his hawkish nose with the other. He commented nasally, "Oh, too bad, it looks like I've missed all the excitement."

Like a frustrated mother scolding a kid in a grocery store, Lt. Ford reached inside and pulled Basil gruffly out into the stair hall. "How many times do I have to tell you that you gotta stay close to me?"

"I'll be sure to do just that from now on." Basil smirked as the police and Eddie Mannix swarmed over Skorzeny like linebackers in a football pileup. "Is this what they mean by 'indoor sports'?'"

Mannix had his knee in Skorzeny's back as Mickey reached around for his handcuffs. "This guy just tried to kidnap Lugosi," the detective said.

"YOU CANNOT ARREST ME!" Skorzeny shouted as Mickey pulled him to his feet. "I CLAIM DIPOLOMATIC IMMUNITY!"

One of the cops clubbed him with his nightstick.

Skorzeny crumpled to the floor.

"Tell it to the Marines!" the cop snarled.

"I see you've got things well in hand," Basil remarked cheerily.

Infuriated by his cheeky disposition, Lugosi glared at Rathbone. "Do not try to fool Bela with your British stiff upper lips." He pointed into the deadly parlor. "Admit you were ready to make water in your pants when those doors closed on you!"

Being annoyingly smarmy, Basil admitted, "I was a *trifle* concerned. However, I deduced quickly that the method used to murder these German chaps was a form of nerve gas, probably experimental, definitely in short supply. I suspected there was only enough gas for one murder attempt. So, apart from being choked to death by the awful stench, I realized I was quite safe."

Mannix joked, "What, you didn't look for a secret panel behind a bookcase or something?"

Lt. Ford nudged Basil kiddingly. "So, is it true about you being a spy?"

"I beg your pardon?" asked Rathbone, obviously taken aback.

The Lieutenant gestured at the unconscious Janika Skorzeny. "That crazy so-and-so said you were with MI6. Pretty funny, huh?"

"Yes," Basil said, smiling nervously, "quite absurd."

"Hey," Bud Abbott said, pulling himself up by the banister, gawking and pointing at the gilded mask next to the parlor fireplace. "Do you see what I see?" he asked. "The mask!"

Basil glanced back at the gilded mask. He shrugged. "What about it?"

"Didn't you see—," Abbott began.

"See what?" Lt. Ford asked.

"I thought I saw eyes in the mask staring back at me," Abbott said.

Mannix smirked. "I kind of had a feeling there would be eyes staring out of that thing sooner or later."

Abbott sighed, lowering himself back on the steps. "I need a good stiff drink."

"I know the feeling," said Lt. Ford. He gestured at Skorzeny. "So, come on, spill it, Rathbone, what's the connection between Skorzeny, the dead Nazis and the gold?"

"Well, Lieutenant," said Basil, "to begin with, this brick—"

Lugosi pushed Rathbone aside and pointed at the mask. "I know whose eyes were staring out from behind the mask," he declared dramatically.

"You do?" remarked Lt. Ford, arms akimbo.

Lugosi turned to gloat at the affronted Basil Rathbone. "They were mine."

"Oh, that's a good trick, how did you manage that?" Rathbone asked, sarcastically.

"I do not mean the eyes now are mine, I mean the eyes once before, they were mine."

Abbott looked up, confused. "I think you've been hanging around Lou too long," he groaned.

Lugosi gestured around him. "Many things in this house look familiar, because they *are* familiar, because they are set pieces from my films."

"Really?" Basil sighed impatiently.

"Yes, really," Lugosi sneered. "That mask, I recognize it now! In one of my RKO pictures with Lionel Atwill, it was an ornament on the wall of a spook house and I watched Alan Carney and Wally Brown from behind that very mask."

"It's from *She*, actually," commented Basil.

"What?"

"The mask, it's a prop from the 1935 film version of H. Rider Haggard's *She*. I recognized it earlier. Apparently your film borrowed it."

Balling up his fists, Lugosi fumed, "There is a Hungarian phrase for a man like you, Rathbone."

"Really? Do tell."

Before Bela could elaborate further, the crime scene photographer ran up the cellar stairs, pointing excitedly. "Hey, you guys, check out the basement! Those glass coffins; there're people, real live people in 'em!"

"Aha!" said Lugosi, "Just as I say before, those freezing cabinets in the basement, they are from *The Black Cat*. Just as I told Costello at the diner—" Bela started, suddenly realizing the implication of the photographer's discovery. He grabbed the man by the lapels and shook him. "These people, is one of them a woman with dark hair?" He reached into his tuxedo jacket and showed the photographer Lillian's picture. "Is it this woman?"

"Yeah, that's her all right. There's another girl there, too, a pretty blonde"

Abbott jumped to his feet. "They got Dee Dee, too!"

Lugosi smiled triumphantly. "Yes! Remember, Mannix, the neighbor man said he saw her here earlier this evening." Bela addressed the photographer again. "Is there also a short bald man?"

"Yeah," said the photographer, nodding.

Lugosi smiled. "That has to be Bobby Barber!" He hurried to the basement, pausing at the door. "That is why the kidnappers kidnapped them! They needed other living bodies in case they had to prove to the Nazis that the waking up process, it works on more than one person! Bela the Detective, he has figured out everything!" He grabbed the crime scene photographer by the arm. "Quickly, take me to them!"

"Please," Abbott begged, "you gotta let me go down there and make sure Dee Dee's okay."

Ford slapped Abbott on the back. "Okay, but get down there fast before Lugosi sets off another one of those booby traps!"

They arrived in time to see Lugosi raging at the photographer. "WHERE IS LIL-LIAN? You said she was here!" He glared at the frost-covered mannequin held in place inside the freezing cabinet by bands of copper clamped across the ribcage, knees and left wrist. The mannequin wore a polka dot dress. The right sleeve was pinned up to the shoulder because the right arm of the mannequin had been amputated. "Can you not tell the difference between a dummy and my wife?"

"There was a real live woman in there," the photographer insisted. "I swear she was right there! And she had both arms! I even got pictures to prove it! She was just as real as those other guys!"

The photographer pointed at the other cases containing the unconscious bodies of Bobby Barber and Joe Glaston.

Bud Abbott hurried to the glass coffin containing Dee Dee Polo and searched around for a latch.

"Help me!" he pleaded as Lt. Ford, Mickey and the cops hurried into the room. He banged on the glass in frustration. "Quick, get her out of there!"

"Get outta the way," Mickey said, as he grabbed a nightstick from one of the cops and swung it at the cabinet. Frosted over glass shattered. Abbott stepped inside and he and Mickey worked to undo the *Bride of Frankenstein*-like copper bands that held Dee Dee upright in the coffin. They soon had her sitting down next to the shivering Bobby Barber and Joe Glaston. "You okay, Miss?" Mickey asked, patting her face until she came around.

Dee Dee nodded. "S-s-so c-c-cold," she gasped as Bud hugged her.

"I'll warm you up," Mickey volunteered, and gave Dee Dee's arms and legs a good rub down.

Dee Dee slapped his face. "Fresh!" she chastised.

"I guess you're feeling better," said Mick, rubbing his cheek.

The coroner gave them a quick once-over and said to the Lieutenant, "They're just frosty around the edges. They'll be fine."

Basil reached inside the cabinet and applied a gentle push, revealing the back of the cabinet pivoted on a center axis.

Barber asked, "W-w-what happened? H-how did I g-g-get here?"

"Don't you remember?" asked Mickey.

"N-n-no," Barber said through chattering teeth. "L-l-last thing I r-r-remember, I w-w-was t-t-talking to Lou on the ph-ph-phone."

Ford said, "Come on, we'll get you guys some hot coffee." He turned to one of the cops. "With all those patrol cars outside, there are bound to be coffee and donuts somewhere." Ford turned to his partner. "Mickey, get their statements."

"Sure thing, Fred." Mickey helped Barber and Glaston to their feet while Abbott took charge of Dee Dee. "Come on. You'll catch your death down here."

"Y-y-you c-c-can say th-th-that ag-g-g-gain," chattered Barber.

"G-g-g-good," Glaston said, "I f-f-feel like I'm a f-f-frozen g-g-ghost!"

Dee Dee began to cry as Bud hurried to wrap her in a parka. "Mike, Lou's accountant, h-h-he put a rag over m-m-my n-n-nose. Th-th-that's all I remember! It was horrible!"

"Don't worry, Miss," said Lt. Ford, "we'll find the bastard that did this."

Lugosi gestured irritably. "Stop standing around and go look for my wife!"

"Take it easy, Lugosi," Ford said. "If she's in this joint, we'll find her, even if we have to tear it down brick by brick."

"BAH!"

Rathbone had taken the policeman's nightstick from Mickey to break the glass imprisoning Lillian's dummy. As he made a closer examination of its features, he observed aloud, "Her face is a perfect likeness, as if it had been cast from Lillian's face."

Lugosi shoved him aside. "Of course this was cast from her face! We are dealing with men who are masters of disguise!"

"Did you notice the dummy is missing an arm?"

Lugosi glared at him. "Yes, I did! They obviously used the dummy to make the substitution." He felt around the back of the cabinet. "There must be a secret panel."

"To borrow the magician's exclamation—" Basil reached inside the cabinet and applied a gentle push, revealing the back of the cabinet pivoted on a center axis. "*Voila!*" Beyond was a hidden passage. "Lillian's disappearing act revealed." Pausing in the doorway, he said cheerily, "Shall we investigate?" and stepped through the hidden revolving door.

Lugosi shook with stifled rage. "I am going to kill that man one day!" He stepped through the secret door and found Basil examining other dummy replicas strapped to the backs of the other cabinets.

"Just as I thought," Rathbone said. "Note that each of these dummies is an amputee." He pointed to the motors that worked the illusion. "Our magician was able to stage the apparent recovery and restoration of his hibernating test subjects with this simple illusion."

Lugosi gestured impatiently down the passageway. "Stop playing around and help me find Lillian!" He glanced down at the dirt floor. "Look! Those tracks, they were made by the wheels of a gurney! Lillian is this way!"

Basil gave Lugosi a cocky smile. "I must be rubbing off on you." He gestured ahead. "Step lively now."

Lugosi glowered.

The passage was buttressed like a mineshaft and lit by work lights strung along the rafters. It followed the contours of the foundation and opened into a makeshift operating room. On an instrument tray Bela saw a glass syringe. He reached for it only to have Rathbone snatch it away.

"Not getting any ideas, are we?" he scolded, holding the syringe out of reach.

Bela snarled. "No, Rathbone, I am not getting ideas about injecting myself! But I am getting ideas that Lillian and the others, they were drugged here!"

"Yes, my thoughts exactly," said Basil, examining a small bottle. "This appears to be a hypnotic of some sort. It seems whoever took Lillian, they made sure she would remain passive."

There were exits leading down two passageways. Lugosi pointed to the one on the left. "The kidnapper, he took Lillian this way! See, the tire marks say so!"

"Bela, wait!" Rathbone cautioned, but to no avail. Bela plunged ahead and literally stumbled into a dead end. He tripped over something and fell into a rectangular depression in the floor. Struggling to get up, Bela grabbed a dangling control box and accidentally depressed a red button. The sound of machinery starting up was followed by a humming noise.

"BELA!" Basil shouted in alarm, pointing up. "Above you! Get out of there!"

Lugosi looked up at a rectangular platform the size of the depression he was lying in as it came pressing down. He let go of the control box and tried to scramble out. The platform was nearly on top of him. Lugosi was halfway out when the platform threatened to cut his body in half. Rathbone grabbed Bela's arm and dragged him to safety.

Lt. Ford's voice echoed from somewhere behind them, "Hey, where the hell are you guys?"

"Right here, Lieutenant," Rathbone called, helping Lugosi to his feet. "Are you all right?"

"Of course Bela is all right!" Lugosi insisted, brushing himself off. "I merely tripped on something."

"You mean, *someone*," Basil corrected as Ford appeared at the entrance.

"Who the hell is that?" the Lieutenant asked, pointing at a dead body near the elevator platform.

Basil rolled the body over.

Lugosi started. "That is Lou Costello's accountant!"

Lt. Ford gestured at the body. "So, if that's Costello's accountant and the rest of the gang is dead upstairs, who the hell took Lugosi's wife?"

"A very good question, Lieutenant," Rathbone said, straightening up. He pointed at the trap door overhead. "He, whoever *he* is, obviously escaped that way." The sleuth gestured at the platform. "Obviously the funeral home fronted for rum running during prohibition. The elevator's original purpose, no doubt, was to smuggle beer barrels down here in the tunnels. The kidnapper used it to escape with Lillian while she was still strapped to a gurney."

"It was Bela who discovered it!" Lugosi peevishly pointed out.

"Yes," said Basil, rolling his eyes, "Lugosi stumbled upon it and, uh, he found it quite a pressing matter."

"What do you think's up there?" Ford asked.

"Shall we find out?" said Basil with an inviting gesture. "There's room enough on the platform for all of us."

Basil pushed the green UP button. Bela felt unsteady on his feet as the platform was set into motion. A looped railing on either side of the elevator pushed open the doors in the ceiling, which became the floor of a carriage house converted into a modern day garage. They found Dee Dee's car hidden under a tarp. Parked alongside it was a hearse. Lugosi opened the rear door, expecting to see his wife. "She is not here!" he exclaimed, then noted bullet holes riddling the side. "Look," he said, "this hearse, there is only one place where it could have gotten these bullet holes; it was on the back lot during the gun battle."

"So that's where they transferred the bodies," said Ford. "Pretty smart. Nobody's gonna search a hearse."

Basil nodded. "The carriage house and elevator provide the perfect cover."

Lt. Ford spotted something. "Hey, what do you think made that?"

Bela and Basil followed Ford to a jagged hole made in the wall at the rear of the carriage house. The Lieutenant stood in the makeshift doorway and raised his derby until the crown touched the topmost part of the hole. "That's gotta be a good eight feet," the Lieutenant figured.

Basil examined the hole, and then pointed outside. "Good heavens. Are those what I think they are?"

Ford turned around and noted a trail of large depressions in the ground. They led to a broken fence and a certain neighbor's crushed flower bed. Bela walked in the depressions. "I am six foot tall, and yet these footprints were made by a man with a greater stride."

Ford marched in the depressions behind Lugosi. "And the guy was wearing square toed shoes, too."

Lugosi pointed at the neighbor's yard. "The neighbor man complained of a monster that trampled his flower bed."

Rathbone smirked. "Perhaps we ought to put out an APB on Frankenstein. I hope Glenn Strange has an alibi."

Lugosi snarled. "Very funny. Big joke."

"Now, now, boys," interjected Ford, "let's all play nice." He pointed back at the carriage house. "I think I saw the garage doors ajar. Maybe whoever took Mrs. Lugosi escaped out that way."

Lt. Ford led the way back to the garage and opened the carriage house doors wider. "See? He tried to get out this way, but look." He pointed at the two Volkswagens blocking the driveway. "There's no way he could drive that hearse outta here, and my heap's blocking the Kraut cars."

Eddie Mannix was standing at the end of the driveway and fit to be tied. "Damn it," he exclaimed, "I left my engine runnin' and my baby right here!" He waved at where his car *used* to be.

Bela lingered by the two Volkswagens and looked at the tires. "These tires," he said, "they are not from the War. The rubber, it is too good."

"Screw the tires!" Mannix raged. "Where's my goddamn car?"

Lugosi ignored him and examined the tires more closely. "They look as though they are extra heavy to carry a great deal more weight than a regular car."

Lt. Ford tried to humor him. "Well, those Nazis *did* use the cars to transport their gold, didn't they?"

"Yes, but look at the tires now. They appear as though they still carry a heavy load. See, the tires are low to the ground."

"So the tires need air, so what? Maybe some kids let the air out."

Lugosi glowered. "You are not fun to deduce with."

Mannix stormed up to them. "Does anybody give a damn that that bastard stole my car?"

Bela glared at him. "He stole your car and my wife, Mannix! You can buy a new car, but I cannot buy a new wife!"

Mannix was taken aback and then gave a slight shrug. "Actually—," he began. But Lugosi wasn't listening; he was following the gurney tracks left in the mud beside the driveway.

"Look," Bela observed, "the wheels stop where your car used to be."

Lt. Ford pointed at something in the bushes. "Here it is." He stepped in and rolled the gurney out.

Bela looked up at Mannix and Ford in alarm. "That means he took Lillian away in Mannix's car!"

"No shit, Sherlock," Mannix grumbled. "I coulda told you *that!*"

Lt. Ford turned to Basil. "Well, Rathbone, where do you think—" Once again the Lieutenant was talking to thin air. "Now where'd he go?"

They hurried back to the garage and found the trap doors closed over the elevator shaft. Mannix asked, "Hey, you don't suppose somebody kidnapped Rathbone?"

Lugosi muttered under his breath, "We should only be so fortunate." He hunted for the buttons that ran the elevator and found the controls hanging from a wooden support. "I fear he has merely gone snooping on his own." He pushed the UP button.

The elevator slowly appeared. "Well, ain't that somethin'?" Mannix marveled. Bela stepped aboard the platform and gestured for the tough guy to join him.

Lt. Ford said, "While you guys look for Rathbone, I'll put out an APB on the car."

"Never mind that," complained Bela. "Call the other police and tell them all to be on the lookout for the car that has my wife!" He pushed the red DOWN button.

"Okay," Ford said with a smile. "Whatever you say." As the doors closed over them, Ford added reassuringly, "Don't worry, Lugosi; we'll get your wife back."

Down in the underground passage, Lugosi doubled back to the operating theater with Mannix following close behind. They turned down the second tunnel and soon found themselves in a combination machine shop and electronics lab. Lugosi glared at Rathbone, who was examining hardware piled up on a draftsman's table.

"Stopping to admire the scenery, are you?" Bela scolded.

"Ah, Bela, Mannix," he said, picking up a vacuum tube, "have a look at this. It seems someone was dabbling in short wave radio electronics."

Mannix had a look-see around. "Yeah, it's somethin', all right." He reached into a box of freshly milled gears. "I'll bet this is where Dr. Fell rigged up that mechanical hand."

Lugosi glared angrily at the two amateur sleuths. "My wife is out there somewhere! This is no time for you two to be puttering around!"

"I am not puttering," Basil insisted. "There may be vital clues about the identity and intentions of the man who took her." He gestured at a series of maps hanging on one wall. "For instance," he said, pointing to one map, "does this remind you of anything?"

"Should it?"

"Hey," said Mannix. "These look like the blueprints Goetz had drawn up when he bought Universal Studios. Those are the plans for the Lubin Lake Frankenstein set."

"Very good," said Basil. "See there? Those red marks? Each 'X' represents the location of a fire bomb."

In spite of himself, Lugosi studied the map. "There are two green 'X's in the middle of the lake," he observed.

"Precisely," Basil said, taking on a didactic tone as he asked, "so what do those 'X's represent?"

Bela irritably jabbed his index finger at the map. "That is where the television camera is."

"Exactly," Basil said. "But what about this *other* 'X'? There wasn't a camera there, and no fire bomb. So what does *this* 'X' represent?"

"How should I know?"

"Why, the only way to know, my dear Lugosi. By hunting for clues." Basil surveyed the room with the eye of a general planning his strategy. "I'll take *these* filing cabinets; you have a look over there; Mannix, over there."

Bela slunk to the opposite side of the room, grumbling to himself, "How did I suddenly become the damn Watson again?"

There were metal shelves teaming with electronics gear, tubes, potentiometers, motors and pulleys of all sorts. To Bela, it was all just a jumble of bizarre-looking gimmicks and doodads, until he spotted a black metal box with a series of buttons on the top and two metal straps bolted to the bottom. It was just like Dr. Alex Zorka's robot control box from *The Phantom Creeps*. Bela glanced up at the ceiling, remembering the hole made in the back of the carriage house. "It cannot be," he muttered as he slipped the device on his forearm. He was about to try the push-buttons when a long wolf-whistle startled him. Bela's eyes darted to Lt. Ford, who stood at the entrance to the room.

"Wow, will ya look at this place?" Lt. Ford marveled.

"Ah, Lieutenant!" Basil said as he examined a roll of blueprints. "Have a look at these, will you?"

Mannix joined Basil and the Lieutenant. "What are those, plans for Buck Rogers' rocket pack?"

"Something nearly as advanced." Basil unrolled the plans on the draftsman's table, using various bits of electronics to keep the blueprints from rolling back up. "Dr. Fell, or whoever our mastermind is, appears to have been working with radio waves and feedback loops." Basil smiled with mock humility. "Mind you, I'm not really an expert on reading schematic diagrams —"

"Amazing," Lugosi jeered as he randomly pushed buttons on the robot control box. "The Master Detective admits there is something he does not know."

Basil cleared his throat and referred to the plans. "If I didn't know better, I'd think these described some kind of guidance system." He directed Lt. Ford's attention to one of the symbols. "See that? I think that represents a gyroscope, and these symbols are the motors that work some kind of steering mechanism." He looked up at Bela. "Why don't you have a look at these, too, Bel —"

Lugosi glared at the three men who were staring at him in slack-jawed astonishment. "Why do you all look at me that way?" he demanded.

"Behind you," Mannix warned.

Lugosi frowned, suddenly aware of the sound of creaking hinges. Turning around, he saw one of the shelves swinging open, revealing a hidden closet, and standing inside it was the eight-foot-tall, bulbous-headed, jagged-toothed, flat-nosed, bug-eyed, heavy-lidded Iron Man from *The Phantom Creeps!*

Lugosi was justifiably annoyed. "BAH! It is just another movie prop," he complained. "But it does explain about the monster." He pointed at the robot's built up shoes. "You see, mud and crushed flowers. And I know only one suspect big enough to wear this costume." He shook his finger angrily at the automaton. "Strange, is that you in there? Show yourself!"

Mannix grabbed a stool and edged up to the robot, poking it with the wooden legs. When the robot didn't react, Mannix waved his hand before its sightless glaring eyes.

"I don't think there's anybody home," he said.

Basil and the Lieutenant cautiously approached. "I say, Bela," Rathbone said, pointing at the control box, "Push another button."

"Why? This control box, it is just a prop, and the robot just a costume."

"I'm not so sure of that. Go ahead, push a button," Rathbone urged.

"Very well, but it is a waste of valuable time."

Bela vaguely remembered how he as Zorka worked the control box, and flicked the toggle switch that was supposed to activate the robot and twisted a knob. The Iron Man responded by advancing as it lashed its pleated rubber arms about, smashing the stool in Mannix's hands.

Lugosi quickly deactivated the robot.

"Damn it, Lugosi," the tough guy complained. "Watch what you're doin'!"

Mannix shielded himself with what remained of the broken stool...

"Shut up," Bela snarled. "This is not so easy to do as I remember."

After fiddling with the controls, and as Mannix shielded himself with what remained of the broken stool, the Iron Man took action much as it did when actor and former circus giant Ed Wolff was inside the costume. It marched forward like a giant windup tin soldier, walking stiffly, swinging its arms. Bela twisted a knob and the robot turned to the right. Twisting the knob to the left, the robot marched to the left, moving in ever widening circles, a mindless puppet.

"Remarkable," Basil said. "Someone has actually equipped the costume with real radio controlled electronics."

Lugosi scoffed, "What good is it to have an Iron Man made of rubber and plastic? It is little more than an oversized toy."

Mannix watched the robot with amusement. "It sure spooked that guy with the shotgun."

Lt. Ford pointed at the rooms above. "It also made a real nice hole in the garage wall."

"So it would seem." Rathbone glanced back at the blueprints on the draftsman's table. "I think there may be another reason besides scaring the neighbors for making this a practical robot."

"How do you mean?" asked Mannix.

Rathbone referred to the plans. "It's quite possible the robot was an early prototype to test the feasibility of a more sophisticated guidance control system."

"A control system to guide what?" Lugosi asked.

"A very good question," mused Basil.

Mannix grabbed Bela's arm and pointed. "Stop it, Lugosi," he warned.

and the House of Doom

The robot's circular marching brought it too near the wall; its swinging arms threatened to pull down the shelves.

"I forget which button turns it off," Bela exclaimed, flipping toggle switches and pushing buttons at random. His fiddling only made the robot's arms wave about wildly, knocking boxes of electronics onto the floor.

Basil pointed. "Try that button, quickly!"

Lugosi snarled, "Who played Zorka, you or me?" as the mechanical giant crashed blindly into the shelving and sent another gizmo clattering to the floor. "I think it is this switch," he said.

The robot's arms dropped limply to its sides as one of the gizmos it knocked to the floor gave off a series of static clicking noises.

"What is that thing?" Lugosi asked, slipping the control box off his forearm. He picked up the clicking box. It had a meter with a needle jumping in time to the clicks, a handgrip on the top, and something like a microphone clipped to the side. He shook it, and the microphone came off. "I think I broke it," he said.

Basil grabbed the device away testily and examined it. His eyebrows arched with alarm. "This is a Geiger counter!"

Lt. Ford examined the device. "What do these characters need with a Geiger counter?"

"I don't know," said Basil, "but earlier, Dr. Fell said the glass in the basement control room was impregnated with lead, supposedly to shield against radiation from his de-animator, but perhaps to really guard against something else."

"Hey," said Mannix, pointing at a cabinet, "I don't know if this means anything, but I found a bunch of film cans in that cabinet over there."

"Film cans?" Rathbone asked.

Lugosi went to the cabinet and examined the flat, round cans and the titles written on tape along their sides. "These titles, they are my films," he said. "Here are all the episodes of *The Phantom Creeps*, as well as *Chandu the Magician*, and — AHA! *Dark Eyes of London* and *Bowery at Midnight*."

"Obviously our mastermind has questionable tastes." Basil pointed the wand toward the robot; the Geiger counter reacted wildly. He pointed the wand away, and the clicking slowed.

Bela glowered, taking umbrage at Basil's careless remark. "Not all of these are *my* films," Lugosi pointed out. "These films, they are German. Two of them are Fritz Lang's films, *Dr. Mabuse the Gambler* and *The Testament of Dr. Mabuse*. He is a quality director who made quality films! Bela's films are in good company."

Lt. Ford frowned. "Dr. Mabuse? Never heard of him."

"The *Dr. Mabuse* films concerned a criminal mastermind," Basil offhandedly explained as he studied the back lot map. "He used hypnotism and other science fiction methods in his attempts to take over the world." He frowned questioningly and glanced back at the *Phantom Creeps* Iron Man. "Much as Lugosi's character, Zorka."

Lugosi spotted something under the drafting table and deliberately shoved Rathbone. "Stand aside," he commanded.

"Excuse you," Basil huffed, approaching the Iron Man with the Geiger counter.

Lt. Ford joined him. "You mean this guy is getting his crazy schemes from movie thrillers?"

"Possibly," said Basil, running the wand of the Geiger counter along the Iron Man's pleated arm. He noted the clicking sounds grew more intense near its metal hands. "This robot has been handling atomic material."

"What kind of atomic material?" Ford asked.

Bela grunted. "Perhaps it is this kind," he said, dragging out a heavy metal box. He heaved it onto the drafting table with a decided thud and another well deserved grunt. The box had PROPERTY OF ATOMIC ENERGY COMMISSION stenciled on the side. "You see there?" Bela said. "It says *atomic*. But I do not know what this other thing means." He pointed at the lid with DANGER FISSILE MATERIAL stenciled on it.

"You got me, Dracula," Mannix said as he felt along the metal box. "But you're right. This thing is made of lead." He grabbed the lid. "Hey, it's unlocked!"

"Don't open that!" Basil warned as he hurried with the Geiger counter. He ran the wand over the box and took a reading. "This is a container for transporting radioactive isotopes. It might still be lethal." He checked the meter on the counter. "The levels seem safe enough." He placed his hands on the lid. "Stand back — just in case I'm wrong." As everyone stood well back, Rathbone cautiously raised the lid while keeping an eye on the Geiger counter needle. "Radiation appears negligible," he said, and looked inside.

From behind the Iron Man, Lugosi said hotly, "Well? Stop milking the scene and tell us what you find!"

Basil announced as he fully raised the lid. "It's empty — now."

As the others approached, Bela looked inside and noted from the depression in the packing material lining the lid and bottom of the box, that it once held something roughly cylindrical in shape. Bela waved dismissively. "The iso-whatever-you-call-it, it is not very big. What harm could it do?"

With a worried expression, Basil approached the map of Lubin Lake. "A great deal of harm, if my suspicions are correct." He asked, "You read what it said on the lid, didn't you, about fissile material?"

"Yes. What is that?" asked Bela.

"It's the kind of isotope you would need for a gun-type fission bomb."

Mannix swallowed hard. "A fission bomb?" he asked.

Ford pointed at the case. "You mean like what they dropped on Japan?"

Lugosi nodded with dawning grim understanding. "An atomic bomb," he said.

They all gazed intently at the map as apprehension gripped their hearts.

"Hey, Fred," Mickey called from the doorway, making everyone jump. Ford whirled around and growled, "Don't do that!"

Mickey jerked a thumb behind him. "Sorry, but there's a phone call for Lugosi."

Bela frowned. "A phone call? Who knows that I am here?"

"Hey," said Mannix, "maybe it's Louie. I told him we wuz on our way over here."

"I dunno who it is," Mickey said, "but the guy says it's important. You can take it on the wall phone in the freezer." He led the way back to the mad scientist lab and handed Bela the receiver.

Putting the receiver to his ear, Lugosi said into the mouthpiece, "Who is this?"

There was a crackle of static as a familiar German-accented voice said, "This is Dr. Kopf."

"Kopf!" Lugosi exclaimed.

"I suspected as much," said Basil.

Bela leered at Rathbone. "How could you have suspected Kopf was behind this?" he challenged.

"It's the only explanation for how Lillian escaped her captors and yet still found herself a prisoner here. She went to the only person she felt she could go to for help."

"Of course," said Lugosi.

"If that bastard scratches my paintjob—," threatened Mannix.

Lt. Ford covered the mouthpiece. "Ask him what he wants."

"And keep 'im talkin'," Mannix whispered. "That radio phone drains the car battery. He'll stall, and then we can catch him easy."

Lugosi spoke into the mouthpiece. "What do you want, Kopf, if that is your real name."

"To make a trade; your wife in exchange for the gold."

Bela covered the mouthpiece. "He wants the gold and he has Lillian!"

Lt. Ford whispered, "Arrange to make the drop."

"To do what?"

"The drop, you know, to get him his gold."

Lugosi nodded and said to Kopf, "Where do you wish us to make for you the drop?"

"Put the bags of gold in the Volkswagens and drive the Volkswagens to the studio. You will drive one of them—"

"I cannot drive," Lugosi interrupted.

Dr. Kopf sighed irritably. "Then *Herr* Mannix will drive and you will accompany him. *Herr* Rathbone will drive the other Volkswagen."

Lugosi's eyes narrowed with suspicion. "Wouldn't police cars be better?" he asked craftily.

"No!" Kopf insisted. "Bring the gold in the Volkswagens. Leave both cars with their engines running outside soundstage number 17. Once I have the gold, I will tell you where your wife is hidden."

Lugosi covered the mouthpiece. "He wants us to bring the gold in the German cars. He insists we use *only* the German cars."

"I don't get it," said Mickey. "How's he gonna drive two cars by himself? His gang is dead."

"Perhaps we should ask him," Lugosi peevishly suggested, and barked into the mouthpiece, "How are you going to drive two cars alone?"

"You will have my robot accompany you. It will drive the other car."

"That big thing? It will never fit."

Again, Dr. Kopf sighed irritably. "Take off the head—it's only decorative—and remove the built-up shoes. They are not needed to operate a car."

"Fine, we take off the head and the shoes."

Mickey started in alarm. "Who's head and shoes?"

Bela hushed him as Kopf instructed further, "And bring *Herr* Skorzeny with you. Leave him handcuffed on the rear seat and put the key on the dashboard."

Lugosi frowned and addressed the Lieutenant. "He says the robot will drive the other car. We take off his head and his shoes so he fits in the front seat. He also wants Janika handcuffed and left in the back seat, and the key he wants left on the dashboard."

Lt. Ford asked, "How'd he know we found his robot?"

"What robot?" Mickey asked.

"There's a robot back there."

"No foolin'? A real robot?"

"Yeah. Didn't you notice it?"

Lugosi cleared his throat irritably. "Did you hear me say that Kopf wants Janika handcuffed in the back seat?"

Mickey put his hand over the mouthpiece. "Say," he whispered, "maybe this is Kopf's way of makin' Skorzeny look like a patsy, when really the guy's an accomplice."

Ford nodded. "Yeah, maybe that's the real reason Skorzeny killed those other three guys; so they go from a four-way split to fifty-fifty."

"It's the oldest con in the book," Mickey said.

Lugosi glowered. "The man is waiting on the telephone!"

"Let him wait," said Mannix. "The car battery, remember?"

"He has Lillian!"

Lt. Ford took Mickey's hand off the mouthpiece. "Hey, Kopf, this is Lt. Ford. We'll do whatever you want, but you're gonna have to give us time to load up the gold."

"How much time do you really need? You're only sixteen minutes from the studio!"

"Yeah, but we kind of knocked Skorzeny out and then there's the bodies you left all over the joint, and we gotta dick around with the robot...."

Kopf grumbled. "Fine. How much time will you need to get here then?"

"What do you say to forty-five minutes?"

Kopf paused. "All of that *and* drive to the studio in forty-five minutes?" There was a longer pause. "I give you sixty minutes."

Ford covered the receiver. "Is sixty minutes gonna be enough?"

"To load all that gold?" asked Mickey. "Ask for an hour and a half."

Ford sighed. "I feel like we're at an auction." He uncovered the receiver. "What do you say to an hour and a half?"

"An hour and a half to load *eight suitcases?*" Kopf complained.

"Give us a break. There were eight German guys carrying them before."

"What about the other police?"

"You said no police."

"I didn't mean they couldn't help you load up the—Fine! Forget it! I don't want to argue anymore! Just get over here with the Volkswagens and the gold! If you are not here by 2:30, I will kill *Frau* Lugosi."

"I make it 2:37," Ford said, consulting his watch.

"Just get over here!"

Lugosi yanked on Ford's arm. "What did he say?"

"He says he's fine with the hour and a half, but if we're late, your wife's goose is cooked." Ford hesitated a moment, then explained, "That means he's gonna kill her."

"I know what it means!" Bela sneered. He grabbed back the handset. "Harm a hair on Lillian's head and I shall find you and kill you with my own two hands! Do you think that the Jews and the War Crimes Commission hunting you is something to worry about? They are nothing compared to how viciously Bela Lugosi shall chase you down! I am a force to be reckoned with! Do you understand?"

"You now have one hour and twenty-nine minutes," said Kopf.

"You are counting now?" Lugosi exclaimed.

Lt. Ford grabbed the receiver back. "We'll be there pronto," said Ford, and hung it up on its hook.

Lugosi turned to Mannix. "Quick, you get the keys to the car and we go."

"Wait," Basil said as he unhooked the receiver and began dialing.

"Wait for what?" Bela griped. "Time is precious, and my wife, she is in danger."

"Which is exactly why I think it's time we called for backup," said Rathbone as he listened to the ring tone.

"What kind of backup?" Lt. Ford asked.

Basil smiled. "Before you asked me whether or not I was a spy. In point of fact, I am. I work for MI6." He nodded towards the exit. "Now if you please, get the gold loaded up. I'll join you shortly."

"How dare you order me around," Lugosi snarled. "I once thought you were an honorable man, if too full of yourself. But now, you are involved in some very shady things. I do not trust you anymore."

"I'm sorry you feel that way," said Basil uncovering the mouthpiece. "Hello," he said, "this is R. One moment please." He gave Bela, Mannix and the two detectives an expectant look. "Do you mind?"

Ford nodded. "I can take a hint." He nudged Mickey.

Mickey hesitated, pointing at Ford and himself. "Maybe you ought to make us spies, too."

"Actually," said Lt. Ford, "that's not such a bad idea. Maybe we could be deputized."

Basil thought a moment. "That might be helpful, at that." He uncovered the mouthpiece. "Sir, there are two members of the Los Angeles Police Department here. They were wondering about being deputized. One is Lt. Fredrick Ford, Homicide. The other is his partner, Detective Mickey— Uh, hold on a moment, please." Basil covered the mouthpiece and whispered, "What is your last name? I'll need it to swear you in."

"Well, don't laugh, but…it's Finn."

Basil gave him a jaundiced look. "You mean to tell me your name is Mickey Finn?"

"Yeah," Detective Finn admitted. "Just no wisecracks, okay, I heard 'em all."

"You have my word." He uncovered the mouthpiece. "Detective Mickey Finn, sir." He paused. "No, I'm not joking." He nodded. "Yes, just like the knockout drops," he confirmed with a sigh.

Mickey asked hopefully, "Ask your boss if we get secret decoder pins."

Basil glared incredulously. "I'm afraid Little Orphan Annie has cornered the market on secret decoder pins."

"Aw, that's too bad."

Lt. Ford grabbed his partner's arm. "Will you come on? We gotta get that gold loaded up." As they hurried up the stairs, Bela could hear Ford scold, "Why do you have to embarrass me like that for?"

Basil eyed Mannix and Lugosi. "If you don't mind, gentlemen…"

Mannix turned to Lugosi. "Come on."

"Please leave us alone," Lugosi said. "I will be up in a moment and I will bring with me the Iron Man. It can load the gold better."

"Good idea. That'll save time—and our backs," Mannix said, and headed up the stairs.

"Really, Bela," Basil insisted, "I need you to leave."

Bela put his hand over the mouthpiece and stared earnestly. "You may think that I am just an old man who likes too much his medicine, but I know the ways of secret police. They do not care who gets hurt so long as their mission, it is accomplished. To men such as you, the regular people, they are only pawns. So know this, Mr. British Intelligence Agent; my wife and son, they are not your pawns. I expect them to be returned to me alive and well. If they are not...."

Bela left the sentence hanging unfinished in the frosty air.

Chapter 19

The Iron Man carried the suitcases of gold with ease. Bela stood by the second Volkswagen, working the remote control, steering the marching automaton to the front luggage compartment.

Mannix smiled. "You work that thing pretty good." Basil emerged from the carriage house. Mannix waved him over. "Hey, Rathbone, watch this."

Lugosi pushed one of the white buttons and turned the knob, directing the robot to load the last of the luggage and close the trunk hatch. "The controls," Bela said, "they work exactly as they do in my picture."

"That's not surprising," said Basil with a smirk. "I suspect whoever made the robot obsessively analyzed every frame of *The Phantom Creeps* to get the buttons on the remote control wired up just that way."

Pushing another button and flicking a toggle switch, Bela caused the robot to stand at attention. "The Iron Man is very strong in spite of the rubber suit." Lugosi cynically eyed the robot. "Why would Fell even bother to cover it with what is nothing more than a masquerade costume?"

Mannix shrugged. "Maybe to scare off nosy neighbors." He spied Connor watching them from behind his backyard fence and pointed. "It sure rattled that guy pretty good."

Basil gestured back at the carriage house. "I had another look in the tunnels. There's a fully stocked makeup studio down there. In fact, Bela, I must congratulate you."

Bela cast Basil a suspicious leer. "For what?"

Basil pulled a foam rubber mask from his pocket. "Your deductions earlier. I found this amongst a collection of other masks. Does this face look familiar?" He slipped it on over his head and adjusted the eye and mouth holes. The mask covered Basil's head and shoulders. He tucked the ends in his shirt collar, completing the illusion of a whole new identity. "Well?" he asked.

Mannix frowned and shook his head. "Don't ring a bell with me. How about you, Lugosi?"

Bela knew the face the instant he saw the blond hair. "That is the face of the blond ambulance man," he said. "The one who struck me. It is exactly as I said; Dr. Fell, he was the other kidnapper!"

Basil smiled beneath the mask; the foam rubber matched his facial muscles perfectly. "Incredible, isn't it? Even close up, you can't tell the difference, particularly if you use spirit gum to adhere the edges of the eye and mouth openings to the skin." He gestured at the foam rubber neck. "This part helped to conceal his neck and body brace. Brilliant, really."

Basil was interrupted by an audible electronic whine that issued from somewhere deep inside the robot. The mechanical man's arms began to spastically twitch.

Mannix jerked his thumb at the machine. "What's wrong with him?" he asked.

"I do not know," Bela said, checking the settings on the control box. "But the robot, it has gone hayseed before."

Basil tugged on Bela's arm. "You mean *haywire*, and keep back."

The robot twitched and fidgeted and sparked for several minutes. Its waving metal hand put a scratch in the Volkswagen's paint job. Then just as suddenly, it stopped its paroxysmal boogie-woogie and resumed its rigid stance, its mechanism humming steadily.

Lt. Ford hurried up the driveway. "I just put in a call to Headquarters. On a hunch I checked to see if the other studios around town filed complaints about missing props."

Bill Connor ran at them with his shotgun—and he looked like he was ready to shoot something.

The Lieutenant took swift action. "Hold it right there, pal," he warned as he drew his weapon and took aim. "Drop it!"

Connor—like O'Connor without the O—turned pale and did as he was told, throwing his shotgun on the ground and putting his hands up. "I didn't mean no harm," he hastily explained, nodding at the robot. "I thought you were being attacked by the monster."

Mannix chuckled. "We owe you an apology, friend," he said. "Turns out there really is a monster, but it's harmless."

"Didn't look so harmless to me," Connor said, keeping his hands up, "not the way it was waving its arms around like that." He indicated his weapon with a nod. "That's why I ran to get my shotgun."

Ford holstered his weapon and waved. "Put your hands down," he said.

Connor relaxed and pointed at his gun. "Do you mind?" he asked.

"Yeah, just watch where you point that thing."

Connor collected his weapon and warily approached the robot. "What the hell is it really?" he asked, poking the Iron Man with the barrel of his shotgun.

"A robot," explained Basil nonchalantly.

"No kiddin'," Connor said.

Ford stared at what he thought was a stranger. "Say, who is this mug?" he asked.

Mannix smirked. "Yeah, he sounds enough like Basil Rathbone to *be* Basil Rathbone."

"He sure does," said Lt. Ford.

Basil smiled. "Mannix is having you on, Lieutenant," he said, pulling the mask off and smoothing down his mussed hair. "It's me." He handed Ford the mask.

"Wow," the Lieutenant said, slipping his hand in the mask and wiggling his fingers out the eye holes. "This thing sure is realistic."

"I found a whole cache of Dr. Fell's masks in the tunnels."

"You don't say."

Lugosi became grim. "That would suggest Westmore or one of his assistants is in the cahoots with Fell."

"Not necessarily." Basil took back the mask. "The supplies I found appear to have all been *stolen* from Universal's makeup department." His eyes narrowed. "This would suggest something impossible; that a dead man may be our prime suspect."

"A dead man?" Connor asked nervously.

"What do you mean by that?" asked Lugosi.

"The serial numbers on Dr. Kopf's wrist, they belonged to a Fredek Vivas, a makeup and special effects man for the UFA film studios."

Ford said, "That sounds like a pretty good suspect to me."

"Yes, except Vivas was gassed, a victim of the Final Solution."

"You don't say," said Mannix. "So if them numbers belonged to a dead guy named Vivas, how'd Kopf get hold of 'em?"

"Elementary," said Rathbone. "Only one man could have obtained those numbers—the Nazi scientist who condemned Vivas to death, Dr. Sigmund Rache, alias Miss Skorzeny's now infamous *Doktor Halál*. So obviously, Dr. Kopf, Dr. Rache, and *Doktor Halál* are all one and the same person."

Connor scratched the back of his head. "What kind of crazy nonsense are you all talking about?"

"Do not interrupt," Lugosi retorted. He glared at Rathbone, pointing back at the funeral home. "Janika just killed the man he said was *Doktor Halál*. If *that* man in there was not *Doktor Halál*, then who was the man pretending to be Dr. Fell without the arm?"

"I'm sure I don't know," said Basil. "But one thing is certain; our perpetrator had access to Universal's prop and makeup departments, which would explain where he obtained the outer shell for our mechanical friend here."

"Universal isn't the only place missing stuff," said Ford, referring to his notebook. "RKO had some of their haunted house gimmicks stolen and," he said, nodding at the Iron Man, "Republic Pictures is missing a bunch of tin robot suits."

Connor frowned. "Do you mean to say there are more of these things stomping around someplace?"

Changing the subject, Basil asked Ford, "Were *you* able to find out anything concerning our late miscreants?"

"So far, Headquarters was only able to pull up priors on Costello's accountant." Ford consulted his notebook. "He's an embezzler with a record a mile long, and he's got a dozen aliases. As far as getting the straight dope about our one-armed stage magician, or the other Krauts, we'll have to wire their prints to the FBI. We won't know anything for sure for at least a week." He looked at Rathbone. "So, Mr. Secret Agent, what do you know about the dead Nazis?"

Basil glared at Ford and pointed at Connor. "Lieutenant, what part of 'secret' don't you understand?"

"Aw, he didn't hear nothing," Ford said, and asked Connor, "Did you, friend?"

"Didn't hear a thing." Connor shrugged. "Not that anybody'd believe me anyway."

"Getting back to the Nazis," Basil said, "they allegedly fled Germany with a cache of stolen Nazi gold."

"What do you mean 'allegedly'?" asked Ford. "The gold bricks are inside the house."

"On the contrary, the gold bricks in there are fakes."

"Fakes?"

"I noticed one of the gold bricks had a chip taken out of it. They're gold-plated lead ingots. The Nazis were pulling what is charmingly referred to as a 'fast one' on our mad scientist."

Lugosi brushed his hand over the scratch in the Volkswagen's trunk hatch and began chuckling.

"What are you laughing at, Lugosi?" Mannix asked. "Don't you get it? If Kopf looks too closely at them bricks, he'll think *we're* the guys pulling a fast one. Your wife's goose is cooked."

"Lillian," Lugosi said, waving confidently, "her goose will be fine."

"You seem awfully sure of yourself," Basil observed.

"You are the Great Detective, so you figure it out why I am so confident."

Ford gestured at the Volkswagens. "I just wish we had radios in them cars. I don't like us not being able to keep in touch in case we got trouble."

Bela smiled. "That will not be a problem. I have an idea."

"*You* have an idea?" Rathbone said with a smirk.

"Yes, Rathbone," Lugosi sneered. "Lugosi has an idea. And it is a good idea, too!" He turned to Ford. "You said you wanted radios in the cars so we can keep in touch, yes?"

"Yeah," said Ford. "I was thinking about tearing the sets out of a couple of squad cars, only the Chief would have my neck."

"Your neck, it will be fine." Bela smiled at Connor. "You said you were a ham radio man. Do you have radios that can be quickly installed in these cars?"

"Since it's for official business, I don't see why not."

Ford rubbed his chin thoughtfully. "Will it take long to rig up?"

"I can do it in a jiffy," Connor assured him. "It's all done with magnets. Stick the unit under the dashboard and the antenna on the roof. Then all you do is plug the radio into the cigarette lighter and you're good to go."

"Excellent," said Lugosi. "Do you have many of these radios?"

"I got all you need. I sell 'em."

"Good. We will need three radios."

Connor nodded. "I'll go get 'em."

As Connor hurried back to his house, Ford asked, "*Three* radios? Why three? There are only *two* Kraut cars."

Lugosi smiled. "Two radios for the Volkswagens," he said, pointing at the carriage house, "and one for the hearse."

Mannix frowned. "What do we need a hearse for? Unless you think we're all gonna get killed."

Bela smiled and patted the robot's arm. "We can transport the robot fully assembled in the back of the hearse rather than taking off the head and the feet as Kopf wants."

"You suspect a trap?" asked Rathbone.

"In case of trouble, I would rather we had the Iron Man on our side."

Ford nodded in agreement. "He's got a point. And while Lugosi gets iron pants tucked in, I'll get a cop to drive the hearse."

"No, Lieutenant," Rathbone insisted. "This is still a Top Secret operation; the less people involved the better." He nodded toward the house. "We'll enlist Mr. Abbott's assistance. He's already been deputized as a field agent."

Lugosi glowered. "You put a comedian in your confidence, and not Bela Lugosi?!" He shook with rage. "I am just as good a detective as you! BETTER!"

"Karloff wanted to bring you in; I opposed it."

"WHY?" Lugosi demanded.

"I felt that your annoying habit of speaking your mind when you're angry made you a security risk. You might have blown our cover."

Mannix nudged the bitter Hungarian. "He's got you there, Lugosi."

"Fine. You keep your secrets, Rathbone." Lugosi smirked at the Volkswagens. "Bela Lugosi, he has his own secrets." He turned to Ford. "May I borrow your notebook and a pen?"

Ford handed the items over. "What for?" he asked.

Bela slipped the notebook in his pocket. "You find out later," he said cryptically. He flicked a toggle switch and turned the knob on his forearm control box. The Iron Man faced him and bowed. Bela chuckled as he patted the automaton's arm with mock affection, recalling his role as Ygor in *Son of Frankenstein*. Still cackling at his private joke, Lugosi pushed another button and marched the obedient Iron Man to the carriage house.

Lt. Ford shook his head sympathetically. "The poor sap, I guess the pressure's getting to him."

Another Brief Interruption

Interior, Lugosi's Trailer
Morning

Costello crossed his arms and grinned at Bela. "Are you trying to tell me *that* wasn't all your imagination, what you said happened? Atomic bombs and an iron monster? I think you've been in too many horror pi'tures, brother."

"It is the truth," Lugosi insisted, tapping his temple. "I remember it clearly now."

"That cop was right, the pressure was gettin' to you." Lou looked to his partner. "Do you remember any of this?"

Abbott shook his head. "Me, I don't remember anything at all. If you ask me, you're both suffering from delusions."

"But you were there," Lugosi insisted. "You saw for yourself, your signature on these very pages."

Abbott shrugged helplessly. "I don't remember signing anything."

"Fine," said Costello, holding up his notes, "but I'm sticking to my version of the way things happened." He glared at Bela. "Now, if you don't mind, I'd like to go on with *my* side of it."

"Very well," Lugosi said. "Please, do enlighten us with your little comedy story."

Costello referred to his notes and related events with the dramatic delivery of a practiced storyteller, "We wuz prisoners of the lady spy and her minions and they had guns on me and Lon Chaney and Bela, Jr.," he glared at the sleeping boy, "who I wish would wake up already so he can back me up."

"Leave my son out of this."

"I wish I could, but he was right there, a prisoner of the Commies...."

Part Three
Strange Confession(s)
Chapter 20

Thursday, 26 February 1948
1:20 A.M.
Suite 204, Hollywood Knickerbocker Hotel

While Zizi slowly paced and absently twirled her diminutive revolver, the Hungarian agents surrounded the couch and kept their guns trained on their American "guests."

"Mr. Chaney tells Zizi much," Madame Z mused aloud. "Bela Lugosi, he was on back lot of studio looking for wife and son, and now Lugosi is on his way to funeral home."

Lou leaned over to Lon and whispered, "Nice goin', Mr. Loose Lips." He frowned. "Wait a minute, I didn't tell you that part about Lugosi goin' to the funeral home." He asked Madame Z, "How'd you know about it?"

Zizi smiled. "Our intelligence gathering methods are, how you say, state-of-art. We have ways of finding out many things without even leaving this room." She winked at Lon. "But sometimes I get bored and fall back on old methods just for fun."

Tovar glared at the prisoners. "Why keep these two men alive? They jeopardize our mission," he complained. "I say we kill them and dispose of bodies before someone comes looking for them."

Zizi eyed Tovar. "Are you questioning my authority?"

Tovar started. "No, Madame Z," he said, his voice trembling, "I was only suggesting…"

Zizi smiled as she slinked up to the agent and said in a deep, breathy voice, "Do you know what it does to Zizi when *anyone* questions her authority?"

Tovar backed away, smiling nervously. "I meant no harm…"

The lady spy put her hand behind Tovar's head as if to draw him in for a passionate kiss. "I tell you what it does to Zizi when her authority is questioned by her underlings," she said, and then abruptly smacked Tovar across the face with the butt of her gun, shrieking, "IT MAKES ZIZI ANGRY!"

Bela, Jr., Lou, and Lon stared in open-mouthed astonishment. Lou leaned over to Lon again, swallowed hard and whispered, "You still feel like flirtin' with this broad?"

Lon shook his head nervously in the negative as Zizi pistol-whipped Tovar into whimpering submission, striking him with the butt of her gun again and again, her breasts heaving, her nostrils flaring, screaming a flood of Hungarian obscenities like a woman possessed.

Lou cleared his throat. "Uh, lady," he ventured.

Zizi was caught up in the throes of passion as she continued to beat her man down.

"Do you see these badges?" she asked.

Lou raised his hand. "Uh, hey, lady," he called, whistling to get her attention.

Zizi whirled around, her arm raised in the act of striking, Tovar's blood spattered over the mounds of her bosom and dripping down the front of her leather dress. "WHAT?" she asked with eyes aflame.

Lou faltered. "Uh, never mind, I forgot what I was gonna ask anyway."

Her mood swung back to seductive as she tried to coax her askew hair back in place. She smiled winsomely at Costello. "It is all right, cute little fat man," she assured him. "What did you want to ask?"

Lou got up the courage to point at the now cowering men. "Are, uh, you their boss or somethin'?"

In response to his question, Zizi holstered her Remington and pulled down the cups of her bustier, proudly displaying her large pale breasts, naked except for two nipple-covering pasties.

Lou quickly used Bela, Jr.'s military cap to cover the boy's eyes.

"Do you see these badges?" she asked.

Lou and Lon stared transfixed, asking simultaneously, "What badges?"

Zizi tossed her head, letting her wild raven locks flip and fall behind her back. "This badge," she said, pointing to a gold badge strategically pinned to the right pasty. "It is the battle axe and bat insignia of the DGSP."

"The what?" Costello asked.

"It means Direction General for the Security of the People and was founded 1944 as covert Romanian branch of KGB, which is why we have bat for insignia." Pointing to the badge pinned to her left pasty, she said, "This badge, the eight-pointed star with outstretched palm, it says that I am Counter-Espionage agent."

and the House of Doom

"Nice concealed weapons, by the way," Lou quipped while ogling her bountiful bosom.

"Thank you." Zizi smiled and propped her boot up on the coffee table to display, not only her shapely leg, but the gleaming Remington in its black leather garter holster. "This lovely concealed weapon was my mother's. An antique, but has great sentimental value." She stepped back and spread out her skirt like a cape, revealing a red velvet lining with many hidden utility pockets. "My other concealed weapons include brass knuckles, teargas grenades, various poison capsules, handcuffs, a spring loaded lead truncheon, razor sharp Ninja stars…"

"Actually, I meant—skip it."

Tucking her breasts back into her bustier, Zizi made the necessary adjustments and then smoothed out her skirt. She posed seductively and proclaimed, "I am Field Commander, First Class, code name Madame Z, and these are my underlings."

She barked a command in Hungarian. The men holstered their guns and pulled back their left lapels, revealing tie tack-sized pins with heart and overlaying battle axe insignia.

"These men," Madame Z explained as she moved down the line, "bear the badges of Special Security." She clapped her hands.

Taking their cue, the agents all pulled back their right lapels, revealing tie tack-sized bat and battle axe pins, all the agents, that is, but Wing Man. "They also wear the symbol of glorious DGSP just like their beautiful commander." She glared at Wing Man, who was exposing only one pin. "Gergo, why are you not showing other pin?"

Gergo shrugged his wounded shoulder, looking nervous. "I cannot move arm to show it, Madame Z."

Madame Z eyed him suspiciously. "Is that so, Gergo?" She reached under her skirt and produced her ever-present riding crop and used it to look under Gergo's right lapel. The pin wasn't there. She thoughtfully tapped the riding crop in her palm. "Cute, Gergo, very cute." Madame Z's dark eyes flashed with renewed rage as she brandished the riding crop, sending the huge man cowering in the corner. "WHERE IS PIN? YOU ARE OUT OF UNIFORM!"

"Hey, come on, lady," said Lou. "That ain't no reason to beat up a guy. I'll bet you've been out of uniform every now and then yourself." As Madame Z hesitated, Lou leaned over to Lon and whispered out the corner of his mouth, "I'm guessin' maybe even more than every now and then."

The villainess lowered her riding crop and considered the matter. "I suppose you are right," she said with a shrug. She kicked away the coffee table and glared at Gergo. "You should lick little fat man's shoes in gratitude that I do not administer punishment you deserve! You should do it until they shine!"

"Yes, Madame Z," said Gergo. He obediently knelt at Costello's feet and extended his tongue toward the comic's shoes.

Lou flinched. "Uh, if it's all the same to you, lady, I'd rather he didn't."

Madame Z frowned as Gergo looked to her for instruction. "Are you sure? Gergo does it very well." She displayed the sheen on her black boots. "See?"

"Uh, thanks, but I know a shoeshine on the corner that needs the business."

Madame Z shrugged. "Very well, suit yourself."

She barked another order. As Gergo stood up, he and the other men gathered around the prisoners and drew their guns.

"Now, where was I?" She returned to her pacing, tapping the riding crop in her palm. "We do not have wife," said Madame Z, smiling at Bela, Jr. "*But*, we have boy, which means we have something Lugosi wants, and cute little fat man can reach Lugosi on fancy American radio telephone owned by decadent American movie mogul."

Tovar grabbed his handkerchief and pinched his nose, keeping his head tilted back in an attempt to staunch the blood gushing from his nostrils. He piped nasally, "A brilliant plan, Madame Z."

The Hungarian seductress went to the telephone and pointed with her riding crop. "Mr. Lou, you will please to call Mr. Eddie Mannix and tell him you find Bela, Jr." She called to Kalara, who was busy with something in the bedroom. "What is number of movie mogul, darling?"

"ALexander-2222," Kalara called back.

Costello started. "Hey, how did she know that?"

Zizi smirked. "Kalara, my pet, show Mr. Lou how you know that!"

Kalara emerged from the bedroom and pinched her nose. "Number plea-uzz," she said in a familiar nasally tone.

"So that was her on the phone before?" Costello asked.

"Yes," said Madame Z. "We intercept all hotel communications."

"So what is it with this dame anyway? I mean, what's with the tattoos I heard tell about?"

Zizi smiled and barked out an order in Hungarian. Kalara responded by unzipping the front of her dress to show off her unusual tattoos.

This time Lou and Lon together covered Bela, Jr.'s eyes with his cap, much to the young man's consternation. "Quit it, you guys," the boy complained. "I *am* in the army, you know."

"Kalara Skorzeny," Zizi explained, "bears the mark of DGSP Technical Operations."

"She's barin' more than that," quipped Costello.

The insignia tattooed on Kalara's naked breasts were just as Lillian had described; the bat and battle axe on her right breast and a telephone in a hexagon symbol on her left breast. The tattoo artist's needle must have been intensely painful considering where those symbols had been inked, but from what Costello had observed so far, maybe that was what Hungarian secret agents liked.

Chaney frowned. "You made that poor girl tattoo those things on her chest like that?"

Kalara said proudly, "I gladly endured the pain to show my submission to the State and to Madame Z! It was the State that rescued me from the Nazis, and it is to Madame Z that I owe my life! I have made the symbols of my rank a part of me forever!"

Costello leaned over and muttered to Lon, "I'll bet gettin' a promotion must be a real pain."

Any further expression of Kalara's loyalty was interrupted by a persistent buzzing that came from the bedroom. Madame Z's ears pricked up. She turned Kalara around and playfully swatted her bottom. "Return to your post like a good girl."

"Yes, my Mistress!" Kalara zipped up her dress and quickly obeyed.

Through the open bedroom door, Lou could see Kalara taking a seat before a mini telephone operator's station mounted inside a steamer trunk. "Number plea-uzz?" she intoned nasally into a headset microphone.

"Okay, that explains about her," said Lou, reaching into his pocket, which made the agents tense. Costello froze and assured them. "I just wanna show your boss lady a card. See?" He pulled out the calling card. "It's just a card. It don't explode or nothin'."

Tovar started. "He has card!"

"Yes, I see card before," Zizi said dismissively.

"Then we must let them go," said Pretty Boy.

Zizi smirked. "He thinks the 'C,' it means 'Communist.' He is not one of Richard's field agents, so it does not count."

"So, wait a minute," Lou said pointing at the door. "The British guy across the hall really is a spy like you said?"

"Richard Septimus Pratt, you mean? But of course! He has been my nemesis for long time. But he is not double agent. That I lie about. He is field commander with Military Intelligence, Section 6." Zizi took Costello's calling card. "The letter 'C' does not mean 'Communist.' It is initial of first leader of MI6, Captain Sir George Mansfield Smith-*Cumming*." She smiled wryly. "Cumming," she mused. "I always liked that name."

"I'll bet I know why," remarked Costello as Chaney nudged him.

"See," Chaney said, "I told you they sounded more like cops."

Zizi bent down and playfully pinched his cheek. "You are pretty quick on the uptake, aren't you, darling? So very handsome and you have brains, too." She gestured at the hotel mini bar. "Can I buy you a drink?"

"Now that you mention it," Chaney said, getting up, "my throat *is* kinda dry."

Zizi helped herself to a bottle of brandy and handed Lon a glass. "I am only Richard's second generation arch enemy." She used her teeth to pull out the cork and poured Lon a drink before taking a swig right from the bottle. "We go back many years. When I was little girl, Richard bounced me on his knee, after he kidnapped me—to use as bargaining chip to retrieve captured agents. I had such big crush on him."

Lou smirked. "You got a big crush on everybody."

"Mother had an opium smuggling ring in Peking called The Avenging Society and Richard was Mother's arch enemy posing as a British consul."

"Wow," remarked Bela, Jr.

"You better believe, 'Wow,'" Madame Z said. "Richard has scar on shoulder blade as reminder of his first encounter with Mother. He led a contingent of British Marines to the docks at Chungking on the Yangtze River to seize a shipment of opium. One of Mother's minions tried to kill him with spear. Richard dedicated his entire time in China to breaking Mother's organization. He was relentless." She took a swig and shrugged. "Eventually, Mother went to India and organized a Thuggee gem smuggling sect, convincing her new followers that she was Shiva, God of Destruction, reincarnated as woman."

Bela, Jr. was riveted. "What was she like?" he asked. "Was she pretty?"

"She was Goddess, infamous throughout Asia as Madame Avinashi, Sanskrit name meaning, 'The Indestructible One,' or Madame A for short." She smirked. "She took under her wing many lovers and often very simple men that she would deflower and inspire to dream of greatness. For instance, H. Rider Haggard was her lover when he was simple unpaid secretary in South Africa. I think Haggard even wrote book about her once." She frowned. "Or was it four times? I never read sequels. He changed her name in book to Ayesha, at her request."

"Wait a minute," said Lou. "Are you tryin' to tell us that your mudder was that dame in Haggard's book, *She?*"

"That is what I am trying to tell you."

Chaney smirked. "If she was lovers with Haggard, that means she was a young woman living in the 1880's."

Zizi nodded. "1878, to be exact, but what is your point?"

"Well, she had to be pretty old when she had you, way too old to have a kid."

"Mother had learned from Oriental mystics long ago how to remain young for very, very long time. She was able to take a lover in 1880's and continued to do so up until my birth, the year I will not disclose, but it was this century. Most of her children are raised by the fathers and the fathers' wives, and never see full criminal potential." She raised her brandy bottle proudly. "I am one of select few that Mother raised personally to continue great family tradition of criminal enterprise."

Chaney held his empty glass out for a refill. "So all this stuff really happened?"

"Is all true," Zizi insisted as she poured him another.

Smiling, he scoffed, "Because it sounds like a bunch of malarkey!"

"Or," said Bela, Jr., "stuff you see in a Republic serial!"

"You are very perceptive, little soldier." Zizi took another large swig of brandy. "Sax Rohmer, one of Mother's lovers, he modeled Fu Manchu and his criminal syndicate on Mother and her criminal empire. But back then no one would believe in female having such power. He changed her sex and gave her beauty to fictitious daughter of evil Fu Manchu." Leaning seductively against the bar and licking her lips, she said, "I cannot tell you how delighted Mother was when Richard Septimus Pratt became her nemesis." She smiled wistfully. "Of all her enemies, Richard Septimus was the only one to truly steal her heart. And he did it by constantly foiling her plans, the only man who ever frustrated her—both criminally and sexually. He refused to succumb to her charms, the only man ever to do that. It made her want him more, and from then on, it was love. She was ever after Hell bent on Richard's destruction. If she could not have him, she said, then no one can. So many stories she told me of the death traps she would set for him." She sighed. "Those were good times."

"It sounds it," Costello said.

"Later on, when I inherit evil empire, I also inherit Richard. So many times I try to kill Richard. Scorpions, poisonous centipedes, piranha fish, but always he would escape. He was born under lucky star, I think."

"So what are you doin' with *this* mob?" asked Chaney, waving his glass at the Hungarians. "I mean, if you got your own evil empire and all."

Madame Z shrugged. "After Richard retired from service, those who succeeded him, they proved much easier to kill. All the fun was taken out of being evil criminal genius, so I lose interest. Then when Communists take over Romania and Hungary after the fall of Third Reich, I saw opportunity to join DGSP. Mostly for prestige, and is very much cheaper."

"Cheaper?" Costello asked.

"Yes. In Mother's day you could start an evil empire with very little capital outlay. These days with inflation, and postwar Europe being what it is—is very expensive. Do you have any idea how much it costs to maintain a pit of deadly vipers in Ukraine?"

Chaney shrugged. "I never thought much about it."

"Nobody does until you need one! Is not only excavating pit, you have to feed vipers, make sure they are not too hot or too cold, and in Ukraine is *very* cold." She shrugged sadly. "I cannot even afford simple death ray." She took another swig of brandy, sighing longingly. "Which is why I join DGSP. Now I let Soviets worry about such things. But enough of this."

Madame Z put down the brandy bottle and went over to the telephone and presented Costello with the handset. "Please to call Mr. Mannix and tell Bela Lugosi that we have his son and to come for him."

"Drop dead, lady," Lou said. "I ain't gonna help you hurt Bats."

Madame Z appeared shocked at the very suggestion. "Hurt Bela Lugosi!" she exclaimed. "We do not want to hurt Bela Lugosi! Where did you get such an idea?"

Lou gestured around him. "Uh, the guns…you kidnappin' his kid…."

Madame Z declared passionately, "We are on a noble mission to bring Bela Lugosi back to his homeland, back to Hungary!"

"TO HUNGARY!" Zizi's henchmen all chanted at once, briskly saluting.

"He is national hero," Tovar squeaked nasally.

"My mother," said Imre, "she saw the great Lugosi on Budapest stage in role of Jesus. To this day, she cries tears of joy at the remembering!"

"Wait a minute," said Costello, trying to wrap his head around this revelation. "You mean, all you guys are Lugosi's *fans?*"

"Not all," Zizi and her comrades glared contemptuously at Scarface. "Vidor, he prefers Boris Karloff," she snarled.

Vidor shrugged. "So shoot me," he said. "I think Karloff is better actor."

"How can you say that?" Zizi nearly swooned as she placed a hand over her heaving breasts. "I would gladly let Lugosi have my body, even if only for one glorious night of passion, anything just to feel his touch on my naked skin, to feel his strong arms crush me in powerful embrace of much sex!"

Chaney put his hands over Bela, Jr.'s ears. "Come on, lady. There's a kid in the room." He said off-handedly to Costello, "Now I know what Glenn was complainin' about before."

Costello pointed at the luggage stacked in the corner. "So that's why you stole Lugosi's luggage?"

"Yes," said Madame Z. "We take from trailer during gun battle with crazy men in ambulance." She eyed Pretty Boy viciously. "During battle it was Imre's duty to keep Mrs. Lugosi and son safe from harm. We would have both wife and son of great Lugosi if not for Imre and his foolish love for decadent American coffee!"

"It was Maxwell House," Imre said in his defense. "Is good to last drop!"

Gergo held up his winged left arm. "Your last drop was to drop on floor! Mrs. Lugosi, she shoots me with *your* gun! And then crazy people, they start to shoot at us!" He gestured at Bela, Jr. "But I get boy back, in spite of great pain, and bleeding all over the place!" He glared at Kalara from the doorway. "And what about Kalara fainting in first place? She was no help at all!"

Kalara covered her headset microphone and glared back at him. "What are you complaining about, Gergo? Because I fainted, Mrs. Lugosi and son were in trailer! It was Janika who suggested how you could take them in first place! His plan was superior to original plan to take them all at fake fund raiser."

"She has point," Zizi said. "The cost to rent ballroom was very expensive. I should probably spare Janika for that alone."

Gergo gave Madame Z a hurt look. "Is so unfair! You do not even discipline Imre for his stupidity. Oh, but Gergo, you give twenty lashes! And look at poor Tovar!"

Madame Z eyed Imre thoughtfully. "Gergo is right, Imre." She raised her riding crop to strike him, but her arm wavered. She lowered her riding crop and gushed, "I cannot do it!" She pinched his cheek. "It is those pretty blue eyes; they just do something to me!"

"Now hold on a minute," said Chaney. "I don't get it. What are you doing all this plotting and sneaking around for? I mean, if you think Bela's such a national treasure, why didn't you just come out and ask him to go back to Hungary with you?"

"He *was* asked," Madame Z hotly insisted. "A year ago our government, they send Mr. Lugosi official invitation to become Minister of Culture, the highest honor we can bestow upon him!"

"You mean you sent that letter Lugosi was cryin' about?" asked Lou.

Madame Z frowned suspiciously. "How do you know about letter?"

Costello tugged at the collar of his shirt as he confessed, "I had Bela's trailer bugged."

Chaney looked at Costello, shocked. "Why'd you go and do a thing like that?"

"I was afraid the guy was a Commie. If I got the goods on him, I was gonna turn him over to the House Un-American Activities Committee." Lou couldn't look Chaney in the eye as he said, "I figured if I named names, the IRS would get off my back."

Madame Z glared angrily. "You would do such a thing, and you say we are the bad ones?" She stiffened. "*We* are loyal to the State, but more importantly, we want only the *best* for Bela Lugosi. Never again would he have to degrade himself making the Poverty Row pictures! No longer would he be forced to cavort around in cape just to earn living! He would have much power and respect!" She grew agitated and paced the room. "But he never answered letter. Our government, they try sending again letter, and again he never answer letter. So I was given glorious mission to bring back Bela Lugosi and entire family, even if by force!" She cracked her riding crop against her thigh. "NOW PICK UP PHONE AND DIAL, YOU SNEAKY, HATEFUL LITTLE MAN!" she shrieked. "I WANT LUGOSI HERE AND I WANT HIM HERE NOW!"

There was a knock at the door.

Costello pointed at the door. "That's what I call service."

Madame Z motioned for Vidor to stand behind the door. The agent waited with his gun drawn as Madame Z opened the door cautiously. A forceful kick sent the door smashing into Vidor. The henchman slid to the floor, unconscious, while Zizi was knocked onto her shapely posterior. She glared up awestruck at the giant standing in the doorway. He was so huge that he had to duck his head down to enter. He wore a cowboy hat and Western duster, a red checkered shirt and Levis with a gun belt and Western holsters strapped to his thighs from which he drew two .45 Colts.

Kalara ran into the living room, her Pistolet at the ready.

"Reach for the sky," the giant commanded with a Southwestern twang.

The Hungarian agents all dropped their weapons and raised their hands.

Madame Z's bosom heaved; her face was flush with excitement. "You are…very… *big*," she breathlessly said.

"Sorry, Ma'am," the giant gave Madame Z a friendly nod, "I didn't mean to barge in on ya, but I guess I had to, seein' that you had pals of mine hostage and all."

Lou, Bela, Jr. and Lon jumped to their feet. "PEE WEE!" they chorused at once.

Glenn Strange smiled broadly. "The one and only!" He gave Costello a chastising shake of the head as he pointed at Bela, Jr. "You oughta be ashamed, Lou, havin' a little cowpoke like this stayin' up past his bedtime."

"It's not like I had a choice," Costello said, nodding at the trembling henchmen.

Holstering one of his weapons with a practiced twirl, Glenn gazed down at Zizi and offered her his huge hand. "Let me help you up, Ma'am."

Strange had Madame Z on her feet in an instant. He tried to let go, but she refused to release his hand. Her eyes were wide with passion, her knees weak as she pressed her body against his.

"You have very big gun with very long barrel," she sighed, caressing the barrel of Strange's gun with her index finger.

"Thank you, Ma'am," Glenn said. "But these are .45s. The Long Colt is a .38."

"I wasn't talking about gun," she said with a saucy smile.

Someone blocked by Glenn's towering figure cleared his throat loudly.

"Oh, sorry," Glenn said, stepping aside.

Richard Septimus Pratt sauntered in and surveyed the situation. Looking behind the door and noting Vidor slumped unconscious on the floor, he bent down and collected Vidor's weapon, and then the other weapons and handed them over to Glenn, who pocketed the guns in his duster.

"So, Zizi," Pratt scolded, "up to your usual shenanigans, I see."

"Why, whatever do you mean?" Zizi asked with mock innocence.

"Hey, look out," Costello warned. "She's packin' heat under that skirt of hers."

"You're tellin' me," Lon said with a smirk.

Pratt looked his adversary up and down. "I know all about Madame Z and her, uh, arsenal." He rolled his eyes. "I often wonder why you don't rattle when you walk."

"Especially the way that dame walks," Costello said.

Madame Z gestured at the mini bar. "Care to have a drink with me, Richard?"

"Whiskey, if you have it," Pratt said, and looked around the room, while reaching into his waistcoat and pulling out a calling card. "Any, uh, *surprises* I should be made aware of?" he asked, displaying the card.

"No, no," Zizi said, pouring Richard J&B on the rocks. "The truly creative death traps, the DGSP have not the budget." She handed him the glass and smiled, clinking his glass with her brandy bottle. "So what brings you here to my lair?" She gazed despairingly around the suite. "I mean to my rooms." She smirked suggestively at Glenn. "Did you bring this big, beautifully rugged man with you just for Zizi to play with?"

"You play a little too roughly. No, one of my operatives suggested we contact Mr. Strange to strong arm the situation."

She gave Glenn a flirtatious wink. "And such a strong arm, too." She glanced out in the hallway. "So is it just you and very big brute coming to visit?"

"My brother and two other operatives are awaiting my return." He addressed Costello. "Which reminds me, I was asked to inform you that your partner is alive and well."

Costello jumped to his feet. "They found Abbott?"

"Mr. Abbott has been working for us undercover."

"So that's why he had one of these here cards," Costello said, producing his calling card.

"Yes."

Zizi said, "Did you say you had brother with you? Which brother? There are seven of you."

Richard sighed. "The famous one. The *actor*. You know, *him*."

"Oh, too bad you knock out Vidor." Madame Z frowned as she gestured at her unconscious operative.

Kalara shook her head sadly. "He is great fan of Boris Karloff. He will be so disappointed to learn how he missed him."

Pratt cast an affronted glare. "Kindly do not use that ridiculous name in my presence."

Costello asked, "What do you got against Boris Karloff, anyway?"

"His name is William Henry Pratt!" Richard vehemently insisted.

"Okay, fine," Costello said, "so why are ya so mad at *William Henry Pratt?*" he asked, mocking Richard's accent.

"My brother shunned Her Majesty's, uh, *consul service* for a career in show business. He said he had *a fire in his belly* for it. I told him not to confuse indigestion for a life calling."

"What's wrong with show business?" Costello asked. "Boris, I mean, *William*, makes a good livin' at it."

"For generations we Pratts have *fought* mad scientists and megalomaniacal fiends for King, Queen and Country, not cavorted on the screen *playacting* them." Pratt gazed heavenward bewailing, "It's such a waste, too. His talents would have made him the *perfect* undercover operative."

"I feel for you, Richard," Zizi lamented with a sympathetic sigh. "For you see, I, too, had a sibling who shunned family enterprise for show business."

"Really?" said Richard. "You never told me that."

"Is true. My half-brother Fredek, Fredek Vivas you spoke of while we listen at door, he had such potential; a master of disguise, a mechanical genius, a keen eye for detail. Mother had such hopes for him." She shrugged. "But he decided instead on career as stage magician, and later a makeup and special effects man." She smiled. "But his loss was my gain. Mother chose me instead as her successor."

"What happened to your brother?" asked Chaney.

"You heard what happened to him while we eavesdropped." Madame Z crossed her eyes and stirred the air around her temple with her index finger, "He was as the Americans say a little *coo-coo*. He was obsessed with Erich von Stroheim, even had surgery to look like him. Then he was taken to concentration camp and used in experiments."

Richard put down his drink and gazed earnestly at Zizi. "The man who ordered his death has assumed your brother's identity—a Nazi scientist named Rache, also known as Dr. Death, or rather, *Doktor Halál*."

"Dr. Death," Zizi mused, "name has nicer ring to it in English. Very dramatic. Mother would have approved." She bit her lip thoughtfully. "Could it be that Fredek only pretended to die so that he might assume proper place as villain and he now calls himself this Dr. Death?"

"Madame Z!" Kalara exclaimed. "*Doktor Halál* is my sworn enemy; mine and Janika, and even poor Vidor's!" She caressed the unconscious agent's long scar. "*Doktor Halál* not only experimented with cryonics, but also the skin grafting and the plastic surgery. He disfigured Janika and Vidor both! Whether he is your brother or not, he must die!"

"There, you see," Pratt urged, "Zizi, we *must* join forces to stop him!" Presenting the calling card again, he audaciously declared, "The need has arisen!"

Madame Z took the card and smiled. "This card is good to honor truce, but if you want us to join forces, we must first negotiate." She tucked the card back in Richard's waistcoat and patted his tummy, and then got down to business. "So this Nazi war criminal, he is not Fredek, but is using Fredek's stolen serial numbers?"

"Exactly."

"And he does this to pose as Holocaust survivor and escape punishment?"

"Precisely."

"That is so—"

"Diabolical?" Pratt suggested. "Fiendish? Outrageous?"

"Clever," Zizi said, her dark eyes sparkling with admiration. "That is *so* clever!"

"Oh, yes. Dr. Death is *fiendishly* clever."

"Really, Richard," Zizi giggled as she shivered and rubbed her arms. "The way you say *fiendishly*, it gives me the goose bumps."

"I'm being serious!" Pratt insisted. "Dr. Death has established a covert criminal organization in Hollywood greater than anything you or your mother ever conceived."

Madame Z smirked. "If it is so covert, how do you know about it?"

"He deliberately left clues that alerted us to his plans."

"Is that so?" Madame Z smiled. "I like his style."

Richard sighed irritably, but pressed on. "There is evidence that hidden on the back lot at Universal-International Studios is some diabolical atomic weapon."

Madame Z's eyes widened with shock. "Atomic weapon! My God!"

"Yes, the prospects are terrible."

"No, I meant that I think I am falling in love." Her bosom began to heave with passion. "Such a man, I *must* have him."

"Will you be serious?" Richard scolded. "Dr. Death has Lillian Lugosi."

Bela, Jr. jumped to his feet. "That rotten Nazi has my mother! We have to stop him!"

"Relax, boy," said Madame Z. "Your mother, she will be hokey dokey."

"You seem awfully sure of that," Richard observed skeptically. "He is no doubt using her to lure Bela Lugosi to his death!"

"Madame Z!" Kalara begged. "We must stop him!"

"Silence, Kalara!" She gave the girl a saucy smirk. "Or tonight it is the clothespins."

Kalara gasped and covered her mouth.

Richard gazed earnestly at Zizi. "How can I impress upon you the urgency of this matter?"

Zizi waved. "This Dr. Death, he likes to play games. He leaves you clues, he takes hostages, he wants you to try and stop him. Obviously he does all this to impress you. I have done the same thing. You should be flattered."

"Be that as it may, will you help me?"

Madame Z extended her hand. "I will."

"Excellent," Pratt said, taking it.

She tightened her grip and gave Richard a cunning smile. "And in exchange, you will help us smuggle Lugosi and his family past American authorities."

Pratt released his grip and glowered. "You know we can't agree to that." He nodded at Bela, Jr. "After all, the young Master Lugosi is an American citizen, and in military school. The State Department would never allow you to just spirit him away."

Madame Z shrugged and took another swig of brandy. "Have fun rescuing Lugosi on your own, then."

Pratt leaned in and whispered, "Come, Zizi, be reasonable."

"I *am* being reasonable." She playfully poked Richard in the waistcoat. "Richard, *dear* Richard, you must offer me something. My superiors, they would expect from me nothing less."

Lon Chaney stepped forward. "Look, why can't you agree to let the lady make Bela the offer? If Bela wants to be the Minister of Culture, then he goes back to Hungary; if he refuses, then Zizi promises not to make anymore kidnapping attempts."

Zizi shrugged. "Sounds reasonable to me."

Pratt sighed and began to pace. "No. If word got out that Bela even considered such an offer, he would be branded a traitor and brought before the HUAC to answer charges."

"Tell you what," said Zizi, "we do this, as the Americans say, on Q.T."

"Actually," Pratt corrected, "that phrase originated in Britain."

Zizi rolled her eyes. "God, Richard, sometimes you are such stick in mud." She added earnestly, "I will agree to leave no paper trail. It is all done strictly talking. I make offer, you be witness."

Costello raised his hand. "Uh, I hate to rush you guys, but didn't Pratt say something about atomic bombs?"

"Yes, you're quite right," Pratt agreed.

"Fine," Madame Z said. "We work together, but I take hostage just to make sure you do not pull double-cross."

"Who?" Pratt asked. He glanced over at Bela, Jr. and then at Zizi, shaking his head. "Not the boy. He comes with us."

"No," the seductress said, gazing hungrily at Glenn, "not the boy."

Glenn frowned. "I just hope the wife don't hear about this."

"I can keep secret," Zizi said with a grin.

Pratt gave Glenn a nudge. "All right, Mr. Strange, give them back their weapons."

Madame Z addressed her agents. "You heard Richard. Arm yourselves, minions, we go."

"Yes, Madame Z," said Kalara. She approached Glenn and held her hand out expectantly. "My weapon, please."

"Not you, Kalara," Madame Z ordered. "You will remain here and look after Vidor."

Kalara's eyes became wild. "No, Madame Z! *Doktor Halál*—"

"That is an order, Comrade Skorzeny! Your emotions make you a liability!" Madame Z pointed at the fallen Vidor. "Imre, Gergo, take Vidor to bedroom. Kalara, you *will* stay at his side!"

A tear rolled down Kalara's cheek. "Vidor, he would *want* me to kill *Doktor Ha-lál.*"

Zizi caressed her cheek. "I bring you back head as souvenir."

"Now that *that's* settled." Pratt turned to Bela, Jr. "Come along, young man."

Costello held the boy back. "The kid stays with me and Chaney. Bats would want us to look after 'im."

"He remains in *our* protective custody," Pratt insisted.

"Where the kid goes, *I* go." The comic put up his fists. "And if you wanna get tough about it, I can still throw a mean punch."

Madame Z smiled. "I like this cute little man, in spite of his politics. He is tough bastard."

With a frustrated sigh, Pratt relented. "You and Mr. Chaney can stay with the boy. Miss Aubert and Miss Randolph can look after you."

Lou relaxed. "Okay, fine." He poked Pratt in the chest. "But you better take good care of Bats." He turned to Chaney. "Let's go, Lon."

"Just a sec." Lon grabbed a bottle of whiskey from the mini bar.

Costello glared at him.

Lon shrugged. "A nightcap won't hurt none."

Chapter 21

Thursday, 26 February 1948
1:39 A.M.
Suite 205, Hollywood Knickerbocker Hotel

Boris Karloff answered the door.

"Ah, Mr. Costello. Lon," he said.

"You never told us your brudder was a spy," said Lou.

"You never asked me," Boris said, and smiled at Bela, Jr. "I see you brought Master Lugosi back safe and sound." He opened the door wider and invited them in.

Lenore and Jane sat together on the sofa. Jane was both striking and casual in slacks and a tight-fitting navy blue sweater with a broad white band across the bust and JR. embroidered over the swell of her right breast.

Costello winked at Jane. "Nice sweater, Junior," he quipped, noting the initials.

"Oh, you," Jane said with a smile.

"Hi, Lenore."

"Hello, Lou," Lenore said, getting up to greet them. "Have you been having fun playing detective tonight?"

Costello put his deerstalker back on. "Like Rathbone says, it's all elemental."

Jane consulted her watch. "It's twenty minutes to two." She covered her mouth and yawned. "I just hope I can get some shut-eye before cast call today."

Chaney smirked. "Well, if we're supposed to shoot on the Phantom Stage, I think it's a safe bet we're gettin' the day off."

Bela, Jr. gave him a worried look. "Why? What happened?"

"It's a long story, kid," said Costello as the contingent of DGSP agents and Richard Pratt gathered out in the hall.

"Billy," Pratt called from the doorway, "you're with me."

"Right," said Boris, grabbing a small tool kit and slipping it into his pocket.

"Jane, Lenore," ordered Pratt, "see to the boy." He gestured at Lou and Lon. "These two have elected to stay with him."

"I'll take good care of them," Lenore said reassuringly.

Boris was about to head out the door when Costello held him back and whispered, "Hey, how much can your brudder be trusted?"

Boris smiled. "I know Richard seems a bit cold, but it goes with his line of work." He whispered, "Frankly, since having retired from his adventures in the Orient, Richard's become something of a recluse. As you can well imagine, he's a trifle peeved about having been called back into active service."

"Don't they have other secret agents in England?"

"Hurry along, Billy," Pratt commanded sharply.

"In a moment, Richard," Boris said, gesturing at Lou. "Mr. Costello has expressed concern about whether or not you can be trusted."

"Oh, did he now?" Pratt said. He gave Lou a challenging look. "Well?"

Costello met the field commander's leer with one of his own. "How come you got picked for this case if you was retired?"

Pratt cast his brother a look of annoyance and snarled, "It's all Billy's fault, he and his accursed Boris Karloff nonsense. I was drafted back into active service, because, as 'C' phrased it, this case centered around Hollywood, and in particular, Universal Studios, and an inside man was vital to its success, and since my *familial connections* put me in direct contact with Universal Studios' top horror man, it made my return to active service an imperative." He addressed Boris. "Now can we *please* get on with it? I want to put this business behind me and get back to tending my rose garden."

"Yes, you're quite right, Richard." Boris wished everyone a pleasant good evening.

Lenore closed the door after them and noted the bottle in Lon's hand. "I don't have any coffee, but could I interest either of you older boys in a cup of Irish tea?" She gestured at a pair of French doors opening into the suite's kitchenette. "I just put the kettle on."

Lon handed Lenore the bottle and in an Irish brogue said, "Sure, just call me Lon O'Chaney."

Costello shrugged. "Eh, why fight it. Make it two."

Jane got up and smiled at Bela, Jr. "As for you, soldier, the boogie-woogie bugler blew taps hours ago. Come on; let's get you ready for bed."

"Do I have to?" Bela, Jr. whined.

"You can stay up a little bit longer," Lenore said with a smile. "I'll make you some hot cocoa. That will put you right to sleep." She was interrupted by the whistling kettle. "That's my cue." She paused at the French doors. "Jane, would you give me a hand?"

Jane smiled nervously. "Do you *really* need my help?" she asked.

"Yes," Lenore insisted. "Right now."

"Okay, then." Jane gave her guests a nervous smile. "Have a seat, we'll be right out." She frowned and joined Lenore in the kitchenette, closing the French doors after her.

Lou patted his pockets for a cigar as he sat on the couch. He frowned, nodding after the girls. "What was that all about?"

"You got me," Lon said, inviting Bela, Jr. to sit next to him. He glanced at Lou. "Did you lose something?"

Poking around inside his jacket, Costello said, "I think I lost my stogies." He paused and snapped his fingers. "Oh yeah, I forgot. Bats took 'em." On the coffee table was a gold cigarette case resting on top of some espionage-related paperwork. Lou noted the initials *L.A.* punctuated by tiny diamond periods on the case. "Hey, do you think Lenore would mind if I bummed a cigarette?"

Lon shrugged. "I don't see why she would."

Costello selected a cigarette and took out the gold lighter clipped inside the case. He stuck the cigarette in his mouth and flicked the flint wheel on the lighter.

A flamethrower-like jet of fire shot up in the air, scorching the tip of Lou's cigarette and the ceiling.

"Hey, watch it!" Lon exclaimed while Bela, Jr. jumped up and sat in a chair by the sofa a safe distance away.

Costello sat frozen with fear, the charred cigarette dangling from his trembling lips.

Lon grabbed a throw pillow and climbed up on the sofa and began beating out the smoking spot on the ceiling. "What are trying to do, burn down the joint?"

The plant blackened, smoked, and shriveled up...

Costello spat out the burnt cigarette and stammered as he threw the lighter away, "I wa-, I wa-, I was just t-t-tryin' to l-l-light a c-c-cigarette." He nervously selected a fresh one from the case. Putting it in his mouth, he asked Lon, "You wouldn't happen to have matches on ya, would ya?"

Satisfied the fire was out, Chaney tossed the pillow aside and climbed down off the sofa. He felt around in his pockets. "I think I grabbed a book of 'em at the diner." He found the matchbook. "Here you go."

Lon sat down next to Costello and gave him a light. The instant the cigarette was lit, a tiny dart shot out of the tip, grazing Chaney's face and striking a lamp near Bela, Jr. The boy cringed as the dart ricocheted off the lamp, off the cigarette case, and finally imbedded itself in a rubber plant behind the couch and near Lou's left shoulder. The plant blackened, smoked, and shriveled up, eliciting mute looks of horror from Lon, Lou and Bela, Jr.

Recovering himself, Costello threw away the cigarette and pointed at the coffee table. "I ain't tryin' nothin' else from that cigarette case," he gasped.

Bela, Jr. said, "I'll bet that's Miss Aubert's spy kit."

Lon pointed a shaking finger at the kitchenette. "M-maybe Lenore keeps the real ones in th-there."

"Good idea." Lou got up and cautiously edged around the coffee table. "I'll be right back—I hope."

Lou hurried to the kitchenette and was about to knock on the French doors when he heard Jane say, "I don't feel right about this."

He peeked through the louvers and saw Lenore and Jane huddled around the counter by the sink. Lenore pulled a pill bottle from her cleavage as she said firmly, "The spy game is a messy business, Jane."

Lou watched intently as Lenore shook some pills in Jane's hand and some in her own. Together the girls divided the pills between three of the five bone china tea cups arranged on a silver service.

"This will take care of them," Lenore said, twisting the cap back on and returning the bottle to her bra. She turned to get the kettle from the stove by the French doors.

Lou gasped and backed away from the louvers and hurried back into the living room. "Hey," he whispered, "whatever you guys do, don't drink nothin'."

"How come?" Bela, Jr. asked.

"Trust me, kid. You guys just pretend to drink what they give you."

Chaney frowned. "Are you nuts?"

"Just trust me, will ya," Lou whispered. "Don't drink nothin', and do what I do."

Lenore and Jane returned. "Here we are," Lenore sang cheerily, carrying the tray.

Jane cleared a place on the coffee table. "Say," she sniffed the air. "Do you smell that?" She picked up the open cigarette case and lighter, glanced up at the burn mark in the ceiling and over at the dead plant and looked questioningly at Costello and Chaney. "Did you boys play around with this?"

Chaney smirked. "Costello borrowed a cigarette. Things kinda got out of hand."

Lenore shook her head as she placed the serving tray on the coffee table. "That was foolish. They arm field operatives with weapons disguised as everyday objects."

Jane closed the case and put it in Lenore's clutch purse. "You're just lucky nobody got hurt."

Bela, Jr. gulped and tugged at his collar. "You're telling me."

"And speaking of dangerous things," Lenore said, handing Chaney a cup, "I make a *potent* Irish tea."

Costello rolled his eyes and muttered nervously, "You can say that again."

"What did you say?" Lenore asked as she handed Bela, Jr. his cocoa.

"I didn't say nothin'," said Costello.

"Drink up, dear," she said to Bela, Jr.

"Thanks," the boy said, sniffing his cocoa. "It smells great."

"I'm having some, too," Lenore said, indicating her cup.

Costello cleared his throat. "Uh, ain't it past Bela, Jr.'s bedtime?"

Bela, Jr. held up his cup. "But I haven't had my cocoa yet."

"It's later than you think, kid." Costello pointed at Jane and made a face. "*Jane* oughta tuck you in *bed… in the other room…* so *Lenore* is out here *alone* with *us.*"

Chaney glared at Costello. "What's gotten into you?"

"Nothin'," Costello insisted nervously. "I'm just tryin' to keep somethin' from gettin' into *you.*"

Jane felt Costello's forehead. "Are you feeling all right?"

"I get nervous when I don't smoke for a while." Costello pointed at the kitchenette. "Would you and Lenore go and get me a cigarette and matches."

Lenore pointed. "There's a box of matches and a pack of cigarettes in the cupboard by the sink."

"Would you both mind gettin' 'em for me?"

Lenore looked askance at Lou. "Why?"

Costello gestured helplessly. "I get all confused in a strange kitchen."

Jane handed Lou his Irish tea. "Why do you want *both* of us to get them?"

"I dunno," Costello said, fidgeting with the cup, "don't you girls do everything in pairs? You know, like go to the powder room, and get stuff from the kitchen?"

"Honestly, Lou," Lenore sighed. "They're right in the cupboard."

"Fine," said Costello, putting his cup down. "I'll go all by myself."

Lou backed away, making sure neither Jane nor Lenore could see him, and then pantomimed a warning about not drinking anything at Lon and Bela, Jr., which was met by a defiant glare from Chaney who reached for his cup. Costello glared right back at him and shook his fist for emphasis. Chaney sighed and put the cup down.

"Why aren't you drinking?" Lenore asked.

"I'm waiting for it to cool," Chaney said as Bela, Jr. shrugged and did likewise.

Costello gave them both the OK and ducked into the kitchenette, shutting the French doors and peaking out into the living room through the louvers.

Lon and Bela, Jr. were doing as they were told, and just sat there and talked.

Satisfied that they were safe for the moment, Lou shut the louvers and found the matches and packet of cigarettes just where Lenore said they would be. He pocketed them and looked around the tiny kitchen for anything that might create a diversion. The kettle was simmering on the back burner of the stove and there was a small hand towel draped over one of two faucets over the sink. Smiling wickedly, Lou grabbed the hand towel, and as he did, he couldn't help remembering the time when he was a kid and accidentally set fire to the family Christmas tree.

Lou set the edge of the hand towel on fire using the blue flame flickering under the tea kettle. He shrugged. "Why should the arsonists have all the fun settin' fires?"

He tossed the burning towel in the sink and then made sure the louvers in the French doors were wide open before hurrying back into the living room. As he did he patted the pocket with the matches and cigarettes and said cheerily to Lenore, "I found 'em."

He picked up his tea cup and saucer and pretended he was about to take a sip.

Jane pointed at the bulge in Costello's pocket. "Aren't you going to smoke?"

Lou shrugged. "I, uh, changed my mind. Maybe later." He sniffed the air. "Uh, speakin' of smoke, do you guys smell somethin' burnin'?" He looked up at the scorch mark in the ceiling and the blackened, shriveled plant. "Somethin' *else* burnin', I mean?"

Lenore frowned as she put her cup down and sniffed the air. "Yes, as a matter of fact I do."

Jane's eyes grew wide with shock as she saw smoke pouring from the louvers in the kitchen doors. "Lenore! Look!"

Lenore sprang to her feet. "Hurry, Jane!"

Costello waited for the two girls to run out of the room, then grabbed Bela, Jr.'s cup and gave him Lenore's cup. "Here, kid, drink outta this one," he said.

"What's the difference?" the boy asked.

"Are you nuts?!" Chaney exclaimed.

"Pipe down, will ya?" Costello snarled, reaching for Lon's cup.

Chaney whispered, "Did you deliberately start that fire?"

"It's just a little fire," Lou whispered back as he switched out Chaney's cup with Jane's cup and emptied his own cup into the drooping rubber plant. Lenore and Jane returned from the kitchenette, just as Costello pretended to finish his tea. "Wow, that sure was swell tea," he said, smacking his lips. "Is the fire out?"

Lenore eyed Lou. "Yes. Fortunately, the hand towel had fallen into the sink. I just turned on the tap and opened a window to air the place out."

"My goodness," said Jane as she stared into Costello's empty cup. "You certainly wolfed that down, didn't you?"

"Yeah." Costello put his cup down and shrugged. "It's like I didn't drink nothin' at all."

Lenore and Jane sat in opposite lounge chairs, with Lou standing between them. Lenore handed Jane her tea and picked up her cup of cocoa. "Now maybe we can enjoy our drinks in peace."

Costello watched intently as the girls put their respective cups to their lips. Lenore hesitated and looked up.

"Is something wrong?" she asked.

"N-n-no," Lou stammered. "Why do you ask?"

"Because you're acting very strangely."

Bela, Jr. gulped his cocoa. His eyes nearly bulged out of his head as he grabbed his throat and began gagging.

"Are you all right?" Lenore asked, putting her cup down.

"You're choking," Jane gasped.

The girls reached to help Bela, Jr.

Costello grabbed their shoulders and forced them back into their chairs. "He's fine!" he said nervously. "It just went down the wrong way! Right, kid?"

Coughing, Bela, Jr. nodded.

Chaney slapped the boy on the back. "You okay, kid?" he asked.

"Uh huh," Bela, Jr. managed to gasp.

Lenore frowned as she stood up and confronted Costello. "What has gotten into you tonight?"

"I'm all upset," Costello whined, "what with Abbott goin' missin' and then findin' out Karloff and you ladies are secret agents. I'm all in a frazzle."

Lenore slapped her forehead. "Of course, how stupid of me! You've all had a horrible experience."

Jane nodded in sympathy. "Especially poor Bela, Jr. Being kidnapped, and worrying about your mother and father, it's no wonder you're all acting so strangely."

"I am an idiot," Lenore said.

Chaney put his cup down. "Aw, don't be so hard on yourself." He handed Lenore back her cocoa and asked, "So, how did you two get involved in this spy business anyway?"

"Lenore only deputized me this morning," Jane said. "That's why we were late reporting to the set."

Lenore poised to drink and shrugged. "As for me, I was in the Vienna Resistance during the war. I was a big star in Austria and I used my position to get information from my Nazi admirers."

She sipped her cocoa. "From Vienna to Paris, where I fought with the French Resistance, using my job as a model and an actress as a cover. I was later recruited by the U.S. Office of Strategic Services."

"Now she's CIA." Jane took a sip of her tea. "I mean, *we're* CIA." She sighed. "I thought being a spy would be exciting and romantic." She frowned at Lenore. "Sometimes some of the things we do aren't very nice."

Lenore took another sip of cocoa, smacked her lips and looked down at her cup. "I can hardly taste the whisky at all," she commented.

"*I* sure did," Bela, Jr. muttered to himself.

Lenore smiled reflectively. "From my first look at the Statue of Liberty I loved my new country. Everyone in Europe knows the United States is a place of real freedom, and I suddenly found myself in a place where I could do whatever I wanted without fear of being questioned by the Gestapo. Or so I thought."

Lou asked, "What do you mean by that?"

She sighed. "Just like Jane said, there are some things I am forced to do as an Intelligence operative that aren't very nice." She finished her cocoa and put the cup down. "I'm sorry, but we had to drug your drinks."

"You what?" asked Chaney, staring at his cup. "You girls slipped us a Mickey Finn?"

"In a moment you won't remember a thing," she said. "It's a special hypnotic drug that induces a total blackout of events that have happened within the past twenty-four hours. In the morning, you will wake up and, if you remember anything at all, it will seem like nothing more than a bad dream. Even if you do happen to recall anything tangible, there won't be any evidence that any of this ever happened."

Costello playacted getting woozy and leaned against Jane's chair.

"You better sit down, Lou," Jane said, and got up to help Lou sit down.

"Yes," said Lenore, "the drug takes effect rather quickly."

Costello flopped into the chair. "That was a dirty trick," he mumbled, and then slumped back. He opened his eye and glared at Chaney.

He did likewise, leaning back and going limp.

Bela, Jr. got the hint and swooned.

Lenore waited a few minutes. "I think they're fully out now."

"Are you sure they're going to be all right?" Jane fretted.

Lenore grabbed her clutch purse and hurried to the telephone. "Positive."

Lou opened his eyes a crack and watched Lenore closely.

She unscrewed the mouthpiece on the handset and dumped the transmitter in the palm of her hand. Setting it aside, she rummaged around in her purse and pulled out a device identical to the transmitter she had just removed, and exactly like the gizmo Richard Pratt was using down in the lobby. She inserted it in the telephone handset, and screwed the mouthpiece cover back on. Then she clicked the plungers repeatedly until she heard a *BEEP!*

She dialed a number and after three rings someone picked up. Lenore said, "All cats are gray at night."

She paused, waiting for the countersign. "This is A. The packages are on their way to Universal-International."

She paused to listen.

"Yes, I administered the drug. They're resting quietly." She looked at Jane. "That wasn't part of the deal," Lenore insisted. "I won't do it."

Jane shrugged questioningly.

Lenore began to sway a bit. "She isn't... a security... risk."

After a moment, she nodded, slowly put down the handset, picked up her purse and pulled out a CIA issue ladies pocket pistol, a Beretta model 418 that had been adapted for a silencer.

"What are you doing?" Jane asked.

Lenore screwed the silencer into the threads reamed into the bore of the muzzle. "I'm sorry, Jane," she said. "But there can't be any witnesses." She took aim.

Jane gasped and stumbled back. "Lenore! No! You can't!"

"I...have to." Lenore's eyelids began to flutter, her arm dropped to her side and her eyes rolled up into her head. She swooned and collapsed across Chaney's lap.

"Lenore?" Jane said just as the drug took effect and she fell back on the carpet in a dead faint.

Costello jumped up and grabbed the handset just as a voice on the other end groused over crackling static, "Hello? Hello? Did you take care of her? We can make things very bad for your husband if you don't. Do you understand that? Now neutralize Miss Randolph if you know what's good for you."

Lou swallowed hard, grabbed his handkerchief and wrapped it around the mouthpiece, and said in a falsetto, "Yes, I did it."

"What's wrong with your voice?"

"I'm getting a cold." Lou coughed. "See?"

"Okay, fine. So are we clear about what you have to do now?"

Lou couldn't place the voice but knew he had heard it someplace before. "Uh, no, can you tell me again?"

"Listen, Aubert, the President himself is counting on this operation to be a success, and he's authorized me to do whatever it takes to insure that success. So do anything funny and we'll have your Jew husband up before the HUAC so fast it will make your head spin! Got it? Now use the firebomb lipstick we gave you and set the hotel room on fire like we planned!"

"Firebomb lipstick, right. I will. Uh, where is it?"

"Where do you think? It's in your purse!"

"Of course it is," he piped.

Lou shouldered the handset and grabbed Lenore's clutch purse. "I was just making sure *you* knew." He dumped out the contents and found the lipstick. "Uh, how do I work it?"

The voice on the phone sighed with exasperation. "Uncap the lipstick and turn the bottom to set the timer."

Costello turned the lipstick over. The knob at the bottom had tiny notches cut into it like an oven timer. The lipstick itself had been replaced by a glass tube filled with a red liquid, no doubt some kind of super hotfoot juice. He held it up for Chaney and Bela, Jr. to see. "Look, it's a bomb," Costello said in his own voice.

"What did you say?" the voice on the phone asked suspiciously.

"Uh..." Costello cleared his throat and coughed and squeaked in a falsetto, "I mean, so it's a bomb."

"Jeez," said the voice, "you oughta gargle with some warm water and salt. You sound terrible."

"Good idea. Uh, after I'm finished setting the fire, what do you want me to do?"

"Meet me at the studio. Skorzeny and the whole stinking spy ring is as good as ours, dead or alive. Guess which one I prefer."

"Dead?" Lou gulped.

"And remember, no witnesses."

"Right, no witnesses....Uh, what witnesses?"

"Karloff, Rathbone, Lugosi, and anyone else who isn't CIA, they're all expendable."

"But what about the blackout pills?"

"Blackout pills," the voice scoffed. "If you want to do things right, remember the old saying, *dead men tell no tales.*"

Lou gulped again.

"Just be sure to stick to the cover story when they debrief you."

Lou was going to make a joke about having his pants pulled down, but thought better of it. "What's the cover story again?" he asked.

"Don't play dumb," the voice warned. "You know the drill. Everybody was killed by Madame Z, and then she and her agents were killed in a pitch gun battle. Now hurry up and get down here!"

A very loud, angry *CLICK!* signaled that the party on the other end of the line had hung up. Costello did likewise. "I think I fooled 'im."

"If that routine fooled him," Chaney said, "then he must be a real dope." Chaney slipped out from under the unconscious actress, got up, and gently laid her back on the sofa. "Help me get Jane in a chair." As Chaney and Costello got Jane up, Lon asked, "So what did the guy say anyway?"

Costello nodded at Lenore. "He wants her to set fire to the room with us still it."

Bela, Jr. glared angrily. "Who was that rotten fink? Do you think he works for the Russians?"

"I hate to say it," Costello said as he and Chaney eased Jane into the chair, "but the guy's on our side."

"What's that got to do with a lipstick?" Chaney asked.

Costello held up the lipstick. "It's a firebomb. You set it by twistin' this thing."

Chaney examined the lipstick and then handed it back, shaking his head. "If I hadn't seen the stuff they did to a cigarette case, I'd say you were nuts."

"I'll bet that guy's a Commie that infiltrated the CIA." Lou slipped the lipstick in his pocket and picked up Lenore's gun. "So we gotta be ready!"

"What do you need that for?" asked Chaney, pointing at the gun.

"Protection," Lou said, and stuck it in the waistband of his pants. He grabbed the cigarette case and was about to slip it into his pocket, then thought better of it and put it down. That's when he noticed a small photograph amongst the contents of Lenore's purse.

In the photo, Lenore was sitting in a booth at a restaurant. Costello recognized the décor as Ciro's. She was posing with two guys and a dame in a mink. One of the guys was Eddie Mannix. The hot dame next to him Lou figured was Eddie's girl, Toni Lanier. The other guy sitting on Lenore's left Lou recognized as Bela Lugosi's agent, Don Marlowe. He picked up the photograph for a closer look. Bela, Jr. looked up and pointed. "Hey, there's writing on the back," he said.

"Yeah?" Costello turned the photo over and saw scribbled in blue ink:

Lou pointed at the inscription and handed Chaney the photo. "Now, who do we know connected with the letter 'M'?"

Chaney shrugged. "Peter Lorre?"

Lou grabbed the photo back. "Not 'M', like the Peter Lorre movie, I mean 'M' like a guy's name." He pointed at the two men. "It's gotta be one of these two guys." Costello snapped his fingers. "Come to think of it, that static on the line sounded kinda familiar."

Chaney glared incredulously. "How can *static* sound familiar?"

"It sounded just like the phone call I made earlier to Eddie's radiophone. So the 'M' is 'M' for *Mannix.*" He shook his head. "I guess I owe Bats an apology. He didn't trust Eddie the whole time."

Bela, Jr. indicated the unconscious girls. "What are we gonna do about them? They'll be awful sore when they wake up."

"I ain't so worried about the girls," Costello said. "If those pills work like Lenore said they do, she and Jane won't remember nothin'." Lou looked down at the sleeping Lenore Aubert. "But we oughta get them pills just in case. They might come in handy."

"I'll go get 'em." Chaney headed for the kitchenette.

Costello whistled and waved him back. "They ain't in the kitchen."

"If they're not in the kitchen, then where are they?"

"Well." Lou mimed putting an imaginary pill bottle in between imaginary breasts. "They're, uh, in her safety deposit box."

Chaney pointed at Lenore. "Aw, now you're not suggesting we…."

"We gotta," said Lou. "It's either that, or we grab her by the ankles and shake her until they fall out."

"I suppose you're right." Chaney frowned, gesturing nervously as he whispered, "So, who's gonna go in and get it?"

Costello chewed on his fingernail as he considered the problem. He suddenly remembered a routine that might get him off the hook. "Tell you what," Lou said slyly. "I'm thinkin' of a number. If you guess the number, then I get the pills. If you don't guess the number, then you get the pills."

"Okay." Lon thought a moment. "Is it a number between 1 and 10?"

"Uh huh." Costello winked at Bela, Jr. and said in his sing-song little boy voice, "He's not gonna get it."

"Is it number 5?" Chaney guessed quickly.

Lou's face fell.

"Aha!" Chaney said triumphantly. "I was right, wasn't I?"

"It always works when Bud does it to me," Costello said, hoisted by his own comic petard.

With a heavy sigh, Lou rolled Lenore on her back and made the tentative reach to feel around inside her cleavage, and then got cold feet, flinched and pulled back. He nervously rubbed his hands together and looked at his companions. "Pinky swear you don't tell my wife," he said, extending his digit.

The three made a pact. "Pinky swear," Lon and Bela, Jr. agreed.

Shutting his eyes, Costello tentatively slipped his hand between Lenore's warm, soft breasts.

Lon covered Bela, Jr.'s eyes.

Lou felt around until he found the top of the glass pill bottle. "Got it," he said, and quickly pulled the bottle out. He looked down at Lenore, who continued to sleep soundly. He noticed his probing had left her breasts askew. Not thinking, he fluffed them up the way a housekeeper fluffs pillows. Once he was satisfied that they were resting correctly in their bra cups, he patted her hand. "There, that's better."

"Wow," Chaney marveled, "she didn't wake up or nothin'."

"This must be some pretty strong stuff," Costello said, holding up the bottle.

"Okay," said Chaney, "we got the pills, so now what?"

"Now," said Lou, pocketing the pill bottle, "we gotta get help, and then get to the studio."

"Help?" asked Lon. "Who are you gonna go to for help?"

Chapter 22

Thursday, 26 February 1948
2:00 A.M.
Suite 204, Hollywood Knickerbocker Hotel

Chaney and Bela, Jr. followed Costello to the suite across the hall. Lou knocked on the door and Kalara answered.

"What do *you* want?" she asked.

Costello pointed behind Kalara at the bedroom. "Is that other guy that got whacked by the door awake now?"

"Vidor? Yes, he has headache, but he is otherwise well. Why do you ask?"

"Your boss lady and my friends are in big trouble. Your brudder's in Dutch, too."

Kalara crossed her arms. "Why would they take Janika to Holland?"

"No," Chaney explained. "*Bein' in Dutch*, it means he's in trouble."

"Right," said Costello. "So we gotta team up. The CIA is settin' everybody up to get killed."

Kalara eyed Lou warily. "I should listen to you the way you feel about Communists? And the way you eavesdrop on Bela Lugosi? For all I know it is *you* who is setting *us* up for CIA."

"Honest Injun," Lou insisted, crossing his heart. "It's the truth, lady."

Chaney pointed at the room across the hall. "Aw, you musta heard it for yourself," he said. "Don't you eavesdrop on all the phone calls in this hotel?"

"There was no such call," Kalara insisted.

Costello reached into his pocket. "Look, Lenore made a call to some guy who's name starts with 'M.'" He showed Kalara the photograph. "One of these two guys. He told her to shoot Jane, only I switched drinks and she got the Mickey before she could do it."

Kalara took the photo and eyed Lou narrowly. "What does cartoon mouse have to do with anything?"

Chaney explained, "He means a Mickey *Finn*, not a Mickey Mouse. It's knockout drops, see." He nudged Costello. "Show her the pills, Lou."

Costello gave Kalara the pill bottle. "Lenore and Jane put these here pills in our drinks." Kalara poured the pills into her gloved hand as Lou explained, "They're also supposed to make you forget stuff that happened."

Kalara touched one of the pills to the tip of her tongue. "Yes, we have something similar," she said. "It creates blackout similar to drinking too much the alcohol." She poured the pills back in the bottle and handed the bottle back to Costello. "You say this Lenore lady just this minute made phone call to CIA agent named 'M'?"

"That's right," said Chaney.

Lou nodded. "Like I said, I switched the drinks around and she got the Mickey and she was knocked out and I got on the phone," Lou resumed his falsetto, "and pretended to be her like this."

Kalara glared incredulously. "You really fool this man with *that* voice?"

Costello nodded and piped, "Uh huh."

The lady agent shook her head and sighed. "CIA must be hard up for operatives."

Costello shrugged. "I dunno. We had a bad connection. I figure it was from talking to Eddie on his radiophone, or maybe the static came from that gizmo she used when she made the call."

Kalara perked up immediately. "Gizmo? What is gizmo?" she pressed.

"It was a doodad about that big. She clicked on the plunger like this," Lou pantomimed as he explained, "and there was a *beep!*"

Kalara drummed her fingers on the doorjamb while she considered things. "Must be new kind of scrambler."

"What's eggs gotta do with it?" asked Lou.

Kalara ignored the remark. "Would be useful to have one," she mused aloud, "so I can 'invent' it and impress superiors."

"Tell you what," Chaney suggested, "if you help us, we'll give you Lenore's gizmo."

"You can't do that!" insisted Bela, Jr. "This lady's a Red. If you give her CIA property, you could go to jail, or worse, get shot by a firing squad!"

Costello gulped. "F-f-firing squad?" he stammered.

Kalara nodded. "Son of Great Lugosi is right. But your treachery *would* be appreciated."

Costello hesitated a moment, and then shrugged. "Okay, whatever it takes for you guys to help us help our pals."

Bela, Jr. stood at attention. "It's my duty to report any Un-American activities that I see, SIR!"

"Get a load of the kid," Lou complained. "He's gonna turn us in."

Chaney tapped the boy on the shoulder. "What if you cover your eyes and you don't see us do nothin'."

"Well," Bela, Jr. said, "I guess that'd be okay."

"Okay," Lon said with a smile, "cover your eyes and count to a hundred."

Bela, Jr. quirked an eyebrow in much the way Basil Rathbone had, and then sighed and covered his eyes. "One, two, three, four...," he said aloud.

"Okay, now that that's settled," Costello rubbed his hands together and smiled at Kalara, "let's you and me go to work, toots."

Kalara returned his smile with a glare of contempt. "Do not *toots* me! Now, it is 'toots,' but before it was 'Commie!' You say you want to help my comrades, but why should you want to help us if you feel the way you do about Communism?"

"Listen, lady," said Costello, "I think what your government does is rotten to the core. You people don't have no freedom at all."

"*Any* freedom at all," Kalara corrected.

"See, even you admit it. But now it looks like we got us somebody on our side doin' stuff like a Communist, and that don't sit well with me. Call me crazy, but I don't think we gotta act like Commies to fight Commies."

Kalara smirked. "You are very naïve."

Costello shrugged. "Okay, maybe I'm bein' a knave, but I still think we gotta work together."

Kalara relented. "Very well. But your government will never forgive you if truth

and the House of Doom

comes out."

"Lady, I'm already in trouble with the IRS. What more can they do to me?"

"Young Lugosi did mention firing squad."

Costello swallowed hard. "Don't remind me," he said.

"Speaking of boy," she said, nodding at Bela, Jr. "What do we do with him?"

"…fifteen, sixteen, seventeen, eighteen…"

Chaney tapped him on the shoulder. Bela, Jr. looked up. "What? I thought you wanted me to close my eyes and count!"

"The lady wants to know if you'd rather wait here while we go rescue your Pop."

Bela, Jr. bristled. "You're not leaving me out of this! I'm a non-commissioned officer and it's my duty to guard our shores from any enemy threat, and save my Dad!"

Lou smiled. "I'll say this for you, kid. You got guts." He nudged the boy. "Close your eyes and count again."

Bela, Jr. grumbled under his breath, sighed, covered his eyes. "One, two, three…"

Chaney pushed the boy into Kalara's suite while Kalara shoved Lou across the hall. "Take me to device."

"Awright! Awright!" Costello complained. "Everybody's all the time shovin' me!"

Entering the suite, Kalara noted the unconscious girls. "So you *were* telling truth."

Lou pointed at the telephone. "Here it is," he said. He was about to pick up the receiver to remove the scrambler when Kalara grabbed the discarded transmitter by mistake.

"Ingenious," she said, examining the transmitter under the light, "it looks just like ordinary telephone microphone."

"Yeah," Costello said, putting the handset back on the hook, "it sure does, don't it?"

Pocketing the transmitter, Kalara assured him, "I tell no one how I get this." She pushed him out of the room and closed the door after them, and then shoved Lou across the hall and back to her suite. "Wait here," she ordered. As Kalara headed to the bedroom to get Vidor up and ready, Bela, Jr. was still counting out loud.

"…thirty-three, thirty-four, thirty-five…"

Costello poked him. "Hey, you can stop countin' now."

Bela, Jr. crossed his arms and shook his head. "I just hope my C.O. doesn't find out about this."

"So what's the plan?" Chaney asked Costello.

Lou shrugged. "I dunno. I'm makin' it up as I go."

Kalara and Vidor emerged from the bedroom with two wooden-stocked submachine guns.

"We are ready," she declared. "What weapons do you have?"

Lou reached into his pockets. "I got a gun and this thing."

Kalara rolled her eyes. "What is so special about lipstick?"

"It's a bomb."

"So it makes chapped lips feel better, how is *that* going to help us?"

"He don't mean a lip balm," Chaney explained. "That's the firebomb the 'M' guy wanted Lou to use to set fire to the hotel."

Kalara handed Vidor her submachine gun. "Wait here, I get you *better* weapons." She returned moments later with a submachine gun for everybody. Handing one to Bela, Jr., she asked, "Do you know how to fire gun?"

Bela, Jr. turned the weapon over in his hands. "Sure. It's a Hungarian variation of the Soviet PPsH41 submachine gun, manufactured in Budapest as the Minta Geppisztoly. It's caliber is 7.6 x 2.5mm with a 40 round staggered row detachable box magazine." He hefted his weapon. "11.9 pounds with a muzzle velocity of 500 to 515 meters per second and a cyclic rate of 700 to 900 rounds per minute."

Kalara sighed. "So short answer is, *yes*, you can fire gun."

Bela, Jr. did a snappy shoulder arms and saluted. "Yes, Ma'am."

"What about you?" she asked Costello.

"Hey, how hard can it be to fire one of these?" He squeezed the trigger by accident and sent a spray of bullets into the air and everyone ducking for cover. Costello screamed over the din of machinegun fire and flung the weapon at the sofa. The room was plunged into silence broken only by a persistent ringing in everybody's ears and the sound of plaster raining down from the ceiling.

Lon glared at Costello. "Okay, I got me a plan of my own," he said, standing up and brushing the plaster dust from his sleeves. "I plan to say as far away from you as possible."

"Is good plan," Vidor agreed as he peered out from behind a chair.

Peeking out from behind the sofa, Kalara said, "So, short answer is, *no*, you do not know how to fire gun."

Costello shrugged. "Maybe not, but I do a routine with Abbott where he's a drill sergeant and I'm a private and he's doin' a rifle drill." He reached for the weapon. "You want I should show you?"

"NO!" everyone exclaimed.

Yet Another Brief Interruption

Interior, Lugosi's Trailer
Morning

Costello was pantomiming firing the submachine gun into the air as he related what he remembered, much to the consternation of Bela Lugosi.

"That could not have happened the way that you say!" Lugosi insisted.

"Sure that's what happened," Lou insisted. "You wasn't there, so what makes you think it didn't?"

Bela gestured impatiently at the ceiling of his trailer. "Because, funnyman, if you had fired a machine gun at the ceiling of a hotel, you would have fired into the floor of the room above you!"

"Who says the room had anybody in it?"

"Somebody, they would have heard you and called the police."

"Maybe Kalara Skorzeny made sure nobody could call out to get the police."

Abbott complained, "Maybe this, maybe that. Come on, Lou. Quit fooling around."

Lugosi glared at Abbott. "Are you certain you have no memories of anything?"

"What? All that business about me deputized as a spy? Certainly not."

Bela shoved the notepaper with Abbott's signature into the straight man's hands. "Look again! There! Your own signature! You must remember something. Think."

"Yeah, Abbott," Costello encouraged. "I'm gettin' tired of tellin' my half of the story all by myself. You gotta read the notes first, and then it'll all come back to ya."

Abbott sighed irritably as he sat down in the makeup chair. "All right, fine. I'll try and remember. But I still think you're both having delusions."

He turned the chair around and faced the mirror as he shuffled through the note pages. He glanced up at his reflection and saw Lugosi standing behind him. Suddenly, he started.

"Do you remember somethin'?" asked Lou.

Abbott gasped. "I remember…driving."

"But you don't drive," Costello pointed out.

"I know!" Abbott gripped the armrests of the makeup chair and started to remember.

Chapter 23

"You are worse than your partner," Bela observed snappishly. "Costello, he drives like a madman while you, Mr. Abbott, drive like a little old lady."

Bud Abbott's knuckles were blanched white from clutching the steering wheel so tight. "I told Rathbone," he moaned, "I told him I couldn't drive. I never have, never could drive, and here I am anyway, drivin', and a hearse yet!" He glanced up in the rearview mirror at the prone *Phantom Creeps* Iron Man. "With a mechanical monster lying in the back!"

"Stop complaining," Bela griped as he jotted something in Lt. Ford's notebook. "It is early in the morning and there is hardly anyone on the road." He glanced over at the speedometer. "Go faster!" They were crawling along at 20 miles an hour on Cahuenga Blvd.

A canvas-covered truck trying to get to the State Highway was stuck behind them. The driver bellowed his horn impatiently.

"Oh, Jesus!" Abbott cried.

"So go faster, or pull over and let him pass."

"But if I pull over, he'll barrel on right past me," Bud whimpered.

"Why is that such a problem?"

"He could force me right off the road!"

Lugosi ought to have been more sympathetic since he himself had never learned to drive, but instead rolled his eyes and carped, "Be quiet. I am trying to compose a letter." He cackled to himself as he wrote, pausing when he felt the eyes of Bud Abbott staring at him. He glowered and pointed. "If the truck bothers you so much, pull over there."

Bud drifted into oncoming traffic as he glanced at Bela's notes. "What are you writing?" he asked, not keeping his eyes on the road.

Lugosi gasped and grabbed the wheel. "We are going to hit those cars! Pay attention!"

Bud started and twisted the wheel, sending the hearse careening all over the road, cutting off the truck, and swerving along the downgrade toward the Hollywood Bowl sign. Bela and Abbott fought with the wheel as the truck driver for *Santa Mira Florists* leaned on his horn and swerved to avoid the hearse and the sign. Sweat broke out across Abbott's brow as he slammed on the brakes, bringing the hearse to a lurching stop amidst a great cloud of dust, and hunched down in shame in the glare of the truck's headlights as the mammoth vehicle rumbled past on its way to the State Highway.

Abbott poked his head over the wheel. "Is he gone?"

"Yes," snarled Bela. "So too is my heart."

"Do you see what I mean, Bela?" he fretted. "I've never driven in my life. I had to drive *one time* for a picture. They gave me a little go-cart to practice in. That's all the driving I've ever done. I'm gonna kill us both, I just know it!"

Bud started and twisted the wheel, sending the hearse careening all over the road...

Lugosi shrugged and quipped, "At least we are in the right kind of car for us to get killed in. Besides, I do not drive, either. Do you see Bela complaining because you are driving?"

"You've been complaining the whole time! What *are* you writing, anyway?"

"Too often Basil Rathbone makes out that he is the Great Detective, and he takes great pleasure in wasting everyone's time by needlessly going over every tiny detail of what he observed, and who it was he suspected."

"Oh, you mean like he does in the Sherlock Holmes movies."

"Precisely. He also likes to take Bela's discoveries and make them his own. Well, this time, Bela will have proof that he is the better detective!" He finished the last sentence and punctuated it with a jab of his pen. "There!" He scribbled the time, day and date. "Now sign your name here."

"Why do you want me to sign it?"

"To witness that I wrote this when I wrote it so Rathbone will know when I wrote it."

Abbott took the notebook, read the opening salutation and frowned. "'Dear Basil Big Deal Celebrity Detective Rathbone?'" he exclaimed, and looked at Bela questioningly. "You want me to sign my name to *this?*"

Lugosi jabbed his finger at the notebook. "Do not criticize my writing, just sign the last page!"

Abbott shrugged and scribbled his name.

Bela took the notebook back and pocketed it, nodding with satisfaction. "Now we see who the better detective is," he said, and then pointed ahead. "Drive. And do it with less complaining and more speed."

Abbott frowned, signaled, and nervously merged onto the State Highway portion of Cahuenga just as Lt. Ford's voice squawked over the jury-rigged radio set, "WHERE THE HELL ARE YOU GUYS? OVER!"

Abbott screamed and let go of the wheel, sending the hearse on a collision course with a roadside palm tree. The collision was avoided by Bela reaching his foot over and hitting the brakes—at least he hoped that pedal was the brakes. As the hearse stopped short, the Hungarian was relieved to discover that indeed they *were* the brakes. He winced as a knife of pain shot up his leg. "Damn, that hurts!" Lugosi complained, grabbing his thigh and rocking back and forth until the knifing subsided.

"What was that?" Abbott asked, looking fretfully around.

"It is just the radio," Lugosi said, indicating a wireless set mounted under the dashboard with a curt gesture. "Answer him!" He hesitated a moment, and then pointed up the street. "On second thought, *you* will drive, *I* will answer him."

As Abbott pulled onto the boulevard once more, Lugosi unhooked the microphone and pushed the talk button. "What do you want?" he demanded.

"You're supposed to say 'over,'" Lt. Ford griped. "Over."

"Over what?" Lugosi asked.

"It means you're finished talking. Over."

"You know I am finished talking when I am not talking anymore!"

"Just say 'over.' Over."

"Fine," Lugosi grumbled. "What do you want? *Over, over.*"

Lugosi heard Ford sigh. "You're just supposed to say 'over' once. Over."

"Fine," griped Lugosi. "What do you want? Over, once over!"

There was a long pause. "Skip it. You're supposed to be following us. Where the hell are you guys? Over."

"It is *your* fault we are late," Lugosi insisted. "We would not have so much of a problem keeping up had Rathbone chosen a driver who can actually *drive*." He added impatiently, "Over, once over, over."

Abbott glanced up at the rearview mirror. A black limousine with diplomatic plates and fluttering Romanian flags was flashing its headlights. "What do they want?" he asked nervously.

"How should I know?" asked Lugosi, as unfamiliar as Bud Abbott regarding the signal to pull over and let the car pass.

• • • •

Rathbone turned the Volkswagen onto Lankershim, keeping an eye on Mannix in the lead car.

Ford had his hands full talking on the radio *and* keeping the antenna from sliding off the roof of the car. He glared at Basil. "Did you know that Bud Abbott couldn't drive?" he asked.

Basil remarked coolly, "There's a difference between not knowing how to drive, and *choosing* not to drive."

Ford sighed and pushed the talk button. "Well, hurry up, Lugosi! We'll be at the Studio in a minute." He glanced out the window. "I'm getting tired holding this antenna on the roof like this!" He shook his head. "Over."

and the House of Doom

Lugosi could be heard chuckling to himself. "Do you not find it strange that the magnet will not stick to the roof? Over, once over."

"I don't see what's so goddamn funny about it," Ford complained. "Over."

"Obviously, neither does Rathbone. Over, once over."

Ford glanced at Basil. "Why's he sounding like the cat that ate the canary?"

"One can only speculate, Lieutenant," Basil said with a shrug.

"Have you awakened Janika yet?" Bela asked. "Over, whatever."

Ford glanced in the back seat. "Hey, Mick, how are you comin' with Skorzeny?"

"He's still out cold," Mickey said. The detective had an open bottle of smelling salts and held it under the unconscious agent's nose. "I think this stuff's lost its potency." He put the bottle under his own nose, took a whiff, and flinched.

"Is it potent?" Ford asked with a smile.

"I'll say."

Ford pushed down on the talk button. "He's still out like a light," he reported to Bela. "Now hurry and catch up! Over."

· · · ·

Back in the hearse, Abbott was nudging Lugosi as Lugosi snarled into the microphone, "Pull over and wait for us, if you are so insistent that we catch up! Over, once over."

"Say," said Abbott. "That friend of yours is having nightmares."

Bela glanced back at the Iron Man as it twitched like a sleeping dog chasing dream rabbits. The Hungarian glared at the microphone in his hand and clicked down on the talk button a number of times, and watched the robot's reaction. Each time he held down the talk button, the Iron Man got spastic. When he let go, it grew quiet.

"So that explains it," said Bela.

"Quit playing with the radio!" Lt. Ford carped. "Over and out!"

"I hope that robot stays where it is," Abbott said, nervously.

Bela hung up the microphone. "*Now* the robot will be quiet," he assured Abbott with confidence.

The driver of the black limousine grew impatient with Abbott's snail's pace driving and swerved around the hearse at the first opportunity, rattling Abbott in the process. The straight man let out a yelp as he lost control of the hearse again.

"What are you trying to do?" Lugosi complained, grabbing the wheel. "Keep us on the road, idiot!"

The hearse ran up onto the curb.

Lugosi gave Abbott a withering stare. "I may regret this for the rest of my life, but I have had enough of your driving!" He pointed with a sweeping gesture. "We switch places! Bela will drive!" He smirked. "And Bela will go where Bela wants to go."

"What do you mean by that?" Abbott asked, getting out.

As Lugosi got out and hurried around to the driver's side, he declared, "I deduce that Lillian is being held prisoner on the back lot! So we go to the back lot! To hell with Rathbone and his ideas!"

Abbott gulped as he got in the passenger seat. "But you said you couldn't drive. Do you at least know how?" he asked anxiously.

Bela ground a few gears putting the car in drive and stamped his foot down on the accelerator, admitting proudly, "No!"

He soon overtook and passed on the right of the black limousine with the fluttering Romanian flags and turned onto Barham Blvd.

• • • •

Kalara swerved to avoid colliding with the speeding hearse, and as she did, she swore a Communist-colored Red streak in her native Hungarian, ending in English with, "Stupid pig dog American drivers!" for the benefit of her passengers.

"That's funny," said Lon Chaney, sitting in back with Costello and Bela, Jr. "The hearse that just passed us looked like Bela Lugosi was drivin'."

Bela, Jr. stuck his head out the window and craned his neck. "That couldn't have been my Dad. He doesn't know how to drive."

"Neither does the stupid American driving that hearse," snarled Kalara. She glared at Bela, Jr. "Sit down!" As Bela, Jr. quickly complied, she asked, "Anyway, what would the great Lugosi be doing driving hearse?"

Chaney shrugged. "Getting a change of pace from riding in the back of one?"

"Are we there yet?" whined Lou Costello in his little boy voice.

"No," said Kalara.

"Are we there yet?"

"No, I said."

Costello paused. "Are we there *now?*"

She eyed Costello's reflection. "*Soon,*" she answered crossly.

Vidor turned and stared angrily. "Listen to Kalara, or we turn right around!"

"Hey," said Chaney, leaning forward, "have you figured out yet where exactly we're goin'?"

"Sit back," Kalara scolded.

Vidor said, "Madame Z spoke of back lot, so we go to back lot."

"So, little fat man," Kalara asked, "how do we get to back lot from here?"

Costello leaned forward and pointed ahead. "See where the hearse is turning off? Go on Barham Blvd. Then you take a bunch of side streets up through Universal City. But it's easier goin' the front way on Lankershim. The back way is a pain in the ass."

She turned onto Barham. "The back way is always pain in the ass," Kalara remarked.

Costello smirked. "Hey, was that a dirty joke? That was pretty good."

"Sit down!" Kalara ordered. "The back way, no one expects."

Lou sat back and nudged Chaney. "Hey," he whispered, "what do you think she'd do if I started kickin' the back of her seat?"

"She'd probably blast ya," Chaney said.

"Oh yeah."

Kalara glared at Vidor. "Remember you ask me once, after moment of passion, about whether what happened to me in Nazi laboratory made me sterile?"

"I do," said Vidor with a nod.

"And that if we should get married and I *can* have children, how many children I want?"

"Yes," said Vidor.

Kalara cast a look in Lou Costello's direction. She shook her head. "No children."

• • • •

Lt. Ford stuck the antenna out the window and turned on the radio. "Lugosi, where the hell are you? Over."

Mickey pointed ahead. "There's something fishy going on with the guardhouse."

The gates were open. Mannix drove right on through without stopping.

Basil pulled up next to the guardhouse and got out. "I'll have a look 'round." He poked his head in the guardhouse window and glance around the tiny office. "The place is deserted," he announced.

Ford pushed the talk button repeatedly. "Lugosi! We're at the main gate but nobody's home. Over." He waited for a response. "Lugosi! Come in. Over!"

• • • •

Lt. Ford's words fell on deaf ears. Lugosi was wending his way down the twisting side roads of Universal City and onto the back lot service road. Abbott kept his eyes shut the whole time. "Tell me when we're there," he whined.

"Stop complaining," Lugosi groused. "Driving, it is not so hard," he said, changing gears without using the clutch. The sound of metal grinding on metal was unnerving.

Abbott reluctantly opened his eyes and pointed at the pedals. "You gotta use the clutch to change gears or you'll break it."

"I thought *that* pedal there was for braking."

"It is. I don't mean break it like you're braking it. I mean break it like you'll break it."

"No more routines!" Lugosi frowned at him. "Just shut up and let me drive."

"Just please slow down!"

"No!" Bela insisted, flooring the accelerator. "There is no time to lose!"

They were almost at the shore of Lubin Lake. Bela recognized what remained of the "Pier on the Island" set. Gaunt rafters of what had once been the boathouse jutted out like ribs of a decomposing animal carcass against the nighttime sky. The firefighters' earlier efforts to put out the blaze had turned the surrounding property into a mud bank. Amazingly, the pier and stone wall portions of the set remained relatively untouched.

Abbott screamed and grabbed Lugosi. "LOOK OUT! You're gonna hit that car!"

A black limousine with Romanian flags was parked by Lugosi's abandoned dressing trailer. Standing by the car were two very familiar figures, one vaguely familiar figure, and a woman with a very nice figure with a tight hold on one of the familiar figures. Lugosi swerved to avoid hitting them.

"Good heavens," exclaimed Boris Karloff.

Richard Septimus Pratt gestured at the hearse and grumbled, "Who is the idiot driving that thing?"

Boris sighed. "That would be Bela Lugosi."

"Lugosi!" Zizi exclaimed.

"But I thought he couldn't drive," remarked Glenn Strange.

"Do you call that driving?" retorted Pratt.

The onlookers watched helplessly as Lugosi sent the hearse crashing through the iron gates of the gothic gateway. The stone wall façade shuddered, creaked and then came tumbling down.

Abbott covered his eyes as Lugosi drove pell-mell down the stone steps and straight onto the pier, crashing into balsa wood crates and barrels.

Abbott peeked, and then wished he hadn't. "YOU'RE GONNA DRIVE US RIGHT INTO THE LAKE!" he screamed.

"Stop distracting me!" Lugosi complained as he slammed on the brakes and brought the hearse to a screeching halt inches from the edge of the pier.

The wooden supports began to creak beneath them. Abbott opened the passenger door to escape, but could only gawk at the surrounding brackish water below. He slammed the door shut and begged, "Get us outta here before the pier collapses!"

"Shut up, front seat driver!" Bela complained as he struggled with the stick shift.

Boris and his brother hurried down to the pier to render assistance. "Bela, are you all right?" Boris called.

"THE CLUTCH!" Abbott screamed as he pointed down at the pedal. "USE THE CLUTCH!"

"I know!" Lugosi snarled. He depressed the clutch and reversed gears and stamped down on the accelerator. The rear wheels spun out, leaving black tire marks as the hearse lurched back at full speed.

Karloff and Pratt reversed gears themselves, dashing up the stone steps with the rear bumper of the hearse hot at their heels.

"STOP!" Abbott screamed. "You're gonna kill Karloff!"

"Be quiet! You are making me nervous," Bela grumbled as he twisted the steering wheel.

"I'm making *you* nervous?" Abbott's nails dug deep into the car seat upholstery as he stared horrorstruck at the rearview mirror.

The hearse careened backward off the stone steps and headed, or rather, tailed, straight for what remained of the boathouse.

"I CAN'T LOOK!" Abbott shrieked as he threw his arms over his eyes.

The imminent crashing into blackened rafters and melted gas drums was interrupted by the hearse lurching to a neck-snapping halt. The rear tires spun freely, digging their way into the surrounding mud bank, that is, until Bela turned off the engine. He smiled and said, "Now *that* is good driving!"

Abbott had had enough. He yanked desperately on the handle, kicked the door open, scrambled out of the hearse, waved his arms about as he tried to keep his footing while stumbling out of the mud and then scrambled up the steps to get as far away from the hearse and Bela Lugosi's driving as he could.

"Coward!" Lugosi called after him. He rolled down the driver's side window and saw Karloff and the old man who looked like Karloff approach.

"Are you insane?" Pratt growled angrily. "You could have killed us!"

"You look alive enough to me," Bela retorted. He scowled at Boris. "It serves you right, trying to keep secrets from Bela. I knew you and Rathbone were up to something!"

"I wanted to tell you," Boris said earnestly, and then glanced at his brother. "But I couldn't for…External Security interests."

"BAH! I find out the truth anyway, because *I*, Bela Lugosi, am a better detective than all of you together!" He eyed Boris narrowly, pointing at Pratt. "So who is this man really? Or is *that* a secret too?"

"Why, this is my brother." Boris made introductions. "Richard Septimus Pratt," he said, "this is Bela Lugosi."

"We've met," Pratt said curtly.

Bela gave the MI6 operative a disdainful leer as he remarked to Boris, "He looks like you, but he behaves like Rathbone." He gave Pratt a hard look. "That was *not* a compliment."

"I'm hurt," Pratt said sarcastically. "Now do you mind telling me what you are doing here on the back lot?"

"Yes," said Boris. "I thought you were supposed to accompany Basil and Lt. Ford to Stage 17."

Lugosi waved impatiently. "They do not need Bela to deliver their gold," adding with a smirk, "they do not even know where the real gold is, but Bela Lugosi, *he* knows."

"You do!" Pratt exclaimed. "Where? It's vital that we know."

Bela smiled fiendishly. "Oh, I cannot reveal such a secret, it would be against External Security interests."

"Now see here…," Pratt began.

Bela scowled and demanded, "Never mind why *I* am here, what is it that *you* are doing here?"

"We're here to find the bomb, of course," said Boris.

"Yes, the atomic bomb that could level this whole valley." Pratt gestured toward the pier. "The green 'X' on the map suggested that we begin our search in the lake."

"Basil briefed us about the map you found," Boris explained.

"Rathbone," Bela snarled. "BAH! He thinks that 'X' on the map means there is a bomb here. But I know what it really means. It means that Lillian is here! I know she is! If you are going to hide someone, you hide them where you have already looked, and we have already looked in my trailer. So Lillian is there. I know it!" He stepped from the car and right into the mud. "Damn, look at my shoes!"

Just then Glenn Strange descended the stone steps with the sexy dark-haired woman in leather on his arm. The deliciously dangerous looking woman asked Glenn, "Are you *happily* married?"

"Very," Glenn insisted. "And I'd appreciate it, Ma'am, if you would give me some space."

"But you are my hostage," the leather-clad woman insisted, tightly hugging his huge arm, and adding with a sly wink, "I must stay close or you might escape my clutches."

Glenn tried to pry her loose but found the vicious vixen's grip tenacious. "Pardon me for saying, Ma'am, but that seems mighty unlikely."

But when Zizi laid eyes on Bela Lugosi, she became like many a starry-eyed bobby-soxer who fainted at the sight of Frank Sinatra. "There he is! There is Bela Lugosi! World's greatest living actor!"

The fickle villainess quickly abandoned Glenn, which suited Glenn just fine. He clenched and unclenched his fist and shook his hand out. "Maybe now I can get my circulation back."

As Zizi ran down to meet Lugosi, she found her way blocked by Pratt. "We really don't have time for this," he vehemently insisted.

Zizi gave her former arch enemy the cold shoulder. "It is my mission," she said haughtily. "I make time!" She added, "You are just jealous."

Pratt grew flush and flustered. "Jealous? Don't be absurd. Why, you're young enough to be my...not to mention that you're completely...and we're on opposite...!"

"You protest too much, Richard." She pushed Pratt aside and reached out to Bela. "Take my hand; I pull you out of mud. Or even better, darling, pull me in and we roll around in it together."

Bela smiled, forgetting about his muddy dress shoes as Zizi helped him onto firmer ground. "You are a fan?"

Zizi sighed, breasts heaving. "Very much so, Great Lugosi." She caressed his cheek and whispered, "I am Madame Z, but you may call me Zizi. You may also call me anytime, day or night." She sighed and then whispered in his ear, "Are you *happily* married?"

R.S. Pratt rolled his eyes. "Oh, honestly."

Boris waved Glenn over. "I say, Glenn, do please help me get this hearse out of the mud."

"Why, sure."

Boris got behind the wheel, while Glenn waded into the mud bank and dug his heels in and pushed on the rear bumper. The tires spun and found some traction and Boris drove the hearse out of the mud bank and up onto the crest of the hill near the limousine.

The smell of burning oil filled the chilly night air as Boris got out and waved. "Much obliged, Glenn."

The mud-spattered Glenn Strange waved back. "Anytime, Boris." He looked down at his boots and duster and chuckled. "Remember that time we were both in the quicksand together?"

"*House of Frankenstein*," Boris said. "I remember."

Glenn shivered. "At least this mud ain't as deep. Mighty cold, though." He chuckled again. "Too bad Lon isn't here. He could give me a shot of whiskey."

"Time is of the essence," Pratt said tersely. "Go get the motorboat ready. We'll need it to search the lake."

"Yes, sir," Glenn said with a cheery salute. He extricated himself from the mud and headed down to the dock.

Madame Z eyed Bela hungrily. "Yes, Mr. Glenn, you get boat; I get Lugosi." She hugged Bela and then jumped up and down excitedly. "I cannot believe it is you at last! You are just as I pictured you!"

Pratt eyed Bela and remarked coolly, "It's probably the tuxedo," and nudged Zizi impatiently. "Well, ask him if you're going to ask him."

Glenn pointed out at the lake. "Hey, the motorboat got loose!" he shouted. The motorboat had escaped its moorings and was adrift near one of the camera platforms.

Pratt called back, "See if you can wade out there and bring it to shore."

"Sure thing," said Glenn. "Maybe I can wash some of this mud off while I'm at it."

Pratt sighed. "Zizi, will you *please* ask Lugosi what you wanted to ask him."

"Ask me what?" Bela said, basking in the woman's adoration.

"Great Lugosi," she said, large breasts swelling, eyes wide and glistening, "I am here on behalf of Hungarian government to bring you and your family back to your homeland so you may assume your rightful place as new Minister of Culture."

Lugosi's eyes brightened. "Aha! The invitation was not a trick!" he said. "You really did want Bela as the new Minister of Culture after all!" He smiled. "Lillian was wrong!"

"Trick?" Madame Z asked. "What trick? What do you mean trick?"

"My wife," Bela explained, "she thought your invitation was a trick and that you really wanted to throw me in a Gulag."

Zizi scowled. "Who wants to throw you in Gulag? Certainly not I! I will kill anyone who would throw you in Gulag!"

Lugosi smiled triumphantly. "But in my heart I knew Lillian was wrong."

Madame Z was beside herself. "Of course she was wrong! My orders come from none other than our illustrious Director, Lieutenant-General Gheorghe Pintilie. He, too, is great Lugosi fan and cannot wait to honor you."

Pratt cleared his throat. "But your Director's *superiors* are KGB."

Zizi turned and eyed him narrowly. "What are you suggesting, Richard?"

"Well, the KGB has their own agenda, Zizi. Mrs. Lugosi has a point."

"Do not try to dissuade me, Richard. I am determined to bring Lugosi home."

"I have no intension of dissuading you. But if your superiors had told you that what they *really* intended was to make an example of Bela Lugosi by throwing him in a Gulag, would you have accepted the assignment to bring him home?"

"Of course not!" Zizi denied.

"Then isn't it possible that they lied to you?"

Bela's renewed hope for a bright future was dashed as the domineering beauty's look of adoration was replaced by expressions of confusion, wavering resolve, and finally, seething hatred.

"No!" she snarled. "It cannot be! And yet, it must be so! I have been played for a fool!" Her fists clenched. "Whoever is responsible for this treachery, I will destroy with my own hands!" She looked longingly into Bela's eyes, stroking his cheek, her voice choked with regret. "I cannot bring you home, not if it means a fate more horrible than Poverty Row pictures."

Just then, a second limousine pulled up.

"We've got company," Karloff shouted, indicating the new arrivals.

"Now who can *that* be?" asked Abbott.

"Karloff!" Vidor exclaimed eagerly as he emerged from the limousine. "Kalara, look! It is Boris Karloff!"

"Not now, Vidor," Kalara scolded.

"ABBOTT!" Costello shouted when he spotted his partner. "HEY, ABBOTT!"

"LOU!" Abbott shouted happily.

The instant Lugosi saw Bela, Jr., he shouted, "SON!" and knelt down and threw his arms wide as the boy ran down the stone steps to meet him.

"DAD!" the boy exclaimed.

Lugosi was close to tears as they hugged. "You are alive! My son! My son!"

Richard Septimus Pratt observed this emotional display with an impatient frown as Lon Chaney hurried over. Together they watched as father and son, and comic and straight man, each shared their own tender moment of reunion.

"Revolting," Pratt declared with British reserve.

"Aw, I dunno," said Lon, patting his chest. "It kinda gets you right here."

Pratt patted his queasy stomach. "You've aimed too high," he said.

Lugosi said, "Son, run and look in our trailer. If your father is right, your mother will be there."

"Mom?" Bela, Jr. called, running up the steps. Lugosi waited as his son searched around inside. The boy stepped out and shook his head in disappointment. "She's not in there, Dad."

"Impossible," Bela said. "She must be there."

With arms akimbo, Abbott complained, "So you nearly killed us both racing over here for nothing?"

Costello eyed his partner questioningly. "What's that supposed to mean?"

"Lou, you have no idea what I've been through. Lugosi's driving nearly killed us both."

Costello jerked a thumb back at the hearse. "You mean, Lugosi wuz drivin'?"

Lugosi looked fiercely at Abbott. "His driving was worse!" he snapped.

"At least I know what a clutch is for!" Abbott snapped back.

Costello wolf-whistled in disbelief. "And here I was on the road with you two guys drivin'." He shook his head. "An' I thought bein' with that Kalara dame was dangerous."

"Kalara!" Madame Z exclaimed. "What are you and Vidor doing here? I ordered you to remain at his side."

Kalara gestured at Vidor with her submachine gun. "He *is* at my side, my Mistress."

Madame Z stamped her foot angrily. "That is *not* what I meant! You will be punished for insubordination."

"Hey!" Costello snapped back. "Be nice to her. We came here to warn ya about the trap!"

"What trap?" Pratt asked with a skeptical leer.

"There's a CIA assassin out for your necks, is what trap. He wants to kill ya all and blame it on this dame," he said, jerking a thumb at Madame Z.

"Who would dare?" Madame Z pointed accusingly at Costello. "Did you know that he had your trailer bugged?"

"What do you mean?" Lugosi pressed.

Costello waved for Madame Z to be quiet as she continued, "He wanted to gather evidence enough to bring you before House Un-American Activities Committee just so he could escape his tax problems!"

Costello chewed his nails and looked shamefaced at the fuming Lugosi as Bela snarled, "So *that* is why you insist that Bela has his own trailer! Not because you think Bela is a big star, but because you are a bugger!" Bela reached into his pocket for the button-sized listening device and testily threw the microphone down at Lou's feet, and then he got in Lou's face. "*That* is why you wanted to be my Watson! So you could spy upon me!" Angrily adding, "BUGGER!"

Pratt laid a hand on the angry Hungarian's shoulder. "That accusation isn't what you think it means, old boy."

Zizi pushed Bela aside and wagged an accusing finger in Lou's face. "You make me so ashamed that I cannot even admire your act of treachery!" She kicked him in the shin. Costello yelped and whined as he hopped on one foot. Madame Z said, "*That* is for giving me momentary feelings of moral uncertainty!" Zizi grabbed Bela from behind, nuzzling him. "Do not fear, my darling, Zizi will protect you from all harm."

Pratt's mouth twisted into a frown. "But who's going to protect him from you?" he asked.

Whimpering, Lou limped out onto the pier, nursing his stinging ankle, when out in the middle of the lake a churning tumult of bubbles and froth erupted underneath the second camera platform.

"Hey, look!" shouted Abbott, pointing out at the lake.

As everyone watched in astonishment, the camera platform parted, and then slowly, majestically, a red cigar-shaped projectile with a hammer and sickle insignia painted on its fins emerged, revealing the platform's true purpose as a façade for a hidden missile silo.

"Dear Lord," gasped Boris.

The capricious Madame Z nearly swooned. "That is V-2 rocket! Where would he get V-2 rocket?"

"Why's it got Russian symbols on it?" asked Abbott.

"Is it not obvious?" Madame Z said. "To make it appear as though Russia wants to start atomic war!" She eyed Lugosi, grabbed him roughly by the lapels of his tuxedo. "We go to trailer," she snarled. "This evil plan is making me so sexy hot I *must* have a man *now!*"

Lugosi admitted to himself that had Lillian not been missing, and had Bela, Jr. not been present, he would have taken Zizi up on her offer in a staked heartbeat. But such was not to be. He said, "I must find my wife." He stroked her cheek and whispered, "But had this been another time, I would have gladly invited you to tour with me as my baby."

Madame Z held Bela's hand and nuzzled his palm against her cheek. "And I would have let you diaper me."

Shocked at the idea, Lugosi quickly took his hand back. "That is not what I meant!"

The frosty night air was suddenly filled with the loud crackling of electricity. Over hidden loudspeakers, a voice with an Austrian accent said, "Testing, testing." Then there was a sharp EEEEEEEEE of feedback, followed by, "Can you hear me?"

Lugosi winced.

"Yes," shouted Pratt, holding his ears. "We hear you. Kindly turn it down a bit. Where are you?"

At a less booming level, the voice asked, "Better?"

"Yes," said Pratt. "Now answer the question. Where are you?"

A large television camera mounted on one of the platforms swung around to focus on them.

"Hey, look!" shouted Abbott, pointing out at the lake.

Boris pointed. "We're being watched."

"I'm watching you from a safe distance," the voice lauded dramatically, "secure within my secret lair!"

"I take it," said Karloff, "that you are Dr. Tod N. Kopf, alias Dr. Rache."

"Or should we call you Dr. Skull, or is it Dr. Death's Head?" asked Pratt.

"Or Dr. Death?" asked Zizi.

Costello nudged Abbott. "This guy needs a press agent."

Abbott gestured for Lou to be quiet.

"You are speaking to the brain behind the skull. Dr. Death was merely the lead player in my great drama of vengeance." He paused dramatically, and then announced, "You may call me *Herr Direktor!*"

"Very commanding," cooed Madame Z as she preened lustfully. "I am most impressed with your handiwork, *Herr Direktor*. It is quite ingenious." She smiled coquettishly. "Do you have a girlfriend? How tall are you? I like tall men. Although, ambitious short men, like Napoleon, they are nice, too."

"I am married."

"Are you *happily* married?"

Costello threw up his hands. "Here we go again."

Richard Pratt frowned reproachfully at her. "Really, Zizi, this is hardly the time for *that* sort of thing." He pointed out at the lake where Glenn was wading back with the recovered motorboat in tow and addressed the voice. "I don't know what you're up to, but I urge you to stop whatever it is you're planning."

"Surely," said *Herr Direktor*, "you have guessed at least some of my plan."

and the House of Doom

Pratt harrumphed impatiently. "All right, *Herr Direktor*, it appears that you're going to destroy some prominent target, a monument or tourist attraction of some sort. You somehow convinced the studio you're making a picture that required a V-2 rocket and you let the special effects and set construction departments do your dirty work for you."

"Oh, that is so clever!" Zizi said. "Think of the money he saved." She turned to Kalara and said with a shake of her head, "Why did *I* not think of this?"

Pratt sighed and continued to address the disembodied voice. "What I find perplexing about this scheme is that you're doing it without making threats, or ransom demands—that you're just blowing up your target! How are you going to profit from this without making ransom demands? That simply isn't done, old boy. Very bad form."

"Fool," said the voice. "Do you think I am doing this simply for profit? I am doing it for *art!*"

"Be that as it may," Pratt said, "where have you aimed that thing?"

"I have no intention of telling you. If I did, you would have the area evacuated. Not that it would help. The countdown has already begun!" He chuckled. "But I *will* tell you that the CIA is going to blame this on Russia."

Costello tugged on Lugosi's sleeve. "See? I told you the CIA was behind this!"

Lugosi yanked his sleeve from Lou's grasp, threatening to strike him. "Stay away from me, bugger," he warned.

Glenn tied off the motorboat and joined the others, asking, "Is he the Nazi you guys have been tellin' me about?"

"I am *not* a Nazi!" *Herr Direktor* denied. "I merely exploited Rache and his co-conspirators as any director would exploit a cast and production crew."

"Then that means," Pratt said, "you really *are* Fredek Vivas!"

Madame Z shook her head. "That is *not* my half-brother's voice."

Kalara's eyes narrowed. "Good! Then you will not mind when I kill him!"

Madame Z sternly hushed her.

The voice taunted, "The tattoo I showed Rathbone and Karloff was a fake! I merely made use of Fredek's serial numbers. Fredek had no further use for them, since I had his arm amputated."

"Why did you do that?" asked Karloff.

"To complete his disguise, of course."

"His disguise?" exclaimed Madame Z.

"Then you must be Dr. Sigmund Rache," Pratt concluded. "The real name of *Doktor Halál.*"

"No," said *Herr Direktor.* "*Fredek* was Rache. They were one and the same! He portrayed the mad Dr. Sigmund Rache, but it was *I* who gave him the role!"

Pratt nudged his brother and whispered, "Rache, by the way is German for 'revenge.'"

"Yes, I know," Boris sniped with brotherly peevishness. "It's also the very first clue used in the very first Sherlock Holmes story, *A Study in Scarlet.*" He shrugged when Pratt raised a questioning eyebrow. "When you spend enough time with Basil Rathbone, you pick these things up."

Kalara sneered at the disembodied voice. "You are the one who gave *Doktor Halál* his orders!" She aimed her submachine gun at the launching pad gantry where a PA speaker was mounted. "Then you should die with him!"

"Kalara, no!" Vidor shouted.

But Kalara was too consumed by hatred to listen. She fired a spray of bullets that blasted the speaker to smithereens.

Madame Z tore the machine gun from Kalara's hands. "You will remain at attention, Comrade Skorzeny!" She waited for Kalara to obey before handing back her weapon. "Shoulder your arms!" She stared the girl down. "That was stupid! You might have detonated rocket and killed us all!"

Kalara stood at rigid attention. "I beg forgiveness, my Mistress," she said. "It is not my place to question your motives." With the hint of a snarl, she added, "Or your family ties."

There was an audible clearing of a throat coming from other loudspeakers mounted in the surrounding trees. "May I continue?"

"Do forgive the interruption," Pratt apologized. "Go on, please."

"Very well," said *Herr Direktor*. "How I came to hear of Fredek Vivas is unimportant. Vivas had a plan to build a criminal empire and he needed my help. I saw this as a perfect opportunity to film the rise and fall of a criminal mastermind."

"Criminal mastermind? Fredek?!" Zizi exclaimed.

"Disguised as an SS officer, I was able to engineer his escape from the concentration camp where he was sentenced to die, and by combining my genius with his talent for magic, engineering, and forging documents, it was easy to convince the Luftwaffe that he, in the guise of Dr. Sigmund Rache, had a new cryonics technique! Of course, his arm with the serial numbers had to be amputated. Nazi scientists do not have concentration camp tattoos. Besides, the mechanical arm he devised was perfect for creating a striking character."

"But all of those deaths!" Karloff protested. "Those horrible experiments in the House of Doom! You arranged to have Rache conduct those experiments *knowing* they were deadly?"

"Death is drama! The House of Doom was the perfect backdrop for the opening chapters of my great film! For the first time, I had unflinching realism!"

"Are you trying to tell us," said Pratt, "that you did it to make a documentary?"

"Not a documentary; a reality piece! I leave mere documentation to the likes of Leni Riefenstahl! Mine is a drama wherein I manipulate real life situations to bring about plot and conflict! That is why I arranged to have Kalara Skorzeny see Fredek Vivas while he was in the role of Dr. Fell. I knew she would recognize him as Sigmund Rache in disguise! Her reaction was real, but the situation was all *my* doing!"

"You used me for a stupid movie!" Kalara snarled. She was about to raise her weapon when Madame Z grabbed the muzzle.

The voice continued, "The conflict begun by Kalara's reaction to Dr. Fell, led to the situation where Janika Skorzeny killed Fredek Vivas in the guise of Rache! It was a true, but completely manipulated, series of dramatic events that made for the perfect closing chapter to Rache's story arc! Do you not see my genius in all of this?"

and the House of Doom

"Genius?" Vidor said, pointing at his face. "Rache arranged for me to endure many skin grafting experiments! This face, it came from a cadaver!" He nudged Abbott and whispered. "The joke, it is on him, because this face, it is much handsomer than my old one." He added, "And Kalara, she likes men with scars."

Kalara jerked her submachine gun free of Madame Z's grasp and ran onto the pier and gave the TV camera a fixed stare of naked rage. "You used us! How dare you! I will hunt you down and kill you with my bare hands!"

Madame Z stamped her foot. "Attention!" she commanded, causing Kalara to hurry back to her position and snap back into line with Vidor. Zizi addressed the TV camera out in the lake. "Was it really necessary to actually kill my half-brother for your picture?"

"When I want my actors to die, they will stay dead!"

Madame Z huffed aloofly, "So *you* are the puppet master."

"Yes."

"You dared to interfere with my mission for your own twisted scheme."

"Yes."

"And you are doing all this just to make movie?"

"Exactly."

"And you are not my half-brother?"

"Certainly not."

Madame Z ran her tongue over her teeth and preened. "Good. Because I am so sexy hot for you right now!" She pulled down the cups of her bustier and flashed the camera. "TAKE ME!"

The voice gasped. "Madame Avinashi!"

Pratt held up his hand to block his view of Zizi's exposed breasts. "Madame Avinashi?" he said, looking away. "What does your mother have to do with this?"

Zizi shrugged. "As you know, Richard, Mother, she got around…a lot." She explained to the disembodied voice, "I am Madame A's daughter, Madame Z." She gave him a saucy smile as she cupped her bosom invitingly. "Play cards right and you can work your way through alphabet." She jiggled them temptingly.

"But that mole," the voice insisted, "that body, I know every curve. You *are* Madame Avinashi."

"Sorry, darling. My mother, she has passed away."

Pratt forgot himself and stared at Zizi disbelievingly, and then recovered himself and resumed blocking his view of her with his hand. "Avinashi is dead?" he asked, a hint of sadness in his usually reserved voice.

"Yes, Richard. Even Madame Avinashi, she cannot live forever."

"When did she…?"

Zizi secured her breasts back in the cups of her costume and gave her longtime adversary a sympathetic smile. "It was a few years after the war. She saw that the world was going to be something very different from what she knew, and well, she arranged to die happily in her sleep. Well, in bed at least." She smiled wickedly. "Actually, there was very little sleeping. Did you ever hear story of Claudius's wife and the many men she bedded at one time?"

"Say no more," Pratt said.

Zizi hugged herself. "What a way to go. I should die so wonderfully."

"Seriously," Pratt insisted, "say no more."

"No!" the voice broke in. "You are lying, playing another of your sadistic games. But it doesn't matter now. All the players are in place, and the cameras are turning, just as you desired."

"I say," Pratt asked, "are you suggesting Madame A has something to do with all this?"

"I have said too much already." The TV camera focused on the motorboat. "I suspect you will want to try and disarm the bomb."

Karloff frowned. "You mean you *want* us to?"

"Of course! It will add to the conflict in this scene!"

Pratt nudged his brother. "He's mad. He's treating us like actors in his film. Just play along."

Karloff shrugged. "It wouldn't be the first crazed director I've worked for."

The voice announced, "ACTION!"

The loudspeakers went silent.

Kalara saluted. "Permission to speak, Ma'am."

"You may speak," Madame Z said.

"Why did you try to seduce the man responsible for the House of Doom? He is my sworn enemy, mine and Vidor's and Janika's, and you seem not at all concerned about our feelings. Your behavior, it is wanton, selfish, and has given me much emotional pain. I have been loyal to you. Why do this to me? Why?"

Madame Z considered the question. She shrugged and said matter-of-factly, "Isn't it obvious?" She gestured at her costume and produced her riding crop. "Because I am sadist. Inflicting pain and taking pleasure in it, it is what I do."

Costello nudged Kalara and said, "The short answer is, she's nuts."

Pratt nodded back at the waiting hearse and second limousine. "All of you go to the studio where you belong. Madame Z and I will handle things here." He held his hand out expectantly. "Billy, give me your toolkit."

"Nonsense," Boris insisted. "I'm staying with you."

"Fine," Pratt relented. "But the rest of you, out!"

"Bela Lugosi is afraid of nothing!" Bela declared, his ego fortified by Madame Z's lustful devotion.

"Is he not magnificent?" the femme fatale gushed. "So brave!" She kissed him and said, "But you must go, my darling. The world must not be denied the genius of Bela Lugosi." She gave Kalara a reproachful stare. "Since you insist on being here, you will keep Great Lugosi safe." She reached under her utility skirt and produced a small flare gun. "You will escort Lugosi to front lot. I will summon Imre, Tovar and Gergo. They at least follow orders." She addressed Vidor. "You will drive other limousine."

Bela, Jr. took his father's arm, glaring at Zizi. "And I'm getting Dad as far away from *you* as I can." He pulled his father in the direction of the hearse. "Come on, Dad."

Bela chuckled and smiled proudly at his son. "Now you see what a good driver I have become."

As they headed up the steps, Abbott blocked their way and pointed at the boy. "Uh, Bela, you're not going to drive with your son in the car, are you?"

Lugosi's shoulders hunched angrily. "Are you suggesting that Bela Lugosi, he is not good enough a driver to drive his own son?"

"No, I'm not suggesting that at all."

"Good." Lugosi brushed Abbott aside and strode up to the hearse.

Abbott quickly blocked his way again. "I'm flat out saying it."

"What! Get away from me." He continued his advance.

Abbott stubbornly followed. "Bela, no offense, but you are the worse driver to ever get behind the wheel of any car ever in the history of automobile driving."

Lugosi had his hand on the driver's side door when he turned angrily on Abbott. "How dare you!"

"It would be irresponsible for you to risk your son's life like that."

Bela glowered as only he could.

Bela, Jr. defused the situation by nudging his father and pointing out, "Dad, come on, you don't even have a license."

Begrudgingly, the stubborn Hungarian said, "FINE! Son, go with Mr. Abbott."

"Believe me, Bela," Abbott said, "you won't regret this."

"I had better not."

Lugosi watched as Abbott took Bela, Jr. to the limousine. The boy got in the back with Costello and Chaney, while Abbott sat up front with Vidor at the wheel.

Kalara approached with her weapon at the ready. "I have been ordered to protect you," she said.

Lugosi smiled, working his hands together wickedly. "Good. *We* take the hearse."

Kalara nodded and stowed her weapon under the seat. She was about to take the wheel when Lugosi snarled, "No!" He pointed at himself. "*I* will drive." He slid in the driver's seat and shut the door. "Despite what Abbott may say, I am getting good at it."

Kalara got in the passenger seat and studied Lugosi questioningly as he turned the key in the ignition.

"What do you mean you are *getting* good at it?" she asked.

"You will see," Lugosi said, stamping down on the accelerator and rooster-tailing clods of dirt in his wake.

Chapter 24

Thursday, 26 February 1948
2:20 A.M.
Stage 6, Universal-International Studios

Nobody that was supposed to see Madame Z's flare saw the sparklingly red arc make a glittering trail in the nighttime sky.

Lou Costello saw it from the back window of Vidor's limousine.

Nobody that the flare was meant to alert saw the burning, glowing ball as it disappeared over the crest of the hill.

Lon Chaney saw it from the same vantage point as Lou Costello and Bela, Jr.

Vidor and Abbott saw the flare in the limousine's rearview mirror as Lugosi's hearse first overtook and then sped past them.

They all saw the flare.

But the DGSP operatives that the flare was meant to signal, namely Imre, Tovar and Gergo, they didn't see it at all. Sadly, they were too busy rendering Eddie Mannix some much needed roadside assistance under the Stage 6 awning that, naturally, blocked their view of the sky and the flare.

Eddie had the hood of his maroon Chevy propped up and it looked to Lou Costello like a bunch of people were huddled around it. There were two Volkswagens parked beside the coupe and a limousine similar to the one Vidor was driving, with Romanian flags and diplomatic plates, and it looked like Basil Rathbone and two other guys were trying to convince Mannix and his new pit crew to drop what they were doing, only they weren't paying any attention. The DGSP agents were too busy clamping the jaws of a pair of jumper cables up to their limousine's battery terminals and were about to do the same to Eddie's battery, when the sound of Lugosi's hearse speeding down Laemmle Blvd. at breakneck speed got everyone's attention.

The hearse was on a collision course with the onlookers, and from his vantage point, it looked to Lou Costello like a frantic Kalara Skorzeny was aiming her submachine gun at Bela Lugosi's head and screaming, "STOP...HEARSE...NOW!"

Always obliging, especially when a gun is literally put to his head, Lugosi stamped down on the hearse's complaining brakes and sent it into a tailspin skid that catapulted the Iron Man out of the back and onto the asphalt with a great thud. The hearse came to a sudden, miraculous stop under the awing and right next to Mannix's Chevy and a shaken Kalara Skorzeny stumbled from the hearse and collapsed on the ground before the startled onlookers.

"Heeeeey, Eddie!" Lou called from the back seat as Vidor brought the limousine to a stop.

Vidor rushed to Kalara's aid as she wanly complained, "That Lugosi, he is a madman."

With their machine guns slung over their shoulders, Chaney and Bela, Jr. and an unarmed Costello approached as Mannix observed good-naturedly, "Well, it looks like the gang's all here." He asked Gergo, "Everyone else I know, but who's the dame with the heater and the guy with the scar?"

"That is Kalara and Vidor!" Gergo exclaimed, and hurried over to help them.

"Oh, yeah," Mannix said, recognizing Kalara as Vidor and Gergo helped her up, "the dame with the fainting spell. She's a real dish, but she sure has trouble stayin' on her feet."

Abbott waved at Ford and Mickey. "Hello again, detectives."

"Quiet, Abbott," said Costello. "Listen up, you guys; the CIA is plannin' a double-cross. And there's some nut who thinks he's makin' a movie—"

"We know," interrupted Basil. "We heard the whole thing. Those public address speakers are set up all over the lot." He stopped to make introductions. "Lou Costello, Lon Chaney, Bela, Jr., this is Lt. Fredrick Ford and his partner, Detective Mickey Finn."

"Hi," Lon waved cheerily.

Bela, Jr. saluted. "Sirs."

Costello did a double take and snickered. "Did you say the guy's name is Mickey Finn?"

Mickey rolled his eyes. "Here we go again with the jokes."

Kalara recovered herself and asked Imre, "Why are you standing here? Did you not see Madame Z's signal? Did you not hear that madman's ultimatum?"

Imre ran out from under the awning and stared at the evening sky. "There was flare?"

"Yes, there was flare! Madame Z is on back lot right now, working to disarm atomic warhead built into war-surplus V-2 rocket. If it should explode, the Americans will blame Soviet Union."

"Hey," asked Lon, "what are you guys doin' here anyway?"

Ford jerked a thumb at Eddie. "Mannix wanted to get his car started in case we have to make a quick getaway."

Mannix smirked. "Yeah, the bastard deliberately let the battery go dead. Hey, Imre, start your car when I give ya the signal."

Imre smiled nervously at Kalara. "I will be only a moment."

He got behind the wheel of the first limousine. With his hand poised on the ignition key and his foot on the gas, he stuck his head out and called, "I am ready, Mr. Eddie."

Vidor spotted a familiar figure in the back seat of Ford's Volkswagen. "Kalara!" he called, pointing. "It is Janika! He is dead, I think!"

"Janika!" she shouted in alarm and ran to rescue him. Mickey hurried to stop her. Kalara responded by leveling her submachine at him. "You will not interfere." she ordered. "And if you have killed my brother I will—"

Mickey put his hands up. "Killed him? Nah, he's okay. He's just a little unconscious is all."

Ford did likewise and raised his hands. "Now take it easy, we're all friends here."

"Is true, Kalara," Tovar said as he pointed to his face and the fresh bandages on his broken nose. "See? Mr. Eddie, he used First Aid kit to fix my nose."

Kalara gave Ford an angry look. "Americans will need First Aid if they have harmed Janika."

Mickey shook his head. "Have a look, lady. See? He's only got—a slight lump on the head." He shrugged. "Okay, maybe a couple."

Mannix checked the jumper cable connections. "Aw, don't let her get your goat. She's okay."

"She's got a machine gun," Mickey pointed out.

Mannix smirked at them. "What? Ya never had a guy cover ya with a machine gun before?" He chuckled. "Sissies."

Kalara said, "Vidor, keep them covered." While Vidor aimed his submachine gun at the crowd, Kalara hurried to rescue her brother. She yanked open the door, slid in the seat beside him and lifted his eyelid to check his pupils.

Janika opened both eyes and exclaimed, "Kalara!"

Lt. Ford kept his hands up and gawked. "You mean that guy was awake the whole time?"

Kalara pulled her brother out of the back seat. He shrugged. "I was waiting for chance to escape," he explained. "I held breath when smaller detective used smelling salts." He twisted around to show his sister the handcuffs. "I had key before, but *they* must have taken it back," he said, nodding at Ford and Mickey. "Probably detective with derby has it now."

Kalara approached Ford and held her gloved hand out expectantly. "The key, if you please."

Ford sighed, glancing over at his trembling partner and at Vidor's submachine gun. He reached into his pocket for his keys and shook his head. "Here we go again," he grumbled, and slipped the handcuff key off his key ring and handed it to Kalara.

What happened next occurred in a split second: So caught up in the moment were both Vidor and Kalara, neither remembered that they had armed Bela, Jr. and Lon Chaney.

Bela, Jr. quickly un-shouldered his weapon and got the drop on Vidor. Vidor stoically kept his weapon aimed at Mickey, while Chaney aimed his gun at Kalara. Kalara aimed at Chaney. Gergo aimed his Pistolet at Mannix, who kept working under the hood. Abbott ducked for cover behind the limousine. Basil quickly drew his Walther PPK from its stout leather belt holster and aimed at Imre. Imre used the armored limousine door as a shield and drew his Pistolet from his shoulder holster and aimed at Basil. Tovar aimed his Pistolet at Costello. Costello reached in his waistband for Lenore's Beretta, but the gun dropped into his pants. He shook his leg until the gun dropped out, and then fumbled trying to pick it up. Giving up, Costello pretended that his index finger was a gun and aimed it at Tovar.

Chaney eyed the comic. "Knock it off," he growled.

Costello responded with a shrug and put his hands up.

Basil arched an eyebrow. "Well, it looks like we have a Mexican standoff."

"We are Hungarian!" Kalara declared.

"Look," said Lt. Ford, smiling nervously, "we're all here to find Lillian Lugosi, right? And we're all here to stop a bad guy, right? So let's quit playing around and work together."

Janika unlocked his handcuffs and tossed them aside. "He is right," he said, adding excitedly, "Kalara, I kill *Doktor Halál!* We have been avenged!"

Kalara shook her head as she kept her gun trained on Chaney. "The madman who calls himself *Herr Direktor*, he is the real mastermind! *Doktor Halál*, he was only a puppet," she said.

"Exactly," said Basil. "So let's all do as Lt. Ford suggested and honor the truce." He holstered his weapon and pulled out his notebook.

"NO MORE CARDS!" Kalara shouted. She aimed at Rathbone. "I am sick of stupid cards!"

Mannix eyed the standoff. "If you guys are finished playin' shoot-'em-up," he said, pointing at the limousine, "can one of you Wild Bills get over here and give me a jump already?"

Imre looked to Kalara. "We must honor Madame Z's wishes," he said.

Reluctantly, Kalara lowered her weapon and nodded. "Lower your weapons," she told her men. "We honor truce—for now."

Mannix got under the hood again, ready to give Imre the signal, when Lugosi came up behind him and shouted, "WE MUST FIND LILLIAN!" startling Mannix, and making him bang his head on the propped open hood.

"Say, what's the big idea?" snarled Mannix, rubbing his head.

"My wife is a madman's prisoner!" Bela gestured at the surrounding soundstages. "While you have all been fooling around, I have been investigating!" Bela gestured at Stage 6. "Lillian is in *there*. We get her now!"

Ford smirked incredulously. "How do you figure that out?"

Lugosi tapped his temple. "Because Bela, he thinks like our adversary who thinks he is a movie director." He gestured at the soundstage. "The castle and laboratory sets are on Stage 17, but Stage 6, it has the dungeon set. Where better to hold a woman captive than a dungeon?" He grabbed Costello's arm. "Come, we go get her."

Lou smiled. "You mean it? Us investigatin' together? So you ain't sore at me no more?"

Bela paused and smiled warmly. "I am nothing, if not forgiving."

Basil eyed them questioningly. "What exactly are you forgiving Mr. Costello for?"

"I'm the guy that bugged Bela's trailer," Costello confessed.

"I see," said Basil.

"You do not see, but Bela sees," said Lugosi. He grabbed Costello's arm. "We must go after Lillian, now!"

"Look, Lugosi," the Lieutenant said, holding him back, "we're not just going to go charging in there, got it?"

"Yeah," said Abbott, "and that dungeon set has lots of places for the bad guys to hide."

"Besides," said Ford, "if we go rushing in there, there's the chance they got another tripwire set up to blow the place sky high."

"Very well," Bela said, turning a dial on the forearm controls. The robot sat up and slowly got to its feet. Twisting another dial, Bela caused the automaton to march forward. "We send in the Iron Man to get her."

Abbott shook his head. "No, Bela, I don't think the set is strong enough to support the weight of something like that."

"If the set can support the weight of a camera, it can support the robot!"

"There's a big water tank set up right in front of the dungeon's revolving door."

"He's right, Bela," said Chaney. "That dock won't hold the weight of something like this."

Lugosi gestured impatiently. "So we sneak in through Stage 17's castle set. They're connected."

"Oh, swell," said Ford. "Go marching onto the set where Kopf is waiting for us to deliver the suitcases." He pointed at the robot. "Besides, I want that thing right here and ready for action in case we need some protection."

Chaney scratched the back of his head. "If only we could be sure how that elevated set was put together, we could plan out our strategy. For all we know, there might be a way we can sneak in under the thing without alerting anybody."

Abbott snapped his fingers. "Say, the drafting office is just over that way. Lieutenant, give me a minute and I'll be right back with the plans."

Ford smiled. "Now that's the first sensible thing I've heard all night."

"I'll be right back," said Abbott.

Mannix drummed his fingers. "If you guys are through playing hero, I got a car to jump." He yanked open the Chevy's driver's side door.

"I'll take care of your car," offered Basil, taking the wheel. "You and Detective Finn have to deliver those suitcases to Stage 17, after all."

Ford checked his watch. "Say, you're right! In all the excitement, we forgot we were on a deadline…with the emphasis on dead."

Hefting his submachine gun, Lon suggested, "Hey, maybe I ought to go along, you know, in case there's a double-cross."

"Say," said Mannix, "that's not such a bad idea."

A second flare shot into the sky and, as the glowing red ball descended, it momentarily illuminated the distant back lot.

Kalara nodded toward her car. "Imre, you, Tovar and Gergo to back lot *now*."

The three agents saluted. "Yes, Comrade," they chorused and hurried to Kalara's limousine. They were soon peeling out at top speed in the direction of the back lot.

Mannix got in the Volkswagen and honked the horn. "Hey, Lou, Bela, come on, you guys. The more, the merrier."

"Right with ya, Eddie," Lou said, reaching for the door handle. He froze when he remembered the incriminating photograph in his pocket. "Uh oh," he said.

"Well, what's eating you?" asked Mannix. "Get in."

"Uh, on second thought, I think I'll stick around right here."

"What's gotten into you?" Chaney asked.

Costello patted the pocket with the photo in it. "It's not what's got into me, but what I got in my pocket."

Mannix griped, "What the hell is *that* supposed to mean?"

Chaney nodded, remembering the photo. "Oh, yeah." He hefted his weapon reassuringly. "Don't be silly, Lou. Nothin's gonna happen while I got this." He waved to Bela as he got in the back seat. "Come on, Lugosi, let's go."

"I'm staying here," Bela insisted, and then turned to his son. "I have a plan. Son, you will go with Chaney and remember, be ready for anything."

"But, Dad, I wanna stay here with you."

"No," Lugosi insisted. "While we make the sneak attack from the rear, you will attack from the front, and together we'll have Kopf trapped in the middle."

"Now hold on, Lugosi," Ford said. "Things are liable to get pretty hairy. Chaney volunteering is one thing, but I don't think you want your kid in the line of fire."

"He is a soldier. He's trained to be in the line of fire!" Bela gestured at Bela, Jr.'s gun. "Besides, he is armed." He smiled down at his son. "I am counting on you to bring your mother safely to me again."

Bela, Jr.'s chest puffed out confidently and he gave his father a snappy salute. "I will do you proud, Dad."

He hopped in the Volkswagen with Chaney. Mannix looked at them in the rearview mirror and smiled. "You guys holding machine guns like that reminds me of my boyhood days with my gang back in the Palisades."

Chaney and Bela, Jr. exchanged looks. "How's that?" asked Lon.

"You don't wanna know," Mannix said. He motioned to Costello. "You comin' with us or what?"

Costello bit his nails, trying to think of a way to get Lon and Bela, Jr. out of the car. "Uh, I'm gonna stay here and wait for Abbott to get back."

"Have it your way." Eddie started the engine as Kalara, Janika and Vidor piled into Mickey's car and both Volkswagens drove up the street and around the corner.

Bela glowered impatiently at the soundstage. "Can we *now* go inside and rescue my wife?"

Ford got in the limousine's driver's seat. "Just as soon as Abbott comes back with those blueprints," he insisted, and turned the key in the ignition.

Bela took Costello aside. "What was that all about between you and Mannix?"

Costello showed Bela the photograph of Eddie, Toni, Lenore and Marlowe. "Your kid just might have drove off with the CIA assassin."

"What!" Lugosi grabbed the picture and read the message. "How could you let my son drive off with him like that?"

"Well, maybe Eddie's innocent. 'M' might be for 'Marlowe.'"

"Marlowe?" Lugosi sneered. "Don't be ridiculous!" He smirked. "But it's no matter. My son will take care of him if he should turn out to be the assassin."

"We better tell the cop." Costello was about to hurry over to Ford when Bela pulled him back.

Bela whispered, "We will keep this to ourselves. Why needlessly upset the Lieutenant over what are, after all, only your suspicions?"

"Are you sure?"

"Yes," Bela snarled. "Say nothing."

Over the revving of the engine, the Lieutenant asked Basil, "How's it coming?"

Basil coaxed the Chevy's engine to turn over. "Ah, success! Now we'll just leave it running for about twenty minutes. That should sufficiently recharge the battery."

Costello looked around anxiously. "Do ya think that nut is watchin' us right now? He's got cameras everywhere."

Somewhere on the lot came the sound of gunshots. Ford got out of the limousine and pulled out his pistol. "That sounds like trouble."

Costello pointed up the street. "Look!"

Behind the hangar-sized soundstage came flashes and the *ratta-tat-tat* of machine-gun fire, followed by screeching tires.

"It sounds like a shootout!" said Ford.

Basil drew his PPK. "Be prepared for anything, gentlemen."

"BAH!" Lugosi exclaimed. "We can no longer wait for Abbott. We must save Lillian now!" He stalked off toward Stage 6 and angrily slammed the stage door after him.

"What's gotten into him?" asked Costello. "He ain't actin' like himself."

Ford sighed heavily. "I better go and bring Lugosi back before he gets into real trouble."

"Watch your back, Lieutenant," Rathbone warned.

"Aren't you coming?"

"I think I ought to wait out here." Basil glanced around cautiously. "This may be Kopf's way of adding drama to his little film. No telling what he has planned for us."

"I guess you're right." Ford stared at the soundstage and then looked to Costello. "What about you, hot shot?" he asked.

Costello pulled his deerstalker out of his pocket and set the tweed cap on his head with a determined tug on the visor. "Bats is my friend, even though I played a dirty trick on 'im with that bug. Now he's in trouble, so I gotta go with ya to make up for the rotten thing I did." He saluted. "Detective Lou Costello, at your service."

Ford slapped Lou on the back. "Thatta boy."

• • • •

The minute Lt. Ford and Lou Costello set foot inside Stage 6, Lou knew things weren't strictly kosher: all the stage lights were on.

Ford closed the stage door.

They walked the perimeter of the huge set together, Ford's gun at the ready, while Lou kept mindful of any sudden movement in the shadows.

As they passed a prop table, Costello whispered, "Hang on a minute." He selected a bottle of Shasta seltzer water from a crate.

"What are you gonna do with that?"

Costello hefted his weapon. "Never underestimate the power of seltzer. And I'm quick on the draw, too."

"I feel safer already," Ford said, rolling his eyes. "Come on."

Costello sidled up close behind. "Wait for me," he said nervously.

Even under the circumstances, it was hard not to be impressed by the handiwork of the Universal Studios construction department. The stone wall façade of the castle turret was covered with fake green moss and glistening slime. Dancing light reflected off an indoor water tank representing a Florida bayou. Rickety stairs led down to a platform and a dock.

Ford shined his light on a large footlocker hidden amongst the set supports. Opening it, he found a cache of gasmasks similar to the kind used at the funeral home. "What do you suppose those things are for?" he asked Costello.

Lou shrugged nervously. "I dunno. Maybe he's plannin' to gas the joint." He quickly grabbed a gasmask, whipped off his deerstalker, slipped the gasmask over his face, and then put the deerstalker on again. He put his hands on his hips, confident he was safe.

Ford looked askance at the anteater detective. "Take that off!"

Lou mumbled something beneath the gasmask.

"What?" Ford asked.

Lou raised the gasmask and repeated, "Better to be safe than sorry, that's what my mudder always says."

Ford grabbed the nose of the mask and yanked it off Lou's head and tossed it back in the footlocker. "Now quit playing around!"

Lou sadly put his cap back on and hefted his seltzer bottle. "If I get gassed, it's all your fault."

Ford shook his head. "It's bad enough you're wearing that stupid beanie. You look like a freshman from Sherlock Holmes U."

Costello shrugged off the comment and started calling out softly, "Hey, Bela. Hey, Bela."

"Not like that." The Lieutenant shouted, "LUGOSI? LUGOSI, WHERE ARE YA?"

Costello grew anxious as he backed away. "Shh. You don't wanna let the other guy know we're here." He tripped on a wire and stumbled. Catching himself, he exclaimed nervously, "Uh oh," and froze with fear.

Ford swung his flashlight around and frowned with annoyance. "What'd you do?"

Lou's lower lip quivered as he pointed down. "I-I-I tripped on a wire." He gulped hard.

Ford held his breath, expecting a firebomb to go off any second. Suddenly from out of the blackness came two tiny glowing green eyes and flapping black wings. Ford and Costello both shrieked and fired their respective weapons at the giant bat as it swooped down on them. It was only after the bat was a wet, bullet-riddled flapping wreck on the floor that they realized it was just a mechanical model flown on the guy wire Lou had just tripped over.

Costello pulled off his cap and mopped the beads of sweat from his forehead. "Oh, jeez, I nearly crapped myself." He set his deerstalker at a comically skewed angle.

"Me, too," Ford snickered with relief. "You look like a dope in that hat."

"At least I'm a live dope."

They had a good laugh together, but it was short-lived, interrupted by a sudden noise behind them. Ford and Costello wheeled around and got shot with a face full of seltzer water. Gurgling and flailing their arms helplessly, Ford and Costello fought and gasped and ranted bubbling gibberish as the unending spray of fizz water knocked the derby off Ford's head and wilted Lou's deerstalker.

"BATS!" Costello exclaimed.

Dripping wet, Ford holstered his gun, bent down and grabbed his derby and growled, "What the hell do you think you're doing sneaking up on us with that thing?"

Smirking, Lugosi hefted the seltzer bottle. "I had to be sure it was you and not Kopf wearing a disguise."

"And what if one of us *was* Kopf?" He pointed at Lugosi's seltzer bottle. "You were gonna maybe bartend us to death?"

Costello nudged him, hefting his own seltzer bottle. "See? I told you not to underestimate this stuff."

Lugosi smirked. "I spray you to make sure *you're* not wearing a mask." Lugosi pinched the fuming investigator's cheek and pulled roughly. He nodded with satisfaction. "No, *that's* definitely your face."

Ford grabbed Costello's seltzer bottle and took aim. "Fine," he said menacingly. "Now it's my turn."

The scene was interrupted by a woman's strangled scream.

"*That's* Lillian!" Lugosi said.

"It came from over there," said Lou, pointing at the castle turret. "That's where the dungeon is."

Ford set the bottle aside and drew out his gun. He searched the elevated set for a ramp or a ladder. "How do we get up there?" he asked.

Costello pointed. "There's a ladder over there."

"Come," said Bela, handing Costello his seltzer bottle, "follow me, I know the way!"

Ford and Costello hurried to keep up with Lugosi as the Hungarian charged up a wooden ladder leading through the wood and metal framed supports and through a trap door leading to the "Broom Closet" set.

Ford shook his head. "The damn fool." He pointed at the seltzer bottles in Lou's trembling hands. "Put those down and follow me if you're coming."

Costello set the bottles on the floor and followed behind Ford as he climbed the ladder. Reaching the top, they spotted Lugosi just as he reached for the knob on the cellar door. Ford hurried over and yanked Lugosi away.

"Now look," he cautioned, "Kopf could have this whole joint booby-trapped." He gave Lugosi and Costello a cautionary look. "So the both of you stay behind me and don't do nothing stupid."

Lugosi scowled. "I resent the implication that *I'd* do something stupid!"

Costello quipped, "I get *paid* to do somethin' stupid."

Ford growled, "Well, just remember you're off the clock."

The Lieutenant took out his flashlight, opened the cellar door and shined his light down the rickety wooden stairs that led down to the dock and bayou water tank. Looking over his shoulder, he asked, "Where's the secret door?"

Pointing down at the section of the wall built to resemble the castle's exterior turret, Lugosi said with a hint of exasperation in his voice, "The hidden panel, *it's* right there."

"Down there?" Ford asked, pointing at the wall by the dock.

"Yes! *I'll* show you."

Lugosi pushed Ford out of the way and took the lead, much to Ford's consternation. The detective took a few steps down and knit his brows at Costello. "Are you coming or not?"

"I'm comin', I'm comin'."

Costello closed the closet door after him and descended the staircase. As Ford and Costello each took his first tentative steps down, they heard what sounded to them like disembodied footsteps and stopped to listen.

Over the sound of a descending series of *clip-clops*, Ford asked Costello, "Is that you?"

Costello shook his head. "Uh uh. Is that you?"

Ford curtly gestured down at his feet. "Does it look like my feet are moving?"

Costello shook his head nervously. "Does it look like *my* feet are movin'?"

Ford paused to listen. "I think it stopped."

Lugosi looked up at them in annoyance. "Well, what are you two waiting for?" he grumbled.

Costello whispered, "We thought we heard something."

"You *did* hear something! My wife screaming! Now get down here."

Ford nodded at Costello and they continued their descent, and suddenly the sounds of ghostly footsteps continue its *clip-clop* down the stairs after them. Ford stopped abruptly on the bottom step, causing Costello to run into him. Costello froze as he listened. "He's comin' closer," the comic whispered anxiously.

They waited for the intruder to catch up. The Lieutenant spun around quickly, pushing Costello against the fake brick wall of the turret and aiming his gun. "NOW I GOT YA!" he shouted.

Costello squeezed his eyes shut and pulled his deerstalker down over his face. "Did ya get 'im?" he asked, trembling.

Ford looked down and saw a doorknob coming to rest beside his shoe. He picked it up, glanced up at the closet door at the top of the stairs, and sighed. "Yeah, I got him."

Costello peeked out from behind the deerstalker and let out a sigh of relief. "Whew! For a minute there, I thought we wuz goners."

Ford eyed him narrowly. "Say, is this a gag they rigged for your picture?"

Costello took the doorknob and turned it over in his hand and saw it had a trigger spring on the end so that it would pop off when the closet door was shut. "Yeah, I guess it is."

Ford grabbed the doorknob back. "Then why didn't you tell me?" he snarled.

Costello shrugged, embarrassed. "Bud an' me, we don't read the script that close."

Pausing by the slime-covered turret wall, Lugosi sneered, "If *you're* both through playing around, the hidden panel is right here."

Ford tossed the doorknob into the water tank as Lugosi pushed open the perfectly balanced swiveling secret door. Beyond was the dungeon set.

A woman's scream echoed within.

"Come, quickly," Lugosi said, and ducked inside.

"Wait," Ford ordered, but Lugosi was gone. He turned to Costello. "You wait out here."

"I ain't stayin' out here alone," said Costello.

Ford jerked his head toward the door. "Well, if you're coming, then come on."

Rubber chains hung from the walls of the dimly lit dungeon. The only source of illumination came from an orange light shining up from an iron grillwork-covered pit in the floor. Steam rising from the pit heightened the spooky atmosphere. Ford searched the hidden room with his flashlight while Costello called out nervously, "Hey, Lillian. Heeeeey, Lillian."

"There's no sign of Lugosi," Ford said, looking around cautiously. "Keep your eyes open."

Ford and Costello skirted around the pit and backed up slowly against the dungeon wall. "Hey, look," said Ford, pointing the flashlight beam in the murky shadows.

A motion picture camera was turning at the far end of the room, capturing their movements.

Costello whispered, "Come to think of it, somebody was takin' pi'tures back on Stage 28 just before it caught on fire."

"Oh, that's just swell," Ford said. He shined his flashlight around the dungeon and called in a nervous whisper, "Mrs. Lugosi. Mrs. Lugosi."

There was another scream that seemed to come from every direction. Ford and Costello backed up and gasped as they felt someone behind them. They whirled around and caught the pretty face of Lillian Lugosi in Ford's flashlight beam; her neck was held fast inside real free standing wooden stocks; her eyes were fixed in a vacant zombie movie stare.

Ford holstered his weapon and waved his hand before Lillian's staring eyes. "Mrs. Lugosi! Are you all right?"

She remained unresponsive.

Costello gulped. "Maybe she's hypnotized."

Examining her pupils, Ford found them fixed and dilated. "More like drugged, I'll bet." He examined her restraint. "How do you open this thing?"

An old padlock kept the stocks locked tight. Ford yanked on it, but the padlock wouldn't open.

"That's the real thing," said Lou. "Jack Otterson, the set designer, he likes everything authentic, even in monster pi'tures."

"Stay with her," Ford instructed. "I'll see if I can find something to break the lock."

Shining his flashlight around the chamber, Ford found a ring of keys hanging from a peg on the wall. "She's as good as outta there," he said. As Ford reached for the keys, he was startled by a woman screaming again. He glanced back at Lillian. "Was that you?" he asked nervously.

Costello shook his head. "It wasn't her."

The scream came again, but Lillian remained mute. "If she ain't screaming," Ford said, "then who's screaming?"

Ford's searching flashlight came to rest on a tape recorder on a rough hewn wooden table. He used his flashlight to follow the wires from the tape recorder to a set of public address speakers mounted out of sight in the rafters. "Well, will you look at that?"

Costello reached over and turned off the tape recorder. "Boy, are we a couple of dopes."

"Yeah, but the point is somebody rigged all this—and that camera." Ford noticed the forearm robot controls resting next to the tape recorder. "Why would Lugosi leave this here?"

"Search me." Costello stepped back and walked straight into a veil of drooping cobwebs. He swatted at them wildly and stumbled backward into a large wooden chair. He jumped up when he realized he was sitting in someone's lap. Whirling around, he pointed at the blanket-covered figure. "There's somebody under there!"

"I got you covered!" Ford said as his gun hand shook. "Put 'em up!"

Whatever was waiting under the blanket made a muffled mewing sound. In *The Brain of Frankenstein*, the Monster was scripted to sit in that chair. Now there was no telling who or *what* was waiting to pounce. Ford stuck the muzzle of his weapon in the figure's chest and barked, "Put your hands up! Police!"

When the figure didn't move, Ford grabbed the blanket and yanked. "I said, put your hands up!"

What Ford and Costello saw made the hair on the back of their necks stand up. "Oh, man," Costello whimpered. "This is bad."

It was Bela Lugosi chained up and gagged. He struggled, snarling angrily, biting down on the gag as his heavy eyebrows and expressive blue eyes suggested danger coming from behind, danger in the form of a second Bela Lugosi, who clapped a large cotton wad soaked in ether over Ford's face. The real Lugosi and a frightened Lou Costello watched helplessly as Lt. Ford's body went rag doll and Lugosi's doppelganger eased the detective onto the stone floor.

"As adversaries go, you are completely worthless!" the fake Lugosi chastised in a lower-class Austrian accent. "Honestly," he told Bela, "it amazes me how unobservant these two fools were." He smiled. "I am a good three inches shorter than you. I even spoke using contractions. You *never* use contractions, or at least very seldom! I even deliberately *emphasized* them! And still they did not discover the truth!" He gave Costello a look of disdain. "And you dare to wear the hat of Conan Doyle's detective."

Costello dropped his comic persona and became the little tough guy again. "You leave the Lieutenant alone!" he snarled. "Or I'll pop you one!" He raised his fists, ready to give the fake Lugosi a fight. "I got the moves of a boxer!"

The fake Lugosi drew an FN-Browning HP-35. "I have the gun of a CIA agent."

Costello reached into his pocket and pulled out the incendiary lipstick. "And I got a firebomb lipstick of a CIA agent!" He stuck his tongue out. "Nyah!" Lou raised the lipstick higher and pointed at it. "I ain't kiddin'! This here is a firebomb direct from the CIA and all I gotta do is turn this here knob and we all blow up."

The real Lugosi went pale with panic. He mumbled through the gag while insistently shaking his head.

The fake Lugosi said, "I believe he is asking how your blowing us up will benefit him."

The real Lugosi quickly nodded in the affirmative, mumbling what were clearly orders to put the lipstick away.

"Do as he says." The madman extended his firing arm and aimed for Costello's chest. "Or I will kill you first and then disarm the lipstick."

Costello smiled weakly and said with a helpless gesture and a gulp, "Okay, you win." He pocketed the explosive.

"Very wise." The fake Lugosi pointed at the fallen detective and over at a wheeled stretcher. "Put him on that operating room gurney and strap him down."

Costello shook his head. "I can't. I got a bad heart."

The Lugosi doppelganger took aim and cocked back the hammer on his weapon. "How bad will your heart be with a bullet in it?"

"Pretty bad."

Costello reluctantly dragged Ford's body to the gurney and huffed and puffed as he heaved him up and laid him out, and then buckled restraining straps around the Lieutenant's chest, arms, and legs.

Satisfied that his prisoner was properly immobilized, the fake Lugosi pointed with his gun. "Un-gag Lugosi," he ordered.

Lou did as he was told. Bela spit out the fuzz in his mouth and coughed.

"I'm sure that feels much better," the fake Lugosi said, and gestured at the turning camera. "I have made certain to photograph your good side."

Lugosi stared menacingly at his evil twin. "How dare you kidnap me!"

Keeping his hands raised, Costello leaned over and muttered out of the side of his mouth, "When did he get ya, anyways?"

Lugosi's eyes narrowed. "As soon as I arrived on the front lot," he snarled. "I look for Lillian and he grabs me from behind!"

"I shoulda figured it wasn't you when you said you and I wuz pals again."

The fake Lugosi smiled. "The time has come for the unmasking scene." He pulled off his Bela Lugosi mask, revealing himself to be Dr. Kopf, still wearing his half-mask. "Well?"

"So you are Dr. Kopf," Lugosi scoffed. "As the Americans say, big deal. I knew that already."

"Yes, that is *partly* who I am." Dr. Kopf smiled beneath the half-mask. "I am wearing *two* disguises. So now, for the sake of my film, it is now time to *fully* reveal myself."

"You ain't gonna drop your pants, are ya?" Costello asked.

Dr. Kopf leveled his gun at Costello. "What I have to show Lugosi is for his eyes only. You may go—and tell Basil Rathbone to prepare for his death scene."

"Nothin' doin'," Costello said. "I'm not gonna leave Bats with a nut job like you."

"Need I remind you I am a nut job with a gun?"

"Oh, yeah."

"Go," Lugosi urged. "I will be fine."

"You're chained to a chair," Costello pointed out.

"Perhaps 'fine' is not the right word." Bela nodded toward the exit. "But you go anyway."

Costello pointed at Lillian. "What about Mrs. Lugosi?"

Dr. Kopf shook his head. "I need her for dramatic tension. Now go."

Bela urged, "Go and warn Rathbone."

Costello hesitated. "Bats," he said, "in case somethin' happens—I just wanted you to know—I'm awful sorry for what I did."

Lugosi sighed, obviously reluctant to let bygones be bygones. Still, he relented, if reluctantly. "Very well," he said, "I forgive you for being a bugger."

Dr. Kopf frowned. "That doesn't mean what you think it means."

Ignoring the villain, Lou said to Bela, "Take it easy, Bats." He leaned in and whispered, "We'll save ya. Just see if we don't."

Costello kept a wary eye on the madman as he edge out of the dungeon.

Once he was sure they were alone, Kopf pocketed his gun and, in full view of the camera, grabbed his wig and the edge of his half-mask, and pulled them off, revealing severely cropped hair and a long forehead scar. Then he peeled away his fuzzy eyebrow and stripped his mustache from his upper lip. He turned and displayed his face to Lugosi. "Do you know my true identity now?" he asked.

"You are Dr. Fell! But you cannot be Dr. Fell!" Lugosi raged. "Dr. Fell is dead! You even said that Janika Skorzeny killed him!"

"As I told you earlier, I am *not* Dr. Fell, nor Rache, nor Vivas. They were all Vivas, and Vivas worked for me. I am *Herr Direktor*," the villain said, and absently felt his

Kopf...grabbed his wig and the edge of his half mask, and pulled them off...

forehead scar with nicotine-stained fingertips. "Vivas got my attention when he deliberately scarred himself to impersonate me in his magic act." He smiled. "I admired his unflinching realism."

"He did not impersonate *you*," Lugosi sneered. "Barber said the magician impersonated Erich von Stroheim."

"Exactly," the madman cryptically replied as he pulled out a cigarette holder. He blew into it to clear out any obstructing ash, and then reached into another pocket for a silver cigarette case with "EvS" engraved upon it. "As I have already explained, Dr. Sigmund Rache was a part Vivas played," he said as he selected a cigarette and inserted it into the holder, "and he was also *pretending* to be the fictitious Dr. Fell," he unclipped a lighter from the case and lit up, "to cheat escaped Nazis hiding in Argentina of their cache of gold." He returned the case to his pocket while drawing hungrily on the holder. As he exhaled curling smoke, he gave the sigh of relief that only a chain smoker denied his habit could evoke. "The gold was to help finance my picture. Uranium 235 is quite expensive, you know. Not so easy to hide in a film budget."

"But what has *that* to do with freezing people?"

"We convinced the Nazis that for a price we could cryogenically suspend their lives indefinitely. Then, in some future age, they could awaken and live again as free men." The villain clenched the mouthpiece of the holder between his teeth. "Desperate men will believe anything. So in exchange for their gold, they were given not cryogenic sleep, but sleep everlasting in Vivas's ingenious death trap. And speaking of death traps," he gestured at the wooden table, "as you can see, the robot controls are there, just out of reach."

He went to the peg on the wall and removed the ring of keys. "And these keys, I will leave on this stool." He dragged the stool just within reach of Bela's right foot. "They are the keys to yours and the *Frau* Lugosi's restraints." He pointed at Bela's legs. "I have taken the liberty of making sure your leg restraints have enough slack to allow you to reach the stool."

Bela frowned. "I do not understand."

"I must stage your heroic escape attempt."

"For your crazy movie, I suppose," Lugosi said impatiently.

Herr Direktor gestured at a far corner of the room. "Now we must have the proper motivation for the scene."

He brought out a time bomb fabricated from a gasoline can, a battery, a photographer's timer, and a mercury switch. "There must be the threat of imminent death. A ticking bomb, as it were," he explained as he switched out the tape recorder for the makeshift explosive, adding with an apologetic frown, "Do forgive the very literal threat of an actual ticking bomb. It's rather obvious, but you must admit it is effective."

"Who are you really?" Lugosi demanded impatiently.

"You may call me what Universal Studios' publicity department labeled me in their garish advertising: *The Man You Love to Hate.*"

Bela scowled. "That is what they called von Stroheim, not *you!*"

The madman smirked as he bent closer. "Look carefully at my face, *Herr* Lugosi. I know I have been away from American screens for a while, and I am older, a little fatter, but surely you must recognize me."

Lugosi shrugged in his restraints. "You look like von Stroheim. So what? The magician, he, too, looked like von Stroheim."

"I do not simply *resemble* Erich von Stroheim," the villain said with a mad gleam in his eyes. He rose up as he proclaimed, "I *am* Erich von Stroheim!" adding calmly, "*Von*, to my friends. You may also call me Von."

Lugosi balked. "Do you take me for a fool?"

"I *am* Count Erich Oswald Hans Carl Maria von Stroheim!" the fiend strongly insisted, punctuating his claim with a curt bow and click of his heels. "Tonight, I will have my revenge."

"Revenge? Revenge on who?"

"Revenge on this town, this horrible town—on Hollywood! How they butchered my films! My masterwork *Greed!* This town denied me my vision, especially *this* studio! How Carl Laemmle fought me at every turn! What they did to *Foolish Wives* was nothing short of criminal! Even Jack Pierce mocked me by giving his Frankenstein's Monster my characteristic forehead scar! But now I shall be avenged, and I shall do it by exploiting the very studio that denied me my glorious creative vision!"

"And just how will you be avenged?"

"I will use my atomic missile to wipe this town off the map! Not by blowing up Las Vegas as that fool Don Marlowe wanted."

"Las Vegas!" Lugosi exclaimed. "Marlowe wanted me to work in Las Vegas."

"The CIA wanted me to send a message to the Mafia. I was to find a way to destroy Las Vegas, the jewel in the crown of their criminal empire, and make it appear as though a foreign power was responsible."

Bela's eyes narrowed as realization dawned. "Marlowe said that if I worked in Las Vegas, I would get a *bang* out of it. So that is what he meant! Are you saying that my agent works for the CIA? He is an idiot!"

"Yes, he is. But that doesn't matter now," Von insisted. "Ground zero will be the Hollywoodland sign! It is from that epicenter that all the rest of this factory town will be leveled!" Raising a fist and shaking it madly, he snarled in defiance, "Give my regards to the Hollywood Reservoir! Farewell, Griffith Park!" He pointed at the camera. "Using both film and television cameras, and my remote-controlled people, I have so far captured every moment leading up to this glorious apocalyptic dénouement! Once all 700 reels of film have been cut together, I will have achieved the greatest triumph the motion picture screen has ever seen: *Son of Greed: The Death of Hollywood!*" He smirked. "It will run for six days, and there will be no intermissions! Food will be brought to the patron! Each theater seat will have its own bedpan! The audience will have all their needs attended to!" He added calmly, "It will debut in Paris, France."

"You are mad," Lugosi scoffed.

"Madness is the handmaiden of Genius." Von smirked. "In a moment, I will leave you to escape in private."

"You *want* me to escape?" Lugosi incredulously asked.

Von seemed nonplused by the question. "For dramatic tension, always the villain's adversary must struggle to escape the death trap." He pointed at the camera. "It will be the high point of the picture!"

Sighing, Lugosi muttered aloud, "I am going to have to re-write those deductions I made for Rathbone." He glared at von Stroheim. "But why do you pick on Bela? I am nothing but an old boogieman, a man crippled by pain and, if you ask Lillian, also I am suffering drug addiction."

Von grabbed a stepladder and made adjustments to the stage lights. "Both Dwight Frye and Marlene Dietrich spoke very highly of you. Excuse me while I find the most advantageous angle."

He went back to the camera, checked the viewfinder, and moved the camera to a new position. "We are kindred souls, you and I. Both of us the epitome of classic screen villainy! For you, the vampire and the mad scientist; for me, I was the very image of the evil Hun. But beyond that, we share something even greater."

"How do you mean?"

Von stared earnestly. "Both of us have been abused by Hollywood, by *this* studio! Used and cast aside as relics of a bygone age, both of us have been condemned by necessity to make cheap horror films and parody our image, all for the sake of our families." With a wicked twinkle in his eye, he added, "And despite the love and devotion we feel for our wives, we are not above seeking gratification elsewhere." He winked.

Bela felt a sudden sting of regret and was glad Lillian couldn't hear this.

"My darling wife Valerie was badly burned," Von explained. "She worked as a beautician in a Hollywood salon. Her clothes caught on fire and when someone grabbed the fur coat of a patron, an actress for this studio, and wanted to use the coat to beat out the flames consuming my wife, the actress said, 'Not with my coat!'" Von shook with rage. "I had to make Poverty Row horror pictures to finance Valerie's treatments. All of those films were pure trash!" His scowl of distaste melted away. "But they were the films *She* greatly admired."

"Your wife, you mean?"

"No, the *She* to whom I am referring was the one great passion of my life. For you, it was Clara Bow, but for me, it was *She*. H. Rider Haggard himself dedicated his classic adventure story to his memories of Her. I keep a token of that film in my house—the mask in the parlor, it reminds me of *She*."

"Who do you mean?"

"Madame Avinashi, She Who Must Be Obeyed! We first met in Austria when I was but a young man. She saw in me the makings of a criminal genius. Our love affair was brief, but passionate. She spirited me away to Her den of sin where She made me into a man." He caressed his forehead scar. "*She* gave me this."

"You must have hated her."

"On the contrary, as I require from my actors a certain discipline and as I have been a soldier in three armies, I not only know how to give orders but also understand how to obey. Avinashi *molded* me, appreciating my sincerity and what people called talent, listened and accepted many of my friendly suggestions until finally I became the man that became known as von Stroheim!" Von smirked. "It was years later, while I was making films in Paris, that my deadly darling Avinashi came back into my life as beautiful as I remembered. She said that ever since She saw *Foolish Wives*, She fantasized about surrendering Herself to *me!* She wore a jeweled dog collar and presented me with the leash, and then got down on all fours."

A faint smile crossed Von's lips as he reached into his Dracula tuxedo and pulled out a rubber bone riddled with human bite marks. "I still keep close to my heart—her favorite squeaky toy."

He squeezed the rubber bone to coax a couple of raspy squeaks, and then shut his eyes and nuzzled it against his cheek. "But it was *I* who was the unwitting slave. That is how she works, you see. I discovered that when I became *Her* master, I had actually surrendered my will to Her. That was how She taught me to embrace my evil side at last, by giving in to my sadistic instincts! And once I became what She wanted, we forged this brilliant plan together."

He pocketed the squeaky toy and shrugged. "And part of that plan was to make something of Her wayward son Fredek. She told me that he had potential, but he wanted a career in show business. He did not understand that She wanted so much more for him. Her only request was that I use Fredek in my scheme, and when I was finished with him, and if he was not clever enough to betray me, I was to see that Fredek died a gloriously poetic death. And he did, killed by one of his victims from the House of Doom."

Von used his hands as a framing device and then returned to the camera and checked the image in the viewfinder. He used a tape measure to check the focal distance between Lugosi and the camera lens. "I approached my role as a villain as I did my other roles, with meticulous research. I made a study of screen villainy, *your* Saturday Matinee serials in particular."

Lugosi stared disbelieving. "Those films were terrible! I only did them because I *had* to do them."

"On the contrary, *Chandu the Magician* inspired me most of all! I still remember the gleam in your eye as you placed your hand on the lever controlling the death ray, and you proclaimed, 'And now I'll be king of all, and this is my scepter!' It gave me chills, and I do not impress easily." He held up a production slate and said, "Cut. Print."

He stopped the camera and quickly switched out film magazines, and then used a piece of chalk to mark the slate anew. Turning on the camera, he stepped before the lens and held up the slate. "Lugosi Death Trap, scene 2103, take one." He clapped the clapper and set the slate aside and collected the exposed film magazine.

The mad von Stroheim set the timer on the bomb and placed the magazine of exposed film on Lt. Ford's chest. "I am counting on you to escape; otherwise the film may not survive the fire. My lair is located on the Stage 17 laboratory set, if you didn't already know. There is a connecting passageway right over there."

He rolled the gurney out. There was the brief sound of Kenneth Strickfaden's machines humming and crackling as the soundproof fire door connecting Stage 6 with Stage 17 slid open and closed.

Lugosi stared anxiously at the advancing timer on the makeshift bomb.

He had less than a minute to live.

•   •   •   •

Rathbone stood watch outside the soundstage just as Costello came running out, waving his hands wildly and pointing behind him. "He's got 'em! He's got 'em!"

Basil glared impatiently. "Kindly use proper nouns and make sense. Who has whom?"

"That Director guy, or Kopf, or whatever the hell his name is. He's got Lugosi and the Lieutenant!"

"Why did he let *you* go?"

"Because he's nuts, that's why. He said I was supposed to tell ya get ready for your death scene!"

Rathbone brandished his weapon. "We shall see about that."

Costello cocked his head. "You hear somethin'?"

Basil strained to listen. They were suddenly illuminated in headlights as one of the Volkswagens turned the corner and sped toward them.

"It's gonna hit us!" Costello shouted.

"I'll get his attention."

Basil stepped out into the middle of the street and fired a warning shot. The car screeched to a halt, the bumper a scant foot from colliding with his shins. Leveling the weapon at the driver, Basil commanded, "Show yourself or I'll fire!"

Neither Mannix nor Mickey was behind the wheel. The driver rolled down the window and desperately waved Rathbone out of the way shouting, "Move it, you ham! They're coming!"

"It's Don Marlowe!" exclaimed Costello. He pulled out the photograph. "That proves he's the guy, he's 'M'! Don't trust 'im!"

"I have no intention of trusting him," Basil remarked coolly, and kept his gun trained on the talent agent. "What brings you here, Marlowe? And why are you driving off with one of the Volkswagens?"

Marlowe's face was pale with fright; his suit was torn and stained with oil. "Look, either get in the goddamn car or get out of my way!" he said. "Didn't you hear what I just said? *They're* coming!" He glanced behind him. "I barely escaped with my skin!"

"*Who* is coming?" asked Basil, resting his free hand on the hood of the car. Marlowe revved the engine. "Last chance, Rathbone! Get in or get run over!" Basil fired another warning. The talent agent took his foot off the gas and raised his hands. "Don't shoot! I'm CIA!"

"Of course you are." Rathbone glanced down and noted a long scratch in the Volkswagen's paintjob, no doubt made by the Iron Man's spastically waving hands earlier that evening. Basil caught the glint of yellow metal. "So that's it," he said, smirking triumphantly at Marlowe. "You're trying to make off with the *real* Nazi gold!"

"Nazi gold?" asked Costello.

Basil pointed at the scratch, "It's a rather long story, but suffice it to say that the Nazis had smuggled out the *real* Nazi gold fashioned into *automobiles!*" He leered at the talent agent. "A fact that our Mr. Marlowe has no doubt discovered."

"Yeah, yeah, yeah!" Marlowe said hastily. "Didn't you hear what I said? I'm CIA!"

Rathbone smirked. "And I'm Doc Savage, Man of Bronze." A sudden pounding on the hood of the front luggage compartment startled him. Basil knocked back. "Hello?" he called. "Who's in there?" Basil opened the hood and found Janika Skorzeny trussed up like a Thanksgiving turkey. He peered over the hood at Marlowe. "Care to explain this?"

Marlowe snarled, "'All cats are gray at night!'"

Basil eyed Marlowe warily as he responded, "'I speak softly, but carry a big stick.'"

Marlowe indicated the gun. "Well, why are you still pointing that at me?"

Basil raised his eyebrow. "Lenore and Jane were our *only* CIA contacts on this case."

"I'm their field commander."

"Is that so?" Basil smirked. "Where are Detective Finn and Eddie Mannix?"

"They were smart! They saw *them* and took off!"

"And Skorzeny?"

"God, don't do this to me! Look, I got orders to bring Skorzeny and his pals in for questioning; it was all part of the plan, only that rat fink von Stroheim double-crossed me!"

"*Erich* von Stroheim?"

"Is there another von Stroheim? He's gone crazy, I tell you!"

"So *he's* our mad director." Basil kept his gun trained on Marlowe. "But never mind about that. Let's have a little chat about *them*—and Skorzeny." He addressed Lou. "Do untie Mr. Skorzeny, old boy." Basil advanced on the nervous talent agent. "Keep your hands up," he warned, aiming his gun right between Marlowe's eyes. "How did you worm your way into the CIA?"

Marlowe was frantic, his eyes crossing as he stared at the gun barrel. "The HUAC needed somebody to give them a list of Hollywood undesirables!"

"So you named names for the House Un-American Activities Committee, eh?"

"Yes! Yes!" Marlowe confessed, nervously glancing behind him.

Costello shook his head as he helped Skorzeny out of the luggage compartment. "Too bad Marlowe's a rat, or I'd say you oughta pin a medal on 'im for taking on the

Commies." He noticed Skorzeny's black-layered look as he loosened Janika's bonds. "Uh, no offense, there." Lou gave the DGSP agent a nervous smile and then ran to hide behind Rathbone.

Basil smirked at Marlowe. "What did you do, give the HUAC your client list?"

"YES! I wanna be somebody! But that's all over with now, because dead men don't tell tales!"

Costello's rubbery face became clouded with anger. *"Dead men don't tell tales!"* He pointed accusingly. "That proves you're the bastard that ordered Lenore to kill us!"

"That doesn't matter now!" Marlowe insisted anxiously.

"I hear noise," Skorzeny said, slipping out of the remaining restraints.

Basil strained to listen. "That almost sounds like men walking in suits of armor."

"Oh, God!" Marlowe fretted. "Hurry and get in the goddamn car! It's our only chance! They'll have us surrounded before you know it!"

"You still haven't told us who *they* are," Basil said calmly.

Costello did a scare-take. His eyes wide with fear, he gasped and pointed. "L-l-l-look," he stammered. He emitted a *chug, chug, chug* of stuttering gasps.

Strange menacing shapes emerged from around every corner.

Rathbone glanced down at his PPK, appraising its effectiveness. "I don't think this will do the trick," he said.

Marlowe frantically honked the horn. "Get in NOW!" he shouted.

Skorzeny, Lou and Basil leapt into the car. The engine revved as Marlowe stamped his foot down on the accelerator. The wheels spun, leaving tire marks and the smell of burnt rubber.

Fingers of blue lightning fired from several directions, enveloping the car and causing the hair of its occupants to stand on end. The Volkswagen spun out and crashed into the limousine, which in turn collided with Mannix's idling Chevy coupe.

"We're dead!" Marlowe cried. "We're all dead!"

"I see it, but I scarcely believe it," said Basil, staring out the back window at the advancing army of animated boiler-shaped robot suits from *Zombies of the Stratosphere*, and dozens of other Republic serials. They were followed by boxy robots with tin hats seen in *The Phantom Empire*. They advanced on the Volkswagen with all the quaint menace of tin soldiers.

Basil quipped, "Does anybody care to whistle Victor Herbert's *March of the Toys?*"

Costello whined, "I feel like I'm in a Saturday Matinee cliffhanger, only there ain't gonna be no rescue!"

Marlowe went into a fetal position under the dashboard as the robot army continued its implausible advance, their claws discharging high voltage Tesla current.

• • • •

Lugosi stared anxiously at the footstool with the keys resting on it and glanced up at the table with the bomb and the robot controls. Obviously Von wanted Lugosi to use his foot to drag the footstool closer and somehow reach down and get the keys. But what Von hadn't counted on was Lugosi's leg pain. His sciatica was in full force now and his thigh muscles and calves were twisted into knots of searing pain.

He tried to fight against it.

"I see it, but I scarcely believe it," said Basil, staring out the back window...

"It is all in your head," Lugosi told himself. "The pain is not real. It is all in your head!"

He moved his foot, and screamed. Pain stabbed at his senses. He fought through it and slowly edged his foot around the leg of the stool. Squeezing his eyes shut, he repeated, "It is all in your head! The pain is all in your head!"

Lugosi's pain shouted back, "IT IS NOT IN YOUR HEAD, IT IS IN BELA'S LEGS!"

Tears ran down Bela's cheeks as his leg spastically kicked the stool, catapulting the keys into his lap. Before Bela had a chance to be appropriately astonished, or work his hands out of his wrist restraints, a figure grabbed the keys.

Through the pain, through the spasm, one emotion came through loud and clear.

"DAMN IT!" Lugosi complained aloud. "IN ANOTHER SECOND I WOULD HAVE FREED MYSELF!"

"Aw, keep your shirt on," Lon Chaney complained. "I'll get to you in a second."

Chaney opened the padlock holding Lillian prisoner and then tossed the keys to Kalara, who hurried to unlock Bela's chains while a man with a long scar around his face disarmed the bomb.

"I know you could have escaped on your own," the lady spy assured Bela. "But we are in a hurry and you must leave this place now."

"How did you—?" Lugosi began, and then saw that the grating in the dungeon floor had been pushed back. His son was climbing out of the pit, followed by Bud Abbott, who was clutching a rolled up blueprint. Getting to his feet, he brandished the plans proudly. "I *knew* there had to be a way to sneak in here!"

Kalara slapped Bud on the back. "It was all thanks to Mr. Abbott and his blueprints that we found a way to save you. He is a brave man."

Abbott shrugged humbly. "Everything was happening so fast, I didn't have time to be scared."

"We found a way to hide under the set and we waited for our chance to save you." Kalara let out a heavy sigh and rolled her eyes. "We also waited for madman von Stroheim to stop bragging about his evil schemes. That man, he would *not* shut up!"

"Tell me about it." Bela eyed Kalara narrowly. "So, I see that you actually speak English, too." He gestured at the man with the long scar. "And who is this?"

"This is Vidor, my beloved," Kalara said.

Bela frowned questioningly. "Then, we are safe now?"

"We have to get out of here, Dad," Bela, Jr. explained. "There's a whole army of robots out there. Fortunately they're pretty slow moving. We saw them coming and Mr. Mannix helped us get away." He frowned. "Dad, that Don Marlowe is a rat! He drove off in the other car and left us to fight the robots ourselves!"

"I know all about Marlowe," Lugosi insisted as he rubbed his leg spasm away.

"The robots, they are unstoppable," said Vidor as he discarded the developer's timer.

Bela, Jr. hefted his submachine gun. "You can't shoot 'em or anything," he said.

Bela stood up and rubbed his sore wrists as he smiled down at his son. "They are not unstoppable, my son." He picked up the robot controls lying on the wooden table. "Your father, he knows their weakness. I show you and Chaney."

"Someone help me up, please," said a silky male voice calling up from the pit.

As a hand appeared, Abbott grabbed hold and helped a security guard climb through the opening, a man Lugosi recognized as Vincent Price!

"YOU!" Lugosi said. "You were the security guard who tried to hide his face!"

"Yes, I was," Price admitted.

"What are you doing here?"

"I came here to help Basil and Boris, of course. They deputized me as an MI6 agent."

Lugosi was furious. "IS EVERYONE A SECRET AGENT BUT BELA?!" he raged.

Price chuckled. "I guess so. They asked me to authenticate Goetz's Van Gogh. It's a fake, of course." He preened his mustache thoughtfully. "And fully insured, with a gas can firebomb just like this one ready to incinerate it. But I managed to disarm the bomb in time." He chuckled proudly, quipping, "Humph. I guess that's one portrait by candlelight that won't be snuffed out."

"Enough talk." Bela gazed earnestly into his son's eyes. "You will find Lou Costello and tell him of my plan." He clipped the robot controls to Bela Jr.'s forearm. "I show you how this works—but first...." He reached into his inner pocket and pulled out a glass test tube that he then put into his son's hand. Closing the boy's fingers around the test tube, he said, "You will need to give this to Costello."

Kalara asked, "What are your orders for the rest of us?"

"You, this man," he said, pointing at Vidor, "and I, we will rescue the Lieutenant. He is a good man. Chaney, you will take Lillian with you."

Kalara hoisted her weapon. "I am ready!"

With Hungarian determination, Lugosi declared, "Now we find that von Stroheim and add more violence to his picture."

A Brief Interlude

Interior. Lugosi's Trailer
Morning

A knock at the door startled Bela, Lou and Bud.

"Now who could that be?" asked Abbott.

Lugosi could only shrug as he reached for the handle. Again it was pulled out of his hand. Bela took one look at the figure standing outside and commented, "It is some minstrel player."

"WHO ARE YOU CALLING A MINSTREL PLAYER?" snarled Lieutenant Fred Ford, his head and shoulders covered in tar, his clothes stained with pie filling.. The detective charged inside and demanded, "What the hell's going on around here?"

Lou gawked at Ford and displayed his own tar stained shoe and pant cuff. "Say, did you have somethin' to do with this?" he gruffly asked.

"I might ask *you* the same question." Ford spotted his notebook on the makeup table and snatched it back. "What are you guys doing with this? This notebook is official police property. I oughta run you all in for doping an officer of the law."

Bud stepped forward. "Now wait a minute, Lieutenant. I can't explain how it happened, but we all woke up with our memories blacked out."

Lou snickered and pointed at the detective's tar covered face. "It looks like he had more than his memory blacked out."

"Yeah, just keep talking, wise guy," Ford snarled.

"But," interjected Abbott, pointing at the notebook in the Lieutenant's hand, "it seems that somehow Lou and Bela managed to jot down notes to jog their memories about what's been going on for the past twenty-four hours."

"Well, what *has* been going on for the past twenty-four hours?"

Lou pointed at himself and his partner. "Abbott and me woke up in each other's trailers."

"Yes," said Bela, "and I woke up in this trailer. And as you can see, my wife and son are still sleeping off some CIA drug we were given to forget."

"CIA? What are you talking about? What's the CIA gotta do with this?"

"It's got everything to do with it," Costello insisted.

"What about you, Lieutenant?" asked Abbott. "Where did *you* wake up from?"

Ford looked stymied as he admitted, "I was asleep on an operating table. It gave me the willies until I figured out I was on a sound stage. But, the screwy part is that waking up on that laboratory set gave me the feeling I was reliving a bad dream I just had."

"What happened in the dream?" Abbott asked.

Lt. Ford strained to remember. "It started…with a smell…"

Chapter 25

Thursday, 26 February 1948
3:20 A.M.
Stage 17, Universal-International Studios

Lt. Ford became aware of a smell that reminded him of his days in the air force, when he was manning the radio set and enemy fire shorted it out. It was the stink of ozone—and there was a distant noise—like bees buzzing lazily in a pastoral field of sunflowers in midsummer. But the buzzing built in ferocity with every passing second, as if a kid had poked their hive with a stick and sent the bees into an angry swarm. The ozone smell grew stronger, too. Blinking to clear his head, Ford realized he was moving headfirst down a passageway that opened out into a large room with crisscrossing catwalks and banks of stage lights hanging from the ceiling. He tried to sit up, but couldn't. He craned his neck to look down the length of his body and saw the buckled leather straps that held him down on a moving gurney. There was a guy pushing the gurney who looked a hellavah lot like Erich von Stroheim in Dracula's tuxedo.

Oh, Christ, he thought, *I seen this all before in* The Crimes of Dr. Crespi! *Only I'm the dope on the operating table!*

He imagined the madman doing to him the kinds of unspeakable things the Breen office wouldn't allow in the movies these days. Von Stroheim maneuvered the gurney into the middle of a huge operating room set and motioned to someone, then hurried to a corner of the room and rolled out an instrument table and basin. Ford felt an involuntary whimper of panic escape his throat as he eyed the array of knives and forceps. They were arranged neatly on sterile white instrument linen, all bright and shiny under the hot stage lights.

He thought, *For movie props them knives look awful sharp!*

The angry beehive drone of Tesla coils was joined by the whirring of camera motors and the playing-cards-in-bicycle-spokes clicking of unexposed celluloid moving through sprockets and a film gate. A high mounted camera rolled uncomfortably near his face for a close-up. The cameramen were dressed in operating room garb, their faces hidden behind surgical masks and caps.

"Where am I?" Ford mumbled as crisscrossing streamers of blue lightning shot from one strategically placed electrode to another in a million volt dance of crackling chaos.

But the cameramen ignored him.

The boogieman von Stroheim slipped out of his tuxedo jacket and scrubbed up in the basin of water. "Smock," he ordered as he towel-dried his hands. The two assistants locked off the camera and hurried to get the mad doctor ready for his "operation."

Ford gulped as the assistants held up a surgical gown while the mad scientist slipped his arms through the sleeves. He turned on his heel with military bearing so his assistants could tie off the smock. He turned back on his heel, held up his hands and ordered, "Gloves." The assistants helped him slip into a pair of thick rubber gloves.

"I said," Ford slurred, "where am I?"

But he was again ignored as the von Stroheim lookalike barked, "Monitors!" and his two assistants began fiddling with controls on a bank of television sets.

"Answer the goddamn question," Ford insisted, getting control of his tongue so he sounded less like a guy coming off a drunk. "Where am I?"

Shaking his head as he approached the gurney, the mad scientist said, "You disappoint me, Lieutenant, your lines are too cliché. 'Where am I,' indeed. We may have to loop your dialogue with better lines later on in post-production."

"Post-production?" Ford asked stupidly.

Von Stroheim pointed at the close-up camera, and at two other movie cameras set up in opposite corners of the soundstage. "You are being filmed," he said. "See there? This camera captures the details of your face; the panic, the anger. The other cameras are for the medium and master shots."

Set up beside the master shot and medium shot cameras were tables made from planks of plywood resting on sawhorses. Lined up on the makeshift prop tables were cream pies and cases of seltzer water. *This is definitely the set for an Abbott and Costello picture*, Ford reflected.

"I want to capture the reality of this moment," the madman continued.

Oh, God, Ford thought anxiously. *This nut is gonna kill me and take home movies of it to boot!* "Dissecting a police officer will get you the chair!" he said aloud, trying to sound tough, but realizing he looked like every ineffectual hero in every Karloff and Lugosi movie he ever saw.

Von Stroheim smiled down at him. "Do you really think *that* is what I have planned for you?"

"Well, you look like you're gonna operate on somebody, and it's me on the table, so I figured—"

The mad doctor picked up a scalpel from the instrument table and held it before the Lieutenant's eyes, letting the lights catch in the stainless steel blade. "You figured that I was going to engage in some amateur anatomy, eh? An autopsy on a living body?" He chuckled as he put the scalpel back on the table, obsessively making certain it lined up perfectly with the row of other instruments. "Have no fear, Lieutenant. I am merely dressed this way to keep dust down to a minimum. Some of this equipment is very sensitive to such things."

"Von, this is getting out of hand," said one assistant.

"He's right," said the other. "I want to call the whole thing off. No prestige production is worth this!" The voice sounded familiar.

Prestige production, Ford thought. *Where have I heard* that *before?*

The mad doctor frowned at his assistants. "Things have progressed too far to simply call the whole thing off," he vehemently insisted.

Ford squinted at the two assistants. Even though their faces were hidden under surgical masks, the eyes of one of them reminded him a lot of Bill Goetz. "Goetz, is that you?" Ford asked.

"Uh, no," said the one while making his voice deeper. "Never met the fellow."

"You got the wrong guy," the other denied in a piping falsetto.

"Is that your partner?" Ford asked.

"Not me," the falsetto insisted.

"Silence!" the madman commanded. "I have not given lines to either of you!" He leaned down and whispered, "Yes, that is exactly who that is."

Goetz pulled down his surgical mask and frowned. "Well, that's just swell! Now he knows who we are!"

"Not me," piped the other. Goetz angrily jerked his partner's mask down, exposing Spitz's face. "What'd you go and do that for?" Spitz complained.

"If I'm going to jail, you're going with me!"

"No one is going to jail," the mad scientist insisted, looking to his right at the main television monitor. He smiled and worked his hands together like a gloating villain in a silent cliffhanger. "Ah, I see my adversaries are trying to stop the rocket."

Ford turned his head and focused on the monitor showing a rocket resting on its steering fins. Smoke issued from its jet nozzles. Searching the hull of the rocket were four people, only one of which Ford recognized, namely Boris Karloff. The others included a big guy sort of dressed like a cowboy, an older gent who looked a lot like Karloff, and a sexy dark-haired beauty in leather.

Ford glared at Goetz. "How the hell did you get mixed up with this screwball?"

With anxious eyes darting to von Stroheim, the mogul said in all earnestness, "I hired the world's greatest director to make our finest prestige picture. But it turns out Von really is just as mad as Carl Laemmle and my father-in-law said he was."

"Did you just called this nut 'Von'?" asked Ford, struggling to sit up. He felt Goetz sliding the handle of a scalpel into the palm of his left hand. "You don't mean to say that guy really *is* Erich von Stroheim?"

"That's exactly who he is," came the startling answer as Goetz used his eyes to signal for Ford to keep things on the Q.T.

Von clicked his heels together and bowed. "Charmed," he said, and then began fiddling with the television controls.

"Oh right," scoffed Ford, keeping the scalpel under his hand, "if he's Erich von Stroheim, then I'm Gloria Swanson."

"He's von Stroheim, all right," said Spitz. "Only instead of making the prestige picture we hired him to film, this guy really wants to blow up Hollywood!"

"With the Hollywoodland sign at the epicenter of the explosion," Von added, not taking his eyes off the monitors. "That is an important detail! If you are going to recap my scheme, do it accurately!" Von tapped the picture tube. "That is my atomic missile armed with an isotope provided by the CIA." He made a sweeping gesture at the surrounding Strickfaden equipment. "And thanks to Vivas's genius with electronics, I had converted all of this do-nothing high frequency laboratory hardware into one huge brain that acts as a remote guidance system for both the missile *and* my army of mechanical men!"

"Mechanical men?" Ford exclaimed. "You mean like that ugly robot we found back at the funeral home?"

"Yes," said Von.

"An army, huh? Made up of those stolen robot suits, I suppose."

"Yes. Observe." With the flick of a switch, the monitor displayed a wider shot of Lubin Lake. Tovar, Imre and Gergo aimed their machine guns at a small battalion of robots that looked like walking water heaters with accordion arms ending in thick claws. The robots wobbled awkwardly on pleated legs ending in boxy metal feet. The camera zoomed in for a closer shot.

"See there?" Von said, tapping the monitor. "Those DGSP agents are trying to fend off my robots." As Ford watched, it became obvious that despite being well armed and crack shots, the agents were helpless to stop the impervious metal men. Von scanned the other monitors. "I wonder what became of Mr. Mannix and your partner. The instant they spotted my army, everyone split up and tried to stage a *coup d'état*. Not that I mind. We need dramatic tension for the third act." A television camera positioned on one of the soundstage rooftops spotted a car parked near the administration building. "Aha!" the mad doctor exclaimed. "*There* is one of my Volkswagens, but no sign of either man. No matter, I will collect the car later."

"That gold's fake," said Ford. "The Nazis played you for a sucker, if that's what this is really all about."

"I know the ingots in the suitcases are fakes. The real gold is built into the bodies of the Volkswagens."

Ford mused aloud, "No wonder that antenna wouldn't stick to the roof. Magnets don't stick to gold."

The mad scientist smirked. "So technically, *you're* the sucker and it was I who played *you*. Now, where is the other car? Yes, there it is!" The camera revealed that the second Volkswagen had been in a three car fender-bender with a parked limousine and Mannix's maroon Chevy coupe. A small army of six ridiculously boxy, tin hat wearing, slit-eyed tin soldiers were surrounding the car along with more water heater metal men.

"Do you see?" the mad doctor said. "Those robots are controlled remotely by these machines."

The camera zoomed in on the immobile *Phantom Creeps* Iron Man.

"All but that one," he explained. "That one is for Lugosi, *if* he breaks free in time."

"Forget Lugosi!" Ford growled. "What about the rocket?"

"If we're lucky," said Spitz, "the warhead will turn out to be a dud and we can forget any of this ever happened."

"The warhead is fully armed," Von insisted strongly, "of *that* I can assure you!"

Ford frowned questioningly. "Well, Goetz? What's the story? How'd you get mixed up in all this crap?"

Goetz explained, "The rest of Hollywood had ostracized von Stroheim, but not me. I wanted to show Hollywood, and especially my father-in-law, that my studio could win more Oscars than anybody, even M-G-M. So I was willing to put up with Von's outrageous demands and his eccentricities, anything, just so long as he gave us the ultimate prestige picture. I let him have the run of the studio, hoping he would give us another *Queen Kelly*, or *Foolish Wives*, or maybe even a sound version of *Greed* in its original length! He ordered all of these TV cameras, drew up phony plans, and got my prop department to get him a V-2 rocket and my set department to build the missile silo out in the lake! I thought he was doing some kind of Atomic Age science fiction picture along the lines of *Metropolis*. He called his film a 'reality piece,' said he was going to stage a fake nuclear war and photograph people's real reactions and turn it into a picture. I didn't realize what he was really up to until it was too late." He positioned his body to block von Stroheim's view of Ford's hand, and reached behind his back to signal for the Lieutenant to act.

Taking his cue, Ford cut on the restraints as he leaned his head back and sighed. "Okay, I get that the studio got their hands on a war surplus V-2 rocket, and that they painted it to look Russian, and that they built the hidden silo out in the lake on the back lot, and you thought it was all for a picture," he lifted up his head and snarled, "but where'd von Stroheim get his hands the atomic stuff to make the warhead? Don't the Atomic Energy Commission keep that kind of thing under wraps?"

Von smirked. "Yes, and just this morning I obtained from the Atomic Energy Commission an isotope of Uranium 235, delivered to me by none other than Bela Lugosi's talent agent Don Marlowe, acting as liaison for the CIA."

Ford burst out laughing. "HAW! HAW! Pull the other one! A talent agent works for the CIA? Now I know you're all nuts!" He smirked at von Stroheim. "Okay, so if this Don Marlowe is really CIA, how'd *you* find out about it?"

Von shook his head disapprovingly. "Because Don Marlowe is a braggart who told everyone within earshot that he was CIA—everyone except Lugosi, it seems. The more I feigned disinterest, the more secrets he told me. For instance, he told me that the CIA used the Mafia as hired political assassins. He also told me how dissatisfied the Agency was getting with the Mafia's success rate, which was appallingly bad—especially for professional killers. *That* was my chance to obtain what I needed! I told Marlowe that I could be a better assassin—and to prove it, I would destroy any target with my missile. You should have seen his eyes pop when he saw my weapon rise from the bottom of Lubin Lake. He immediately picked Las Vegas as the target. I told Marlowe all I lacked was radioactive material for the warhead. I then laid out my plan to use an atomic missile with Russian markings to destroy Las Vegas and blame the Russians for the sneak attack. Then the United States could declare a Third World War with guaranteed public and international support. This would lead to the total eradication of the Communist bloc. No more dividing up a war-torn Europe. Before you could say 'mushroom cloud,' my plan was given the green light and now I'm ready to launch my missile at *my* chosen target!"

Ford asked in a patronizing tone, "But what's that gotta do with all the fires you've been setting around the studio?"

"*Herr* Goetz was having financial problems, so I exploited that to gain his cooperation. If I learned anything from making *Greed*, it's that desperate men are very easy to convince to do anything—if you offer them a quick and easy solution for their troubles. I told him that in exchange for his cooperation, I would arrange to have his least favorite, and yet, most heavily insured production, *The Brain of Frankenstein*, burnt to the ground."

"And I'll bet you were gonna pin the rap on Chaney by putting him at the scene of one of the fires, right?"

"Yes. I spiked Chaney's many hidden reserves of whiskey with the CIA's amnesia formula, just a pinch, and placed some blood that I obtained for authenticity by the doghouse so that even *Chaney* would be convinced that he was guilty of not only murdering Bobby Barber, but committing arson!"

"What about the surveyors? Why'd you rub them out if everybody thought your missile was just a movie prop anyway?"

"The DGSP was responsible for that. But the surveyors' deaths proved useful. When I had their bodies moved from the lake to the boathouse and then destroyed the boathouse, it kept you from looking too closely at the lake. If I learned anything from having once played a magician, it is what the magicians call misdirection."

Ford grimaced at Goetz. "So you went along with all this just to collect the insurance, huh?"

Goetz stood shamefaced and silent as Von said, "*Herr* Goetz also recently purchased what he thought was a newly discovered Van Gogh. It was a fake, of course."

Ford eyed Goetz. "A phony, eh? But I'm figuring it's insured for plenty."

"*Herr* Goetz fancies himself a patron of the arts. If it became known that he wasted a fortune on a worthless painting...."

Spitz nodded. "His father-in-law would have a fit."

"Yes," Goetz finally admitted. "Von told me to leave the blasted painting to burn along with Abbott and Costello's movie. I hadn't planned on Karloff and Rathbone getting in the way."

"Enough talk," Von insisted. "Things are getting interesting at the Lubin Lake location."

The camera zoomed in on Karloff and company as Pratt found an access panel on the rocket's hull. Tapping the screen, Von explained, "Boris Karloff you know already. That fellow is Richard Septimus Pratt, MI6 secret agent and Karloff's brother. And the woman there in leather, she claims to be the daughter of my beloved Avinashi, but I think it actually *is* Avinashi, only she is playing one of her mind games again. The tall one there in the denim and the cowboy hat, that is Glenn Strange."

Glenn was using an oar from the motor boat like a club, knocking the boxy metal men back into the water as they clumsily tried to pull themselves up onto the camera platform. Hidden microphones picked up their conversation as Strange said, "I can't hold these things off forever."

"This won't take long," Pratt assured him.

"Here are the tools," Boris said, producing the tool kit and holding it open.

Pratt rubbed his fingers over the hexagonal holes on the access panel screw heads and stared at the array of tools in dismay. "Blast! We need a hex key. This kit doesn't have a hex key."

Zizi smiled as she reached for the top of her bustier. "Always, Madame Z, she comes prepared." She unzipped a hidden zipper that ran down the length of her shiny leather corset, revealing an inner lining of secret compartments containing, amongst other things, a complete miniature tool kit, including a full set of Allen wrenches. Her tapered leather-clad fingers hovered over the L shaped tools. "What size, darling?"

Holding his hand out expectantly, Richard said, "1.25 standard metric, please."

"Certainly," said Madame Z, slapping the tool handle-first into Richard's waiting hand like an operating room nurse.

Von smirked. "He thinks that he will foil my plans. But little does Pratt know that I have a trap door right where he is standing." He flicked a switch on his control console and twisted a dial. Pratt's lucky star must have been shining, because nothing happened. "What?" Von slapped the side of the monitor cabinet and pounded on the top. "What's wrong with this thing?"

Lt. Ford chuckled. "I guess they just don't make trap doors like they used to."

Pratt and Karloff quickly removed the access panel.

Pratt pointed at a tiny metal box with a clock face on it. "That's the timer."

"Can you disarm it?" asked Boris.

"Of course I can disarm it," Pratt said, obviously insulted.

Several robots managed to climb on the platform and one of them yanked the oar right out of Glenn's hands. It held the oar high and snapped it in two.

"Whatever it is you're gonna do," warned the cowboy heavy, "you better do it quick."

Glenn drew his .45 Colts and fired. The bullets penetrated the boxy robots' tin armor, but ricocheted off the armature beneath. "Real quick."

He emptied both shooting irons into the advancing robots. When that failed to stop them, Glenn resorted to throwing his guns at the robots. They bounced harmlessly off their metal hulls.

Pratt grimaced as he worked on the timer. "How am I expected to accomplish anything with that racket going on?" He held his hand out. "Billy, a pair of wire snips, if you please."

Boris was about to comply, when a metal claw knocked the toolkit out of his hands. He looked up in alarm and saw a water boiler robot appear from behind one of the rocket's fins.

"Richard! Boris!" Zizi exclaimed. "Get down!" She drew her Remington from her garter holster and prepared to fire.

"Zizi, please," Pratt sighed wearily. "That toy of yours will hardly make a dent in it." He quickly drew a huge Ruger .44 magnum from his shoulder holster hidden beneath his loose-fitting tweed jacket. "Now *this* is a weapon with some fire power behind it."

Zizi smirked as she holstered her Remington. "It would appear somebody is compensating for something."

Pratt cocked both an eyebrow and the hammer on the gun and aimed for the robot's chest plate. He fired point blank. Despite the sizable hole made by the Ruger, the robot continued to press forward. "I see," Pratt said, holstering his piece. "So it's going to be that way, is it?"

The robot's arm lashed out. The MI6 agent easily dodged the snapping metal claw and with a swift judo move, tripped it up and sent its metal appendage into the electronics inside the rocket. Sparks flew; the robot shuddered and stumbled back, the timer mechanism clutched in its metal claw. The robot teetered on the edge of the platform, trying to right itself. Richard very calmly grabbed the timer and tapped the robot with his index finger. It fell backward into the water.

Pratt peered over the edge, hefting the timer and observed, "Not exactly the wire snips I asked for, but that sufficed." He frowned. "Mr. Strange, kindly stop playing with those things and tidy up."

"Sure thing, Mr. Pratt," Glenn said.

As the remaining robots advanced on him, Glenn snarled, "Okay, you iron varmints, I guess if I can't shoot ya, I'll have to rassle ya."

Glenn grabbed the nearest boxy robot and got it into a modified fireman's carry and then spun around so that it's kicking metal arms and legs knocked the other robots back into the drink. Once the platform was cleared of metal monsters, Glenn did a "spinning bulldog" and threw the robot overboard.

Dropping to his knees, he rubbed his lower back and said, "That's sure gonna smart something fierce in the morning."

Boris and Zizi helped him up. "I'll personally pay for a masseuse."

Zizi gave Glenn a saucy smile. "Save your money, Karloff. I will gladly do it for free."

Von watched the television monitor and worked his rubber gloved hands together. "I'd like to see Republic Pictures outdo that!"

Lt. Ford sneered. "Well, well, it looks your countdown is down for the count." Von patted the monitor cabinet. "Fool. I can launch the rocket myself by remote control. That timer was merely a device to create suspense!"

Ford knitted his brows. "So what's blowing up Hollywood gonna get you, anyway? Aren't you gonna blow yourself up right along with it?"

With a mad gleam in his eye, Von said, "I have planned for everything! The surrounding Santa Monica Mountains will focus the blast away from us and aim the shock wave at Hollywood and Beverly Hills!" Clapping his hands together, he rejoiced, "They will be flattened, but the San Fernando Valley will be left relatively unscathed! Those who survive will be terrified, devastated—ready for a new leader to help them rebuild this factory town—*me*, Erich von Stroheim, the King of Hollywood! Not Clark Gable, ME! What would this town be without my genius? NOTHING!"

Ford shook his head. "Brother, *you* are a mental case."

Von smiled as he reached for a large knife switch mounted on the side of the television monitor. He tightened his grip around the fatal lever. "Now I'll be King of all!" he said, quoting from *Chandu the Magician*. "This lever is my scepter. Roxor, NO! *Von Stroheim*, the God whose hand deals death!" He started. "No, wait!" He hurried to his discarded tuxedo jacket and searched the inner pocket. He pulled out the rubber bone squeaky toy and kissed it. "I'll keep you with me for luck." He laid it on the instrument tray near Ford and grabbed the lever again. "As I was saying, this lever is my scepter!"

"Like I said," remarked Ford, "*you* are a mental case." He squinted. "Hey, what's going on there?"

On one of the monitors, robots were attacking the Volkswagen with electric bolts. Ford could see the heads of Rathbone, Costello and Janika Skorzeny hunkered down inside the car to avoid electrocution. He would have seen Don Marlowe, had the agent not squeezed himself under the dashboard. Suddenly, the Iron Man sprang to life and advanced on Mannix's car.

"Ah! See that!" Von exclaimed excitedly. "Lugosi has obviously escaped and has retrieved his control box!" He released his grip on the fatal lever. "We must give him a moment to exercise his futile plan. Better for dramatic tension." He blinked in disbelief. "What?!"

On the monitor Von saw not Bela Lugosi, but his *son* with the robot controls. Bela, Jr. was standing in the doorway to the soundstage with Lon Chaney. Chaney had the slumped form of Lillian Lugosi in his arms while Bela, Jr. gestured and gave Lon instructions. Lon nodded, and while the boy pressed a button on his forearm controls, the Iron Man responded by punching a hole through the window on the passenger side door of Mannix's Chevy coupe. With a mighty yank, the robot ripped the door off its hinges and casually tossed it aside.

"Now why would he make it do *that?*" Von wondered.

"I dunno," remarked Ford, having almost worked the sharp blade of the scalpel through the heavy leather strap, "but Mannix is gonna have a fit when he sees what that thing did to his car."

With eyes wide, Goetz pointed at the screen. "Is that thing calling the police?"

Von looked askance at the *Phantom Creeps* Iron Man as it reached for the handset on Eddie Mannix's radio telephone and brought it up to its ear.

The robot army and the Iron Man suddenly became possessed with mechanical fits.

Accordion pleated arms flailed wildly as the robots wandered aimlessly and bumped into each other. "Very clever," the director marveled. "Lugosi has exploited their one weakness; my mechanical men and their sensitivity to other high frequency radio sources!"

Chaney dodged around the stumbling robots and ran to the hearse parked just where Lugosi had left it, with the back hatch hanging open. He slid Lillian inside the cargo space, slammed the door shut, and then hurried around to the driver's side. He got behind the wheel and sped up Laemmle Blvd.

Meanwhile, Bud Abbott and Vincent Price, armed with Hungarian machine guns, appeared in the stage door behind Bela, Jr. and, at the boy's signal, ran to the Volkswagen to aid its trapped passengers. While Abbott kept the spastic robots covered, Price pried open the doors and got the men to safety. Bela, Jr. shouted to get Lou Costello's attention. The comic hurried over and listened as the boy gave him instructions and pointed up at the roofline of the soundstages.

The roof-mounted camera zoomed in on Costello as Bela, Jr. handed him what looked to Ford like a test tube; they talked. Costello smiled and patted his pocket and then made a run for a ladder on the side of Stage 17.

Von wondered aloud, "What can they be planning? I love the uncertainty."

He twisted a dial that made the roof-mounted camera pan around, giving him a sweeping view of the Stage 17 double flat-topped roof. Before long, Costello's head peaked out over the edge of the roofline. He clung to the ladder, huffing and puffing, but appeared determined to do something. He threw a leg over the roof ledge and struggled to pull himself up and over until at last he paused to catch his breath by flopping onto his back. As he lay there he looked like a beached whale—or at least a very tubby minnow. After a minute, he rolled over on his stomach and slowly got to his feet. He stumbled forward, obviously in too much of a hurry to notice a bucket filled with tar and a long-handled brush left behind by workmen water-proofing the roof. Lou tripped over the handle of the brush, stumbled, and got his foot stuck in the bucket of tar. He supported himself by leaning on the brush handle and tried to shake the bucket off his foot, but found the tar a formidable adhesive. Lou looked straight into the camera and shrugged in defeat, and then limped his way across the roof using the handle of the brush as a walking stick.

"I hope I don't run out of film," Von commented. "This makes terrific comedy relief." He frowned. "But what is he doing?"

He watched as Costello hobbled along until he came to one of the square aluminum air vents dotting the rooftop. He reached into his pocket for the test tube and used his teeth to pull out the rubber stopper. Then he dropped in a lipstick, put the stopper back in, shook up the test tube, and then shoved it through the louvers guarding the vent.

Overhead, Ford heard the distinct sound of something clattering down the aluminum air ducts. He relaxed, satisfied that only a very minimal amount of force was needed to rip open the leather strap and free his left arm.

"How strange," Von said, looking up at the ceiling "Now I wish I had placed cameras in the ducts." He thought a moment and then raised his eyebrows with dawning realization. "*Mein Gott! Herr* Costello said that lipstick was a firebomb!"

There was a muffled explosion that sent gray clouds of dust and accumulated debris spilling out of the vents and every joint along the air duct system. Von screwed up his face and sniffed the air. "What is that terrible smell?" He looked up and saw purple smoke pouring in from the ventilation shafts. It spread quickly, choking the air with noxious fumes.

Covering his mouth, von Stroheim gasped, "That horrible gas! That is what Lou Costello put in the vents!" Von reached under the instrument table for three gasmasks. "But it will do them no good!" He secured one over his face and handed gasmasks to his co-conspirators before again grabbing the knife switch. Von's voice muffled under the gasmask said, "Now to launch the rocket!" Which to Ford sounded more like, "Mmmph mm mmmph mm mm mmph mph!"

Seeing his chance, Ford flexed his arm and broke the strap. He grabbed the rubber dog toy and thrust it between the blades of the knife switch and the contacts, rendering the knife switch ineffective. Von Stroheim gasped, "No! Not my token!"

As Von reached out to save his precious fetish toy, Ford grabbed Von's wrist and refused to let go. Von pulled the wheeled gurney along as he tried to break free of Ford's iron grip. The director had to resort to bracing his foot against the gurney and kicking Ford across the room, gurney and all. While Ford struggled to unbuckle the remaining straps, Von quickly extricated the dog toy from the knife switch and anxiously squeezed it. He was relieved to find that it retained its wheezy squeak. He stuck the toy in his pocket and threw the fatal switch. "Now, the rocket will launch and the Hollywoodland sign will be nothing but a memory!" He added with a shrug, "It was falling apart anyway. It's an eyesore, really." To Ford, it all sounded like, "Mummph, muph, mmuph, muph, muph! Murmur, muph, muph, mmuph."

Von waited with bated breath for the big bang, but the cigar-shaped projectile stubbornly remained on the launch pad. "What has gone wrong?" Von asked himself as he repeatedly threw the switch to no effect. "Unless!"

Von panned the camera covering Lubin Lake to the shoreline where robots writhed on the ground. A hearse sat with its engine idling by the edge of the lake. Von zoomed in and saw Lon Chaney at the wheel with a now conscious Lillian Lugosi climbing into the passenger seat. Lon was holding down the talk button on the hearse's radio set while Lillian laughed at the wild dancing robots. Von said with a muffled snarl, "They're jamming my signal!"

Spitz shook von Stroheim. "Forget the rocket. Let's get out of here!" Which sounded to von Stroheim like, "Mmmph mm mmm! Mmm mmm mmph!"

"What? Speak up, man!" Von asked snappishly as he remained frozen to the spot, staring at the impotent rocket. Spitz took off running, while Goetz ran to help Ford, who was nearly free of his restraints.

The great director shook himself from his reverie and hurried to the nearest exit. He and Spitz were stopped dead in their tracks by two Boston cream pies that hit them squarely in their faces. With pie filling obscuring the lenses on his gasmask, Von pulled it off and saw four figures in similar gasmasks: Bela Lugosi standing by a prop table of pies with his son, both ready to let fly with more tasty projectiles; and Kalara and Vidor aiming bottles of seltzer at the temperamental film director and his associate. Which they did, with not so deadly accuracy.

"Is that how it is?" Von glowered angrily as he ran to a second prop table and made ready to do battle.

Kalara turned to Lugosi, hefting the seltzer bottle. "I prefer machine gun," her voice muffled by the mask insisted.

Von grabbed his own confectionary ammunition and waved Spitz over, handing him a pie. "Help me, man!" he ordered.

Soon a barrage of pies and seltzer flew across the No-Man's Land of Stage 17 with Lt. Ford and Bill Goetz caught in the crossfire as Goetz helped Ford off the gurney, each getting a face full of lemon meringue from Bela's side, and custard from von Stroheim's side. The homicide detective wiped meringue out of his eyes and grumbled, "Jesus H. Christ, all we need now is the goddamn Three Stooges!"

Bela Jr.'s last seltzer bottle fizzled out. So did Kalara's. So did Vidor's. Lugosi became aware that he had thrown his last pie.

"HA!" Von lauded as he made ready to let fly with a custard pie. "You are out of ammunition! What will you do now?" He and Spitz were poised to deliver the final barrage on their hapless foes.

"This!" said Lugosi. He grabbed the seltzer bottle from his son, took aim and threw it at von Stroheim's head. It connected with a sizable *clink!*, stunning von Stroheim. The mad director fell backward against one end of the plywood tabletop behind him. The saw horses acted as a fulcrum and catapulted the remaining custard pies across the stage—where they scored direct hits at Belas senior and junior, the pretty Hungarian agent, and her paramour. The plywood slab knocked Spitz in the head, rendering him unconscious. He fell over backward and flopped on top of the inert von Stroheim.

Pulling off his pie-covered gasmask, Lugosi looked around. "Did we win?"

Pulling off *his* gasmask, Bela, Jr. squinted and said, "We won! They're out cold!"

"Victory!" Kalara exclaimed, her fist in the air. The four protagonists exchanged congratulatory handshakes.

Choking on the descending fumes, Ford coughed and scowled at Lugosi. "How long were you standing over there?"

Lugosi shrugged. "We were there almost the whole time," he said. "We had to wait for the right moment."

Red-faced, the Lieutenant ordered, "Never mind, just get outta here." He pointed at the exit. "Scram!"

Polishing the lenses, Lugosi put his gasmask back on and said, "Come, son!" Bela, Jr. did likewise, and father and son hurried out.

Goetz grabbed an extra gasmask, giving it to Ford. Kalara and Vidor stayed behind. Fumes now completely obscured their vision as the four of them grabbed the two unconscious foes, one taking the underarms, the other the legs, and together they piled von Stroheim and Spitz on the gurney. They opened the large soundstage loading door and pushed the gurney through. The sudden influx of outside air forced the plume of purple smoke out of the soundstage.

As they emerged from the purple fog, the Lieutenant, Kalara, Vidor, and Goetz were unexpectedly conked on their heads with fire extinguishers.

Ford grabbed his aching noggin and dropped to his knees while Goetz flopped down and joined the bodies on the gurney. Kalara and Vidor collapsed, stunned.

Bud Abbott and Vincent Price had been lying in wait just outside the soundstage loading door. "We got 'em! We got 'em!" Abbott rejoiced, brandishing his weapon.

Lugosi spotted his unconscious allies and complained, "Fools! You just struck down the detective and my accomplices!"

Janika hurried to his sister's aid while Ford pulled himself up by the gurney and slipped off his gasmask, glaring menacingly at the now nervous straight man. "You wanna try that one again?"

"I-I didn't realize!" The flustered Bud Abbott apologized as he reached to help Janika help the stunned Kalara to her feet.

She shoved Abbott away angrily and uttered a disdainful, "Capitalist swine!" She and Janika helped the stunned Vidor to his feet and brushed off his clothes. "There, there," she said. "We go home now."

Ford grumbled. "First I get hit with a pie, and now I get hit with a fire extinguisher! What else could hit me, I wonder?"

A bucket filled with tar flew in a wide arc from the roof and landed squarely over Lt. Ford's head. Lou Costello appeared at the edge of the roof, propping himself up with the brush handle and shaking his now freed-up foot.

"I thought I'd never get that bucket off!" He called down and asked, "Did the plan work?"

Basil Rathbone waved and shouted through cupped hands, "Yes." He gave Lt. Ford a smirk as Abbott and Price struggled to get the bucket off the fuming detective's head. "With only minor casualties. But the plan worked perfectly!"

Lugosi leered at Rathbone. "Of course it was perfect! It was Bela's idea!"

Costello crossed his arms and smiled. "I guess that'll show those guys not to mess with us!"

With Abbott holding Lt. Ford by the waistband of his trousers, Price braced his foot on Ford's shoulder and grabbed the bucket by the rim. Price counted, "One, two, three, now!" They heaved together and out popped Ford's head, his hair matted down with tar. He straightened up and rubbed his now sore shoulder and snarled, "The first guy who makes any Tar Baby cracks is gonna get a snoot full of my fist!"

"Humph," Price chuckled, "I wouldn't dream of it, Lieutenant."

"You won't hear anything outta me either," Abbott swore earnestly.

"Good!" said Ford, and shouted up to Costello, "Get your ass down here before you kill somebody!" He reached behind his back for the handcuffs clipped to his belt, ready to arrest von Stroheim and his movie mogul cronies. He looked at his unconscious prisoners and shook his head. "You're really taking all the fun out of arresting you guys."

Marlowe chose that moment to push forward and affect authority. "All right, everyone," he said, flashing his ID, "this is all under CIA jurisdiction. Consider everything confiscated."

Basil arched his eyebrow. "I see you found your spine—now that the danger's passed."

"Can the comedy, Sherlock," Marlowe said. He clapped his hands and announced, "We're taking everything, people; the robots, the missile, the remote control equipment, the film, the cameras, everything." He snapped his fingers in Rathbone's face. "You heard me, get started with collecting all this stuff."

Costello clung to the ladder and emitted a sharp whistle and pointed at a cloud of dust approaching from the back lot. "Hey, they're comin' back!"

"Good," said Marlowe, and pointed at Rathbone. "You can help me arrest those enemy agents."

"I'll do nothing of the kind."

"Now look," said Marlowe, hooking his thumbs in his belt loops, "I'm in charge. I'm CIA. You do what I say or else."

Ford crossed his arms and stood defiantly. "Oh yeah? Sez who? If what von Stroheim told me in there is true, this whole mess is your fault!" Ford jabbed his forefinger in Marlowe's chest. "*You're* the guy who spilled top secrets! *You're* the guy who got von Stroheim the uranium! So by my way of thinking, *you're* the guy who ought to go to jail!"

"Now hold on—," Marlowe sputtered.

There was a honk, not from the approaching cars, but from the second Volkswagen. Mannix was driving and Mickey was the passenger. "Hello, boys!" Eddie said, waving.

"Where the hell have you guys been?" asked Ford.

"Watching movies," came Mickey's unlikely answer.

Bela glared angrily. "We have been risking our lives and you have been watching movies?"

Mannix parked the Volkswagen and got out. "We've been looking at some interesting dailies."

"Yeah," said Mickey as the hearse and limousines approached, "the dailies to Erich von Stroheim's latest picture."

Mannix jerked his thumb behind him. "The guy's got reels and reels of film hidden in the vaults."

"And he already had footage all threaded and ready to go in one of the projecting rooms."

Don Marlowe pointed at the Volkswagen. "That car is CIA property."

Richard Septimus Pratt emerged from the first limousine, holding a metal box with wires dangling from it. "The missile is disarmed," he announced. "This is the remote controled fuse." He handed it to Rathbone. "I suggest someone call the Atomic Energy Commission to remove the uranium core in the missile's warhead."

"Don't bother," said Ford. "The Atomic Energy Commission gave that nut the uranium in the first place." He pointed at Marlowe. "It was hand-delivered by *this* guy."

"I see." Pratt sighed and turned to his brother. "Well, Billy, it looks like we'll have to do the cleaning up ourselves."

Boris checked his watch. "We don't have much time. Makeup call starts at 6 A.M."

Glenn moaned. "I'm gonna be dead on my feet all day."

"At least you'll look the part," quipped Costello.

"Now, Lou," Abbott chastised.

"What?"

Pratt grimaced as he shook his head. "It will take an army to put things right again."

Lugosi gestured at the Iron Man. "Perhaps you can clean things up using the robots."

"Oh, yes, I forgot about the robots."

Bela took the forearm control box from his son and showed it to Pratt. "This control box, it is easy to work. Anyone can do it."

Pratt nodded his approval. "Yes, this just might do the trick."

The hearse pulled up just then. Lillian got out and ran to her son and was about to embrace him when she noticed his uniform was covered with custard. "Bela George! What happened?"

"Mom! It was great! There was a pie fight! Evil robots! Spies!"

Lon Chaney hurried over with Lillian's coat and Bela, Jr.'s cap. "Hey, Lillian, you're gonna catch your death." He wrapped the coat around Lillian's shoulders as Lugosi eyed Chaney with green-eyed venom.

"Chaney, keep your hands off my wife!" Bela demanded.

Lillian thrust a scolding finger in her husband's face. "Bela, you've got some explaining to do! What has been going on around here? I don't remember a thing, but," she added, shivering and clutching her coat around her, "I'm pretty sure *stocks* were involved!"

"Lucky girl," Madame Z quipped as she sashayed over.

Janika handed Kalara her submachine gun as they hurried to join their Comrades.

Don Marlowe blocked their way. "You're all under arrest on a charge of espionage." He pointed at Kalara's weapon, and the weapons of the other agents. "You can pile your weapons over there."

"Who is annoying little man?" Madame Z asked Pratt.

"Oh," he said, making brief introductions, "this is Don Marlowe, talent agent and CIA mole. Mr. Marlowe, Madame Z."

"I know who Madame Z is." Marlowe produced a pair of handcuffs. "Baby," he said, grabbing Zizi's wrist, "this 'annoying little man' is taking you prisoner. I'm CIA."

"Oh, really?" said Madame Z. Amusement flickered in her eyes and then veered sharply to anger. With one quick judo move she broke Marlowe's hold and grabbed his wrist, giving it a quick twist and a jerk around until the talent agent was on his knees and screaming in pain. Madame Z's stiletto heel pressed into the back of his neck as she glared at him with burning, reproachful eyes. "I EAT CIA FOR BREAKFAST, LITTLE MAN!" she shrieked, and before Marlowe knew it, he found himself wearing his own handcuffs.

"The tables are turned now, yes?" She pressed down on his head with the heel of her boot, making Marlowe eat dirt. "Feel my boot?" she snarled. "NOW LICK IT!" She pulled him up gruffly by his handcuffs, threatening to dislocate both shoulders. "NOW!" she ordered.

Marlowe whined, and reluctantly stuck his tongue out and winced as he started licking the toe of Zizi's boot.

"Say, 'Yes, Mistress!'" Zizi commanded.

His face flushed with humiliation and anger, Marlowe sputtered and said, "Es, Miss-us," spitting to get the mud out of his mouth.

Costello nudged Strange and observed, "Not using a regular shoeshine, this dame must save a fortune in nickels."

Mannix cleared his throat to get everyone's attention. "Well, like we wuz sayin', Mickey and me wuz sampling some of von Stroheim's rushes."

"Yeah," said Mickey, bending down to smile in Marlowe's face, "the guy filmed everything that happened on the lot over the past couple of weeks."

"Turns out," said Mannix, "that our CIA stoolie's been planning a little heist all his own with these two guys," he said, pointing at the unconscious Goetz and Spitz.

"He was playing both ends so they could meet each other," said Mickey.

Rathbone frowned. "You mean, playing both ends against the middle?"

"Yeah, whatever," said Mannix. "Seems this guy was gonna double-cross the Feds and split the Nazi gold with Goetz and Spitz."

"You mean," said Ford, pointing at Von, "*this* nut job filmed *that* nut job planning a double-cross, and then he let the guy do it anyway?"

Von stirred awake and stared with bleary-eyed determination. "It created the right sense of drama for the final act!" he declared before crossing his eyes and falling back into unconsciousness.

Ford shook his head. "That does it. I'm putting in a transfer to someplace where they never *heard* of movies."

Mannix chuckled. "At least now we know why all the gold bars was fakes. They're just props for von Stroheim's picture."

Bela smirked knowingly. "Yes, that must be it."

"Erich von Stroheim!" Zizi smiled. "So he is the one, the brains behind this glorious scheme?" She pulled Marlowe up and snarled, "ANSWER QUESTION!"

"YES!" he said, "He's the brains!"

She released her hold on Marlowe and started ministering to Von, patting his face to stir him awake. As he roused, she shook him. "You are the genius, yes?" she asked.

Without a trace of humility, Von said, "Yes, I am the genius! I am Count Erich Oswald Hans Carl Maria von Stroheim!" As his eyes began to focus, he looked at Zizi closely. He brightened with recognition. "Avinashi! My Mistress! You *have* come back for me!"

"You are mistaken," Madame Z said, petting his cheek. "As I have already told you, I am her daughter."

Von sat up and took her hand, holding it against his cheek. "A remarkable resemblance. You could be her twin." He reached into his pants pocket for the squeaky toy. "This was your Mother's," he said, presenting the dog toy to her.

Madame Z put the toy in her mouth and bit down. It squeaked in raspy whistles. She held the toy and smiled warmly. "So Mother even took as her lover the great Erich von Stroheim. And you mean to say you did all of this for your art?"

Von took back the dog toy and earnestly declared, "Nothing matters more than my film." He kissed the toy and stuck it back in his pocket. "Except my devotion to Madame Avinashi."

Kalara watched this display with a look of disgust.

Madame Z reached into her bodice and produced her own DGSP version of the MI6 calling card and handed it to Ford. "I claim your prisoner as my prisoner. The need has arisen."

"Really, Zizi," scolded Pratt. "Aren't your personal feelings getting in the way of your assignment? It's Lugosi you're after, not Erich von Stroheim."

Bela, Jr. hugged his father. "I won't let her take my Dad away!"

Madame Z smiled and chucked the boy under the chin. "At ease, little soldier. The Great Lugosi need have no fear." She looked apologetically to Bela. "I cannot take chance that my Government wants to throw you in Gulag. But they have no reason to do same with von Stroheim." She smiled at Von. "So I extend invitation for von Stroheim to become new Minister of Culture." Madame Z caressed the director's cheek. "This man, this criminal genius, he will make fine Minister of Culture. He will stop at nothing to fulfill his artistic vision! My Government will be very happy if he accepts." She glanced at Ford over her shapely shoulder. "We will also confiscate all cans of von Stroheim's film. They are now property of DGSP."

Pratt asked warily, "What if von Stroheim refuses?"

Madame Z shrugged. "Then I spirit him away to old secret lair until, as they say in decadent gangster films, heat is off—but heat will be on in different way." She snarled like a tigress in heat. "If you get meaning."

Lt. Ford squinted at the card with its bat insignia. "So what do I do with this thing?"

"You show to your government card if there are questions," Zizi explained as she got Von to his feet and brushed him off. She licked meringue off his cheek with one long, lingering, cat-like caress of her tongue. "Mmmm," she said smacking her ruby lips, "there is treaty no one but people who matter knows about. They will not question my authority." She pinched Von's cheek. "We have nice long chat. You will like my form of interrogation." She steered the dazed and confused film director toward her limousine and shoved him into the back seat.

"NO!" a voice shouted. All eyes turned to see Kalara leveling her submachine gun at Madame Z and Von. "You will *not* let him escape my vengeance!" Her brother stood by her, aiming his Pistolet, but looking uneasy about it. "Madame Z," Kalara warned, "stand aside or die with him!"

Madame Z was taken aback. "Wow. I did *not* see this coming."

"Really?" asked everyone else simultaneously as they all raised their hands.

Not one to be easily intimidated, Madame Z produced her riding crop and used her own body to shield von Stroheim. "Put down your weapons, Comrade Skorzenys, both of you."

Janika quickly obeyed, but Kalara tightened her grip on her weapon, training her sights on Zizi's ample chest. "If I have to shoot through you to get to *him*, then I shall!"

Cracking the riding crop against her thigh, Zizi fearlessly snarled, "Lower your weapon! I command it!"

"No," Kalara snarled back through clenched teeth. "You do not know the tortures I have suffered because of that madman!" She glanced at Janika. "Keep them covered!" she commanded.

As Janika reluctantly raised his weapon again, Kalara lowered hers and bit down on the tip of the slender index finger of her left glove and slipped her hand out. She spat out the glove and displayed a hand with fingers amputated at the furthermost knuckles, the skin blanched and cracked. "Do you see now?" she asked with fervor as she used the disfigured appendage to raise her weapon. "Frostbite from the Nazis and their low temperature experiments have robbed my whole body of sensation!" Tears welled up

Bela stepped between Kalara and Madame Z. "Put that gun down!" he commanded.

in her eyes as she said, "Both my fingers and my toes are nothing but stubs! And von Stroheim, he is to blame!" Her grip tightened on the muzzle of her submachine gun. "I cannot experience the pleasure of a tender caress! Vidor cannot even tickle my feet! There is no tender feeling anywhere! Only the most intense pain gives me pleasure now, all because of *him!*" Her finger slowly squeezed the trigger. "And *your* mother," she snarled.

Bela stepped between Kalara and Madame Z. "Put that gun down!" he commanded.

Janika looked anxiously to his sister. "Kalara, you cannot mean to shoot Bela Lugosi."

"Shut up, brother!" Kalara snapped. "I have bullets enough for everyone." She added ominously, "Including you and me."

Richard Septimus Pratt stepped forward. "Miss Skorzeny —," he began.

"NO!" Lugosi demanded. "You will stay back!"

"Bela," Rathbone warned, "don't be foolhardy. Let Commander Pratt handle this."

"Stay out of this, Rathbone!" Bela sharply insisted. "These are my fellow countrymen — and countrywomen. They are also my fans. I must act alone." He gazed at Kalara, making trance-inducing passes with his hand. "Kalara, you *will* put your gun away."

"Are you crazy?" fretted Marlowe.

Lillian clutched her son close. "Bela!" she scolded.

"Dad!" Bela, Jr. called.

"You really can't hypnotize people," Lillian pressed. "Now get over here!"

"Silence!" Bela commanded as he kept his penetrating gaze on Kalara. "You will obey," he insisted strongly, making gestures with his tapered fingers, "obey—for your will is *not* your own."

Kalara began to perspire. The muzzle of her submachine gun began to waver as she became nervous. "Do not make me shoot you," she pleaded as stinging sweat ran into her eyes.

"You will listen to me," Lugosi commanded as he approached, now fully immersed in the role of Count Dracula. "Your will is mine. You will obey me. You will put down that gun. I am your Master."

Vidor stood transfixed. He leaned close to Imre. "You are right," he whispered. "Lugosi *is* better actor than Karloff." He looked to Boris. "No offense."

"None taken," Boris remarked absently, intent on the scene playing out before him.

Marlowe was a nervous wreck. "Lugosi's out of his mind. He's going to get us all killed!"

"Shut up," Lillian angrily retorted.

Lugosi stalked Kalara with all of Dracula's intensity. He was no longer a 65-year-old character actor teetering on a life of drug addiction and endless road company tours; nor was he an actor standing in a rumpled tuxedo covered in custard pie stains; he was the magnetic and irresistible Dracula.

"Obey me, Kalara," he intoned sternly, making hypnotic passes, "I am your Master. I am—Dracula!"

Janika turned to his sister. "Listen to Lugosi, Kalara," he pleaded. "It is time we put behind us those horrible days. We have new lives before us. Even in that evil place, you found happiness with Vidor. I have avenged us. That should satisfy you." He motioned to Vidor. "Tell her, Vidor."

But Vidor was too caught up in Lugosi's acting.

"Vidor!" Janika barked.

Snapping out of it, Vidor said, "Oh! Yes!" He stepped forward. "Darling Kalara, I regret nothing from those terrible days because this man," he said, gesturing at von Stroheim, "and his twisted schemes are what brought us together. Please. I do not wish to lose you." He added hopefully, "And we do not even have to have children. I just want you. And if you should be sent to Gulag, we go together. Siberia would be heaven with you beside me."

"Listen to him," Bela said in low, spellbinding tones, "he is your lover. You will listen." He was close enough to touch the muzzle of the submachine gun. His mesmerizing hand hovered over the barrel.

Everyone held their breaths for what seemed like an intolerably long moment of hesitation. Kalara wavered. "I will obey," she said, and then lowered her weapon.

Lugosi seized the gun and passed it along to Madame Z. "Take this, please. I think I am going to faint now."

His knees buckled. Lillian rushed forward to catch him.

"That was amazing," she said, cradling Bela in her arms, "incredibly *stupid*—but amazing." She kissed him. "I told you. You *are* Dracula." She glowered angrily. "But if you ever do that again, I'll kill you myself!"

Costello patted Lugosi on the back. "That's our Bats," he said.

Madame Z handed the weapon off to Tovar while directing her steely gaze at the lady agent. "Comrade Kalara, come here," she commanded sternly.

Bowing her head in submission, Kalara approached Madame Z, ready to receive her punishment. She dropped to her knees. "Yes, my Mistress," she said. "Send me to the Gulag. I am ready to accept my fate."

Zizi cradled the girl's chin and looked intently into her eyes as she raised her riding crop. "What happened just now—," she snarled.

"Now, Zizi," warned Pratt, "don't be too hard on her. Show some mercy."

"—has made me so incredibly aroused I cannot stand it!" Zizi gushed.

Pratt sighed wearily. "Or take her as a lover. Either way."

Zizi whispered in Kalara's ear as she pulled her to her feet, "Vidor and I will share you later." She kissed her cheek and pointed at the other limousine. "Ride in *that* car. I am going to keep you and von Stroheim apart." She turned Kalara around and gave her bottom a swat with the crop.

"Yes, Madame Z," Kalara said, relieved. She and Vidor hurried to the car together. Costello blocked their way.

"If I wuz you," he whispered to Kalara as he handed her the discarded glove, "I wouldn't show that scrambler to nobody." He cleared his throat as he patted her hand. "You grabbed the wrong gizmo back at the hotel." As she looked at him questioningly, he explained, "You've had enough trouble in your life, kid. I don't want you to get in any more."

Kalara smiled warmly and kissed Lou's cheek. "For Capitalist swine, you are not so bad."

Blushing shyly, Lou said, "For a rotten Commie, you ain't so bad yourself."

Kalara and Vidor got in the back seat of the second limousine together, while Tovar got behind the wheel. Zizi returned her amorous attention to the maniacal director.

"As for *you*—," she said, kissing him, "we have a little fun on ride back to hotel."

As she prepared to slide in the seat next to him, Pratt stepped forward. "Now, Zizi," he cautioned, nodding at von Stroheim, "he's a national treasure in France—and he's married—*happily* married," he added with a shake of his finger.

Von smirked. "That has never kept me from enjoying a young lady's company."

Zizi tapped the tip of Von's nose. "I like the way you think, darling!" She shoved his head back in the car and reassured Pratt, "He will not disappear." She added with a sexy smirk, "But when he reemerges again, he will be *much* happier." As she got in and closed the car door, Zizi was heard to ask her new companion, "Do you like girls who are very ticklish?"

Gergo got behind the wheel and Imre took the front passenger seat. With a signaling honk from the lead limousine, both cars drove away in the direction of the film vaults, no doubt to collect von Stroheim's footage.

Mannix shook his head. "I don't know what that dame's thinkin'. It'll take a bunch of moving vans to cart away all that film."

"Madame Z has her ways," Pratt remarked cryptically.

"Look," Marlowe warned, "you can't let those people go! They're enemy agents! When I tell the Agency, they'll—"

Costello nudged Pratt and presented the vial of amnesia pills. "Hey, you think we oughta give this guy a taste of his own medicine?"

Pratt took the vial and poured some of the contents into his palm. "Oh, yes," he said, taking a taste of one of the pills with the tip of his tongue and giving his lips an analytical smack, "we've been hearing rumors about this. It's a lysergic acid derivative with a mixture of hypnotics." He gave Don Marlowe a very wicked, very Karloff-like smile. Fear stark and vivid glinted in Marlowe's eyes. He backed away and bumped into Lon Chaney and Glenn Strange. The two men held Marlowe as Pratt approached. He pinched the talent agent's nose until his mouth gaped open and then popped in four pills. Pratt clapped his hand over Marlowe's face, ordering sternly, "Swallow!"

Having no choice in the matter, Marlowe swallowed. Pratt released his grip, allowing Marlowe to gasp and sputter. "You just gave me an overdose!" said Marlowe, his eyes wide with horror. "There's no telling what that'll do to me!"

Pratt turned the vial over in his hands and smiled with a rare mischievous twinkle in his eye. "You're quite right. I'm afraid I gave you enough to erase more than the usual 24 hours of memory. I'd say you'll forget, oh, a week, perhaps more, perhaps even that you were ever CIA at all." Adding with a shrug, "And you'll have more than your fair share of nightmares, too, I shouldn't wonder."

Marlowe's eyes crossed and rolled up into his head until the two orbs displayed nothing but bloodshot whites. He collapsed against Strange and Chaney like a marionette whose strings had just been cut. The two men held the handcuffed agent up by his armpits.

Glenn shrugged. "If this was one of my Westerns, they'd have just strung him up."

Lon frowned at the British field commander. "Say, are you sure giving him all those pills is safe?"

"Frankly," said Pratt, sticking the vial in his waistcoat pocket, "no."

As if dreading the work ahead of him, Rathbone asked, "*Total* cleanup?"

"*Total* cleanup," Pratt confirmed, patting his waistcoat pocket. "But first," he gave Lugosi a searching look, "Before, you intimated that you knew where the real Nazi gold was. Well, where is it?"

Bela smirked. "So you want to know the truth, do you? Very well. Bela will tell you what he learned. And he will go over every detail. It was all perfectly simple—"

Basil rolled his eyes. "Honestly, Bela, stop milking it and tell them that the Nazis smuggled the real gold past customs by fashioning it into the bodies of those Volkswagens."

"Damn you, Rathbone!" Lugosi snarled.

Boris shook his head disapprovingly. "Basil, really."

"I'm sorry, Boris," Rathbone said irritably. "But we really don't have time for Bela's longwinded explanations."

Bela was taken aback. "*My* longwinded explanations? You, all the time you are always over explaining things!"

"There's nothing to over explain, dear fellow. A scratch in the paint of Marlowe's getaway car revealed the yellow metal beneath. My discovery was purely based on chance…and a keen eye."

Lugosi was beside himself with rage. "Back at the haunted house, *Bela* saw the scratch in the paint first!"

Ford smirked and pointed at the soundstage. "Don't give us that, Lugosi. You heard von Stroheim tell me about it when he had me on the operating table in there."

"Bela has *proof* that I deduced the secret before any of you!"

"Oh, really?" asked Rathbone. "And what proof is that?"

Pratt loudly cleared his throat and got everyone's attention. "It really doesn't matter who discovered what, when. We have to attend to a total cleanup operation." He patted his waistcoat pocket, "including blacking out the memories of all those who haven't a 'need to know' status."

"Yes," said Rathbone. "But we'll have to do it properly, removing any traces of evidence about what transpired in the past 24 hours."

Pratt smiled. "I see you've read the reports about this drug, too. Yes, we must stage their awakenings exactly so, otherwise the censored memories could reemerge. Now let's get started. The robots should make the cleanup go quickly." He looked for Bela. "Where did Lugosi go? We need his control box."

· · · ·

Lugosi was hurriedly pulling the protesting Lou Costello around a corner.

"Lay off the suit, will ya?" the comic complained. "It's bad enough I got tar on my pants! I gotta wear this suit for the shoot later today!"

"Did you not hear what Karloff's brother said? He made Marlowe forget and he plans to do the same thing to all of us." Lugosi reached in his tuxedo pocket and forced Lt. Ford's borrowed notebook and a pen into Costello's hands. "Write quickly, funny-man," Bela insisted.

"Write what?"

"Write down quickly what happened to you and I will save the papers along with my statement. That way, we remember everything!"

"You think I wanna remember any of this crazy business?" Costello shoved the pad and pen back at Lugosi. "Let 'em dose me!"

"We *must* remember," Lugosi insisted. "What are we if not our memories?" He pressed a note in Costello's hand.

"What's this?" Costello asked, holding the folded piece of paper.

"Something only *you* can decide if you wish to remember." He gazed earnestly. "It is my findings about your son and why his knees were not scraped."

Lou pocketed the note and, at Bela's urging, quickly scribbled short memory-jogging phrases in Lt. Ford's notebook concerning what had happened at the Hollywood Knickerbocker Hotel, and anything else he thought was important. He signed and dated his written testimony, tore the pages out of the notebook and gave the pages to Lugosi for safekeeping. Lugosi quickly wrote down what had just happened moments ago, tore out the pages and stuck the notebook back in his pocket.

"Now, do as I do," Lugosi instructed as he balanced himself against the soundstage wall and pulled off his shoe. He stuffed half of the pages in one shoe, and the rest of the testimony along with the MI6 calling card Karloff had given him in the other.

Lou did the same thing to Lugosi's scribbled note without reading it.

"Do you not want to read it first?" Bela asked.

"I'm afraid to," Lou said, tying his shoe. He looked up and pointed. "Psst. Cheese it!" he warned.

Lugosi felt a hand with long tapered bronzed fingers rest upon his shoulder. He turned around and stared into Boris Karloff's earnest, gaunt face.

"Bela," he said apologetically, "I'm afraid my brother would like a word—"

Lugosi stood erect and straightened the lapels of his custard-stained tuxedo. "It was nice to work with you again, Karloff," he said. "Too bad I will not remember it."

"I am sorry," Boris said. "If it's any comfort at all, I've been put in charge of placing you boys back where you belong—and seeing there's no evidence left behind either in your trailers..." He gazed at Lugosi until an understanding passed between them. "...or on your person."

"You are not going to take clues away?" Lugosi asked. "Why?"

"It's the reason I never joined the family trade. I don't believe in secrets. Secrets foster more secrets, and in that kind of an atmosphere there's no accountability. Then the real horrors can occur where our own Government thinks it's above the law."

Costello waved. "Sounds like a lot of Liberal malarkey to me."

"Call me a Liberal if you like, but the spy business just doesn't sit well with me." Boris patted Lugosi's arm. "I'm sure Lugosi, the Great Detective, will put the pieces together again quickly enough." He gestured invitingly. "This way, gentlemen."

"Wait," said Bela, eyeing Boris narrowly. "Is it true that *you* wanted to tell me about this spy business?"

"Yes. In fact, I suggested to my brother that you be deputized as an operative."

"You did?"

"Of course," said Boris. "I argued that if he needed an inside man at Universal Studios, *you* were the obvious choice."

"So you say," Bela scoffed. "And yet it is *you* promoting *my* film instead of Bela promoting his own film."

"MI6 arranged all that to give me a reason to be on the lot."

"Bah!"

"It's true," Boris insisted. "It was either promote your film, or agree to play the Monster again. And that meant taking the role away from Glenn. Well, obviously *that* was out of the question. Believe me, Bela, if I had my druthers, you would have been Richard's top operative."

Bela thought about this and finally relented. "I will remember this, Karloff."

"I hope so. Now, if you'll both come this way...."

Bela followed Boris. Costello cleared his throat nervously, fidgeted with his tie, and followed Lugosi.

• • • •

Boris brought them to Pratt, who gave Lugosi an earnest look. "Now, where is the robot control box?"

Bela gestured at his son. "I gave the controls back to Bela, Jr., so to take on the role of Dracula, I had my hands free."

"Good. That ties everything up neatly then." Pratt uncapped the bottle of amnesia pills. "Now hold out your hands, both of you. This is for the best really."

"Just a moment, R.S.," Rathbone interrupted. He smiled at Lugosi. "I say, Bela, old boy, earlier, you mentioned you had proof about exactly when you made your observations about the golden cars. What proof is that?"

"Yes," Bela boldly declared. "I have...," he was about to say, "...deductions dated and witnessed by Bud Abbott," when Costello cleared his throat and shook his head.

"Well?" urged Rathbone. "What proof do you have?"

Lugosi grimaced and rolled his eyes, snarling through clenched teeth, "Forget it. I have nothing. But," he said, giving Pratt a wicked leer, "before you make me forget, I have something to say for *you* to remember."

"Oh?"

"I think this Madame Z, she has played on you a trick."

"I beg your pardon?"

"Think about it, did not von Stroheim insist Madame Z bore an uncanny resemblance to her mother?"

Pratt shrugged, unimpressed. "Zizi *does* rather resemble her mother. But so what?"

"Von Stroheim said he knew every curve of her body, and recognized Madame Z as the one he met again in Paris, even when Madame Z steadfastly denied it. I think this Madame Z, she knew that her mother and von Stroheim were lovers once, and she impersonated her mother to get von Stroheim into her power."

"That's ridiculous."

"Is it? You have known her mother, this Madame Avinashi. Is she the kind of woman to wear a dog collar and give to any man a leash, and then get down on all fours and chew on a dog's squeaky toy?"

Pratt sniggered incredulously. "Madame Avinashi? I should hardly think so."

"Well, that is what von Stroheim said Madame A did when she renewed their love affair in Paris. And Madame Z, she strikes me as a woman who likes to be both dominated and to dominate. She would get down on all fours if it suited her purpose."

"Yeah," Costello said. "I noticed that about her myself."

Pratt rubbed his chin thoughtfully. "Zizi is rather that way, actually. I believe in the parlance of S and M, it's called being a 'switch.'"

"Exactly," said Bela. "And you will recall that Madame Z was very eager to chew again on the squeaky toy. I even think I saw that her teeth fit perfectly into the bite marks already there!"

Pratt balked at the idea. "You couldn't have seen a detail like that from where you were standing. Besides, what has she gained from any of this? Absolutely nothing. She didn't get the gold, she didn't get the atomic warhead, and she didn't get *you*. She got absolutely nothing out of it."

"Well," interrupted Costello, "she got rid of her brudder."

"What do you mean?" Rathbone asked.

"Back at the hotel, she said that she was picked by her mudder to take over her criminal empire after her brudder Vivas decided to go into show business instead."

Pratt furrowed his brow as he considered this. "Did she?"

Lou shrugged. "Well, supposin' it was like von Stroheim said, Vivas had a plan to start a big criminal empire all his own, and Zizi got a whiff of it, and she decided she didn't like the competition."

Boris frowned. "Richard, you don't suppose…I mean, after all, she *did* have the right hex key for the access panel on the rocket."

Pratt shook his head vehemently. "No, she carries around all sorts of things like that all the time. As Zizi likes to say, she is always prepared…always…prepared." His face fell as a dreadful realization took hold. He sighed and began rubbing the bridge of his nose. "Oh dear, I think I'm going to be deathly ill."

Costello slapped Pratt on the back. "Hey, don't let it bug ya. Look on the bright side."

Pratt grimaced. "There's a bright side?"

"Sure there is. There might be another reason she done it, *if* she done it." Costello snickered like a little kid and said, "Maybe she done it to get ya out of retirement so she could have fun fightin' wit'cha. It's like she said back at the hotel, remember, when you and her was talkin' about Dr. Death and the games he wuz playin'? He leaves you clues, he takes hostages, he wants you to try and stop him? Maybe she done all this so it was like the good old days, when she could afford to t'row you into a pit of deadly vipers an' stuff like that."

Pratt folded his arms and considered the matter. "She said that Dr. Death was obviously trying to impress me. She even said she had often done the same thing herself." He rolled his eyes. "Oh, dear lord, I've been a stupid old fool! That woman played me like a violin."

"Hey, don't take it like that," Lou playfully scolded. "She said you oughta be flattered. And you oughta be, too. I mean, a hot dish like her, and she done all of this, and right here in Hollywood, just so's you'd have to come out of retirement because your brudder is Boris Karloff."

Boris chortled as he said, "You have to admit, Richard, you *have* been getting rather set in your ways, puttering around that rose garden and keeping to yourself all these years."

"Now hold on a moment," Basil hotly interjected. "This isn't just some silly game she's been playing like spin the bottle. People have died, and have been tortured. Property was damaged."

Costello shrugged. "Hey, it's like she said, she's a sadist, it's what she does."

Basil ignored the remark and asked Commander Pratt, "Are you going to let Madame Z get away with this?"

With his jaw set, and his eyes bright with renewed purpose, Commander Richard Septimus Pratt said, "I should say not! A diabolical woman like that, I don't dare leave her to inexperienced operatives. Why, she herself said that those younger agents were far too easy to kill."

Costello gave Pratt a cherubic smile. "Yeah, about all them death traps you escape from, the ones Madame A set for ya, and later Madame Z, I'll bet the mudder and the daughter let you escape 'em on purpose."

"What!"

"Sure. It wasn't because you wuz born under a lucky star like Madame Z said you wuz. It was love, brother."

"I must agree with my Watson," Bela said. "What they did, they did to create the illusion that you are indestructible, and it was this reputation that would insure that only you would be assigned by your agency to thwart their evil plans."

"And if that ain't love," said Costello, "I don't know what is."

Pratt's face grew red with indignation. "Well, we'll just see about that!" He plunged his hands in his pockets and began pacing furiously. "I'll have to have a word with 'C' regarding a more permanent reinstatement. If Zizi wants a worthy adversary, she's jolly well got one." He stopped his pacing and scowled. "I'm going to bring that woman to the gallows if it's the last thing I do!"

Costello gave Pratt an encouraging pat on the back. "Thatta boy! You tell 'em!"

Pratt became all business and brandished the bottle of amnesia pills. "Never mind about that. Just take these. The less anyone remembers about all this, the better."

Eddie Mannix's exclamation of, "MY BABY!" diverted everyone's attention.

Lugosi saw the tough guy on his knees, mourning the mangling of his maroon Chevy coupe.

"What the hell happened to my baby?! My beautiful car!" Mannix looked angrily at the Iron Man, now crumpled on the ground, and then at the other robots. "LUGOSI!" he bellowed, jabbing a stubby digit in Bela's direction. "DID YOU DO THIS TO MY CAR?"

Bela pointed at the bottle in Pratt's hand. "Is Mannix getting a forgetting pill too?"

"Yes," said Pratt. "Now hold out your hand."

As Pratt shook an amnesia pill into Bela and Costello's waiting palms, the Hungarian said a silent prayer of thanks to the Blessed Virgin that Eddie Mannix was going to be made to forget.

Soon, Bela was enveloped by darkness, a deep and profound and welcoming darkness.

Epilogue

Dead Man's Eyes

Interior, Lugosi's Trailer
Morning

"And that," said Lugosi, "is the last thing that I remember before waking up."

Abbott pushed back his fedora and shook his head. "That's a pretty farfetched yarn."

"Yeah," said Ford. "Do you think all that crazy stuff with von Stroheim really happened?"

"Sure it really happened," Costello insisted, holding up the note pages. "How else do you explain why you was sleepin' it off on the lab set? Or how Abbott and me woke up in each other's trailers?"

Lillian and Bela, Jr. began to stir.

"Hey, Bela," said Abbott. "Your wife and son are waking up."

"Good," said Costello, "now we can get their side of it."

"No!" Bela hastily shooed the comic duo and the detective out the door, and as he shut the door after them, he urged, "It is enough that *we* remember everything. When we talk to the reporters, we just leave my wife and son out of the story. Why burden Lillian or Bela, Jr. with the truth?"

"Wait a minute," Ford balked. "What reporters?"

"All the big newspapers, they should be told. We are heroes. We saved Hollywood."

"Are you nuts?" exclaimed Costello.

"If you ask me," said Abbott, "I think we oughta just let sleeping dogs lie."

Lugosi eyed the straight man. "What does that mean?"

"It means," said Costello, "we never let on that we know nothin'."

"I gotta go along with that," said Ford. "Because if Rathbone, or anybody else who might be wise to all this catches on that *we* catch on, we're all liable to get in real trouble."

Bela grabbed back his notes from Costello and shook them at Ford. "You want to just pretend that this never happened?" He made a sweeping gesture at the surrounding lot. "We ought to be decorated as heroes," he pointed at Lou, "and you should not have the tax problems you do, because we saved everybody in Hollywood from crazy von Stroheim!" He jabbed a finger in Ford's chest. "And what about you? It could mean for you a big promotion."

"Or we could all wind up in a federal prison," Ford countered.

"I am willing to take that chance!"

"Well, not me!" Costello angrily snatched the papers back. "Fighting the IRS is bad enough. I ain't takin' on the CIA!"

"Those notes belong to me," Bela demanded. "Give them back!"

"Nothin' doin'. I ain't gonna put my family at risk just so you can feel like a big shot!"

"Look at it this way, how much worse for the three of us can things get?"

"Look," said Ford, "you three clowns do what you want, just leave me out of it. I gotta call in to headquarters. There's no telling what kind of cockamamie cover story this Richard Pratt told the Chief about me."

Abbott pointed down a side street. "Go to the makeup department. They have a telephone and they might be able to get the tar off of you."

"Say, that's not a bad idea. Thanks." Ford hurried off, leaving Abbott, Costello and Lugosi to ponder their fate.

"What do you intend to do?" Lugosi asked Costello.

Lou searched his pockets. "I'm gonna burns these notes, see? An' you're gonna play along—or I'll see you never work in Hollywood again, you got it?" He looked at his partner. "Abbott, you got any matches?"

Suddenly the trailer door opened and Lillian stuck her head out.

"Bela!" she shouted. "Why is our son sleeping on the floor? He's waking up now, but he's not acting right! And why am I sleeping in my clothes? What's going on?"

Bela was about to open his mouth when Costello stepped in and said, "It's my fault, Lillian! See, last night, as a gag, I arranged to sneak you guys on the lot and set you up in the dressing trailer while you guys wuz asleep."

"You what!" Lillian exclaimed, eyeing the comic narrowly.

Bela affected a devil-may-care attitude. "You will have a hangover, but it will not last," he assured her good-naturedly. "It was a joke that was not so funny as Mr. Costello led me to believe to it would be."

"A joke!" Lillian sharply retorted, hands on hips, "You think kidnapping your own family this way was funny?!" She tasted the cotton in her mouth and felt her forehead.

"Of all the thoughtless things!" She turned on her heel and slammed the trailer door after her.

Costello shrugged. "Sorry," he said, "it was all I could think up."

Bela nodded wearily. "The next few days, they are going to very bad."

"I guess now *you're* the guy in the doghouse." Costello reached into his jacket but came up empty. "Where are my stogies? I usually have a pocket full of stogies."

Bela produced three glass tubes from his tuxedo pocket and handed them to Costello.

"Where'd you—" He waved. "Skip it." He handed one to Abbott and one to Bela just as Lillian threw open the trailer door, her overnight bag in one hand, and clutching a groggy Bela, Jr.'s hand in the other.

"We're staying with my parents," she announced as she shot daggers of anger at her husband and then noted the cigars. "Celebrating your little practical joke, are you?"

The mortified Bela hastily snatched the cigar from his mouth and gesture helplessly. "It was only meant to be for fun," he explained lamely. "No harm was meant."

Lillian brushed Bela aside and said to her son. "Come, Bela George," and pulled her son after her.

"Mom," he asked, still in a daze, "what's going on? Why's my uniform all messed up?"

"I'll explain in the car," she said, giving her husband the coldest cold shoulder she could muster, reviving vivid sense memories in Bela of the chilly air in Dr. Fell's cryonics lab. Lillian ushered her son toward the parking lot, and then halted, looking around, frowning, unsure. She looked back and met Lugosi's gaze with an angry frown. "WHERE AM I PARKED?!"

Bela could only point in the direction of where Lillian was already heading. She turned on her heel and dragged her son to the parking lot.

"This is bad," Lugosi insisted, and looked down at his cigar. "I had better enjoy this now," he noted with Hungarian fatality, "because for the next few days, there will be little for Bela to enjoy."

"Ah, cheer up," said Costello, sticking his cigar in his mouth. "Wives are all alike. You're in the doghouse for a while, and then they forgive ya."

Bud tapped Lou on the shoulder. "Say, what was in that note that got you so hot under the collar? You never told me."

Costello smiled grimly and nudged Bela. "Go ahead, read it to 'im."

"Are you sure?" Bela asked warily. "This was meant for you alone."

Lou nodded. "Read it, go ahead."

Bela sighed, and then reached into his pocket for the letter and began to read it aloud. "Dear, Lou: I have thought very carefully about your son Butch and how he was found…" He hesitated, but with an encouraging gesture from Costello, continued to read. "I have the solution to the problem of his knees and why they were not scraped. The only way that his knees were not scraped by crawling to the edge of the pool is that he did not *crawl* to the edge of the pool at all, but was *walking*."

Bud nodded solemnly. "That makes a lot of sense."

"Shut your yap, will ya?" chastised Costello as he listened.

Bela continued, "Your little son, I believe, was taking his first steps on that horrible day. It was he, and not your wife or your secretary, who left open the playpen.

The boy *himself* opened the playpen and he did it when he pulled himself up to his feet. The sock on the ground is the evidence that this is so. He lost it when he toddled out of the playpen and to the edge of the pool, attracted, I think, by the shimmering water. As most children his age do when they walk for the first time, he stumbled and fell in the water, and that is how he drowned. This is Bela's solution, and I hope it gives to you the peace of mind that you have sought. But I fear that it may only make you feel sadder, because had you not recovered from your illness to do your radio show, you would have been home to witness your son's first steps, and the drowning would never have happened."

Lou shook his head sadly as he took the note and stuck it in his pocket. "I don't know why I never seen it that way."

Bud put his arm around his partner's shoulder. "Are you okay, Lou?"

Costello solemnly put his cigar in his mouth, rolled up the memory jogging note-paper and held it out. "Hey, Bud, I need a light."

Taking his cue, Abbott reached into his pocket for a book of matches. Bud struck a match and set an edge of the paper tube alight. Costello used the burning paper to light his cigar and offered the makeshift lighter to Bela. "About you an' your wife, you can stay at my joint 'til the heat's off."

"Thank you." Lugosi leaned in and lit his cigar.

Costello offered a light to Abbott and mused, "Since that note about Butch was in my shoe, I guess I wanted to remember about it. Now I gotta decide if I oughta tell Anne what Bela thinks. I mean, it's really just your theory, right? Maybe that's what happened, and maybe it ain't. But it makes a hellavah lotta sense. So if I tell Anne, maybe it'll make things easier for her, maybe it won't. I gotta have time to think."

Abbott puffed away thoughtfully on his cigar. "That's probably for the best, Lou," he said.

"Yeah," said Costello as he dropped the burning papers to the ground.

Lugosi stared at the burning pages and at their cigars. "Three on a match," Lugosi observed as he exhaled blue smoke through his mouth and nostrils. "That is very bad luck." A gloomy foreboding kept him from enjoying the flavor of the expensive cigar.

He glanced back at the trailer, remembering the calling card hidden under the makeup table, and realized that without the written testimony to explain its significance, the card alone was worthless. Gone were his chances of restoring even a modicum of domestic harmony. He also vaguely wondered if Eddie Mannix was awake at his home now, his memory wiped clean, and finding a brand new maroon Chevy coupe in his garage to replace the one ravaged by the Iron Man. He also wondered what had become of the Iron Man, and the other robots. Were they gutted and returned to their respective studios?

Bela mused aloud, "Do you suppose that it all really happened the way we re-member?"

"How do you mean?" asked Abbott.

"Do you not find it strange about finding the Iron Man just as it was in *The Phantom Creeps*, as a real robot and not just a man in a suit, and von Stroheim acting like a mad scientist from one of my pictures? As for this Madame Z, she may be a collection of memories of other women Costello and I have known in our past. I remember her acting very much like Clara Bow back when she and I had a torrid love affair."

"I get ya," said Costello. "And the way I remember it, Zizi coulda been like some stripper I met from when Bud and me was working the burlesque circuit." He smirked. "It would sure explain the pasties she wuz wearin'."

Abbott frowned. "So what you're saying is the stuff you said happened didn't really happen the way you think it happened? That it all got mixed up with other memories and movie plots?"

"Yeah," said Costello, "they're just pipe dreams from that drug they gave us." He eyed Bela. "But we wuz given drugs, right? And look at ya," he said, gesturing at Bela's pie-stained tuxedo. He took a sniff, "and smell how ya stink. There really was a stink bomb, and a pie fight." He gestured at the soundstage, "And that police detective woke up on the laboratory set," he pointed at the notes as they curled up into blackened ashes, "and some of them notes there was written before you wuz drugged. So we know they're on the up and up."

"Yes. That cannot be denied," said Bela. "There *was* a Dr. Fell trying to cheat you out of money to finance a plot to steal gold from Nazis hiding in Argentina, but as for the rest about Karloff's brother being a secret agent, and the atomic bomb, and the V-2 rocket…" Bela could only shrug, until he remembered the calling card. "But *somebody* gave to us a drug to make us forget. So perhaps…"

Costello smiled at him. "Relax, Bela," he said. "Maybe it's better that we don't remember nothin' like it really happened. It'll keep us out of trouble."

A gust of wind carried the smoldering pieces of notepaper up into the morning sky. Lugosi watched the ashes soar on the wind like dancing fireflies. "I cannot help feeling a sense of impending doom…for all of us."

"Aw, don't be such a gloomy Gus." Costello gestured at the floating ashes with his cigar, asking philosophically, "Look at it this way: how much worse for the three of us can things get?"

Bela stared glumly through tired, dead man's eyes.

"How much, indeed," he asked with a wistful sigh, and tried to summon a dash of hope, only to feel the pain once again shoot up his legs. He winced and remembered a line from Basil Rathbone's film *The Hound of the Baskervilles* that had escaped the censors: "Watson, the needle." And Lugosi thought of the morphine, and wished to follow Sherlock Holmes' example and lose himself in the swirl of shadows and fog.

He plunged his hand in his trouser pocket and felt something stick his finger. He turned around and pulled out something that had escaped his notice when he first searched his pockets—a strange gold pin. On it was a bat with outstretched wings with a battle axe emblazoned across it. He recalled the DGSP and its strange bat insignia and Mannix's joke about "Dracula's tiepin."

"You okay there, Bats?" asked Costello.

Lugosi put the pin back in his pocket and gave Bud and Lou a reassuring smile, while inside he felt the crafty Lugosi reemerge.

Maybe, he thought, *there is evidence to support my story after all.*

His leg pain subsided as hope was renewed.

"Everything," he told them confidently, "it is fine."

THE END
A Universal International Picture

Who's On First...?

Separating Fact from Fiction on the way to Third Base.
(Warning: Contains spoilers)

THE BRAIN OF FRANKENSTEIN—was re-titled *Bud Abbott and Lou Costello meet Frankenstein* on February 27, 1948, after William Goetz complained that the original title sounded too much like a real horror movie. Audience testing of the new title proved that having Abbott and Costello's name prominently in the title along with Frankenstein suggested a movie both funny *and* scary. Production wrapped on March 20th, 1948, and the movie was previewed at the Forum Theatre, Los Angeles on June 25th, 1948. The movie premiered in the Los Angeles area on July 24th, 1948, and in New York City on July 28th, 1948, and was a smash hit. Information regarding the production was gleaned from both the *Universal Filmscripts Series, Classic Comedy – Volume 1: Bud Abbott and Lou Costello meet Frankenstein* by Gregory William Mank and from original production reports provided by Bob Furmanek and Ron Palumbo, authors of *Abbott and Costello in Hollywood*.

DGSP—Yes, there really was a Romanian branch of the KGB called the Direction General for the Security of the People (although most reference sources say *General Direction* for the Security of the People, but that doesn't fit the acronym). It was officially begun in August of 1948, but there is evidence that the covert spy organization existed as early as 1944. But as for Madame Z and her cohorts, they are all pure fiction. Eventually the DGSP was replaced by the SRI. The described insignia are all real.

MI6—Military Intelligence, Section 6 and its insignia described in this book are real. The get-out-of-jail free aspect of the calling cards and friendly truce is pure fiction. Although I would like to think there was some kind of honor amongst covert operatives, this was the Cold War and not World War I. No one saluted anyone during the Cold War when an adversary had fallen. My main source of information for both MI6 and DGSP was *The Secret Services Handbook* by Michael Bradley.

EMERGENCY RADIO TELEPHONES— Yes, there really were radio telephones. Commercial mobile telephony began in 1946. The cellular radio concept was published in 1947. The type of radio telephone I described was used in Sweden by country doctors in late 1949. However, early models were very expensive and rather unwieldy. And, yes, that particular model as described in this story did run off the car battery and, as a result, frequently caused car batteries to go dead if used too much. Telephone booths were more prevalent at the time and infinitely more practical. Telephone booths also offered certain advantages lost in our modern cell phone world, such as a place for private conversations that no one else could overhear, a convenient changing room for Clark Kent, and a place for large numbers of college students to crowd into at one time.

TELEVISION— Yes, there was such a thing as television in 1948. Still in its infancy, the average cost of a TV at that time was around three hundred to two thousand-one hundred dollars, a fortune in the 1940's and comparable to the cost of some plasma screen TVs today. GE offered a "Daylight Television" that boasted a picture tube that allowed you to watch TV even in broad daylight. Most consoles offered an AM/FM radio and phonograph combo and many offered cabinets in both "blond" and "mahogany."

SCHWAB'S PHARMACY—Although songwriter Harold Arlen wrote the lyrics to "Over the Rainbow" by the light of its famous neon signs, and Harold Lloyd and Charlie Chaplin often played pinball in the private back room, and F. Scott Fitzgerald suffered a heart attack at Schwab's while buying a pack of cigarettes, the drugstore was most famous for an event that never really happened. Lana Turner was allegedly discovered while sitting at the soda fountain. Pharmacist Leon Schwab started that rumor himself, hoping to attract customers. Ever since then, other starlet wannabes set up shop at the very same soda fountain, praying that lightning might strike twice. The location was featured in Billy Wilder's 1950 noir classic, *Sunset Boulevard*, which also featured Erich von Stroheim as the chauffeur and manservant to Norma Desmond, played by Gloria Swanson.

THE HOLLYWOOD KNICKERBOCKER HOTEL—opened in 1925 to meet the needs of a flourishing film industry; the eleven-story hotel was a popular haven for Hollywood hopefuls and has-beens alike, even if those has-beens became that way from having died. Legend has it that the tango dancing specter of the late Rudolph Valentino haunted the Renaissance Revival bar, while up on the roof, on Halloween night in 1936, Bess Houdini held her final séance before millions of radio listeners, hoping to finally make contact with her late escape artist husband. It is said that after Bess declared Harry was a no-show, the illusionist made his final bow in the form of a brief and unexpected display of thunder and lightning. D. W. Griffith had a heart attack and died in the lobby. The hotel was also the hub for Hollywood scandal perpetrated by the living. In 1943, "Paramount Pretty" Frances Farmer was dragged half-naked through the hotel's sumptuous lobby by police, having failed to report to her parole officer for an earlier drunk and disorderly conduct conviction. Her reaction was just as disorderly, as she screamed obscenities on her way out the door. The glamorous Hollywood landmark has since been converted into a rather unglamorous apartment house for senior citizens. However, for $5.00 a ticket, the All-Star Café holds an annual Houdini séance on Halloween night.

BUD ABBOTT and LOU COSTELLO—Except for getting mixed up with foreign spies and mad scientist plots, everything about the boys, the production, their families, and their home life is true, including, tragically, the death of Lou Costello's only son. However, Bela Lugosi's proposed theory to explain the circumstances surrounding Butch's death is purely the author's own deduction and is not the official verdict. The cause of death was accidental drowning. The concern about the baby and his not hav-ing scraped his knees was raised by Chris Costello in her book, *Lou's on First*, which also provided the author of this book with details concerning Lou Costello's mansion and home theater.

LOU COSTELLO'S ACCOUNTANT—Mike is a fictitious name for an accountant kept anonymous in Chris Costello's book *Lou's on First*. In reality, there really was a young accountant that Lou hired without references and that his secretary Dee Dee Polo did not trust. Indeed, the accountant was embezzling from Lou Costello Enterprises. As for the rest of the accountant's shady connections in this story, pure fiction, and so, too, was his death in this novel.

RICHARD SEPTIMUS PRATT—Boris Karloff's brother, middle name Septimus for being the seventh son, was born on October 11th, 1882, retired from the consul service 1936/37, and died on the 15th of December, 1975. He was indeed a British consul for China. He really did lead a battalion of British Marines to the docks at Chunking, and he really did receive a spear to the back and a brick to the head for his trouble on March 18th, 1927. Opium had nothing to do with the incident, however. Pratt led the unarmed battalion to seize a cargo of stolen naval stores from a band of "coolies." So, I'm afraid there was no Madame A, no supplies of opium—officially. Pratt refused a knighthood and reportedly had a marked dislike for China and the Chinese and was longing to retire, which he did at the age of 54. Officially, he was never with MI6. But it ought to be pointed out that British Intelligence often used consuls and diplomats to work covertly as spies…so, use your imagination. I did. All information regarding R.S. Pratt was given to me by Stephen Jacobs, author of the upcoming authorized biography from Tomahawk Press, *Boris Karloff: More Than a Monster*.

BORIS KARLOFF—born William Henry Pratt on November 23rd, 1887 – died February 2nd, 1969. Boris Karloff was best known for his classic portrayal of Frankenstein's Monster in three Universal films (not counting stock footage appearances in other sequels). He was also a co-founder of the Screen Actors Guild. Boris decided to follow his ambitions as an actor, shunning the family tradition of entering the consul service, much to the consternation of his father and brothers. His brothers tried to talk him out of a career on the boards by pointing out the tragic end suffered by brother Charles Pratt, who died young while struggling to become an actor. Fortunately for all of us classic monster fans, Boris kept to that "fire in his belly" and eventually became the classic stage and screen star we know today. He is survived by his daughter Sara Jane Karloff Pratt, head of Karloff Enterprises. Naturally, all this business about helping his brother with a covert spy mission is pure fiction.

BELA LUGOSI—born Béla Ferenc Dezső Blaskó in Lugos, Austria-Hungary on October 20th, 1882. The facts presented about Lugosi are essentially true, gleaned from biographies and copious production reports provided by Bob Furmanek and Ron Palumbo, authors of *Abbott and Costello in Hollywood*. He really was late for work that morning on February 25th, 1948, but the reason for being late had nothing to do with a plot to kidnap him by the DGSP. The plot concerning the Hungarian Government and their invitation for him to return as their Minister of Culture was suggested by a deleted scene presented on the DVD to the 1994 Tim Burton film *Ed Wood*. Bela and Lillian divorced on July 17th, 1953. Lillian eventually took up with actor Brian Dunlevy. Lugosi committed himself to the State Hospital to kick his morphine addiction. While staying there, he received encouraging fan letters from a woman who signed them: "A dash of Hope." After leaving the hospital cured, he sought out and married his fifth and final

wife Hope Linninger in 1955. On August 16th, 1956, Hope came home to their small Los Angeles apartment and found Bela Lugosi dead from a heart attack. He was allegedly found reading a script by Edward D. Wood, Jr. ironically titled, *The Final Curtain*.
BELA LUGOSI, JR.—was indeed a student at the Elsinore Naval and Military School and was a frequent guest on the set during the filming of *Bud Abbott and Lou Costello meet Frankenstein*. He eventually became a prominent Los Angeles attorney. Although he never took up arms against DGSP agents, I'm sure he would have acted as bravely as his fictional counter-part.

BASIL RATHBONE—born June 13th, 1892, in South Africa, Basil really was in Military Intelligence in the Great War. He was best known for playing Sherlock Holmes, first for 20th Century Fox and later for Universal Studios with Nigel Bruce playing Dr. Watson. He continued playing the consulting detective both on radio and later in a disastrous stage production that convinced him it was time to retire from the role. He never actually solved a real case, nor did he continue his work with MI6—as far as I know. He really did, in fact, break his wrist in New York City while walking his dog. At Ninety-sixth Street and Fifth Avenue the park is some eight feet off the ground and somehow on the morning of November 13th, 1947, Rathbone lost his footing and took a plunge that ended with a severely broken wrist. He had to appear that evening for opening night of *The Heiress*, and in the best tradition of The Show Must Go On, he appeared on stage wearing a cast and his arm in a sling. The description of the incident inspired me to imagine he was actually injured fending off some attack by person or persons unknown, hence its inclusion in this story. After a long and distinguished career managed by his beloved wife Ouida, Basil Rathbone passed away on July 21st, 1967.

LON CHANEY, JR.—born February 10th, 1906 in Oklahoma City, Oklahoma as Creighton Chaney, Lon Chaney, Jr. is best known for playing The Wolf Man, the only creature in Universal's pantheon of classic monsters to be portrayed in all the sequels by the same actor who originated the role. Lon was also the only actor at Universal to play all the other monsters in subsequent sequels, including Frankenstein's Monster and Dracula (or rather, the Son of Dracula, Count Alucard). Lon really did have problems with alcoholism and actually did hide liquor in spirit gum jars, as it was revealed on *Biography*. This occurred during his most embarrassing moment on the small screen when he portrayed Frankenstein's Monster on the anthology series *Tales of Tomorrow*. This was a live broadcast, but Lon was under the impression the show was only a dress rehearsal and played his part as such, pretending to smash breakaway furniture and smirking at the camera. When he learned the awful truth about the broadcast, he was devastated. His final role was as Groton in the ultra-low budget shocker *Dracula vs. Frankenstein*. He died of liver failure on July 12th, 1973. Despite many ups and downs in his career and personal life, Lon will be much loved and remembered as the tragic Lawrence Talbot in *The Wolf Man* and subsequent sequels and spinoffs, including a reprisal of the role on TV's *Route 66* in the Halloween episode *Lizard's Leg and Owlet's Wing* with fellow boogiemen Boris Karloff and Peter Lorre.

VINCENT PRICE—born May 27th, 1911, in St. Louis, Missouri – died October 25th, 1993, just shy of Halloween. He was indeed a collector of fine art and an art expert.

and the House of Doom

He did not, however, appraise the authenticity of Goetz's painting, or take part in an espionage plot. He *did* make a cameo appearance of sorts at the end of *Bud Abbott and Lou Costello meet Frankenstein* as the disembodied voice of The Invisible Man and actually got the last laugh (literally). He began his career as a straight dramatic actor, but soon branched out into comedies and historical dramas including *Tower of London* with Rathbone and Karloff and *Dragonwyck*. Price's long career spanned just about every medium and genre there is, including guest appearances as the egg-stremely egg-sellent villain Egghead on *Batman* and as Vincent van Ghoul in *The 13 Ghosts of Scooby Doo*. He also appeared in three Tim Burton projects including the stop motion animated short subject *Vincent* and in the feature film *Edward Scissorhands* as the Inventor, as well as the voice-over in Michael Jackson's *Thriller*.

WILLIAM GOETZ—No, Bill Goetz did not get involved in a wild plot orchestrated by Erich von Stroheim, nor did he condone arson to collect the insurance money on a film he detested and a fake Van Gogh he couldn't resell, but he *did* indeed buy a fake Van Gogh. That much is true. In fact, he would sue anyone who dared to suggest *Study by Candlelight* was a forgery. Everything else, including his marrying Louis Mayer's daughter and his feelings regarding Bud Abbott and Lou Costello are true.

LEO SPITZ—Facts presented about Spitz are true; his role in this plot is not.

LENORE AUBERT—Ms. Aubert's role as a covert agent for the CIA, and her working in the Resistance during the Second World War, are fiction. The rest is true. She really was married to a Jewish man that she loved, she really did come to America hoping to find a new life away from the Gestapo, and she really did tell Sam Goldwyn to go to blazes when he tried to get her on his casting couch. As a result, Lenore was blackballed and forced to work in B-movies for Republic. Information about Lenore was obtained from both ballyhoo in the Filmscripts book and the commentary track by Gregory William Mank for the DVD release of *Bud Abbott and Lou Costello meet Frankenstein*.

JANE RANDOLPH—was never deputized as a spy. Both she and Lenore Aubert *were* a half an hour late for work that morning on February 25th, 1948, on Stage 17 according to production reports.

ERICH von STROHEIM—born September 22nd, 1885 - died May 12th, 1957. Although he was known as The Man You Love to Hate, the perfectionist silent-film director never had an affair with a sadistic criminal femme fatale or tried to blow up Hollywood with an atomic missile. But then again, how can we know for sure? Erich von Stroheim frequently exaggerated his credentials and personal history when asked about his background. He was also dictatorial, a chain smoker, had nearly bankrupted Universal and M-D-M Studios with his extravagant productions, and eventually fled to France where he was honored as a genius. His wife Valerie really did suffer severe burns while working in a Hollywood beauty salon, and sadly, there really was a prominent actress who refused to let anyone use her coat to beat out the flames while Valerie burned. Sometimes truth *is* stranger than fiction. Von Stroheim was also known to have affairs. But he never did a massively long film for William Goetz, nor did he get mixed up with escaped Nazis or atomic weapons. The bit about his forehead scar inspiring Jack Pierce to use the same scar for the Frankenstein Monster is purely this author's speculation, but you have to admit, they look the same. Von Stroheim had something in common with both Boris Karloff and Bela Lugosi—he also played Jonathan Brewster in a touring production of *Arsenic and Old Lace*.

DON MARLOWE—He really was Bela Lugosi's agent, he really did claim, when asked by interviewers, to have shamed studio executives into giving his client the role of Dracula in *The Brain of Frankenstein*. He also had a reputation for exaggeration. However, he never got involved with the HUAC and he never tried to steal a solid gold Volkswagen, or become an agent for the CIA. The Don Marlowe in this book is purely fictional.

GLENN STRANGE—Born August 16th, 1899, in Otero County, New Mexico, the six-foot-five cowboy heavy was possibly the most beloved Frankenstein Monster next to Boris Karloff. In fact, it was Strange's portrait as the Monster that graced some of Boris Karloff's obituary notices. He is best known for his later TV work on *Gunsmoke* as Sam the Bartender. The series starred fellow former monster actor James Arness (the titular Thing in *The Thing from Another World*), and it was said that one day between takes, Arness quipped to Strange, "Well, look at us, Glenn. We're just a couple of old monsters." Strange was known for being a good-natured fellow to work with and shared memorabilia with collector and gorilla actor Bob Burns, who still has one of Glenn's Frankenstein forehead pieces in his collection along with a pair of his Frankenstein boots worn in a spook show. To quote Burns, "Hey, they're Frankenstein's boots. You can't get cooler than that." Indeed, you can't. Glenn died on September 20th, 1973.

COMING SOON
by the same author:

Bela Lugosi's Final Curtain

Bela Lugosi

About the Author/Illustrator

DWIGHT KEMPER is the writer, producer, director, and performer of Murder Mystery Theater for special events like the Arts Festival in North Charleston, South Carolina, where he has appeared for an unprecedented three seasons in a row as a returning performer. He conducts mystery weekends for Bed and Breakfasts like The Inn at East Hill Farms in Troy, New Hampshire, The Benjamin Prescott Inn in Jaffrey, New Hampshire, and The Edge of Thyme Bed and Breakfast in Candor, New York. He also appears in mystery dinner shows for hotels like the Chestnut Inn at Oquaga Lake, Deposit, New York and at the Holiday Inn Arena in Binghamton, New York. As a member of the International Brotherhood of Magicians, Mr. Kemper includes magic with his mysteries. He has written over sixty mystery plays since starting The Repertory 2 Theater Company in 1989.

Mr. Kemper recently learned that writing ability runs in the family when the Judah L. Magnes Museum in Berkeley, California informed him that his great-great aunt on his father's side was author Gertrude Stein.

His previous novel, *Who Framed Boris Karloff?* was nominated in the Best Book of 2007 category by the Rondo Hatton Classic Horror Awards.

Mr. Kemper is also an artist and works in a variety of media including oils, pastels, clay, and pen and ink. The 25 illustrations gracing the inside of this volume were drawn by Dwight Kemper over a two-month period using India ink felt-tipped pens on smooth 100 lb. Bristol paper. He is also available for commissioned work.

Visit Mr. Kemper online at www.murdermysterytheater.com.

IF YOU ENJOYED THIS BOOK
PLEASE CALL OR WRITE
OR E-MAIL
FOR A FREE CATALOG.

MIDNIGHT MARQUEE PRESS, INC.
9721 BRITINAY LANE
BALTIMORE, MD 21234

410-665-1198

WWW.MIDMAR.COM

Bela Lugosi

3150021

Made in the USA